THE
ACCIDENTAL
WAG

Maggie Parker

http://www.facebook.com/maggieparkerauthor

Paperback Edition First Published in the United Kingdom
in 2020 by aSys Publishing

eBook Edition First Published in the United Kingdom
in 2020 by aSys Publishing

Disclaimer

This is a work of fiction. Names, characters, businesses, places,
events and incidents are either the products of the author's
imagination or used in a fictitious manner. Any resemblance to
actual persons, living or dead, or actual events
is purely coincidental.

ISBN: 978-1-913438-38-8

aSys Publishing
http://www.asys-publishing.co.uk

Sandra Gault.
This one is for you my friend.

CHAPTER
ONE

5 p.m. Tuesday 23rd February

'Fill it up again Gemma!' Willie Ogilvy pushed his glass to the front of the bar, he sat on the high chrome stool rocking unsteadily, his speech slurred, and his face flushed from an afternoon drinking whisky.

'Don't you think you've had enough Uncle Wull?' Gemma Gibson asked, her pretty face showing she was concerned but disgusted. 'You've been here since lunch time, it's nearly five o'clock and you're really drunk. I think I should go upstairs see if Uncle Frankie is back and get him to put you to bed.'

Willie stared at her and banged his fist on the bar. 'WHO DO YOU THINK YOU ARE? Just get me a drink and do what I pay you for. This is my bar, my glass, my bottle. Do you get it? Just give me a drink before I SACK YOUR SKINNY LITTLE ARSE. Whether I drink or don't drink is my business, not yours.' There was a moment of stunned silence before Gemma's face collapsed; she burst into tears and ran from the bar.

Chris Craig, the bar manager, walked towards Willie shaking his head. 'Boss, you need to calm down, Gemma was only trying to help.'

1

'Hey Kemosabe! What's going on?' Willie turned around, trying to focus on the person standing behind him. Frankie Dastis put his hand heavily on Willie's shoulder. 'What the fuck is eating you? What are you doing making the wean greet?' Rolling his eyes, he dismissed Chris with a wave of his hand. Tall and good-looking, his tanned skin and dark eyes alluding to his Mediterranean heritage, Frankie adored Willie and thought of him as a brother, the feeling was mutual. Franco Dastis and his twin brother Alfonzo had been best friends with Willie since nursery school. Growing up as neighbours and schoolmates on a Glasgow east end council estate, they had shared many life experiences along with Gemma's father David Gibson who was Willie's cousin.

The four friends had, as young boys, played football together. It had been clear from an early age Willie possessed a natural talent for the game. Despite a difficult home life, he had gone on from schoolboy football, to a career in Scotland and England, before moving to play in Germany and Spain. Among the first of the big money super players Willie had been capped more times for Scotland than any other player in history. Known affectionately to his fans as Willog, he had played professional football from the age of sixteen until his late thirties when he then moved with ease into management. He was as famous now at forty-seven for his off the pitch activities, as he had been for his footballing prowess.

In his teens Willie had become a pin-up boy for British football. Standing just over six feet tall with dark hair which was now speckled with grey; his bright blue eyes sparkled, his generous mouth curved upwards naturally, and his perfect white teeth showed when he smiled. Willie Ogilvie smiled a lot. Blessed with pop star looks and a sportsman's talent and physique, some said that if he had not been so interested in wine, women and song, he could have been up there with the greats. Willie never cared though; he loved football, but he had played to live.

Having the confidence and personality to match his looks, Willie had been in relationships with some of the United Kingdom's most beautiful women. His first wife Corinna had been his childhood sweetheart. During his early playing days Corinna had followed him around the country with their three young children. She had been devastated when Willie had been unfaithful with the woman who became his second wife, beauty queen Hailey Alcraig, whom he met when he was a judge in a Miss United Kingdom competition. Hailey didn't win the crown, but she did go home that night with Willie.

Corinna remained dignified; returning to Scotland where she quietly divorced him. Later, she married Bernie Johnstone who had been one of Willie's teammates during his Old Firm days. Willie had married Hailey in a blaze of publicity and gone on to have a daughter, Jade, before yet again he cheated. Hailey discovered this particular indiscretion when a tabloid newspaper named Willie as the father of stunning soap opera actress Belinsa Blackstock's new-born son Euan. Willie and Belinsa had married when his very public divorce from Hailey had been finalised five years later. The marriage lasted only a few months before Belinsa left him for a fellow soap opera actor and sold her story to a tabloid newspaper. Their fighting over money and Euan had taken three years, and their acrimonious divorce had finally been completed just six months previously.

Having returned to Scotland to live permanently when his playing days were over. Willie Ogilvy being appointed as Scotland team manager had caused widespread debate amongst followers of football. Opinion was split between those who felt that his lifestyle would impinge on his ability to steer the team and those who recognised Willie's football knowledge and natural leadership abilities.

In his early playing days, Willie put up the money for the Dastis' twins first pub. They proved themselves to be entrepreneurs, with hard work and David Gibson's financial expertise, they built their portfolio of businesses. Over the last twenty-five years the company they formed with Willie as a silent partner, had built their empire to the point where they controlled most of the popular nightlife in Scotland, as well as a successful European hotel and nightclub chain.

David, like Willie, had married his childhood sweetheart but unlike Willie he remained married to Lesley, who was also a schoolmate of the men. The couple had gone to university in Glasgow gaining accountancy degrees and eventually started their family, making Willie Godfather to their daughter Gemma.

Frankie, the more outgoing of the twins, was well known as Willie's wingman. He was in an on and off relationship with Lynne Lockhead a popular journalist and BBC news anchor woman. Frankie lived mostly alone in a luxury flat above the flagship club where they now stood. Alfie had settled down and married the love of his life. Alfie, his wife Betty and their young family had settled in Spain where they ran the European side of the business.

Standing in the opulent surroundings of the Glasgow flagship club, his arm around Willie's shoulder, Frankie looked at his friend and shook his head. 'What the hell are you playing at Willie? Have you been on the Columbian marching powder, mate?'

'Piss off Frankie, you know I never touch that stuff. That's your department, not mine.' He lifted his empty glass and threw it at the gantry. 'This is my poison.' The glass shattered against the mirror and fell to the floor. 'I just wanted a drink. That little besom wouldn't give me any. Sack her.'

'Wull! What is wrong with you?' Frankie gasped, 'that wean is in bits. What is with you mate?'

Willie slammed his fist down on the bar. 'I'm sick of women, that's what. Sick of them.'

Frankie pulled his friend to his feet. 'Not sure I know what you mean Wull. Has Belinsa upset you? You've been far too good with her, giving in to her demands.'

Willie shook his head. 'Yes! No . . . I don't fucking know Frankie? It's nothing to do with Belinsa. I met a woman and I scared her off. But I don't care. Why should I care? I can have any woman I want; can't I mate?'

'You sure can. You just don't have to marry every woman you sleep with more than once though bud.' He tried to make light of Willie's mood, which was as alien to Frankie as it had been to Gemma and the bar staff, who were now all staring at Willie. 'Right, show's over!' Frankie called. 'Get back to work, now!' He turned back to his friend. 'Okay mate tell me about it. You've been a bit secretive recently. You know we're only joking when we laugh about your women, Willie. You're just shite at picking them, apart from Corinna. Letting her go, that was your biggest mistake, but you were young, stupid and got your head turned.' Frankie shook his head and sighed heavily. 'It's not another fucking actress, is it?'

Willie put his head in his hands. 'This one, she was different Frankie, a little doll, beautiful and intelligent, a bit like your Lynne. I blew it.' Willie staggered to his feet. 'She was different Frankie. She didn't know who I was when I met her. She doesn't care who I am. I was so stupid. I tried to move too quickly, she kicked me into touch. I didn't think, I didn't consider she was different.' He slapped his forehead with his hand. 'How could I have been so daft?'

'Christ mate, you have got it bad! Come on let's take this upstairs, people are starting to look at you.' Frankie motioned to Chris who stood watching silently, his arms crossed, a look of confusion on his face. 'Chris, go and check on Gemma. Send her to the staff room for a while, stay with her until I deal with Willie. Don't let her phone her mother whatever you do. I don't need Lesley here tonight. If Willie needs a boot in the balls, I'll do it.' Frankie led Willie through the VIP area. He made to unlock the security door leading to the upstairs of the club, and his flat. He looked around the club, noticing it was relatively empty.

Willie staggered and sat down heavily in the corner seat next to the door. Sinking into the smooth brown leather he lay back and put his feet on the table in front of him. 'I'm staying here Frankie boy; I'm going to party now. Where's your woman Frankie? My Frankie, my man,' he slurred heavily, now starting to look worse for wear.

'Willie, we need to get you out of here. It's Tuesday, and this place will start to fill up in an hour or so with punters coming in after work. There's a quiz tonight so it'll be extra busy. You can't be seen in this state, the SFA will get to hear. You might be Golden Balls, pal, but they don't like you bringing disrepute on them either. You're still on that warning, remember? Now come on, let's go upstairs. You can relax and hopefully sleep it off.'

'Sleep! I don't need to sleep! I need to party. Fuck her! If she don't want me, others will. Five months I have been taking it easy with her. Who waits these days?' He looked sadly at his friend. 'It made me want her more. She was a prick tease that's what she was. I told her she was frigid, she told me to go fuck myself! Frankie, I never wanted a woman as much in my puff. Do you know what else Frankie? I don't give a flying feck what the SFA think! My personal life, it's got nothing to do with them. They can sack me if they want, but no one has done better with the national team than me. Not ever Frankie, not ever.' He put his head back in his hands. 'Frankie, it's not as though I need the money or the kudos, is it?'

'Wull, you really are wasted. This woman must be something special for you to be in this state over her!' Frankie smiled and nudged Willie, 'or have you just never had a woman dump you before? Was she the one who was at your house last weekend? I saw her drive in when I left.'

'Yeah, she's a social worker. Has a face and an arse that you would never get tired of looking at, but she had principles. I rushed it and blew it. I tried to push it with her, she went ape shit at me. I said some things. I fucking blew it.'

'Aye, you said,' Frankie laughed. He was, in all honesty, relieved the problem was female. Willie's behaviour had scared him. 'Look, you're Willog, national treasure! Everybody loves you. It'll work out. She'll miss you, want to see you again, you'll see.' Frankie sensed Willie was starting to calm down. 'How did you meet her anyway? Not your normal type of bird, is she?'

'No, she's not, her name is Ally and I've never met anyone quite like her. It was one of those charity things, Children in Need lunch, last year.' Willie smiled, remembering. 'I sat next to her because she was the only female at the top table without a moustache. I was there cos it was positive publicity, the SFA thought it would improve my profile. It was a good cause but bloody boring. We ended up getting drunk together. She's a tiny wee thing, but she can drink and then some. It was at Ayr Racecourse. We broke out, ran away like kids. We went for a walk along the beach with a bag of chips from the harbour chippy. I ended up kissing her in a shelter then I called a cab to take her home. When we got to her house, she said goodnight and goodbye. I chased her for weeks before she would go out with me, been seeing her ever since.' She's not glamorous or anything, at least not in the normal sense. She doesn't need to be, she's beautiful, super intelligent. She has a PHD actually, that makes her a Doctor and . . . ' he tailed off, 'not speaking to me now.'

'A social worker? Like Lynne's mother? She's a social worker . . . she hates me you know.'

'Who? Lynne?' Willie slurred.

'No, her mother, you prick. Lynne loves me.'

'Where is Lynne? Is she upstairs? She understands me, she gets me Frankie. Where is she? I need to speak to her.'

Frankie his expression turning serious looked at his friend. 'She's working Wull. There's been some incident at a school in Ayrshire this morning. Where have you been? It's all over the news. Lynn has been called out. A big explosion but there are people trapped, loads of kids got hurt, there are folk dead as well. Some nutter fell out with his missus and started shooting at people. Look, there's my girl.' Frankie stood up, he walked towards the big television, picked up the remote and turned up the sound. His girlfriend appeared on the screen. 'Chris! Turn the music off mate,' he shouted across the bar, as Lynne's familiar voice filled the room. A sad look on her face, Lynne stood in front of what looked like a building site, blue flashing lights lit up the sky behind her.

'Evil came to this quiet Ayrshire seaside town this morning. Just after ten fifteen, a man began shooting in Whitefield primary school. Shortly afterwards an explosion ripped through the building which was reduced to a pile of rubble. The adjacent Ayrshire college annexe was also affected by the blast and subsequent fire. All day, bodies have been pulled from the debris. At this moment there are twenty confirmed dead, most of them children. Some are believed to have been shot, but most of the casualties we are told are as a result of the explosion. It's thought the gunman may have shot through an exposed gas main.' Lynne began to speak to a policeman who advised there were still people trapped in the rubble. He told Lynne a major incident had been declared. Rescuers were trying to find trapped children and adults.

'This is a very distressing situation and one where there appears to be no known motive,' Lynn continued. 'It's believed two social workers are among those missing. One of them managed to use his mobile phone to say he and his colleague were alive under the rubble.' Two pictures filled the screen. 'Survivors informed us Steven Marshall and Alyson Campbell were last seen leading children to safety shortly before the blast. It is feared they are in grave danger, buried deep within the rubble. As darkness closes in, the rescuers continue to search for survivors of this unbelievable incident.'

Lynne began to make comparison to the Dunblane school massacre. The scene shifted to news coverage of this and interviews with survivors of the 1996 atrocity when a lone gunman with a grudge murdered sixteen innocent young children and their teacher and injured many more. Library pictures of the horrific incident at the small Stirlingshire town popped up. Lynne's face was serious as the film ended and she spoke again. 'As darkness falls, however, the death and injury toll is set to rise. As the evening begins, the sense of anger and shock is evident in this quiet community. Lynn Lockhead, reporting from Ayrshire, for BBC Scotland.'

'Fuck, Willie, this is awful, dead kids! Puts your thing into perspective, doesn't it?' Frankie said, turning around. The couch was empty; the faint trace of Willie could be seen as an indent in the brown leather. 'What? Where is he?' Frankie called to Chris and Gemma, looking around the bar area, he walked towards them.

Chris shrugged and walked towards Frankie. 'I thought he was going to the can, but he went out the door. What 's wrong with him boss? I've worked here for six years, and he has never been like that before. Even during his divorce, when Belinsa was taking him for everything, telling her version to the papers, he was never a nasty drunk. He was well out of order with Gemma by the way.'

'Are you okay babe?' Frankie asked Gemma who had come around from the bar where she had been talking to other staff.

'I'm fine uncle Frankie,' Gemma said smiling through tears. I hope he is okay, where has he gone?'

Frankie shrugged and put an arm around Gemma kissing her head. 'He's probably gone home. I've known him all my life. I could count on one hand how many times I've seen him angry; I've never known him to be like that before. He has the hots for some bird, she's dumped him.'

'He's upset over a woman?' Chris gasped.

Frankie smiled and let go of Gemma who walked back towards the bar, he waited until she was out of earshot before speaking again. 'Unlike you and I mate, I don't think Willie has ever had a woman dump him. It was already over between him and Belinsa before she went off with that tosser, so he really has never experienced rejection.' Frankie smiled, remembering. 'Even when we were kids, he was the one who got all the chicks and we all just tagged along. This woman refused his amorous advances by the sound of it. He's going nuts over her.' Frankie scratched his head. 'Never, ever, seen him lose it over a woman before.'

'She must be something else Frankie! Belinsa is nuts but she is gorgeous. Hailey was Miss Scotland. So, what's this one like?'

Frankie shrugged and pursed his lips. 'Not sure mate, I only saw her in the car, and it was getting dark. She looked quite small. At first, I thought it was a kid driving the car! That's what drew my attention to her. Willie didn't realise I saw her. I took the accounts over to him at the Loch house a couple of weeks ago, I had stopped at the end of the drive to phone Lynne. It was dark, she didn't quite come up to his shoulder, so she's only about five feet. I've hardly seen him recently, so haven't had a chance to ask him but she's small, with long dark hair.'

'Just Willie's type then?' Chris laughed.

'The hair? Nah, if she's female and has a pulse, that's Willie's type! Granted, all the wives have been dark-haired but the others!' Frankie shook his head. 'He's done them all, short, tall, blondes, brunettes, redheads, fat, thin, ugly ... What can I say? The guy's a walking sperm bank. He would be a billionaire if he stopped marrying them. At least he's been cut off at the mains now, so he can't get them pregnant. That's the only reason he married any of them, the kids. Willie just likes the thrill of the chase. He nails them then pretty soon afterwards he gets bored. He was a kid, just fifteen, when he got Corinna pregnant. That was an accident. Hailey and Belinsa? Well, Alfie and I reckon they both got bairned deliberately to trap him.'

'They are stunning looking women though Frankie.'

Frankie pursed his lips and shrugged his shoulders. 'Thing is young Chris; beauty is only skin deep as my old ma says. Willie's last two wives have been with him because he is famous, not for who he really is. Nasty cows the pair of them. I actually think he's had some sort of episode or something. He never usually cares, he's not bad to them, if anything he's too good to them, but he just ... oh I suppose he just likes to have a good time.' Frankie stretched, took his mobile phone out then walked around the bar, dialling Willie's mobile as he walked, the message informed him it was switched off. Frankie put the phone back in his pocket. 'Chris, throw us the keys for the staff car, pal. I can't be bothered going upstairs for mine. I'd better go look for him, he's switched off his phone. If he doesn't calm down, he'll end up in a cell again.' Suddenly Frankie stopped. 'Fuck! Chris! It's the social worker, the one who's been hurt in the blast!' He quickly rewound the television report and looked at the picture. 'Shit! It could be her; he called her Ally, she's a social worker he met her in Ayrshire.' He pulled his mobile phone back out from his trouser pocket and dialled Lynne's number. It went straight to answering machine. 'Lynne, it's Frankie, please call me as soon as you get this. I really need to speak to you honey.'

***

Willie was already in a taxi, moving slowly through the rush hour traffic over the Kingston Bridge, heading towards the M77 and Ayrshire. He suddenly felt sober despite the amount of whisky he had consumed. He fiddled with his phone, trying to get the latest news, then switched it off when he couldn't. 'Can you turn on the radio mate? Put on the news? Radio Scotland.'

'You okay Mr Ogilvy?' the taxi driver asked . . .

'A friend of mine's been involved in that explosion in Ayrshire.' Willie sighed. 'I need to know what's happening. I want to get down there.' He leaned back in the seat, putting his head back to try to stem the tears threatening to fall. He was now sober enough to know he had to be careful with what he shared.

'It's really shady,' the taxi driver gasped. 'I mean what kind of man does that? Goes into a school and shoots weans? They reckon he shot through a gas main and blew the place up on purpose. I had two sun journo's in the cab earlier. They're saying he's an Irish terrorist whose wife ran away, he found her, killed her and her boyfriend and then went on a shooting spree looking for his kids.' Taking Willie's silence for agreement he carried on speaking. 'Nutter! I hope he's dead and frying in hell tonight. They reckon there could be as many as fifty folk dead. How could this happen here . . . after Dunblane? How could someone just walk into a school and do this? You'd think that there would be security, wouldn't you? If your friend is hurt Mr Ogilvy they might have been taken to the southern . . . what's it called now, the Queen Elizabeth they were taking people there.'

CHAPTER

TWO

Ayr 9.30 a.m. Tuesday 23rd February—nine hours earlier

'Where have you been Ally? Are you okay? They're waiting for you in the conference room. Gerry's furious. I know you've had a rough time this week, but you knew this meeting was today. Gerry called you himself yesterday, so you also knew it was a nine thirty start.' Ruby Weir shook her head as Alyson Campbell ran into the office, her long hair still wet from showering after her workout.

'Sorry Ruby, the traffic was terrible coming from the gym this morning. I'm fine by the way. I've had a good night's sleep, a workout and swim this morning. You're right, I need to get over it, move on. Thanks for letting me work from home yesterday.'

'He called here. I spoke to him and asked him not to call back.' Seeing the look of horror on Ally's face she added quickly. 'Oh, don't worry, I didn't let on. I just did the boss thing. You know? *'Please do not call here, Mrs Campbell is not allowed personal calls.'* Ruby shook her head. 'There's a bouquet of flowers in my room for you. They came this morning.'

'Thanks, I sent the ones he sent to the house, back. I'm so sorry Rubes. Thanks for the other night too. What I told you was the drink talking. It wasn't him; it was me. Still, it's all for the best. It was never going to work, was it? I couldn't face him now anyway, after the way I carried on.' Noticing Ruby's raised eyebrow, Ally made a face, 'you knew that didn't you?'

Ruby sighed. 'What, that you were overreacting? Or that it wouldn't have worked?' She pulled Ally over and hugged her kissing her cheek, letting her friend go she whispered. 'We can talk later, after the meeting. You had better get your beautifully toned butt in there. I told Gerry you had to do an early child protection visit. Hope no one notices your hair's wet when it's not raining. Stevie's making them all coffee to try to stall them. Where's the Driske file by the way?'

'In the first cabinet in our office. Stevie would be hoping Gerry went to get it. It's filed under B for Belfast, its area's this month, street names, place names for out of area.'

'I never asked him Ally. He was too busy trying to cover for you.' Ruby laughed and shook her head. 'Don't know why I couldn't work out Stevie's crazy filing system! I'll be glad when we finally go paperless, he won't be able to do it then.'

Ally smiled and shook her head. 'He'll find a way; it's become a challenge. You know he only does it to wind Gerry up, and it works! He changes his system each month. Don't know how he can be bothered.'

'Oh, it's just Stevie. He's got to keep dreaming up something new. When Gerry or I challenge him, he says he does it for data protection. Now, you'd better get through there and start talking.' Ruby laughed as Ally ran down the corridor. 'You've far too much energy for a forty-four-year-old woman, never mind at this time in the morning, especially as you've obviously spent at least an hour in the gym.'

Ally slowed down and sedately entered the conference room. 'Sorry for the delay,' she said, 'I had an early visit.'

Gerry O'Hare looked up from the report in front of him. "Thank you for gracing us with your presence, Ms Campbell.' Taking in her wet hair he added, 'I didn't realise it was raining! I know you're busy, but we really need to get moving on this. Whilst Stevie serves the refreshments can we quickly do introductions please?' Stevie Marshall, Ally's colleague and friend, entered the room with a tray of mugs and began to hand them out. Gerry shook his head. 'You must be the highest paid tea boy in Scotland Stevie.'

Stevie put the tray down. Ally smiled at him, he grinned back. Stevie pushed back his black hair from his face. He knew he needed a haircut, but he preferred it longer. The clean-cut, suited and booted Gerry hated his scruffy look; Stevie knew and loved this fact. 'I aim to please Gerry, and if it's just coffee then I can do that.' He sat down across from Ally, his jeans, trainers and fleece jacket out of sync with the rest of the professionals in the room. Stevie didn't care though. He'd not shaved for a couple of days either; again, the fact that it irritated the very anal, rigid Gerry O'Hare made him happy. He stretched his long, slim legs out under the table and leaned back in the chair, grinning at Gerry.

Ally looked around the table; she guessed the two strangers at the end of the long conference table were the police officer and child protection social work manager from Belfast. She had only had a brief discussion with Gerry last night in respect of some new, vague information that had come from the workers in Northern Ireland in relation to the family she had been care-taking for them for several weeks. Ally had spoken to the services weekly, but today was her first face-to-face meeting. She nodded cordially at the two men.

'Okay!' Gerry said, looking at his watch, '9.45, let's get started. Better late than never. Now, can we please do introductions? I'm Gerry O'Hare, senior social work manager with responsibility for child protection. I will be chairing this meeting in respect of the Driske children. Gavin aged fifteen, Jenny aged eight , Alexis aged seven, and their sixteen-year-old sister Seonaid, she's still in education so classed as a child.' Gerry looked to his left.

'I'm Anne Lightbody, admin manager and today's minute taker.' The small blond women with the notepad said.

'Stevie Marshall, social worker, senior practitioner.'

'Ally Campbell, social worker, senior practitioner.'

'Pauline McKnight, family support worker.'

'Annie Williamson, Children's reporter

'Louisa Parkinson, school nurse coordinator, senior child protection advisor.'

Stevie made a face. He and Ally did not get on with the school nurse, who they felt was more interested in furthering her own career than she was in the children in her care. She had set herself up as an NHS expert in child protection. Her strategy was mainly to recommend removing children and letting them be adopted by what she considered to be better parents, which, in theory, neither Stevie nor Ally had any real difficulty with, if they had tried everything to sort out the situation first and failed. The problem with Louisa was she was judgemental, she concentrated on families meeting her view of how they should be living and often ignored the emotional intelligence of the parents. Stevie and Ally mainly disagreed with her; they both found her precious about herself. Stevie often said that Louisa's ego, far outweighed her ability.

The tall, good-looking man across from Ally spoke and interrupted her thought train. 'Cameron O'Sullivan, detective inspector, family protection, Police Scotland, based in Ayr.' He winked at Ally, she smiled back, the social work team were proud of the relationship with the police Family Protection Unit; despite the difference in social work and police values, both Ally and Stevie were highly regarded. Cameron, known as Cammy, was a divorcé and had tried a few times to persuade Ally to go out with him, but they remained friends despite her refusal.

All eyes fell on the two strangers in the room. 'I'm Detective Inspector Jamie Johnstone, Police Northern Ireland.' the tall, thin young man said, his face serious he nodded at the others in the room.

'I'm Bill Magill, senior social work manager, West Belfast Trust.' The small, balding man, who looked as though he would not be a lot of fun to be around. He looked miserable, Ally glanced up at Pauline, whose eyes sparkled in silent mirth; they had spent the last few months imagining what Bill Magill looked like. Pauline insisted that he had such a deep, gravelly voice, he had to be handsome and sexy. He clearly was neither. Poker faced; Ally nudged her friend. Gerry glared at them both.

The door opened; a slightly built young woman rushed into the room. 'Sorry I'm late!' She said breathing heavily, 'there are so many problems with the new building,' shaking her blonde hair from her eyes, she sat down across from Ally. 'This morning the power cut off at the new school, and it affected the old school too. The site foreman says it was vandalised during the night, the fuse was taken out apparently the one that controls the security system, the box has been vandalised so it could take all day to fix it. All these cuts, they don't have a night watchman during the week now. Honestly, it's a mess, they're also in the process of re-routing the gas supply just now, so we have to keep the kids away from the office area because they've lifted the floor,' she glanced at the two strangers in the room, then at the minute taker. 'Gabby Ballantyne head teacher Whitefield's primary school.' She said quickly. 'Sorry folks you are getting the full force of my frustration,'

'Oh, that's okay Gabby. We know how busy you are. Can I get you a hot beverage?' Gerry asked. Stevie made a face at Ally. Ally smiled back, she liked Gabby, who at thirty-one was one of the youngest head teachers in Scotland. The difficulty for Stevie was Gerry appeared to be besotted with the young head teacher; despite the fact he was old enough to be her father. Gerry glared at Ally. 'Something amusing you Ally?'

'No, nothing at all.' Ally lied, kicking Stevie under the table.

'Okay then, do you all know Ruby?' Gerry said, as Ruby entered the room with the orange file in her hand and sat down.

'Ruby Weir, I'm senior social worker, child protection.'

Gerry looked up from the laptop in front of him. 'Can we please get started? Thank you to our colleagues from Northern Ireland for coming over. We've had so many problems with the new video conferencing systems, but I'm a bit old fashioned anyway, I prefer good old face-to-face contact in meetings. Bill, perhaps we should start with you. Would you like to give us the history of this case and a summary of your involvement?'

Bill Magill shuffled some papers in front of him. 'Okay, the family came to our notice some years ago.' His deep Northern Irish accent filled the room as he spoke. 'The mother is Sally Driske, she's thirty years old. She married at sixteen, shortly after the birth of her second child, Gavin. There were major domestic violence concerns, she was seen with quite extensive injuries, and always refused medical assistance. She denied that her husband, one Seamus Driske, was abusing her. He is quite a bit older than her, there is a long history of him targeting young, vulnerable women and abusing them.'

'Is he all the children's father?' Louisa asked looking around, 'there is quite an age difference between them. The children I mean.'

'Driske has always denied fathering the two eldest children but we know they are his. Sally was pregnant at fourteen, and she had Seonaid and Gavin a year apart. If he acknowledged parentage, then we could have him for abuse of a minor. When they married, he was thirty-five? There was a lengthy separation,

I think it was about six years. This was due to Seamus serving a prison sentence for violence, we tried to get her to leave then, but she was too scared of him. When he was released, she was pregnant and bruised again within weeks. She had the two younger girls, again just a year apart. She would possibly have kept having children, only there was a problem after Alexis. We suspected Seamus beat her up which caused her to deliver early. She told us at the time she was run over, and she looked as though she had been in a car accident. The result was, however, a hysterectomy, so no more children.

'She admitted recently that Seamus beat her up for talking to a male neighbour and actually kicked her repeatedly in the groin,' Ally put in, 'So, you were correct in your assumptions.'

Bill nodded. 'Despite her bravado we knew she was terrified of him, and she had good reason to be. Anyway, social work continued to be alerted by the health visitors, nursery and school to concerns about the children. The children were well turned out but always scared, like little mice. We held back a bit because each time we visited we suspected Sally got a hiding from Seamus. They wouldn't speak out; we never had any real evidence that there was abuse. Things came to a head three months ago when it was noticed that Jenny, who's eight years old, was having some problems at school, continually asking to go to the toilet, so the school nurse spoke to her. She reported that she was having problems passing urine. Sally took her to the GP and when examined it was clear she had been sexually abused. Subsequent medicals of Alexis revealed she too had been assaulted. It was obvious Sally didn't know. We spoke to Seonaid. After some prompting, she disclosed Seamus had been sexually abusing her too.'

'Can you tell us what has occurred since then Bill?' Gerry asked.

'The disclosures of abuse were the turning point for Sally. She was willing to take Seamus' abuse of her but not her kids. Young as she is, she knew that she had to protect them. We couldn't get enough evidence initially to proceed with rape charges, mainly because the children were too afraid to face him in court, but we began to work with them on this fear. This is a dangerous man, and we needed to get the evidence to put him away for a long time. The only way to do that was to get the family out of Belfast. Sally has no one. She was in care as a child, usual story, very vulnerable, moved around a lot.'

'So how did they get here then?' Louisa asked. 'Surely you should have kept her in her own country? Wouldn't it have been better to have just removed the children; she obviously can't keep them safe.'

'We brought Sally over to Scotland because it was essential to keep them safe. She is a good mother and the children and her need to be together. Sally herself suggested coming here, she had lived here with her grandmother for a few years, they returned to Belfast when her grandmother was diagnosed with inoperable cancer. When her grandmother died there was no family willing to look after Sally, so she was taken into our care. She was around 11 years old, but she had happy memories of Ayrshire.' He sighed heavily, 'probably the last time she was happy. Anyway, Ally has quickly built up a great relationship with the family, monitored and supported them for us.' He smiled and his whole face changed. 'It's good to put a face to your voice, you too Stevie. They've taken things slowly; with Cameron's assistance they've gained evidence through building a relationship with the family.' He looked around the table and smiled again. 'Great job guys.' He looked at Gerry, 'as you are aware they started interviewing the children and Sally which meant we were able to begin building up a case. It didn't take long to get enough evidence to charge Seamus. The other thing that has made a difference is, Sally has recently begun a relationship with one of her neighbours, David Prentice. By all accounts he seems like a decent man and although it's at an early stage, he's having a positive influence on Sally and the kids.'

Stevie nodded. 'I know Davie Prentice quite well actually. Not through any concerns. He runs Whitefield's Youth Centre and does a lot of mentoring for us. He's a great guy. Davie grew up in Whitefield's, his parents still live here. He trained as a community education worker, married a local girl, but his wife died, leaving him with a young family to bring up. He took the community job in Whitefield's because it fitted in with his life. He could get support from family with the kids. He is what would be classed as a good neighbour too. When Sally and the kids moved in, he helped them settle in and gradually built up a friendship. He has, to my knowledge, not been in a relationship since his wife died about ten years ago.'

'What's he like Stevie? Should we be worried? He's quite a bit older than her?' Louisa asked. 'He wouldn't be the first professional to get involved with a vulnerable woman? He lives in Whitefield's after all, it's not exactly a des res, is it?'

Stevie looked annoyed, but he contained it and answered quickly. 'Davie's not a sexual predator. He was worried that he would be classed as one by narrow minded people. That's why they spoke to me about their relationship. It's really a friendship just now. He's helped Sally and the kids to trust Ally and me. She initially told him more than she did us. He convinced her and the kids to speak up, tell us everything.'

Bill smiled. 'Because of all of your efforts and David Prentices help, last week we were able to pass all the transcripts of the interviews to Police Northern Ireland. We did it . . . they charged Seamus. However, he got lucky and was bailed yesterday. He got a sympathetic magistrate or a biased one and he is, in the opinion of PNI, a very dangerous individual. Jamie will fill you in on Mr Seamus Driske.'

Jamie Johnstone looked serious. 'This was never meant to happen. We thought the family would be safe in Scotland, but we think someone was hired to find them, and possibly through paramilitary links here, did just that. However, when Seamus was charged on Friday night everything changed. His comrades became very nervous. You see, despite their criminal activity, they see themselves as honourable men who defend family values. Abusing children, especially sexually, is taboo. It's a great big no-no.' He smiled wryly. 'Drug dealing, gun running, giving the wife a wee slap on a Friday night are fine, but don't harm a hair on a child's head or at the very least you'll be knee-capped. Given what Seamus has been charged with, he's likely to be murdered. Problem is, our informer advised us yesterday that Seamus already knows where the family are, so we'll have to move them again before he gets to them.'

'What else do we know about Seamus?' Gerry asked, looking concerned.

Bill sighed and shook his head. 'He's a nasty piece of work. He is I'm ashamed to say a product of the care system; he was a bit of a tearaway as a child and educated in what I think you would call a list D residential school. We know that a lot of the boys in this particular establishment were physically and sexually abused, so from what we know about the abuse that went on, there is a distinct possibility that he was left damaged by this. The social work records from the time say he was a bit of a thug and a bully . . . but there could have been a reason.'

Jamie Johnstone sighed and looked around the room, 'I agree to a point, but he is a nasty individual. He was a young man towards the end of the troubles, he was recruited and heavily involved in some terrible things. Before the peace agreement we thought he was a bit of a dangerous lad who the paramilitaries used when they wanted nasty work done. Afterwards when information started to get out about those times, we realised he is most likely a psychopath, no empathy, no thoughts of how anything affects anyone but him.' Jamie looked over at Bill, 'I know your lot think it was damage in the care system and early years experiences that caused it, but Bill, the facts remain. He has no boundaries, a liking for alcohol, cocaine and very young girls. One of the things we charged him with was statutory rape. Sally told us that he was thirty when he first had intercourse with her, she was just twelve years old.' Jamie continued, looking serious. 'She also gave us leads to other young women who she was in care with. This allowed us to charge him on three other counts of sex with an underage girl.' Jamie paused and shook his head. 'I know how Seamus Driske thinks. He is the type of man who is cruel and controlling. First, he will be angry she has left him and blabbed, but he will be even angrier if he thinks that she has another man. Amongst other things he is a classic domestic abuser.'

'How dangerous is he?' Gerry asked, looking at Jamie, he moved his gaze to Ally and raised an eyebrow.

'Please don't minute this Anne.' Jamie put down his own pen and continued. 'We suspect he killed his first wife. She vanished, leaving three young sons. Her family are sure she's dead. However, they were also involved in terrorism at a high level, so they don't talk to us. They got the children from that relationship, who are now adults.' He shook his head. 'Not great ... but from what we can gather, they agreed that they would not do anything if Seamus handed over the kids.' Jamie looked around the table. 'I'm ashamed of my countrymen on a daily basis, as some of the things that were done in the name of the Troubles are deeply disturbing. However, as I said, on both sides of the argument children are important and protected after a fashion. We had hoped someone had bumped Seamus off. We do have informants and they tell us that his comrades are looking for him too.'

'What could that mean for Sally and the children?' Stevie asked looking around the table, 'I'm concerned, could they be in more danger than we thought, real danger? Life and death stuff? No wonder they were terrified.'

'Why weren't we told all of this Jamie, Bill? Cameron did you know?' Ally asked looking along the table.

Jamie sighed, 'We couldn't tell anyone, a lot of what we knew about Seamus was hearsay, we had no proof. We were also unsure of what Sally knew, and how involved she was, today was to tell you all of the history, but . . . well . . . events have kind of overtaken that.'

Gerry looked angry, 'you have put my workers at risk, you told us he was a domestic abuser, but murder of a previous part-ner? Terrorism?'

Bill looked sheepish. 'Would you have taken the case if you had known?'

Jamie nodded sadly, 'We really did think they would be safer here.' He looked uncomfortable and sighed before continuing. 'I'm afraid there's more . . . most worrying folks . . . is the fact that Seamus also has had access to guns and explosives. He'll not be afraid to use them, he has very little to lose now.' He looked across and made eye contact with Cameron. 'That makes him extremely dangerous to Sally and the children . . . and anyone who gets in the way. Intelligence tell us he was still in Northern Ireland last night, but those of us who know him think he'll be trying to get to Scotland. The Port Police are watching for him at the ferry terminals and the airport, but we can't guarantee that he won't get over here someway.' Jamie looked along the table. 'There are so many sympathisers in Scotland folks, they may be helping him. They certainly found the family for him. To be fair to them, he is a very persuasive man.'

Gerry looked pale and worried; he glanced at Ally who was also visibly shaken by what she had just heard. 'Ally, anything to add?'

'Yes Gerry. Why are we sitting here having a meeting when Sally and her kids are in danger? We need to move them and do it this morning.'

'Ally, I hear what you're saying, but we had to plan it.'

Ally stood up. 'Let's just go and get Sally and the children, bring them back here. I think we'll all feel better if we have them as safe as we can make them. We should have done that first. We can make plans for them once they're safe.' Ally tapped the Fitbit on her wrist. 'Ten fifteen. She'll have put the kids out to school and gone to college herself.'

Stevie shook his head. 'It's a late start today. Rosie was going around for ten fifteen to do some work with Sally and Davie on coping with Jenny's introverted behaviour.'

'Ally, we'd better have a police presence standing by,' Gerry said quickly.

Ally nodded, she inclined her head to Stevie who looked back and shrugged. 'Let's go,' he said quietly, taking a drink from his coffee mug.

'I'll call it in!' Cameron walked to the door, taking his mobile phone from his pocket, you'll have to go through 101 and that'll waste time.'

Gabby stood up. 'I'll head back to the school, lock it down as well. Although, with the power cut the security system went down and all the doors were open.' Gabby looked at Cameron. 'Do you think it might be better if we just close the school, send the children home and just blame the security system failure?'

Cameron shrugged. 'Not sure Gabby. If it's been fixed, then it should be one of the safest places there is. Why don't you head back and if it's still off, you can start the process of closing the school? Ally, Stevie, you two go for the children, Jamie and I will go to the house for Sally.'

'Stevie and I will come and get the kids in ten minutes,' Ally said, touching Gabby's arm. 'Are you okay?'

Gabby smiled and nodded. 'You read about this sort of thing but don't expect it on your own doorstep. See you in ten minutes then!'

Ally, Stevie, don't take any chances, this man is dangerous, just collect the kids and bring them back here. Bill come upstairs to my office and we can start thinking about where we can take the family.' Ruby looked at her two workers. 'No heroics folks.'

'Of course, we won't be silly,' Ally said, she nodded at Stevie who followed her from the room.

The Whitefield's area was a run-down council estate populated by many people who were known to social work. The social work office was ideally placed to provide support and protection to the people of Whitefield's and the surrounding area. The four-in-a-block houses were mainly Housing Association owned. Due to the high unemployment in the area most of the residents existed on benefits. There was, however, despite the problems and the poverty, a very strong community spirit.

Outside in the car park Jamie Johnstone searched in his pockets for car keys. 'Forget it Jamie,' Cameron said inclining his head, 'we'll be quicker on foot, the centre of the estate is not car friendly.'

Ally looked at them. 'Pauline will go with you to Sally's house. Rosie apparently left a few minutes ago to go see Sally, so she will be there. Stevie and I will go get the kids from school. The college annexe is next door to the school Jamie, so we can get Seonaid too.' They separated, and Ally and Stevie walked quickly around the corner to the school.

Jamie, Cameron and Pauline crossed the road, walking towards Sally's house; as they approached, the front door flew opened, Rosie Nelson stumbled from the house. Immediately realising there was something wrong, Pauline ran towards her. Rosie vomited into the bushes at the side of the garden. Her face ashen, she gasped that Sally was dead. 'Oh my God, Pauline!' she sobbed. 'She's been hacked up, there's blood everywhere. I tried to help them, but it was too late.'

Rosie's hands and clothes were covered in blood., words rushed out of her mouth. 'Seonaid and Davie Prentice are in there too. Oh God, it's horrible. I went in because the door was open. Who would do something like this?' She sobbed, 'thank god the other kids are not there, Jenny and Alexis are in school, because I saw them earlier in the playground. I don't know where Gavin is, but I think he might have had an induction at the college. I called the police, so there should be someone on their way.' She vomited again as a police car screeched into the street.

'Cammy what about Ally and Stevie? It has to have been Seamus Driske who did this?' Pauline gasped. 'Who else could have done it, who else would want to?'

'My god, he could have gone to the school,' Cameron cried. 'Ally and Stevie are going to walk right into him. He won't know who they are though will he?' An ambulance siren could be heard approaching. 'Get help!' seal off the area,' Cameron shouted to the two police officers who were now walking towards them. 'Get someone round to Whitefield's school, control have pictures of the suspect. Get them to send them to you and let the Chief know.' Cameron and Jamie left Pauline helping Rosie, who was now sobbing and shaking, to sit down.

Meanwhile, Ally and Stevie attempted to use their council swipe cards to enter the school building. They both helped at after school clubs and breakfast clubs so had clearance to be in the school. 'Gabby will have let the staff know that we're coming so we can just go to the classes and get them. No point in waiting for the staff to bring them up.'

'That's strange, it's not locked. They must have seen us coming on the camera and opened it,' Stevie said, as he waved up at the camera.

'Did you not hear Gabby say the electricity had short circuited and had cut off the security system Stevie?'

Immediately on entering the school they realised something was very wrong. A young girl ran towards them, screaming. They could hear banging noises, a car backfiring. Ally stumbled. When she looked down Gabby lay on her back, her eyes staring, a single red mark on her forehead and blood oozing out over her blonde hair. 'There's a bad man with a gun,' the terrified child cried.

Suddenly aware the noise they had heard was gunshots, they could hear children screaming. 'Get outside!' she said to the girl, 'Don't stop! Run as fast as you can. Stop the first adult you see, get them to call the police.'

Stevie used a chair to wedge the fire doors open as more children ran towards them. 'Keep going! Get out!' he shouted.

Children ran down the stairs and began to scramble through the doors out into the playground. The school was an old one, spread over two floors it was due for demolition at the end of term; the new building twenty yards from the current school was almost completed. Ally saw Alexis Driske coming down the stairs. Running towards her, she lifted the little girl off her feet and into her arms.

Ally looked around. A man carrying a handgun appeared in the doorway of the corridor behind her, blocking their escape route. Ally still carrying Alexis, grabbed another little girl's hand and looked in the opposite direction, pushing children in front of her. 'Keep going,' she cried. She could see the second outside door. She was not aware of where Stevie was, her only thought was to get the children out of harms reach.

'Alexis come here right now you little bitch!' The man shouted.

Ally seeing the fear on Alexis's face held her closer and ran, suddenly she was aware of children around her. The little girl she held by the hand suddenly fell forward with great force, letting Ally's hand go. Ally looked down thinking she had fallen. To her horror the child lay on the floor, her eyes wide in terror, dark red blood oozing out onto the grey tiled floor. The sudden realisation of the situation hit Ally like a sledgehammer. 'My god!' she cried out loud, 'he's shooting at them!' Something hit her shoulder and the force spun her around still holding on to Alexis. She realised immediately she had been shot but felt no pain. Ally knew she had to keep going. Seconds later a shot hit her at the top of her leg, and she fell to the ground near to the old janitor's room. She pulled Alexis close to her, crawling towards the door. Suddenly Stevie was beside her. Pulling her and Alexis along, he pushed them into a recess under the staff stairs then jumped in beside Ally.

In the chaos the gunman missed this and passed by, still shooting. Ally saw a little boy, covered in blood, trying to move. She crawled out, dragging her damaged leg, which was bleeding profusely and reached the boy. Wrapping herself around him she began to crawl back towards the recess, pulling the little boy with her. Stevie noticing the trail of fresh blood following her across the floor jumped to his feet. Ally looked up as she reached the stair recess and realised that the man was heading back towards her. When he was a few feet away, she saw the gun point at her. Suddenly Stevie flew past her and rugby tackled the gunman to the ground. She saw the bang of the gun rather than heard it. Ally felt the ground shake, was aware of debris all around her, everything was in slow motion.

CHAPTER

THREE

In the darkness the first sensation Ally felt was pain; she was not sure where it was coming from. She tried to move but was quickly aware that something heavy lay across her thigh; Ally realised she was trapped. She could hear groaning from behind her head and tried to move. 'Who's there?' she whispered. Her lungs filled with dust and she began to cough, her head and chest hurting when she did.

'Ally, where are you? Thank God you're alive!'

'Stevie?' Ally whispered. 'What just happened?'

'Not sure, something blew up. I can't move much, there is something on top of me, but I can move my arm and get my hand out.'

Ally felt her arm being touched and grabbed the hand knowing it was her friend. Pain ripped through her arm and shoulder as she did. She gripped his hand tightly despite the sickening pain. 'What just happened Stevie? Is this real? I'm confused. What happened?' she asked again. The pain in her body was intense. She felt as though her head was about to explode and tried to tell herself that this was a dream.

'Ally there was a big explosion and then nothing. Stevie held her hand. 'I'm right above your head. The ground is wet but

I'm not sure whether it's oil from the central heating radiator or something else.'

'Is anyone else here?' Ally cried out; there was silence. 'Alexis, are you there?'

Ally tried to move her other hand, but something was pinning her down. 'My head hurts. It's really bad, burning like it's on fire or something.' Stevie moved his hand and searched around. Ally felt him touching her head.

'Ally, you're bleeding! I think that's what the liquid is. You must have lost a lot of blood. You need to stay calm and not move.'

'Stevie, I think I was shot in the shoulder and leg as well. How could anyone shoot at little children? I can understand, on some level, anger spilling out and him targeting us, but he was shooting children. Was it Seamus?'

'Ally, don't speak, just listen. We've both been shot. I think he blew the school up; we are buried under it. We need to listen out, there'll be help coming. We also need to conserve energy, try to be ready for them to rescue us.'

'Dear god Stevie, the children! Alexis . . . where is she? Wee Bobby Russell? He was alive when I went towards him. They were beside us.'

Stevie let out a sob, he knew however he sounded calmer than he felt. 'Ally listen to me; we have to stay calm. Please don't think about it. The explosion was huge. The blast could have moved them further away from us. I feel as though we have been here for hours, but it could just be minutes, I don't know.'

They lay, listening for any sound of a rescue attempt. Every now and then Stevie would ask 'Ally, are you okay?' Her voice, when she answered, sounding weaker and further away as time passed. When there was no response, he cried out; 'Ally, please answer me!'

'Stevie I'm okay, I just feel so tired. I feel as though my life is ebbing away with the blood.'

'Fuck sake, Ally, stay with me. Please Ally, stay awake. Stay with me.'

'Stevie, I love you, you do know that don't you? I just want you to know, I think I'm going to die. Tell the boys I love them and look after them for me Stevie. Can you tell my dad I was grateful for everything he has done for me?'

'Ally, you have to stop thinking like that, you're not going to die. You can tell them yourself.'

'I'm going to die without doing all the things I meant to do.'

'Well don't then, don't die. You're strong-willed and head-strong, will yourself to live. Ally, answer me!' Stevie realised Ally had possibly slipped back into unconsciousness or worse. Stevie managed to get his hand to her chest and rested it there. He could tell she was still breathing; he kept his hand on her chest, feeling it rise and fall.

Suddenly she gasped, coughed again and cried out in pain. 'Ally stay with me! Tell me about what you did at the weekend!' he called out in desperation. Stevie knew he was panicking; he also knew from a recent first aid course, he had to keep her awake. 'What did you do on Friday night? Remember Ally?' he urged. 'You didn't want to go out for a drink after work with Ruby and me because you were meeting someone. Who did you meet? Ally, please, just keep talking. I think you've been seeing someone? Ruby wouldn't commit to an answer when I asked her. I had a missed call from you, but you didn't answer when I called you back. Norma in reception said you got flowers yesterday and Ruby said she wasn't to tell anyone.'

'Yes, I've been seeing someone for the last few months. We had a big argument at the weekend, I finished with him. I really liked him, but it was never going to work. He wanted me to sleep with him. I wasn't ready for it. I thought I was, thought I wanted to, but I haven't slept with anyone since Ralph died. I tried but I was too scared, then I over-reacted and made a fool of myself.'

Stevie listening intently, heard the hint of a sob in her whisper. 'Oh Ally. I'm sorry I shouldn't have asked.'

'I couldn't tell you, but I actually called you on Saturday night because I needed to speak to a man I could trust. I knew you were out, so I called your mobile, but you didn't answer your phone, I switched mine off because he kept calling me.' Ally's voice sounded strange, calm, far away almost. 'Now, I'm going to die, I wish that I had had sex again. Is that strange?'

'No Ally, it's not strange. We're all sexual beings. Once and for all Ally, you're not going to die.' Stevie's heart ached. For a long time, even before his marriage ended four years ago, he had hoped that his friendship with Ally would develop into something more. He had never told her how he felt, too afraid he would lose her friendship which he valued. He didn't want to know who Ally had been seeing. There had been men over the years, but they never lasted long, over the last few months, he had realised there was someone. Ally's sons had also told him about a male calling the house for her. He knew though that he needed to keep her talking. He could hear life draining out of her voice, knew that it was imperative he keep her conscious due to the amount of blood she was losing.

'Who was the guy Ally? I asked you if you were seeing someone, but you denied it. Why? I thought we were good enough friends for you to have told me there was someone special! It's not Cammy O'Sullivan, is it? I was out drinking with him at Christmas, and he kept asking how to get into your knickers!'

'You wouldn't have understood Stevie. You would certainly not have approved, no it isn't Cammy,' Ally whispered, trying to focus on her words which were, she realised, coming out confused and slurred. She struggled to speak. 'I met him at that charity radio Children in Need lunch thing in the summer Ruby made me go to. They were donating money for Christmas toys to us. Remember? We tossed a coin at the team meeting, I lost and had to attend. Well I got sat next to him. He made me laugh, I enjoyed his company. I had no idea who he was at first. We got drunk, ended up running away. He wasn't used to not being recognised, and I would never have given him the time of day normally. I spotted he was trouble straight away, but it was so boring. He was just as bored as I was. He was different from anyone I knew. I ended up down the shore with him, we were really wasted, we got a bit carried away. I wasn't going to see him again then thought what the hell! I never take chances. I've never been into bad boys. It was just a game at first. I wanted to see how far he would go trying to sleep with me. He saw me as a challenge. We were both playing a game then I started to fall for him. I really began to enjoy his company and, probably because we were hiding, we became friends.'

'Who is he Ally? Do I know him?'

She took a deep breath. 'He's well known. His name is Willie . . . Willie Ogilvy.'

'Willog! You told me you never spoke to him at the do, I asked you, you said Willie who? I showed you the photograph from the local paper of you and him and you said . . . He's the Scotland manager? You said you were just at the same table and he was a prick!' Stevie gasped. 'He was my football hero when I was a boy. He's a bastard to women. He's been married a few times, always has some model or other on his arm. He's also usually drunk, falling out of nightclubs. Sorry Ally, I wouldn't have thought he would have been your type.'

'He's not what you think Stevie, he is quite sweet actually.'

'He's a womaniser who has a shocking reputation Ally. What possessed you?' Stevie hissed, shock overtaking fear for a second.

When Ally didn't answer, Stevie began to panic. 'Ally are you okay stay with me, tell me about him? Ally? Talk to me.'

When she answered her voice sounded strong again, more like herself. 'Stevie, I was lonely I think, and it was coming up to the anniversary. I fancied him, I liked that he was chasing me. I know you and I are friends, but it's not the same as having someone there to love you, sexually, I mean. I miss intimacy, I miss having a sex life. Stevie, it's been fifteen years, suddenly I missed it. I think I just wanted to be touched by someone.'

'I don't know what to say Ally, I kind of thought that you weren't interested in men?'

'I don't really know what happened, Ralph, well you know what he was like, he was really tactile. You used to laugh at him being touchy feely and well, we had a good sex life. I've never met anyone else I wanted to sleep with. Willie, well he was a perfect gentleman, he never forced the issue about sex, he kissed me oh I don't know ... it was the first time I've ever felt I wanted to be touched by someone else.'

'Are you sure it wasn't just the novelty?'

There was a long pause, when she answered, Stevie could hear that she was in pain, her breathing again heavy and laboured. 'No, I thought that at first, I started going for massages to see if it was just, I needed someone touching me. When you are not in a relationship no one touches you,' Ally's voice was merely a whisper as she added. 'I still just wanted him to do it. I can't believe I'm telling you this Stevie, but I don't want to die without saying it. I need someone to tell Willie I'm sorry for the way I behaved. I was embarrassed. I made such a fool of myself.'

'Ally you are going to be okay, stay calm,' Stevie knew her voice was weakening; her breathing increasing, 'shoosh' he whispered, 'don't talk anymore just try to stay calm.'

'Stevie, I have a funny feeling in my head. I can't feel my legs or my arm.' She squeezed his hand. 'Stevie I'm scared! I'm drifting away, I can't stop. The pain is . . . it's.' She cried out, howling like a wounded animal. 'Stevie, it hurts. I thought dying didn't hurt but it does. Help me. Oh god, please help me!'

'Ally, please keep thinking, keep saying who you are.' Panic overtook his own pain. 'Ally, please answer me.' There was no reply, however, Stevie realised she was still breathing. 'Oh please, dear god, don't let me lose her now,' he said out loud. 'If you live Ally, I'll do anything for you. Please Ally!' He pushed her chest, she gasped and coughed. 'Ally, please try to stay awake. Please Ally, don't die on me.' She didn't answer this time though. Stevie continued to try to wake her but quickly realised that he was fighting a losing battle. He was not sure how long they had been lying in the rubble of the school but guessed that it was running in to several hours. Suddenly Stevie remembered his phone was in his pocket. He let go of his hold on Ally and reached for it; he needed to know the time. He managed to bring it up to his face and pressed buttons. It immediately lit up, showed the time then a low battery warning. He gasped when he realised it was 3 p.m. which he knew meant he and Ally had been buried for nearly five hours. He looked around him, moving the phone to light his way. He could see they were still in the recess under the stairs; some of the steel of the stairwell had bent around them providing a protective cage. Stevie's heart lurched as he realised that there were bodies too. He could see a child's foot sticking out of the rubble to his left; a man's shoe lay beside his head. He moved his head to the side and could make out Ally's face in the darkness. She was still, her eyes closed, blood covered half her face. He was sure, for a few seconds, that she was dead, then he was aware of her breathing breaking the silence. Suddenly he noticed a message on the phone's screen: it said, *'emergency services only.'* He tried to dial 999 and to his amazement it rang; he got through to a control room.

'Which service?' the operator asked.

'Anyone, I don't know or care who!' Stevie gasped. 'My name is Stevie Marshall, I'm a social worker. I'm trapped in Whitefield's Primary School. There was an explosion.'

'Hold on Stevie!' the operator gasped. 'I'll put you through to the incident room.'

The line went dead for a few seconds then Stevie heard a familiar voice. 'Stevie? It's Cammy. Where are you?'

'How the fuck should I know! We were near the Crammond Street door when the explosion happened Cammy. Near the janitor's office. We are under a stairwell. Can't you follow the signal? You need to get us out. Ally is in a bad way; she was shot a couple of times and she has a head injury.'

Suddenly the line went dead, and the light on the phone went out. Stevie realised his battery had run out. 'Shit! Shit! Shit! Why did I not charge it up this morning?' Stevie began to panic. '*She was right!* he thought. '*We're both going to die here.*' He reached out and pushed Ally. 'Ally! Ally! Wake up!' He knew he was shouting now; he didn't care. 'Ally, they know we are here, you've got to wake up. We'll get out of here. They know we're alive, so they'll be trying to dig us out. Ally, please wake up.' Although there was no response, he could still feel her chest moving up and down, so he hung on to the knowledge that she was still breathing.

Stevie's mind was in turmoil. Ally was a beautiful woman with a great personality, but what on earth was she doing with Willie Ogilvy? Why, he asked himself, had he never had the courage to ask Ally about relationships? Ralph had been one of Stevie's best friends. He had been working with them for a few years before Ralph died. He helped her through the aftermath of the road traffic accident where she lost Ralph, her mother and her baby daughter. Ally had been badly hurt in the smash but had recovered and brought up her boys on her own.

Stevie, married with a daughter much the same age as Ally's boys, had remained a friend of the family. They had even gone on holiday together with his wife Laura and the children a few times. His daughter Kiera was close to Ally and her boys, who she viewed as brothers. Ally had been there for him four years ago, when Laura told him she was leaving him to live with an old boyfriend who she'd rekindled a relationship with through Facebook. At fifteen, Kiera was infinitely sensible, she had not been too interested; she moved easily between her mother and father. Now nineteen, Keira was at university in Glasgow, studying social work and sharing a flat with Scott, Ally's eldest son, who was a business studies student at the same university. This allowed Ally and Stevie to share the bills for their respective children. Ally's younger son Danny was currently studying for Highers, hoping to take up a place at another Glasgow university in September and then occupy the third bedroom in the flat.

Stevie tried to move his foot; the pain ripped through his body like wildfire. He realised how badly he was hurt. He knew it was broken but was also aware that he'd been lucky. He was unsure of how many times Ally had been shot. He had tried to pull her back when she rushed out from their hiding place to rescue the little boy. Stevie realised that in the split second between that and him rugby tackling the gunman, she may have been shot in the head. He began to sob quietly to himself. He heard a groan, then a child's cry. 'Mammy! I want my mammy.' The strong Northern Irish accent was unmistakable.

'Alexis, is that you darling?'

'Stevie!' the child whimpered, immediately recognising his voice, 'I'm scared. I want my mammy.'

Stevie realised Alexis had most likely been unconscious since the blast and had just woken up. 'Are you hurting Alexis?' he asked gently.

'This is all my fault. My daddy said that everyone would die if I told, so he did.' She began to sob. 'My back hurts and my head.'

Stevie felt his heart would break at this little girl's pain. 'Listen to me honey, no matter what has happened, it is not your fault! Sweetheart listen to me please? I can't move to reach you, but you need to try to stay calm. The police, they'll get to us. They're searching for us now. But you must keep very still and quiet, so we can listen for sounds then if we hear something we yell as loud as we can. Can you move Alexis?'

'Something is on my leg, but my hands are okay. My head hurts. I think I was sleeping; I feel tired. Stevie, I'm scared. What if he is still there? It was my daddy, so it was. I saw him, he saw me. He shot the boy beside me, told me to come with him. I ran away. He had Gavin and Jenny; they were scared Stevie. Then I saw you and Ally. She picked me up and we ran away.' Alexis began to sob again, 'it's all my fault.'

'Alexis please listen to me. Everything is going to be okay; this isn't your fault; you were very brave to run. You need to stay calm sweetheart. We've been lying here a long time, so you have been asleep, but you must not go back to sleep.' He tried to follow the sound of her voice, but he could not work out where she was. He thought her voice was coming from behind him and wondered if it had been her foot he could see when he had the phone lit. Knowing Alexis was there and could hear him though, meant he remained calm, at least on the surface.

'Alexis, keep talking to me.' There was silence once again. 'Alexis? Alexis?' he called out, but this time there was no reply. Stevie lay in the darkness, listening to the silence around him; he guessed that as he could not hear any other noise, they were well buried in the rubble. This made the fact that he had got through on the mobile even more amazing. He imagined emergency vehicles would be there with sirens, and he could hear nothing. He reached out again and touched Ally's face; he heard her groan. 'Ally, are you awake?'

Stevie viewed Ally as one of his closest friends. His male friends laughed about the friendship; they could not believe that he had never made a move on her. Stevie could not imagine a world where she was not in his life. He began to cry quietly as the fear of losing her became more real. He wanted to scream out loud, but knowing Alexis was alive nearby, opened the possibility that there were other children around who could hear. He touched Ally's cheek, checked again and realised that although she was still breathing, her breaths were slower. He took her hand again and felt for her pulse; to his amazement it appeared to be strong, almost normal. This gave him hope she would survive. He was trying not to think about Ally being with Willie Ogilvy, but despite this the picture kept coming into his head. Stevie made up his mind he would tell Ally how he felt as soon as they were rescued. '*Ally, I love you! Please don't die Ally. I don't care if you are with that prick footballer,* he said to himself. *If you're still alive, I'll be there for you.*' Stevie was not a religious person. He had always cursed religion for the atrocities he felt it caused, but he found himself praying. He realised he felt dizzy; it occurred to him that it was now several hours since he had eaten. Stevie had been a diabetic since childhood. He knew his blood sugar levels would be getting low. He reached down into his jacket pocket and managed to pull out a couple of biscuits he had taken from the meeting.

CHAPTER
FOUR

1.45 p.m. Tuesday 23rd February

Ruby Weir stood with Cameron O'Sullivan, the local chief constable and the leading fireman. They watched in stunned silence as the rescue squads worked carefully, moving rubble and pulling bodies from the mass of twisted wood and metal. 'Why are we still waiting for the heat-seeking equipment to come through?' Cameron shouted into his mobile phone. 'We need it now! With it we'll be able to locate any survivors.'

There was a commotion behind them. Ruby turned around to see Ally's younger son Danny pushing his way towards her. 'Ruby, what's happened to my mum? I was supposed to meet her for lunch and when she didn't turn up . . . I phoned the office, they told me that the police were looking for me. They wouldn't tell me anything. I heard about this on the radio, I just knew mum would be involved. Please tell me she's alright Ruby. Where's Stevie?'

Ruby put her arm around Danny. 'I tried to call you but got no answer. The police have managed to contact Scott and Kiera.'

Ruby tightened her grip on him. 'Stevie was with your mum, Danny, they were in the school. We don't know where they are but love . . . we are assuming they are somewhere in there. We haven't managed to reach your granddad. He wasn't at the house. This is Danny, Ally's youngest son.' Ruby told Cameron, who put out his hand for a handshake.

Cameron looked into Danny's eyes and spoke calmly, 'We're waiting for heat-seeking equipment to come from Glasgow. Meanwhile we are digging carefully and quietly, so we can hear. We are bringing out survivors and, unfortunately, bodies.' Cameron shook his head. 'This is not a nice scene Danny. There are a lot of dead and badly injured. The fire brigade think that perhaps a gas main was fractured and that caused an explosion. It's strange, the force of the blast brought the building down, but the little bit of fire blew itself out.'

'I heard there was a gunman?' Danny said, looking at Ruby, tears building up in his eyes.

'There was. We know who he was. Your mother and Stevie had come here to get some children.' Ruby looked at the handsome young man; she had known him since birth. She had been Ally's line manager for the last six years but was also her closest friend. Ruby, as usual, was struck by how much eighteen-year-old Danny resembled his father; Ralph Campbell, who had been only thirty years old when he died. Ally was a widow at twenty-eight; Danny had been nearly three years old and his brother Scott, five. Ralph, Ally and Ruby had been at university together, studying to be social workers Ally and Ruby in the same year and Ralph two years ahead of the women. They had become close friends. Ruby had watched their romance develop. When Ally had become pregnant in her last year and she and Ralph had decided to marry, Ruby been bridesmaid at their wedding. She was also Scott's godmother. She loved Ally and her boys; they were her family. Ruby had been there with Stevie, supporting Ally in the dark days after the tragic accident where her family were killed. Ally had supported Ruby through the heartbreak of infertility and her divorce. Ally shared her pain when Ruby's ex-husband had babies with his new wife. They were best friends, they shared everything. Ruby loved Danny and his brother as though they were her own.

Ruby was the only person Ally had told about her dates with Willie Ogilvy. Like Stevie, Ruby could not believe Ally would get involved with someone like this womanising football player. However, Ally was her friend, so Ruby said nothing. When Ally had come to her on Saturday night in tears and had been honest about her feelings for this man, Ruby had urged her to forget about him for a while and then see how she felt in a month or so.

'Kiera, we're over here!' Ruby called out as she saw Kiera Marshall searching faces in the crowd. Behind her, Scott Campbell, Ally's elder son. Scott hugged Ruby tightly; he looked pale, and he trembled as Ruth quickly filled them in on the situation.

Kiera began to cry as Cameron told her about her father's last moments before the blast. Cameron looked at Ally's sons. 'A lot of the children who got out tell us that it was because your mum and Stevie helped them.'

Danny began to pace up and down. His brother put a hand on his shoulder. 'Dan, have you eaten? Have you had your insulin?'

Danny nodded, looking annoyed. 'Don't treat me like a kid, Scott, I'm eighteen and I'm fine. I don't need to be reminded to take my insulin or to eat.'

Scott Campbell shook his head. 'It's just the stress Dan, you can forget. We don't need you getting sick.'

Two firemen passed by and Danny grabbed one by the arm. 'Can we do anything?' he asked. 'Our mum and her friend are trapped in there.'

The fireman looked at him. 'The more help we get, the quicker we can rescue people,' he said, 'but it's pretty bad son, lots of bodies and bad injuries. If you report over there at the rig, they'll get you some PPE and tell you what to do.'

Kiera looked at Ruby. 'We need to do something don't we? I'll go mad just standing around waiting.'

Ruby nodded. 'The social work emergency response team are in the new school, dealing with relatives and taking information. We could help with that. Come on, we'll go over now,' Ruby said. 'Cameron, when there's news can you come find us?'

Cameron nodded. 'I'm going to help dig,' he said to his commanding officer, 'there's no point in just standing here watching everyone else work.'

The chief constable shook his head. 'Cammy, I know what you're saying, but you're more use to us in the control room. I need you to stay there, you know the area and you know the inside of the school. You also were involved with the emergency response team formation.'

Cameron shrugged, but looked annoyed. 'I'll do as I'm told sir, but I know a lot of these children, and Stevie and Ally have worked with us for years. We're friends as well as colleagues.'

***

Just after three o'clock, Cameron ran out to the site, a plan of the school in his hand. 'There's been a call from the rubble. One of the social workers has managed to get through on their mobile. They're trapped somewhere in this area we think.' He showed the rescue team the map and highlighted the janitor's office. Danny and Scott stopped and listened intently as Cameron O'Sullivan told them their mother was alive under the debris, although she was hurt; Stevie was with her.

CHAPTER

FIVE

Light was beginning to fade. They erected floodlights and continued to painstakingly move the rubble. Danny and Scott worked tirelessly, along with the emergency services and other volunteers, slowly moving rubble so the firemen and paramedics could pull bodies from the mess of wood, steel and masonry that had, until this morning, been Whitefield primary school.

There was despair one minute, when a small child's lifeless, broken body was gently lifted onto a stretcher, followed by elation a few minutes later when another was found alive. No one involved with the rescue would ever be able to forget the horror they had been exposed to.

It was 5 p.m. when they found Stevie. He was weak but still conscious. 'There's a child here, she has been drifting in and out of consciousness. Also, my friend Ally,' he gasped. 'Leave me, get them out. Ally ... Alyson Campbell is badly hurt, but still breathing. Please get to her, leave me, I can wait. Alexis Driske is here, to my left, above my head, I think. She's seven years old. Ally is on the right, just at my side. Please get them first. I just need some glucose, I'm diabetic. I had some biscuits in my pocket ... but that was hours ago.'

'Hey, stay calm mate, you owe me a pint for this.' The paramedic joked with him. Scot here tells me you like your beer,'

Scott Campbell bent down and looked sadly at Stevie, 'I'm so glad you are okay Stevie, just relax now, Alex here will see to you.' He nodded at the green suited paramedic who knelt beside him. 'They know about your diabetes, so they have everything ready. I'll see you later once you are out. Fuck Stevie . . . it's been awful. I can't believe what's happened.'

'I know, buddy.' Stevie whispered, 'not what I expected to be doing today either.'

'Sorry mate, I'm going to have to take the pin prick from your ear, can't reach your hands,' the paramedic said. He looked at the blood glucose monitor. 'It's amazing you're still conscious . . . 2.9 . . . not too bad considering. I'll give you a shot of glucagon.'

'Can you get me some water please? My mouth is dry!' Stevie asked as the ambulance man injected him.

Seconds later, as the ambulance man put a straw in his mouth, Stevie became aware of Danny Campbell talking to him. 'Stevie, thank God you're alive. Scott and I have been helping to dig people out. We've been worried sick. Kiera's here too, helping in the centre with the relatives. She's frantic about you and Mum, Ruby is keeping her busy.'

Danny stood up. He watched the firemen lift another child from the rubble and place the body on a stretcher. Suddenly he realised that this wasn't a child, it was his mother. Danny shouted to Scott, and together they watched in terror as a paramedic put a cannula in her hand and after placing an oxygen mask over her face, he quickly checked her over. 'She's breathing and only just alive.' he heard a medic say quietly. 'Get her out of here.'

'They've found mum she's breathing,' Scott whispered to Stevie, he stood up watching the paramedics wheel her away. 'They are taking her to the ambulance.'

Stevie grabbed Scott's ankle. 'Please go with her, she shouldn't be alone. I'm not as badly hurt. I was shot in the shoulder, but I think she was shot a few times. Keep calm mate.' he whispered. As Scott stood back up and disappeared from view, the firemen pulled Stevie free. Stevie suddenly was aware of his head spinning and then darkness enveloped him.

In the ambulance, a doctor quickly worked with Ally; he began to look for injuries. Danny Campbell stood at the ambulance door, tears running down his face. He had never really thought about how small his mother was. At just over five-foot-tall and a natural size eight, she had looked tiny on the stretcher. Her auburn hair was matted with blood and dirt, her face grey from the rubble; blood dripped from her head. She was so still it was difficult to know if she was breathing or not. The medic intubated her in seconds and hooked her to a monitor before instructing his colleague to get her to hospital.

Danny jumped into the vehicle; the paramedic blocked his way. 'Sorry mate, we can't take you. Is this your sister?'

'No. My mum!'

'I'm going to need to take the medic with her, she's really badly hurt. We'll get her to hospital and stabilise her. She is likely to have to be transferred to the major trauma unit in Glasgow, probably by helicopter. It will leave from the hospital. Do you have transport? You can follow us up to the hospital by car. We need to stabilise her before we can assess her.'

'Is she going to die?' Danny asked, the pain of having to ask this question etched on his face. The trauma of the day lay heavily on his mind; the strain of hoping, each time they found someone alive. He had seen things he could not make sense of, had his hopes raised and dashed many times.

The medic looked up. 'Hope not. Look pal, her pulse is strong, but she's in a bad way. She'll need surgery, but she's holding her own here.'

'She's a very determined and strong lady!' Scott said over his brother's shoulder.

'That will help buddy, she'll need that strength.' He shut the door, and the ambulance moved away, its blue light flashing.

'What about Stevie?' Scott suddenly asked. 'He was fine and talking to me.'

Danny shook his head. 'I don't know Scott. I never even asked, I think he was fine, he was talking, they gave him glucagon.'

Moments later Kiera ran towards them. 'Can you take me to the hospital with you? They won't let me go with Dad. Scott, his heart stopped! They were running with him on a trolley, pumping his chest, trying to get it started.' She began to cry. Scott put his arm around her, his own tears falling unchecked onto his cheeks.

Ruby appeared from behind them as a paramedic passed by carrying a little girl, her face streaked with blood, dirt and tears, but she was alive, and a little boy who, obviously breathing, but unconscious, was placed on a stretcher.

***

'Cameron, we've got your two social worker friends out,' the chief constable cried, coming into the control room. He put down his hard hat and gloves and unzipped the fluorescent yellow safety jacket he had been wearing.

Cameron jumped up. 'Alive?'

'Yes. Alyson is barely there, but they're working on her. She has multiple injuries by the look of her and if she lives, well...we can worry about that later. Steven, well, it would appear he was conscious the whole time then his heart stopped when we were pulling him out. Something to do with whatever they injected him with for his diabetes. They shocked him back, they think he will be okay.' The chief constable called over to Gerry who was inputting information on a computer. 'Gerry they're alive but both in a bad way I'm afraid. Do you want a lift to the hospital? Cameron and I are going to need to go up there.' He nodded at Jamie Johnstone, who had also been helping with the rescue. 'They think they got Seamus Driske, he's alive, but with multiple injuries. He's being taken to accident and emergency, so we need to go. Cameron, can you hand over now? Come with me.'

Gerry stood up; wearily he lifted his jacket. 'I'll take my own car up if you don't mind and meet you there.'

'Okay if you're sure?' Cameron said, putting his hand on Gerry's shoulder as he passed him. 'Thanks for your help Gerry, see you up at the hospital?'

***

Gerry walked towards his car and got in, his mind in turmoil, the day had been so busy he had not really had time to think. Although he was relieved they were alive, Gerry spent a lot of his working life angry at Stevie and Ally. He knew they were fine social workers, but Stevie especially wound him up with his reluctance to conform. Gerry had always been someone who followed orders and process; he found it difficult to understand people who refused to do so. If he was honest, he was in awe of Ally. Other workers in the team and in the department tended to seek her out for advice and guidance. Gerry had never really acknowledged her PHD. Not having her academic ability, he knew he would never have managed to study the way Ally had. Gerry never used Ally's academic title, but he knew that others did especially when trying to prove a point. Dr Alyson Campbell had been a thorn in his side for the last few years. He had discussed it many times with Ruby, whom he managed. She had been adamant that she would not push Ally towards promotion, because Ally did not want to apply for promoted posts.

Gerry knew, with Ally's experience and PHD, she should have been in senior management or teaching social work. However, Ruby pointed out that in social work considering the high burnout rate among children and families' workers, Ally and Stevie were unique.

He and Ruby had argued recently about it and Ruby told him, 'the average child protection social worker is twenty-three, childless and with two years' experience. Ally and Stevie have been doing this for over twenty years. Leave it be. We're lucky to have been able to keep workers of this quality in the team. The other social work staff look up to them and they're both natural leaders. If they don't want promotion, leave them alone Gerry, it's not as though they stay because they can't go elsewhere, any other team would snap them up. You should be proud of them, not trying to push them out.'

If Gerry was honest with himself, he was jealous of them, their ability, their friendship. He wondered if they were a couple, they were so close. Gerry had also worked with Ally's husband Ralph many years before, although him and Stevie Marshall had been friends, Ralph had been someone Gerry admired as a person and a social worker. Ally to his knowledge had been on her own since Ralph died. Stevie was he knew, divorced. Everyone was astounded by the accounts of two friends bravery today. When Gerry thought about it, he really wasn't surprised by what they had done. They were both fearless in most situations.

Children who had escaped told their rescuers Stevie and Ally had run into the line of fire helping them to get out. One child said they saw Ally and Stevie carrying children shortly before the blast. Gerry knew that if they lived, he would make sure that their bravery was acknowledged and rewarded.

***

'How is the community going to recover from this?' Ruby Weir whispered to herself. She was following Danny's car as it sped after the ambulance up the hill toward the hospital; a major trauma receiving centre had been set up to receive the casualties of the day.

Ruby waited to turn into the hospital public entrance and watched as a helicopter came down to land in the hospital grounds. Hospital staff pushed trollies out to the helipad with children on them. Television cameras were everywhere taking pictures, presenters lit by floodlights, spoke to cameras in front of the hospital. Ruby parked her car in the street. '*They can give me a ticket, I don't care,*' she said to herself. '**Fuck off!**' she yelled at a female police officer walking towards her.

A taxi screeched to a halt beside her and Ruby gasped as she saw Jimmy Jackson, Ally's father, getting out of it. 'Where is she? Is she alright, Ruby? I was in Glasgow. I saw it on the news.'

'We've been trying all day to reach you Granddad,' Scott said, coming up behind them. 'You really do need to switch on that mobile Mum got you. She's alive, they're working on her. The doctor I spoke to reckons they'll airlift her and Stevie straight to Glasgow. They're badly hurt Granddad.' Scott began to sob, his body shaking as he gasped for breath. 'She looked awful. I saw her, she was covered in blood and dirt, she wasn't conscious. Stevie's hurt badly. He was conscious the whole time, but he suffered some sort of seizure when they pulled him out. The paramedic said it can happen when someone is trapped for a long period. The blood rushes apparently, they had to give him glucagon when he was trapped and that made the risk higher. They said . . . they said, if there is already a head injury that can cause more problems. He's not conscious either now. Granddad, how could this happen? Ruby, what was Mum doing in there?

The police said she and Stevie knew there was a problem before they went to the school. Why did no one stop them?'

Ruby put her hand on his shoulder. 'Try to calm down. She appears to have gone straight to the school, heard the shooting and still gone inside. There are kids who got out because of her and Stevie. Boys, you know what her and Stevie are like!'

'Oh, fucking great. They can be dead heroes,' Danny burst out crying.

His grandfather grabbed his arm and shook him. 'Danny son, you need to stay calm. You know your mum wouldn't listen to anyone. Danny, have you eaten? Have you had your insulin?'

Danny nodded. 'I'm fine Gramps. I'm just so worried about Mum and Stevie.'

Jimmy put his arm around his grandson. 'She's a tough cookie. If anyone can survive, it's your mum.'

Kiera Marshall stood shaking by the side of the car. Scott walked over and put his arm around her. 'Come on Kiera, let's go and face it together. Coming Ruby? Granddad? Danny?' The others followed as he walked through the electric doors of the Accident and Emergency department.

A police officer stopped them. 'Sorry, you can't come in.'

'Oh, we can, and we are going to,' Ruby said wearily. 'I have two staff members in there, these people are their family. We *are* going in.' Ruby looked at the young constable sternly over the top of her glasses.

'It's okay Colin mate.' Cameron O'Sullivan, accompanied by the chief constable, came through the car park towards them. 'They're with us, just let them through. He is only doing his job,' Cameron said, looking at the small group of people.

'I know!' Danny said wearily. 'But can you try to find out what is to happen with Mum and Stevie. The medic at the school reckoned they would airlift them straight to Glasgow.'

He glanced over to where a helicopter was taking off. 'How did they manage to pull all this together so quickly?'

'Each area has an emergency plan which involves all the emergency services and can be brought in within a very fast time frame,' Cameron told him.

'They did well then?' Scott observed.

Cameron nodded. 'We did better than we thought we would in the emergency response. You know, you practice these things over and over, but it's with the hope that you never have to use the emergency plans.'

The chief constable was on his phone. Danny looked at Scott and then at Cameron and watched as the two policemen walked to the corner of the room, out of earshot the chief inspector looked around and then said quietly. 'They've recovered firearms from the scene, and they'll most likely be unlicensed and illegal. They'll not be traceable. It will give us evidence of the terrorist connection to the perpetrator, say nothing yet though,' he whispered to Cameron.

'Is he dead?' Scott asked as the two police officers joined the small group, 'the man who did this?'

Cameron shook his head and made a face. 'Don't know yet Scott, we've not been able to account for all the adults found in the rubble,' he lied, making the decision that Scott didn't need to know yet that the gunman was alive; in fact, he was being treated only a few feet away from where they stood. 'There are so many casualties, it's not possible to say if he is dead, among the survivors, or still buried in the rubble. '*God forgive me!*' he thought. He looked at Scott again. 'Luckily, colleagues from Police Northern Ireland were here for the meeting we were having about the family, so they can identify him. If he's alive, we'll make sure they throw away the key. Hopefully, he is alive, in order to allow some closure for the survivors and the victims' families. There are around thirty dead, most of them young kids and that number will most likely rise as the night progresses,' Cameron choked on a sob

Ruby reached over and touched Cameron's arm. She looked at Scott and Danny. 'You'll all need some help dealing with this,' she said gently, 'you've experienced the very worst of human nature today, and you saw some really awful things, please remember that big boys can cry, all of you.' Ruby sighed, I'm going to go get some fresh air, I'll be back in a moment.'

Cameron nodded watching Ruby leave, he turned to the two boys. 'You two have done so well today. Trained police officers twice your age struggled with what they were seeing. But Ruby is right, we are all going to need help to deal with it all.'

'At least we felt we were helping,' Scott sighed. 'It was really bad. How can someone do that to a school full of little kids? Mum and Stevie too? They really care about people; they go out of their way to help.'

'If there's anything I can do, just ask,' Cameron said quietly.

'Hey Cameron, you could maybe advise Danny. He wants to join the police after university. Would he be able to with his diabetes?'

Danny punched his brother on the arm. 'Leave it for now Scott. This isn't the time.'

The chief constable smiled. 'The general rule is that if it has been controlled over a period of time you can apply,' he looked at Danny. 'Let's get your mum sorted out, then you can come and speak to me about it. I have a feeling you would be exactly the type of young person we would be looking for.'

'I hope you don't think I'm looking for favours, sir,' Danny stammered. 'I'd never do that.'

'I believe that son'

Gerry sat in the hospital car park staring straight ahead. Paralysed with fear; he could not get out of his car. Gerry was a big man, over six feet tall. Stopping smoking two years ago meant he'd gained weight. He was aware most of his shirts strained under the girth of his gut, and he had taken to wearing sweaters over them to hide it. Gerry felt separated from his team. Most of his career he'd been a manager, but he sometimes struggled with the emotional side of managing staff. He was a social worker at heart though and found working with child protection rewarding. Trapped in a marriage, which had become a relationship of convenience rather than passion, he was desperate for some female comfort. However, he was aware that this made him a figure of fun amongst his colleagues. Gerry had never been good at reading signals from the opposite sex; he had grown up with a strong, overbearing father and three older brothers. His mother had left when he was four years old, and the young Gerry had struggled to make and sustain relationships with women. He'd met his wife at church and initially thought they had a lot in common. However, they had been unable to have children. Eventually they had both developed interests away from the marriage but remained together as friends. Gerry, at fifty, felt that life was passing him by.

Gerry remained in the car, trying to compose himself as the shock of the day's events played on his mind. Tears ran down his face. He wished he had treated Ally and Stevie better than he had; they were both good people and dedicated social workers. He was . . . he now realised, jealous of their close friendship; he had never been able to relax with his colleagues. Gerry snapped out of his thoughts, realising someone was tapping the window. He looked up; Ruby stood shivering outside the door. He put down the window and looked up at her.

'Can I come in and sit with you? I don't want to intrude in the family stuff, but I don't want to be alone,' she admitted. Gerry nodded, Ruby quickly walked around the car and slid into the passenger seat beside him.

'I know we've both stopped, but I had these in the car.' She offered him a cigarette which he took and lit from the car cigarette lighter. Taking a deep draw, Gerry pressed the electronic window button on his side of the car, lowering both his window and the passenger one. He tilted his head back and let out a long slow stream of smoke.

Neither of them spoke for a few minutes, but eventually Gerry broke the silence. 'Any news?' he asked, his voice gruff with emotion.

Ruby nodded. 'Ally is critical but stable. They're waiting for the air ambulance. Stevie had some sort of seizure. His heart had to be shocked to bring him back, but they've stabilised him too. They're taking them to the Queen Elizabeth Hospital. They reckon that that's the best place for them. Ally has a serious head injury and Stevie may have one. Gerry I'm so scared. I can't believe what's happened here.' She began to cry, Gerry put his arm around her and pulled her close. He felt tears prick at his own eyes again. He couldn't speak; the day had been traumatic for everyone. 'How do we start to deal with this?' Ruby whispered into his chest.

Gerry kissed the top of her head and she could feel the wetness of his own tears in her hair. 'You are a tough cookie Ruby Weir, you will . . . we will deal with this . . . leadership that's what it needs. You can do it, and I can too if you are on my side.'

Ruby quickly composed herself and pulled away from her boss's embrace. 'Thank you Gerry, I needed that.'

'Do you want to go to the hospital Ruby? I'll go with you if you like.'

Ruby nodded. 'I think I would Gerry, I need to know they're alright. Also, I need to make sure their families are supported. I just had to take a moment away from it all.'

'Me too.' he admitted. 'It's a lot to take in, isn't it? I keep thinking I should have stopped them going out this morning. I should have done more, Ruby.'

Ruby looked at him and shook her head. 'Nothing you said would have made any difference Gerry, they would have gone anyway.' She sighed. 'I'm so fucking angry at Ally . . . She went into the school. Cammy showed me the CCTV footage. Stevie, he would do anything she suggested. They should have left it to the police. They must have heard the gunshots?'

Gerry sighed. 'It would appear though there are quite a few children who are alive because they *did* go in Ruby. Alexis Driske and Bobby Russell certainly survived because of Ally.'

'I saw Ally when they pulled her out Gerry. She's in a bad way. She's been shot several times, lost a lot of blood, and there are all sorts of injuries from the explosion. The medic in there just told Jimmy that if she had not been unconscious, she would have died from the blood loss. Apparently because she was not moving, it slowed and clotted. God, Gerry, what on earth happened? Why didn't we know that this man was as dangerous? How did he manage to get here without the port police being aware?'

'Ruby, these are all questions for later. Right now, we just have to hope and pray they both come through.' Gerry sighed, 'and if they don't we will deal with that too.'

Ruby wiped her eyes with the tissue that Gerry handed her. 'They reckon there are about forty dead, Gerry, most of them young kids. Kids we know. How will the community ever recover from this? Fuck, how will any of us be able to forget what happened today?'

'Don't know Ruby, but we'll recover. As will the people in the Whitefield's, they've a strong community spirit.'

'Is Seamus Driske dead?' Ruby asked.

Gerry shook his head, blowing smoke out the window before he spoke. 'He was pulled out unconscious but alive. He's been taken to hospital. Hopefully, they'll stabilise him, and he'll live to go on trial and be punished for this. He needs to be, everyone will need closure. The police told me what they found at Sally's was gruesome. Rosie is having treatment for shock. It looks as though they had been taken by surprise, they were all tied up and gagged. Sally had been sexually assaulted then knifed. Seonaid too. Davie Prentice had been castrated, his penis had been hacked off and put in his mouth whilst he was still alive. He bled to death they reckon. Fuck I'm sorry, you didn't need to hear that.'

'It's okay Gerry, you are in shock too, and it kind of all fits with the kind of animal who could have killed little children. It's barbaric, they were right in their diagnosis of a psychopath. We were totally out of our depth with this. We should have known, should have been prepared.'

'Nothing could have prepared us for this, it's not like anything that we've ever experienced is it? It's totally out of kilter with our knowledge of the world. As I said all of these questions will be asked and hopefully answered later.'

Ruby wiped away tears with a tissue, 'Okay Gerry, let's go and see how Jimmy and the kids are coping. There must be some news now. Then we will need to go to Glasgow.' She looked at Gerry and sighed, it's going to be a long night, you'd better call your wife. She'll be worried. I know she was ill, is she back at work yet?'

'She's due back at work next week. I might as well tell you . . . it's kind of complicated, she's in Majorca,' he sighed, 'with her latest girlfriend, Ruby. Oh, it's a long kind of sad story. Not that she won't care, we are not you know, a couple. We've stayed together out of convenience and out of her not wanting anyone to know she's gay. She teaches at a catholic girl's school as you know, well she was a bit worried that they would find a way to get rid of her if they knew. However, she has told them, her bosses have been supportive, and we have decided to end the charade. So, no I don't need to call her yet, I would imagine she will hear it on the news and call me.'

'I'm sorry Gerry, that must be hard?' Ruby sighed, 'I kind of wondered about you and her I suppose. You never seemed happy but it's really none of my business. Thank you for sharing it with me though, I'm kind of proud you felt able to.'

'Oh, I'm fine with it, we are friends her and I. It's not that there's any animosity, and to be honest, it didn't come as a shock when she came out. It's just that there was no reason for either of us to leave before she met her current girlfriend and it became serious. She's a nice lady Bria, that's her name, I think we will be friends, but I kind of don't want her to move in with us, because that would be weird, so I'm in the process of moving out to a flat. Anyway, I would appreciate if you could keep that to yourself Ruby, I'm, not sure I want to be the subject of office gossip.'

CHAPTER
SIX

2.30 a.m. 24th February

Lynne Lockhead sat in the front of the news van, her hands around her hot coffee in a polystyrene cup. She was freezing; she wanted to just go home and go to bed. She had been out since lunchtime the day before, and she was due to present the early breakfast news bulletin at 6 a.m. She looked at her watch, 2.30 a.m. so not much point in going home to bed she realised. Lynne decided to try to get some rest in the front seat of the van, pulling her coat around her she lay back in the seat. Earlier the news teams had been promised a progress report from the hospital giving details of the adult survivors' progress. Lynne like most people, was still in shock at the senseless waste of life, unable to believe that anyone could commit the sort of evil atrocity which had taken place at the school.

'You okay Lynne?' Graham her cameraman asked, quietly taking the empty polystyrene cup from her and throwing it over his shoulder into the back-storage area.

Lynne nodded, 'I'm okay Graham, just cold and a bit shocked, it's all so terrifying, you never get used to the evil that people can do, it's so desperately sad. Can you start the engine and put the heater on please?'

Graham did as he was asked, 'oh the glamourous life of an award-winning BBC team.' He said wryly as the engine revved up and cold air blew into their faces.

They'd been at the children's hospital for several hours earlier in the day. They'd been given their last update at eight o'clock; press teams were asked to be back at 8 a.m. for a press conference. The Queen Elizabeth Hospital promised to update them every few hours and had announced that they had several people in surgery, including the gunman and the two social workers. The hospital spokesman had advised they would give an update on their progress as soon as possible.

'Fucking sick bastard!' Graham said as he looked at the written update on the progress of the gunman that they now knew to be Seamus Driske, a fifty-year-old Northern Irish man who had been a known terrorist and had recently been charged with sexual offences and domestic violence. He had a long criminal history of violence. 'I would do the operation without an anaesthetic if they would let me. As would any one of the parents of the dead kids.'

Lynne looked at Graham and nodded. 'There are no words,' she said as she took the sheet of paper from him and put it on the dashboard. The world's press was beginning to descend on the city of Glasgow, where the more seriously injured had been brought the thirty-five miles from Ayr due to the surgical facilities available to them in the city hospitals. Lynne lifted her mobile phone and switched it on. A missed call alert flashed up: Frankie at 6 p.m. then three times since, with the last being a few moments ago. She pulled her coat around her, stepped out of the van, pressing call back as she did so.

'Lynne, thank goodness! You finally got my messages then?'

'Frankie, you do know I'm working, don't you? This better not be another 'bring me a curry call!'

'As if. It's too late, all the curry houses are closed,' Frankie said. 'This is important. Where are you?' Without waiting for her to reply he added, 'do you know anything about the social worker who was hurt Lynne?'

'Which one?'

'The woman, Lynne.'

'She was in surgery the last time they updated. Her condition was critical though, and it was touch and go. Why, do you know her?'

'No, but I think Willie does. He has cracked up today over a row with her.'

'Christ Frankie, I knew I had heard her name before. I just thought my mum had maybe mentioned her. She is the one he has been chasing after. He really likes her. I've not seen him this keen ever, he never said she was a social worker, he ordered flowers when he was with me and said her name on the phone.'

'You knew?'

'He spoke to me about her last month. Remember that night he was in after the Romanian game, there was the fight in the club, and you sent him upstairs whilst you dealt with it? Well, he told me about her then. He just said her name was Ally. I'd forgotten all about it, his women don't usually last these days.'

'Well she dumped him. I don't know what he did. Willie reckons he moved too fast for her, and they fell out. He was devastated. Then the news came in that she was hurt. I don't know where he went. I've been to his flat, tried to call him, but nothing. Where are you?'

'The Queen Elizabeth. She's out of surgery, critical but stable. We just got an update.'

'Lynne, he might head there if he knows that's where they've taken her. Can you keep an eye out for him and let me know? I'll come and get him.'

'Frankie, I'm not his babysitter and neither are you! Willie is an adult. He needs to deal with his own messes.'

'Lynne! A wee bit compassion wouldn't be amiss here?'

'No Frankie, I'm serious. I love Willie as much as you do, but his love life is like a flaming train wreck. He needs to grow up . . . oh leave it with me and if I see him I'll call you, if not you can come and get me after six if you are still up.' Lynne stepped out of the van, she put her phone in her pocket, sighed and looked at the entrance to the hospital accident and emergency unit. She shook her head and walked towards it. He was standing near to the front door, a cigarette in his hand, his jacket collar turned up against the cold February air. 'Wull, are you okay?'

'Lynne, it's her, Ally, the one I told you about. She is in there, in surgery.' Tears began to roll down his cheeks. He wiped away the tears with the back of his hand. 'Lynne, she can't die. I really do love her.'

'Willie how much alcohol have you had?'

'I'm not talking through drink Lynne. I had a lot earlier, but I'm sober now.' He looked miserable and frightened. 'Lynne, I'm really scared for her. They won't tell me anything because I'm not a relative. I need to see her.'

'You're going to owe me big style,' Lynne said as she disappeared into the foyer of the hospital. She came out a few minutes later. Willie jumped up from his seat on the low wall and flicked his cigarette butt away. Lynne handed him a plastic card. 'You'd better not get caught. I've a friend who works here, I've explained the situation, and she's given me the swipe card from the desk of another member of staff. You're to leave it on the reception desk on the way out and tell no one how you came to have it if you get caught. Alyson is out of surgery and has been taken to high dependency. Here's the directions, and a packet of mints, you stink of whisky and fags.'

He kissed her cheek, then popped two of the mints into his mouth. 'Lynne I'll never be able to thank you.'

'Wull, come out to the van and let me know, yeah?'

Willie nodded as he disappeared through the doors.

When Willie arrived on the ward he was immediately recognised. He explained that he was a close friend of Alyson Campbell's and needed to know how she was. The policeman on the door luckily was a big football fan and was only too happy to show Willog to her room. He entered; it was empty apart from a nurse sitting on a stool at the foot of the bed and the woman he had come to see. Ally lay in the bed, surrounded by machinery, looking small and vulnerable. Her face was deathly white and badly bruised. He noticed a cut held together with stitches above her right eye and another large, stitched cut ran in to her bandaged head from her forehead. 'Her son has gone for something to eat,' the nurse sitting at the foot of her bed told him. Willie sat down, putting his hand under hers as a cannula stopped him from holding it; both her arms were encased in plaster. 'She has multiple injuries,' the nurse told him.

'How bad is it?'

The nurse turned to Willie and sighed. 'You really shouldn't be here without her family's permission Mr Ogilvy. I can't really tell you anything other than what they have released to the press without speaking to her son first. Her condition is critical but stable, she's holding her own, I'm sorry but you need to wait outside in the waiting area.'

Willie kissed Ally, glancing at her head which was heavily bandaged. 'Ally, I love you!' he whispered in her ear. 'I'll do anything for you, just live.' He kissed her cheek, unable to kiss her lips because of the breathing tube.

One of the first things Willie had noticed about Ally was her skin, it looked and felt like porcelain. When he first met her, Willie had initially thought she was a lot younger than he was. He'd been amazed to find only a few years separated them, and she had two adult sons. They'd spent a lot of the last three months together talking and finding out about each other. This had been unusual for Willie. He loved her company; because they hadn't moved beyond anything more than kissing, he'd got to know her. He was absolutely sure he wanted to be with Alyson Campbell but was not sure what had happened at the weekend to spook her and make her react the way she had.

'Hey, who're you?' Willie looked up; a tall, thin, young man stood in the doorway. 'Willie Ogilvy! What are you doing in my mum's room?'

'I'm sorry Mr Campbell I was just asking Mr Ogilvy to leave.' The nurse said quickly.

Willie stood up. 'I'm a friend of your mum's.'

'You're the guy who's been calling?' the younger man gasped, his face showing his surprise. 'I don't believe this, what would you want with my mum?' Scott Campbell looked warily at Willie. 'My mum's not your kind of woman!'

'Oh, she is son. I need you to understand she's very important to me. I want to help.'

Scott shook his head. 'I don't want to be rude, but we really don't need your help Mr Ogilvy.'

'What son are you?' Willie asked. 'I'm guessing you're Scott, because she said you'd be the calmest about us when you found out. Look, I know this is a shock . . . I didn't want it to be like this either . . . but I needed to see her.' To Willie's horror tears started to fall from his eyes. 'I love your mother, I really do. I've been seeing her for a few months,' he said, his voice breaking with emotion. 'She was worried about how to tell you and your brother. I know there's been no one serious since your dad . . . and I'm not, well, I'm not exactly the sort of person a son would want their mother to be seeing.'

Scott stared at him. He was tired, emotional, weary and had seen things yesterday he did not understand and would never forget. This for him, however, was as strange as a gunman going into a school. All he could think was, it was lucky he'd sent Danny home with his granddad when their mother had come out of theatre. The surgeons who had operated on his mother had advised them that it would be a long, slow process but were hopeful she would survive. They recommended the two boys and their granddad take turns sitting with her and get plenty of rest. Kiera had stayed at the hospital to allow her grandparents to go home. She and Scott had just been to the staff canteen to grab some food then she had left him to sit at her father's bedside in the next room. Stevie had also been in theatre and had several serious injuries, including a skull fracture and some broken bones, but overall, his injuries had been less severe than Ally's. However, his heart had stopped from shock, so he was being kept sedated to allow some healing to take place. Stevie also had the added problem of his diabetes.

Scott sat down on the remaining chair. The nurse, who had watched the scene in stunned silence, looked at the two men. 'Mr Campbell, if you want security called, I'll get them? I'm so sorry I had no idea you didn't know him.'

Scott shook his head, 'Mum wouldn't want us to be rude and I know she was speaking to him a lot. I would hear her laughing when he was on the phone and she's been happier the last few months.'

Willie looked at the nurse then at Ally's son. 'Scott, they won't tell me anything about her condition without your permission. If you want me to go I will. I just wanted to see her mate, I'm sorry this was a shock. I wouldn't have come if I hadn't been desperate for news, I hope you understand?'

'I don't understand any of this,' Scott said looking sadly at Willie, 'but I recognise your voice now, she said you were someone from work. I knew your voice was familiar? This is unbelievable.' He nodded at the nurse, 'just tell him what you told us, I don't remember most of it anyway. She'd want him to know, I guess.'

The nurse sighed and picked up a clipboard. 'Mrs Campbell's arms are both fractured. Her right leg is broken in two places. Her left leg has a bullet wound in the thigh, which has shattered the bone. She also has fractures to her left ankle and pelvis. Several of her ribs are broken, her right lung collapsed and there has been a lot of internal bleeding. There's a bullet wound in her shoulder and a serious head injury. They removed a large clot. A bullet grazed her head, but they think she banged it in the explosion too.' The nurse looked at the two men, her face serious. 'She's lucky to be here. Any longer buried and she wouldn't have made it. She was in theatre for six hours and is not out of the woods yet. The next forty-eight hours are crucial. I'm about to change shift and hand over to another staff nurse.' She asked them to leave whilst she carried out her checks on Ally.

Scott followed the older man who, although he had only ever seen him in the newspapers or on television, was as familiar to Scott, a keen amateur footballer, as some members of his family. Scott had debated the world's greatest football player many times, and Willog was up there. However, he had been what the tabloids referred to as a *'serial adulterer,'* and a notorious party animal. Scott could not think what this man would have in common with his strong, feminist mother. As they sat outside the room Scott's mind was in turmoil. He'd known a man had been calling his mother in the last few months, but he had never in his wildest dreams imagined his mother knowing Willog, never mind being in a relationship with him. When he had asked who Willie was, realising his voice had been vaguely familiar, Scott and Danny had been placated when his mother had said, someone she met through work, and he was just a friend. They had both known it was more than that, they knew she was happy. They had in turn been happy there was someone and had not pursued the issue.'

Scott and his brother had always hoped their mother would meet someone. Scott barely remembered his father; he was just a face in a photograph and some hazy memories. Danny had no memories of Ralph Campbell at all. Their mother though, had never appeared interested in a relationship. She had spent years working towards her PHD, devoted to her job in social work whilst looking after the two brothers and their grandfather. When she had finally been rewarded with her PHD four years ago, Danny had asked her then if it was now time for her to settle down and find a man. Ally had laughed, saying she was not interested. She told the boys their father had been the only man for her, and she could never find anyone like him. Scott was perplexed. How on earth had she gone from that to dating, albeit in secret, one of the most famous misogynists in Scotland? Yet the tears had been genuine Scott thought, and the way Willie had kissed his mother's face was gentle and loving. He also recalled his mother's recent happiness and hearing her laughing whilst on the telephone.

Shaking away his feelings, Scott turned to Willie. 'You might want to go home, get some sleep. She's not going to waken up tonight. They'll possibly try to reduce the drugs a bit in the morning to see how she responds, they said it'll be about three or four days. That's if there are no setbacks, before she'll be alert enough to even know you're there.' Scott looked Willie in the eye. 'I'm going to stay around. Look, I'll be honest with you. If you go home, it'll give me the chance to speak to my brother and my granddad about you. My granddad will be okay I think. He's a big fan of yours.' He smiled wryly. 'My brother, well, that's a whole different ball game Willie.'

Willie smiled sadly back. 'I know. Ally . . . I mean your mum, was going to tell you first about us then get you to tell him.'

'I can't believe she never told us about you, but we thought she was seeing someone, and it might be serious. I understand now why she was being so secretive, we thought maybe she was seeing a married man or something like that. She's never been in a relationship to my knowledge. Danny and I thought that we were the only special men in her life.' He looked at Willie and smiled sadly. 'If you stick around, you'd better be good to her, or my brother will hunt you down, believe me there will be nowhere to hide.'

A young male nurse appeared beside them. 'Hello, I'm Stan, I'll be taking over your mother's care Mr Campbell. I'll just go and do the shift change.' He nodded at Willie. 'If you just give me a few minutes you can come back in.'

Outside in the relatives' area, Willie looked at Scott. 'You look tired mate, you need to take care of yourself too, or you'll be no use to your mother when she wakes. Would it be wrong of me to offer you the chance to have a sleep at my flat in the city? It's not far from here.'

Scott shook his head. 'No, I'll be fine here. Thanks for offering, I do appreciate that. My granddad and my Aunt Ruth are coming up first thing with Danny. Once we've seen the doctors, Ruth will take me home. She's like our second mother. I need to stick around because I'm mums next of kin. I have to sign any consent forms; they are bringing in some trauma expert from London too. I was waiting to speak to him, but it looks like he's been held up.'

Scott left the room whilst Willie said his goodbyes.

Willie kissed Ally gently on the cheek. He looked at her sleeping form. 'Is she in any pain Stan?' he asked the nurse.

Stan shook his head. 'No, she's being kept unconscious to allow her internal organs to heal. Shock can be more of a killer than the trauma, so the idea is to keep the patient sedated until their body is healed a little and the pain and shock is lessened. She's a very brave lady Mr Ogilvie and a very strong willed one. By rights she should be dead.'

***

Scott looked at Stevie who lay sleeping peacefully, his broken leg raised on a pulley at the end of the bed and his face swollen and bruised, a stitched cut noticeable under his left eye. He put his arm around Kiera and pulling her towards him, kissed her forehead. 'Fuck Kiera, he is even scruffier than usual. Look at the length of his hair.'

Kiera smiled. 'I know, but he's handsome too. I can't believe your mum has been going out with Willie Ogilvy. I've been in his clubs a couple of times in Glasgow with Sharon and Lyra and I've seen him. He's a bit of a show-off and always happy.' She looked at her father's sleeping form and brushed a stray lock of his black hair away from his face. 'You know? I always thought Dad and Ally would get it together someday.'

Scott sighed. 'Yeah, we did too, they do a lot together. He never has a girlfriend for long either. I wonder if he knew about Willie? Are you alright Kiera, you look tired?' He stopped and turned as they heard a groan.

Stevie stirred and opened one eye. 'Have you two got nothing better to do than stand here gossiping?' he whispered. The nurse observing him from the corner of the room got up and moved over to him. She took his pulse and checked his blood pressure and temperature. Stevie's eyes moved across the room. 'Scott! Your mum? Where is she? Is she?'

'She's alive and in the room next door Stevie. She's still unconscious, but she has come through six hours of surgery and is holding her own.'

Stevie closed his eyes then opened them again. 'Are you okay Dad?' Kiera asked, bending over him and kissing his cheek.

Stevie smiled. 'I'm fine sweetheart. I'm sore and tired but more worried about Ally than anything else.'

Scott looked at him. 'It's looking hopeful Stevie; they're telling us she'll live. We'll just need to deal with whatever she is left with later.'

'Thank God Scott, I was really worried about her. Has she got a lot of injuries?'

'A few, but she also has a boyfriend we didn't know about. Did you know?'

'Willog?' Stevie nodded, 'she's been seeing him for a while in secret. Scott, I didn't know, she only told me while we were trapped. She didn't think I would approve. Ruby probably knew though. Apparently, your mum and him had a fall out at the weekend. I'm not sure what it was about but Ruby might know more about it all.'

'Well, he doesn't realise they aren't talking . . . because he's with her now . . . he isn't like I thought he would be Stevie.'

'Your mum is a sensible woman, son. She wouldn't get involved if she didn't see something she liked. Let's just concentrate on getting her back to health, she does like him a lot, amazing though it might seem, because he's not her type. Well I'll rephrase that, he's not what I thought her type would be.'

Scott stood up and took Stevie's free hand. 'I'm going back to sit with Mum now. I've asked him to go home so I can tell Danny about him. I'm not sure how this bit of news will go down, you know what Danny's like? I'll look in later this morning, before I go home . . . let you know if you need a flak jacket! Thanks for saving my mum Stevie.'

'I wish I could take credit for it Scott, but your mother is the real hero. She carried on trying to save kids, and even after she was severely injured, she crawled out trying ... to reach ... a wee boy.' Stevie's voice tailed off; he closed his eyes. Within a few seconds he was asleep again.

When Scott returned to his mother's bedside, the nurse had gone out of the room. Willie sat holding Ally's hand; he bent down, whispering to her and kissing her cheek before moving away. He shook hands with Scott. 'It's good to meet you at last though I'm sorry it's in these circumstances,' he said. 'I feel as though I know you, your mum has told me so much about you.'

'Wish I could say the same mate,' Scott said quietly.

CHAPTER
SEVEN

Outside the hospital, there was a frost in the air; a white, sparkling coating covered the pavement and road. Willie suddenly felt tired and wanted to sleep. He saw doctors in white coats and operating scrubs talking to television cameras. Willie looked at his watch, 5.55 a.m. He could not believe what the last twelve hours had done to him. He stood against the front of the BBC news van, smoking a cigarette and watching as Lynne spoke to the camera. She finished her presentation and walked towards him wrapping her arms around him. He kissed her cheek. 'Thanks for your help, Lynne.'

'How are you? You obviously got in to see her? Graham, can you take the van around to the children's hospital? Bert will be ready to film there. Monica Girvan's presenting. Come on Wull,' she said, linking her arm through his. 'I'll buy you a coffee then we can wait for Frankie. I've just messaged him, asked him to pick us up. He's been really worried about you. Hopefully, my tabloid colleagues will think you're here to meet me.'

They sat down in the hospital coffee bar watching the news coverage of the incident. Lynne's interview outside the hospital was played; she and Willie watched in silence until it ended. The news reports were understandably full of nothing but the tragedy. Willie looked at Lynne, 'I can't believe that the bastard who caused all this is in this hospital. How can that be right Lynne?'

'Because that's what sets us apart from savages Wull. Besides, he'll live to pay for what he has done . . . which was something that was denied the Dunblane families. The coward who killed all those kids and their teacher, killed himself.'

Willie shrugged. 'It won't bring any of those kids back, nor will it make Ally's poor broken body feel any less pain. She's in a bad way Lynne. If she lives, recovery will take months. Ally was in a serious road traffic accident fifteen years ago, her six-week old baby died. Her husband and mother were also killed. She was in a coma with a head injury then. She also had multiple fractures and was off work for ten months. How fucking unlucky can you get?'

'The press hasn't picked that up yet, but they will, they'll start digging. Within days, they'll find out about her relationship with you too. Willie, it might be better if you speak to someone, or better still, get Bernie to do a statement.'

'Nah Lynne, I prefer they just make up their own stories, it makes for interesting reading.'

'That's fine for you hun,' Lynne said gently, touching his arm, 'you have to think about her family though Willie. You also need to speak to your kids. They shouldn't hear about Ally and you from the press. Are you coping Wull? You must be right out of your comfort zone with all of this?' Lynne looked into his eyes and paused, considering her words carefully. 'Willie, do you really love this woman?' she asked, her voice betraying the doubt she felt.

'Yeah, I think I do Lynne. I don't think I've ever felt what I felt last night. I knew that I couldn't lose her. I've never experienced the feelings I had when she fell out with me either. This is hard for me to talk about Lynne, it's all new to me. She dumped me two days ago because I tried to move too fast.' Willie took Lynne's hand and patted it. 'Know what? I don't care if she never sleeps with me, as long as she's alive. I'm in love with her, I think she felt it too. I don't think she's been with a man for years, not since her old man died. She kind of went nuts at me.'

'Why Willie? What did you do? What does *moving too fast* mean?'

'I got a bit too amorous with her, I'm not sure what happened, she lost it with me. I thought I was being gentle and loving, oh I don't know maybe I just got a bit too excited.'

Lynne looked sympathetic. 'Willie, you need to be careful here, you can't just treat this like your other relationships. Ally's been through a terrible ordeal, she'll need support, help and understanding.' She paused and looked at him. 'She's, from what I can gather, also very unlikely to put up with your nonsense.' Lynne smiled, again choosing her words carefully. 'You're a lovely guy Willie, but ... well what can I say?'

'I'm a self-centred, selfish prick where women are concerned.' He finished for her. 'You think I don't know what I am?'

'I never said that.'

'No, but you're thinking it. For what it's worth Lynne, I really do love her.'

Lynne nodded then sighed. 'I can see that Wull. But will you be able to put her needs before your own? I'm sorry but you've never managed it before. You've really hurt all the women in your life. I know Belinsa left you, went public about it all, but you did treat her like shit and sleep around. You've made a mess of all your marriages through your inability to be a grown up.' She looked at him. 'Willie, you drink too much, you party too much. You've never been faithful to a woman. Despite what you think now, all your women, all your wives, cared deeply for you.'

Willie looked at her, a thoughtful expression on his face. 'Maybe, Belinsa never loved me though, Hayley probably did at first. Corinna definitely did, but it was young love. She still loves me you know but as a friend. She luckily found real love with Bernie.' Willie sighed. 'This is different, Lynne. I never loved any of them. I don't know if I was capable of loving anyone but myself.'

Lynne looked at him, raising her eyebrow. 'So how do you know now? How can you tell? Are you sure it's not just the thrill of the chase Willie?'

'I'm serious Lynne, I'm nuts about her. I was like a lunatic yesterday when I thought I'd lost her. Before I knew she was hurt.' He put down his paper cup and stared at it. 'I've never loved a woman before. I've liked them, cared deeply for them.' He looked Lynne in the eye. 'I've lusted after them, but love . . . well . . . I thought I knew what love was.' He shook his head and sighed. 'What I feel for Ally is the real deal. It's like Lesley and David, Alfie and Betty. It's . . . despite what you think . . . what you and Frankie have. Me, I've been in relationships with some of the most beautiful women in the country, but I never loved them. Ally has something my last two wives never had.'

'A personality, looks and a body that didn't come from a surgeon? Sanity?' Lynne quipped.

Willie grinned. 'Yeah, and a lot more. She has me hook, line and sinker. I'm in love Lynne.'

They were so engrossed in their conversation that they didn't notice the coffee shop door open. 'Well there you both are.' Frankie Dastis kissed his girlfriend, then leaned over, put his arms around Willie's neck and kissed his cheek. 'You had me fucking worried, daft prick.'

'I'm really sorry bud, I just lost the plot. I'm up to my armpits in this. I love her, and I was upset at her dumping me. I didn't know how to cope with that, so I turned into Mr Angry. It scared me Frankie, the way I reacted.'

Frankie shrugged, he sat down and pulled Lynne towards him, kissing her gently, she leaned back into him, Frankie smiled at Willie shaking his head in disbelief. 'If it wasn't so tragic, it would be funny mate. The original Mr Laid Back! How is she? I heard on the telly that it was touch and go. She was in theatre.'

'She's out of theatre but unconscious and critically ill. I've seen her. I'm going to go home, get a shower, then sleep for a couple of hours before I come back here. Thanks for coming for me mate!'

'I didn't, I came to pick Lynne up. You're just an added extra, daft arse.'

After Frankie dropped him off, Willie showered and changed his clothes. Unable to sleep, he sat drinking coffee in his riverside penthouse lounge. He looked around his flat, suddenly ashamed. It was merely used as somewhere to entertain the opposite sex. Willie owned a large family house on the shores of Loch Lomond but, apart from recently when he had been going there with Ally, he didn't use it much. He usually only stayed at the house when he had all his children with him. Luckily, his five children got on and the three older ones liked the two younger ones a lot. Having them all together was normally a good time for Willie. He wondered what his kids would make of Ally. Frankie had asked him in the car if he intended to marry her. Willie had told him yes, if she would have him, he would. He knew; however, he did not need a marriage licence to prove how much he loved this woman.

CHAPTER

EIGHT

'**Willie Ogilvy?**' Danny Campbell gasped, staring at his brother. 'You must be fucking joking? Mum would never be into him, he's a moron, an arsehole. He's only interested in football, partying and glamour models. I read his unauthorised biography a couple of years ago. He's been married three times, has loads of kids, and he's cheated on every woman he has been with. He was a brilliant player and the best manager Scotland has ever had, but that's not going to help mum, is it? Fuck sake, what was she thinking?'

'Danny, calm down Bro, it's really nothing to do with us. If that's what she wants, then we will just have to accept it. Stevie said she was with him, but they had fallen out just before this all happened.'

Jimmy Jackson smiled. 'Well, well, Willog and my girl, what a shock. He's a brave man indeed.'

'Granddad you surely can't approve of this?' Danny gasped, staring at his grandfather.

Jimmy shrugged his shoulders. 'Your mother has known her own mind since she was a toddler.' He chuckled. 'No one could get the better of her you know? Not even your dad. He did as he was told and liked it.'

Danny shook his head. 'You two are bloody mad.'

Scott sighed and leaned back in his chair. 'Danny, our mother could have died yesterday, but she didn't. I personally will be happy with anything or anyone she wants because she's still here.' Scott laid a calming hand on his younger brother's shoulder then looked over at his grandfather. 'He seemed okay . . . Willie I mean, I think he really does care for her. Oh, I don't know what to think, like I said, it's so out of character for her, Stevie says they've been seeing each other for months. She didn't tell him until yesterday when they were trapped, he kind of implied, she thought she was going to die, and told him.'

'Oh, come on Scott, you think this is right for her? You've got to be joking? I can't believe she could be that stupid, he's a prick, she doesn't know anything about football, maybe she doesn't know?'

'Your mother is nobody's fool son,' Jimmy said, putting his arm around his grandson, 'she'll not get involved with someone who she thinks is a loser. Like Scott, I'm only glad she's alive.' Jimmy shook his head and smiled. 'Christ, she hates football too.'

'Auntie Ruby, what do you think? I take it you knew?' Danny asked, calming down slightly.

Ruby nodded and sighed. 'I can't say that I was impressed when she told me but your granddad's right, your mum's not naive boys. She said Willie was really quite sweet. She's also not the type to be impressed by status or anything. Actually, she knew nothing about him. When she first met him, it was at a fundraiser last summer, and she told me she went home and Googled him to find out. I guessed she was seeing someone, so I asked. I was as shocked as you are when she told me. She was different though, happier than I've seen her in years. She said it took her by surprise how she felt about him, she knew how you were going to feel folks, so she wanted to be sure before she told you.'

'Look Danny, it would appear she cares for him, we are going to have to just wait and see what she says.' Jimmy said looking at his grandson. If she has been seeing him for months, then he must like her a lot. She has never done this before, has she?'

They all looked at Ruby, who shrugged, 'not to my knowledge boys, however she didn't tell me for months either. I only found out on her birthday because a present and flowers arrived at the office.' Ruby smiled remembering. 'She returned the present, though she did keep the flowers.'

Jimmy looked at his grandson and then spoke sternly. 'I'm warning you Danny, you need to stay calm and deal with this. This is a shock to me too, but know what? She must have had her reasons. She's told both Ruby and Stevie she cares for him. Let's just give him the benefit of the doubt just now until we know more. If he doesn't treat her well, then I'll be the first to sort him out.'

'Speak of the devil,' Danny muttered as he saw the lift doors open and Willie Ogilvy stepped out looking strained and tired.

Willie realised instantly the young man glaring at him was Danny. Knowing he had to tread carefully, he offered his hand, Danny took it.

'You hurt my mother,' Danny growled, 'you'll have me to answer to.'

Willie nodded. 'I can live with that Danny.'

The older man with them stepped forward, also putting out his hand to Willie. 'I'm Jimmy Jackson, Alyson's dad. It's good to meet you Willie.'

'I'm Ruby, Ally's friend, and her manager.' Ruby said, nodding at Willie. 'We spoke on the phone.'

'How is she?' Willie asked, pulling off his quilted jacket and scarf.

'Much the same, but the doctors told us there wouldn't be much progress this side of the week. She's holding her own though.' Scott sighed. 'She doesn't look too pretty now either, the bruising is starting to come out and her face is swollen.'

'You can go in if you like,' Danny said gruffly. 'You know where she is?'

Willie nodded. 'Thanks.'

Willie gasped when he entered the room; Stan was wiping Ally's face with a soft cloth. The breathing tube cord was tied in a bow at the side of her chin which was swollen. Angry, purple bruising was coming out on her cheek and forehead. Her head was still bandaged tightly, only a wispy bit of auburn hair escaped under the bandages. Willie bent and kissed her gently on the forehead, then pulling over the chair he sat down. Willie nodded acknowledging Stan who sat back down on the stool at the foot of her bed observing her.

Stan nodded back. 'It looks worse than it is.'

'What?'

'The bruising and swelling, it looks worse than it actually is. She's doing really well all things considered.'

'She looks as though she's in pain,' Willie observed.

'No, she is pretty much out of it.'

A female in a white coat appeared in the doorway. She smiled at Stan, then at Willie. 'Are you Mrs Campbell's partner?'

'I'm a close friend,' Willie said quietly.'

'I'm Carrie, surgical registrar on duty today. The consultant will be around in about ten minutes. Mr Ruthven, who's a top London neurosurgeon, has flown in this morning and he will take over the management of Mrs Campbell's care. He used to work here, so we know he's the best there is, don't we Stan?' Carrie said, smiling at the nurse. 'We need to give her more blood, we're just waiting for it to come through. Stan, could you go check on whether it's come up yet? I'm going to see another few patients.'

When they left, Willie was alone. He took hold of Ally's hand and sat down beside her. 'You need to hang on in there,' he whispered in her ear. He kissed her cheek gently and touched her hand. The machine beside her bleeped and the numbers on it rose slightly. 'Ally! Can you hear me? Are you hearing my voice?' He tightened his grip on her hand. 'Ally, squeeze my hand!' To his amazement, her fingers curled around his. Tears began to flow as he held her hand, his words coming out in a jumbled rush, vocalising everything he had been thinking over the last twenty-four hours. 'Ally, I love you, I promise you I'll never hurt you. You need to get better. No one will ever hurt you again. I swear that while there is a breath in my body I'll love and protect you. Ally, I need you to believe me. I don't know how much you're hearing or understanding, but I'm here, your boys and your dad know about you and me. I want you to get better darling. I've never felt like this before, all I want is to be with you.' He began to sob quietly. Again, he felt her fingers tighten around his and then relax. He rang the buzzer at the side of the bed and a nurse rushed in, quickly followed by Ally's sons and her father. 'I spoke to her, asked her to squeeze my hand, she did it!' he cried. 'Is she coming around?'

The nurse switched the buzzer off. 'She could be in a lighter coma, which happens sometimes. She won't be responding as such Mr Ogilvy, but she may hear things.'

'I asked her to squeeze my hand, she did it three times.'

The nurse adjusted the drip in Ally's hand. 'It's possible that medication fluxation caused her to respond. She's in a deep state of unconsciousness. We need to keep her there for now. Her consultant Mr Ruthven is on his way. Oh, you're here Clive.' The nurse smiled as the door opened.

A large man entered the room, followed by three young females in white coats and the registrar who had visited earlier. 'What's happening?' he asked, looking around the room.

Willie explained what he had witnessed.

'I'm Clive Ruthven. I'm going to be managing Mrs Campbell's care now.' Willie looked at the surgeon. He was a big man with a moustache and close-cropped grey hair. Willie noted his expensive looking grey suit was crumpled and stained. He noticed Willie looking at him and he laughed, his blue eyes twinkling. 'Sorry about my attire, I'm afraid I came straight off the London Shuttle this morning, the red eye, I believe it's called, I'm a bit bedraggled. I was keen to get here, so came straight from the airport. I've been in theatre, although I did not operate on Mrs Campbell. I'm afraid that it was too much of an emergency for them to wait.'

Willie looked him in the eye. 'I don't care if you came in a pair of speedos mate! What you look like, well it's not that relevant to Ally's care is it? I know she responded to my voice!' Clive walked over to Ally and lifting her eyelid, he shone a small torch, took her pulse then asked them all to leave the room.

Outside in the relatives' area Jimmy and Scott sat down. Danny went to the counter and poured himself a cup of coffee. 'Anyone else want a drink?' he asked, holding up the pot.

Willie began to pace up and down. Jimmy sighed, 'Willie, one maniac in here is enough. Danny can do enough pacing for us all, and he's calm.'

'I know she responded to me Jimmy. I spoke to her, she moaned then I said, 'if you can hear me squeeze my hand', she did it. I was holding her hand, speaking to her earlier, there was no response. I know she heard me this time.'

Danny handed him a paper cup filled with coffee. 'We don't doubt it. If anyone can come through a coma it's my mum.'

The nurse appeared in front of them and asked them all to come back through. Mr Ruthven stood at the side of the bed. 'You're right, she is hearing. She appears to be fighting the medication. But . . . I have to tell you,' Clive said, taking a deep breath, his expression alluding to the fact this might not necessarily be good news, 'I have to make you aware it could be a sign of something more sinister.'

They all looked at him. 'Like what?' Jimmy asked.

Clive Ruthven sighed. He looked at the four men, choosing his words carefully, hoping he sounded more confident than he felt. Clive knew that there were indicators that all wasn't well with his patient. He also knew from experience he had to do the investigation and assessment to provide himself with as much evidence as he could. 'I'm going to try to bring her round over the next few days, but if she gets distressed or is in too much pain then I'll put her out again. I've taken the breathing tube out as it appears to be distressing her. We'll carefully monitor her to make sure that she's breathing normally, and her oxygen levels are stable. I'm being told that there was nothing concerning on her last scans. However, I may do another scan to check.'

She may come around now, or she might need to be put into deeper sedation. I have no way of knowing until I try this. Is Alyson normally headstrong?'

Jimmy gasped and laughed. 'You could say that.' Scott and Danny both smiled despite their fear.

Willie slumped into the chair by the side of the bed. 'Put it this way Doc, you wouldn't want to go home to her with a broken pay packet.'

Clive Ruthven turned to face them. 'This is only the beginning gentlemen, there's a long way to go. She is in no way out of the woods. This won't be straightforward, as Alyson has suffered major trauma we need to proceed with care. She remains critically ill. I'm sorry it's not better news, but I must be truthful, this is a waiting game now. I would ask that you only sit with her one at a time, allow her some space. A nurse will be with her at all times. Whilst we are reducing the sedation, she needs to be observed every few minutes. I would like quarterly recordings.' He smiled at the nurse. 'It's good to see you again Stanley.'

'You too Clive, it's been too long. I'll catch up with you later,' Stan said, smiling warmly.

Clive looked from the nurse to the registrar, who moved in front of the other white coated medics. 'Carrie, every fifteen minutes throughout the day, be here, check the stats personally.' He turned to the four men. 'Please do not distress her in any way. If she comes around, she shouldn't know anything that may upset her. Stan, you know what to do.'

Willie turned to the big man. 'Can she be treated privately? I want her to have the best care there is.'

Clive Ruthven looked at Willie over his glasses. 'Mr Ogilvy, I don't want to be rude, but I would never dream of telling you how to play football or manage the national team.' He glanced around at the others. 'Alyson will get the same, if not better care at this stage as she would in a private hospital. If, when she is out of danger, you want to move her to a private clinic, and if that is what she wants, then it can happen. Believe me, Alyson will get first class nursing care here. When she is out of danger If you want to pay for a better view or a bigger bed, I won't be stopping you, but I would be treating Alyson the same way no matter where her bed is. If you want my opinion though, keep your money for services you can't get unless you pay. My services come free.'

CHAPTER
NINE

As the day progressed, they all took turns to sit with Ally; she never opened her eyes despite stimulation from them. Scott went home with Ruby eventually. Mid-afternoon came, Willie decided to go home and shower. He found himself warming to Ally's sons and he told Danny to go home when he returned after dinner. 'I'll sit with her tonight. I'll call you if there's any change.' He offered Danny the use of his flat, but Danny declined, informing Willie that he really needed to go home and get showered, changed and pick up more insulin. Danny also admitted his blood glucose levels were erratic. Willie urged him to take things easy.

Kiera came in to see Ally with Danny as she was travelling home with him. Willie politely asked about Stevie.

'Dad is doing well thanks. He'll be laid up for a while yet. He keeps falling asleep mid-sentence, but his nurse says it's the pain medication.' She looked at him from under her dark eyelashes. 'You could go in and meet him you know? He says you were his boyhood football hero.'

Willie smiled. 'I'll do that. I'd love to meet him, he's my hero now. He obviously looked after Ally whilst they were trapped.

The stories about his bravery that are coming out are way beyond anything I've ever achieved.'

After Danny and Kiera left, Willie was alone with Ally in the early hours of the morning, when she became restless. Stan, who had come back on duty, took her temperature and pulse then checked her blood pressure. Ally began to try to move around the bed, despite being restricted by the machinery monitoring her. Stan advised that he'd have a doctor to look at her as a precaution.

Carrie, the young female registrar, could not hide her concern and telephoned Clive, who returned shortly afterwards. After examining Ally, Clive asked Willie to come back through to the room. 'She isn't progressing as well as we had hoped. The sedation is reduced but she's not coming around. She's distressed, her vitals are not good. It may be nothing, but I need to be sure.' He moved outside and spoke to the registrar on duty and when he returned to the room, he looked concerned. He turned to Willie, 'I'm going to have her taken down for a scan shortly. I'm just waiting for the duty radiographer to come back on shift.'

'Should I be worried Doc? Should I be calling her family?'

The big doctor sighed. 'My being concerned is concern enough just now Willie. I'm just not sure what's going on, best wait until after the scan. She's showing signs of something. I need to investigate whether there is a sinister reason for it.' He looked at Willie, 'then I can make decisions. I wouldn't alert her kids and father yet; I think we need to let them rest for now. I'm sorry I can't be more precise.'

Shortly before 2 a.m. a porter appeared in the doorway. Willie stood up and went out into the waiting area. He watched as Stan and the porter wheeled Ally away, before taking himself downstairs to the staff dining room. He nodded at some of the staff from the ward, who were obviously on their break before going over to the vending machine and selecting a pack of sandwiches. Willie sat by himself away from the staff; not wanting to be rude, he wanted to be alone with his thoughts for a time. As he ate, he picked up a newspaper someone had left behind. The paper was almost entirely devoted to the incident at the school. The newspaper asked the same questions the world was asking. 'How could this have happened?' Willie read security at the school may not have been updated due to the opening of the new school which had been set for Easter. The council had, the newspaper claimed, been trying to save money and had disengaged the security system as the new school had been expensive to build and maintain. They had also decided to re-route the gas mains in the school rather than lay new ones, so there was an area in the school where the floors had been lifted, exposing the gas connections.

The floor plan showed where the explosion had taken place and where Ally and Stevie had been found. Willie looked at the pictures of the dead which covered two pages now. There were thirty-five children and six adults dead, another forty, including Ally and Stevie, injured. The large school, he read, held 420 pupils and fifty-five staff, so many had escaped the carnage. Ally and Stevie were credited with helping children to escape and were being hailed as heroes. Willie stared at the pictures of the victims. As a father himself, he realised nothing could compensate for the loss the families of these children had suffered. He also knew he had to do something constructive or he would be eaten up with pain at the senselessness of the tragedy. Ideas began to take shape in his head. With his sports connections, he could organise a testimonial game of football. With his entertainment connections through the clubs, he decided he may be able to put together a fundraising concert, start perhaps a campaign with proceeds going to help the families and the community towards recovery. He ate his sandwiches without really tasting them and then returned to the ward. Ally's room was still empty. Walking out to the relatives' area, he poured himself a coffee and taking it back through to the room, he sat down. The door opened, the porter and nurse wheeled Ally's sleeping form back into the room and settled her. 'How did it go Stan?' he asked the nurse.

Stan looked uncomfortable and avoided eye contact. 'Mr Ruthven is on his way up Willie, he'll tell you.'

'What is it? Stan? Stan, tell me what it is? Tell me I'm not going to lose her mate?'

'It's okay Stan, I'll explain,' Clive Ruthven said as he came into the room, his face serious. 'We'll need to take her back to theatre. I've asked them to call Scott to come in to sign the consent forms. Hopefully, he'll get here in time.' Clive took a deep breath. He laid his hand on Willie's shoulder. 'I'm sorry Willie, it's not good. Alyson has a large aneurism on her brain. I was afraid of this, because there were signs, she was just not responding as well as we had hoped.' He cleared his throat. 'In layman's terms Willie, there's a significant bubble of blood in an artery, if it bursts it will flood her brain and she'll die almost instantly. If we leave it, it will undoubtedly rupture. She's heavily sedated now, that's the best way to keep her calm until we can operate.'

Willie sat upright in the chair and looked Clive in the eye. 'What are her chances Doc?'

Clive looked at the ceiling, before sitting down on the edge of the bed. 'Fifty-fifty I'm afraid. It's close to the base of the brain, which is not the worst place to operate in, if I get it right ... if we are successful then her chances of full recovery are high.'

'If you get it wrong ... what?'

'Let's not go there!'

Willie took Ally's hand and squeezed it, there was no response. He looked at the big man perched on the edge of the bed. 'You have to make her better Mr Ruthven. She has to live.'

Stan cleared his throat. 'If anyone can do it Willie, it's this man.'

Clive Ruthven smiled sadly. 'I'm glad you have faith in me Stanley. It's heartening, if not a little frightening.'

'She's come so far Mr Ruthven; I can't lose her now.' Willie was afraid, more scared than he had ever been in his life. The last few days being around Ally's family had been, although difficult, a comfort to him. He couldn't believe they had accepted him into their circle, shared their loved one with him. Willie was lucky enough to have a close circle of friends and family who loved him, never judged his behaviour, but were honest with him. He hoped Ally's family and friends were as genuinely accepting of him as they seemed.

The big doctor stood up and put his hand on Willies shoulder. 'I need to go get prepared. It's a bit like you picking the national team. I want the right people there. Stan, you up for it? You've assisted me before.'

'Of course, I'll start preparing.'

'Willie,' Clive said quietly, 'can you let the boys know when they get here that the paperwork is at the nurse's station?'

Willie nodded and shook the doctor's hand. 'I know she's in safe hands.'

Clive sighed and looked at Willie. 'The operation could take a long time Willie. Can you possibly get the family out of here? Don't have them hanging around waiting!'

'How long Mr Ruthven?' Willie asked. 'Will it be a long operation?'

'Hard to say. With recovery Willie, it could be a full shift.' He looked at his watch. 'It's seven a.m. now. We'll get her prepared, aiming to get her down to theatre about eight. I have staff coming in specially to assist with this procedure. The positives are I've got the pick of the best medical team available. People have flown in from all over the world to assist because of the seriousness of this incident.' He put his hand on Willie's shoulder and squeezed it lightly. 'Willie, my name is Clive.'

Willie was still sitting with Ally, holding her hand and watching her sleeping, when Scott, Danny and Jimmy came into the room. 'She has really small hands,' he said out loud.

Jimmy nodded, choking back tears. 'Her mother was the same, even smaller with the same slight build and tiny hands. We had to get Ella's wedding ring made from a bigger ring as they didn't stock adult rings that size. She has tiny feet like her mother too.'

'Willie, what did the doctor say?' Jimmy asked. 'Please don't give us false hope.' Willie stood up and walked over to the window. To his horror, he couldn't speak. He began to cry as he tried to impart the information Clive had given him. In the end, Stan intervened and gave them the news. Danny and Jimmy looked stunned.

Scott sat down on the side of the chair Willie had vacated. He reached over and touched his mother's head, bent over and gently kissed her forehead. 'She can't die Granddad! It's not fair. She can't die now, not after what she's been through.' Scott began to sob.

Willie watched as Jimmy held his grandson's head close to his own chest. 'Scott, she has a fighting chance. Anyway, when did your mother ever give up? She won't leave us without a fight.'

As they watched Ally being wheeled away, all four men were silent, not knowing if they would see her again. Willie stood up. 'Look, there's no point in us sitting here waiting. Clive said it could be hours, the surgery, then recovery, she might not be through until late afternoon. Why don't we go downstairs for breakfast, then I'll take you to see around the stadium?'

Danny began to protest, but his grandfather stood up. 'I think sitting here waiting will drive us all mad. Willie you're right, it will pass some time. Jimmy looked sadly at the other three men, 'there's nothing we can do folks, it's in God's hands now.'

'It's in Clive Ruthven's hands actually!' Willie said. 'Come on, sitting looking at the empty space in this room will make it seem longer!'

Scott nodded; he stood up and wiped his eyes with a tissue. 'Can we go into the VIP areas?' he asked. 'I've always meant to go and see the museum too; will that be possible?'

Willie's smile he hoped disguised how miserable he felt. 'Don't see why not, its closed today, there will be no one else there. You just happen to be the guests of the Scotland manager.'

Despite the hearty breakfast served in the hospital canteen, none of the men managed to eat much. Their appetites lost; stomachs, hearts and heads filled with fear and dread. Wearily they climbed into Willie's light blue Range Rover Sport and he drove them across to Hampden Park. The mood became slightly lighter as Willie took them through the public areas and into the behind-the-scenes offices and dressing rooms. He led them out onto the football field and found a ball to kick around. Danny kicked the ball to his brother. 'Let's show this amateur how to play football!' Willie ran onto the pitch and found that both boys were surprisingly good players.

'I thought you said there was no one else here?' Jimmy shouted. 'There are people watching from the top of the stand. Look!' He pointed, drawing their attention to the far end of the park from where the three men were kicking the ball.

Three figures stood watching them from the highest seats. 'Maybe it's a scout come to watch us play,' Scott said, smiling.

Willie looked up and when he looked back again the people had vanished. Jimmy shook his head. 'There were people there, a man and two kids, I didn't imagine it!'

Willie shrugged. 'We all saw them. Probably cleaners, they can be like that.'

When they left the stadium, it was 1.30pm. Willie drove them around the corner to a local restaurant; due to the missed breakfast, they all felt hungry. 'Thank you for looking after us Willie,' Danny said, shaking his hand. 'You've really managed to take my mind off Mum this morning. I didn't think that I would be able to do anything but think about it.'

Scott looked up from his fish and chips. 'We should get back now though, there must be some news surely.' He looked at his mobile then at his brother. 'What'll we do if she doesn't make it?'

'Scott, no news is good news.' Jimmy sighed. 'Your mother is as tough as they come. She survived the crash all those years ago, I told you, she's not going to leave you now without a fight.'

'This must be bringing all that back for you Jimmy?' Willie said quietly, looking at the older man.

Jimmy nodded. 'It was touch-and-go for a few days then as well. I had these two to deal with, they were too young to understand what had happened. I'd lost my wife, my granddaughter, my son-in-law, and my only child was fighting for her life. Ella and I were both only children, we don't have a lot of family.' He shook his head. 'Not a great time. Ruby and Stevie really helped, that's why we are all as close now. They were there for us, and we got through it.'

CHAPTER

TEN

Ally fought her way through the fog. She felt a breeze on her cheek, someone kissed her, asked her to squeeze his hand, she heard Willie's voice, he was upset she knew he was crying, something wet dripping on her forehead, his voice sounded far away and echoed. 'Ally I love you, Ally can you hear me?' She tried to open her eyes. but they were stuck, she felt immense pain in her body, then found herself falling.

Ally was awake and alert, there was still fog but also bright light ahead, sunshine on a cloudy day. She was not sure where she was or where she was going but she knew she had to move towards something. She could hear someone calling her name. She felt light and happy; there was no pain and she knew she was safe. She came through the clouds and she could see a figure in the fog ahead, then another. They were familiar; even in this dull light she knew it was Ralph and her mother. She looked at them. 'Am I dreaming? Am I dead?'

Ralph smiled. 'Neither. You've been through a terrible ordeal darling, but it's all going to be okay.'

'How did I get here? What happened to me, did something happen to me? The boys, dad? I can't leave them.'

'Come on Ally Bally, start fighting back,' her mother said; she looked young and carefree. Ally looked at the two people standing in front of her, she knew she had to be dreaming. Ralph looked like he had when they first met at Glasgow University, Fresher's Week, however both were wearing the clothes they had on the day of the accident, the day they died.

'If I'm not dead, where am I?'

Ralph looked down. Ally followed his gaze and realised she was looking at herself. At least, it was the back of her head; she was lying on her side on an operating table. A large man was mopping blood from her head. Suddenly a man in blue scrubs sitting on the other side of him began to shout.

'We're losing her! Quickly, get back. I need to shock her again!' Ally watched as they restarted her heart. The big man, his hands outstretched in front of his chest, watched on a monitor as it stabilised. The smaller man lifted his head. 'Okay folks! She's stable again.' He was holding a mask on her face, watching the dials on a monitor. 'Okey-dokey Clive, you can go back in now but be quick. Anything that can be left till later, leave it.'

'I'm going to sort it all Deke, I don't want her opened up again. I was nearly there anyway. Christ this girl is one hell of a fighter.'

'Fuck! She's going again Clive!'

The scene changed. Ally found herself high up in a stadium, standing between her mother and husband. Ralph smiled at her. 'You've done well with our boys Ally; you should be proud of yourself.' Ally looked down, on the far side of the stadium three figures kicked a ball around. She realised immediately that the fourth figure standing on the side-line was her father.

'He needs to find another woman Ally,' her mother said. 'You need to help him accept he needs female company his own age, help him to do it. He's been far too long on his own.'

Ralph sighed. 'You've both mourned too long.'

'Is that Willie with the boys?' Ally gasped. 'What's going on?'

'Ally, you need to follow your heart with Willie. He's in love with you. This is the path you're meant to follow. It's time to move on. Don't be afraid. I sent him to you.' Ralph looked at her and smiled again.

'Where's Abby?' Ally asked. 'Why isn't she with you?'

'Ally, you've done a great job with the boys and Jimmy, but you need to move on now, do something for your own happiness. Abby will find her way to you. It happens sometimes.' She felt his kiss on her forehead. 'Loving Willie and being loved by him will lead to the next love of your life.' His breath in her ear as he whispered felt cool, he kissed her again, and moved away from her. 'Nothing is forever except love Ally. Just follow your heart, this is how it is meant to be.' Suddenly the fog surrounded her again, darkness, the light was gone.

'Mum? Ralph? I can't see you anymore! Please come back.' Ally felt herself falling through the air.

CHAPTER

ELEVEN

As Willie and the others walked back onto the ward, the first person they saw was Clive still in his theatre greens. He smiled as he walked towards them. 'She's in recovery boys. It was touch-and-go. Her heart fluttered a couple of times, but she came through it with flying colours. She has an extraordinarily strong spirit.' They hugged each other and shook hands with Clive. Willie felt an immense sense of relief, and he knew this was shared with the three men beside him.

As soon as the porter and Stan brought Ally back to the room, Willie knew she would be alright. Her face, although badly bruised and still swollen, looked calmer. He could see that she was not in pain anymore. Scott and Jimmy went home, Danny remained with Willie. Clive Ruthven looked in a few hours later and sat with them. 'She'll be okay now boys, I am sure of it. We've scanned her from head to foot. I'm one hundred percent sure that there's nothing else we've missed. I've looked at the earlier scans and it was there, but exceedingly small, they missed it and it increased quickly. That happens sometimes with pressure. This woman is one hell of a fighter though!' Clive looked around them all, his face showing relief. 'Ally's recovery may be slow, but she will recover. All her physical injuries will mend, I don't

97

think she will have any real brain injury, but I can't tell until she is awake. The emotional part of it though will be down to you lot. She's been through a terrible ordeal, so she may be left with some fragility. Be patient with her. Give her the time and space to get over it.'

When Clive returned to the room at 8 p.m. he found Willie and Danny still sitting by Ally's bed. He looked at Danny. 'Are you alright Daniel? You need to check your blood sugar and not ignore it. I think you look very tired young man; you need to go home and sleep. Willie, you too, you've had a lot to contend with this week. You've had no sleep for what, forty-eight hours? Alyson is not going to get any worse. Her vitals are good now we've released the pressure on her brain. We'll keep her sedated for the next few days and then gradually bring her around. You two need to get as much rest as you can because she'll need you to be there for her. Now, both of you please go home and get some sleep.'

Danny stood up and looked at Willie. 'Can I take you up on the offer of a bed Willie?'

Willie smiled, delighted at the request. 'Of course, you can. It's only ten minutes from here. If we need to get back quickly, we can.'

Clive sank into the chair Danny had vacated. 'You won't need to get back quickly boys; I can assure you of that.' Clive smiled broadly. 'What part of she is out of danger did you not understand? I'm so confident of that fact, I'm about to go outside and give a statement to the world's press. Just one problem though? I need to ask?'

'What?' Danny said, looking at Willie then back to the big doctor.

Clive grinned. 'Does this tie go with my jacket?'

***

After Danny and Willie left, Clive sat for a few minutes looking at his patient. It had not been an easy day for him. After operating on Ally he'd been called to an emergency, performing an operation required to save the life of Seamus Driske. 'She really is exquisite.'

'You too Clive?'

Clive turned his head; Stan had come back into the room. 'Did I say that out loud?' He smiled and shook his head, 'as if! She is way out of my league Stanley, destined to be a WAG it would appear.' He stood up and made wearily for the door. 'Are you going off shift for your days off Stan?'

'Yes, I'm off tomorrow for a rest day but I've cancelled the rest of my leave Clive, too much to do here just now,' Stan said, grinning. 'What're you thinking?'

'Fancy a game of poker? Some of the registrars and the orthapods have organised a game in the basement. I'm going down once I've done my media thing and checked on my other patients.'

'Oh, yes Clive. I've missed those all-night poker games.'

CHAPTER
TWELVE

'Good, you are doing well Mr Driske, it looks like you're on the mend. We can arrange for you to be moved now.' Clive turned to the policeman sitting by the bed side then pointed at the double handcuffs securing him to the bed on both sides. 'Are those really necessary? He is not going anywhere. He has a spinal injury.'

'He's killed over forty people, mainly little kids and maimed the same again, Doc. If he gets out of here, you and I are for the high jump.'

'Are you treating those social workers?' Seamus asked.

'Who I treat Mr Driske, is my business not yours.'

'It *is* my business. Busybodies sticking their noses into people's lives, they caused this, so they did. They think they're so special. She was scared of being fucked you know? She kept my wife and my kids away from me. She was a frustrated old cow, that Ally one, scared of sex. I could have shown her how to do it. Her and fucking Willie Ogilvy. I was lying there listening to her and that Steve talking, I heard it all.'

Clive looked at him. 'That's not my concern Mr Driske. I have no idea what you are talking about.'

Seamus pulled against the handcuffs, 'I would have had her back if they had not interfered.' Saliva ran down his chin from his mouth as his anger rose. 'Sally was my wife, my property to do with what I wanted, so she was.'

'Mr Driske, this is none of my business. My concern is your health. Getting you fit enough to stand trial for what you are accused of.' Clive moved forward to adjust the drip on Seamus's arm. 'You were quite ill and almost died.'

Seamus spat in Clive's face. 'You're going to wish you never saved me doctor. You just wait, you've seen nothing yet, pompous bastard.' Clive quickly left the room. He could hear Seamus shouting after him. 'You tell those two fucking busybodies I will get them one day. Maybe not yet, but I'll get them, they'll suffer. I've lost everything through them. My kids are dead because of them. What I did to that fucker who was shagging my wife is nothing. Tell them I'll get them, especially tell the woman. I'll fuck her brains out when I get her, and I will get her.'

Outside in the corridor, Clive stood wiping the spit from his face with a tissue. He was visibly shaken by the venom in Seamus Driske's statements. 'He's mad,' one of the armed police guards, said. 'That's why he's handcuffed. Get him well enough for us to move him Doc. As soon as you give the word, he will be in the hospital wing up at the big house. We're here as there could be a revenge attack from someone because of what he's done. If it was up to me, I'd take him back to Ayrshire and drop him off where he did it. As you can see, he has no remorse or insight into the atrocity. He's blaming the people who tried to help his family. He's little more than an animal, Doc.'

Clive shook his head. 'But we're not animal's sergeant, are we? The ability to not do to others as they do to us is what makes us superior. The fact that we are heuristic is a given, how we use it is a choice. His fate will be decided by a court. He'll be ready to move tomorrow, late morning. I would suggest you have the

101

prison medical staff to come see me first thing. How does he know about the two social workers being here?'

'Television in his room I expect.'

'Why is he being allowed to watch it? Surely he shouldn't be able to see any coverage?'

'He's not, but it's a long day for the cops in with him. They would be watching it while he sleeps, he must've been pretending to sleep. As soon as he's awake, we switch it off.'

Clive returned to the room. Without speaking, he walked over to the television on the stand next to the bed and pulling the cable roughly from the wall then wheeled the screen and controls out into the corridor. He pushed it at the police sergeant. 'If anything happens to anyone else involved in this tragedy, I'll come looking for you. Do you understand? Now arrange to have him out of this hospital by tomorrow, mid-day.'

CHAPTER

THIRTEEN

'Wow, this is something else Willie, I'm impressed,' Danny gasped. 'It's real luxury. Our whole house would fit in this living room. You must be able to see the whole of Glasgow from here!'

'It's okay. It is what it is, but yes, it has a great outlook. I like the view best when you stand on the roof terrace. It looks right down the river and you can see the Squinty Bridge on one side and the Finnieston Crane on the other. In fact, you're right, on a good day you can see most of Glasgow. It's not actually mine, it belongs to my company. We own a couple of flats in this building. It was a tax dodge more than anything else. My mate Alfie initially bought this penthouse when he was single then he got married, started having babies and it wasn't practical, so he was selling up. We just bought him out then added it to our portfolio. I always liked it, so I took it on when I came back to Scotland.' Willie chuckled, 'it's a real anthropological study, this building. The class system is alive and kicking here in River Heights, Danny.'

'The class system?' Danny asked smiling, 'this building with the concierge in uniform and all the trimmings. The foyer looks like a high-class hotel.'

Willie walked towards the double patio doors in the lounge and pulled them open. 'Floors one and two have five three-bedroom flats. Three, four and five have three four-bedroom flats. Six and seven two flats each and this is the only apartment on this floor. So, the more money you have the higher up you get. Ten years ago, when Alfie sold it to us it cost two hundred and fifty thousand. Today you are looking at oh, probably about two million.' He switched on the soft lighting and motioned with his head for Danny to follow him through onto the terrace.

'Wow!' Danny gasped, taking in the patio area with the barbeque and the smoked glass panels in front of it joined to the wall, the lights of Glasgow twinkled all around them as he looked over the glass barriers. 'Is that a hot tub too? Its huge.'

Willie laughed and patted the covered up hot tub. 'When you sit in it you can see through the glass and across the river. It was such a babe magnet that thing, it has seen a lot of action.' He looked at Danny and smiled. Seeing a look of concern crossing the younger man's face he added, 'I do love your mother Danny, I won't hurt her. I never want to chase another woman. Don't ask me how I know, but I just do. I've made a lot of mistakes in my life son, but she's not one of them.'

Danny smiled wryly. 'You're just not what I thought you'd be like Willie.'

'I am, or was, exactly what you thought I would be like before I met your mum Danny. What happened to her this week has changed me too. I knew before that she was special, but now I know it's forever.'

'What if you're not changed though Willie? This could just be a reaction to what has happened.'

'Nah, I knew I wanted be with her before this happened. She's dumped me by the way. So, when she wakes up, I'm going to have to convince her she should trust me.'

'Why did she dump you?'

'Hmm . . . I don't think I want to tell you Danny, your mum wouldn't want you to know. It's kind of personal. Let's just say I acted like a wanker and leave it at that. There's no one else involved by the way; just in case you think it's that. Actually, this is the first time I've been able to say that after a relationship breakup.' Willie shook his head and smiled as he led Danny back into the lounge area.

Danny shrugged and picked up one of the picture frames from the baby grand piano in the corner. 'Don't fancy your chances Willie if you've pissed her off, she's really stubborn.' Danny nodded at the piano, 'do you play?'

'No, it was Alfie's. He can't play it either, he just thought it looked good. It was a nightmare to get up here, cost a fortune to do it, so he just left it when he moved.'

'Are these your kids?' Danny asked, looking down at the large silver framed picture in his hands.

Willie nodded. 'I have three daughters and two boys. Oh, and three ex-wives to go with the kids.' Willie pointed to another picture, a large canvas on the wall with all his children together. 'That was their Christmas present to me this year.' He smiled and touched the picture, 'Leah, she's my eldest.' Willie chuckled, 'she's thirty-one, but more sensible than I am. I was only sixteen when she was born. She has a daughter now, my granddaughter Caitlin, who is nearly three. She's the toddler at the front. Caitlin's father Archie Simpson plays for Stoke. Leah played football too, she has been capped for Scotland, but she stopped playing when she got pregnant. It's hard for female footballers, they make a fraction of what the men do, and they don't get the recognition. Leah is a sports presenter now. Korrie is next. She's twenty-seven, a real wild child. She has all my bad habits, constantly in the papers. She's a talented singer, but too lazy to work hard at it. Then there's Billy, my eldest son, he currently plays for Manchester United. He's twenty-four and is a lovely boy, nothing like me.'

'He's a great player too Willie.'

Willie nodded. 'Their mother is Corinna who was my child-hood sweetheart and is now happily married to a guy who treats her the way she should be treated. Next is Jade, she's fourteen, beautiful and going on twenty-one, she plays football at national level too. Her mother is my second wife Hailey. Then finally there is our Euan, he's the youngest, he's nine. His mother Belinsa was my third wife. Euan's probably going to be a better player than me or Billy. He's showing real promise. He's train-ing with Man U football academy. If he continues to develop, they'll put him on their books when he's old enough. He lives in Manchester with his mum, I see him one weekend a month and school holidays. Corinna still talks to me, but the other two, well I'm kind of a bad word in their vocabulary. I've no one to blame but myself so I can't complain. My kids luckily all get on though. The older three don't resent the younger ones, and the younger two adore the older ones. Do you want a drink? I'm going to have a whisky.' He pulled open a drinks cabinet. 'I have most things.'

Danny smiled. 'Vodka and diet coke please.'

'Can you drink when you have diabetes? Does your mother know you drink?'

'Yes, to both. I'm eighteen and legal, but I need to be careful with it. I think we deserve one though.' He laughed as Willie lifted a bottle of Grey Goose out of the cabinet.

'Never touch the stuff myself, vodka I mean. I'm a whisky drinker when I do spirits. Sometimes I forget to stop drinking.' He reached into his jacket pocket and brought out a packet of cigarettes. 'I'm also a social smoker. I have one a day. Except on Tuesday when your mother got hurt, I had ten. I like a cigarette with a drink, so I treat myself every day. I very rarely have more than one, sometimes I don't have any. Depends how much I drink mainly, as to whether I remember.'

Danny grinned. 'Just as well you didn't go into PR Willie, you're not exactly selling yourself as a prospective stepfather.'

'I believe in honesty Danny, and I really don't take myself too seriously. There are always stories about me in the papers, a lot of it is true but some of it is far-fetched even for me.'

They sat talking about football for the next hour before Danny began to look tired. Willie showed him to a guest bedroom. 'I think everything you'll need is here. This is the en-suite and there should be towels and anything you need there. If you need clothes in the morning, help yourself.' He pointed at the built-in wardrobe which stretched across the room. 'I have loads, designers and sportswear companies give me free stuff, I just put it in there. My mates raid the wardrobes every time they visit. You and I are about the same size, I think. What size shoes are you?'

'Ten,' Danny replied.

'Same as me, so help yourself. There's trainers and shoes in that bottom cupboard. I could never wear the amount I'm gifted.'

'I think I'll be okay, but thanks for offering.' Danny said smiling as Willie closed the door.

After Danny had gone to bed, Willie poured another drink and sat outside on the terrace. He looked at the lights of the city twinkling below him and sighed. Right now, he wanted to go to his house on the loch or to Majorca to rest up. He knew though that he couldn't leave Glasgow. He also knew his whole life was about to change. He wasn't sure why he knew he was ready for it. He stubbed out his cigarette and made his way through to his bedroom.

***

Willie woke as he heard the front door slam. He realised it would be Brenda, his cleaner. He pulled on his jeans and went out to the lounge.

'Willie, how are you my lovely?' Brenda called as she hung her jacket up. The strength of her Irish accent amused Willie as Brenda had lived in Scotland for thirty-five years or so but still sounded as though she had just arrived.

'There's a friend staying here Brenda, well a friend's son, actually. Could you lay off the hoover until he gets up? His mum's in hospital and we were visiting. He lives in Ayrshire, so I offered him a bed to be near the hospital.'

Brenda shook her head smiled then turned Willie with a knowing look on her face, her hands on her hips. 'Oh, I know so I do Willie, tis all over the papers today so it is. Does that lovely lady know what she is taking on?'

'What?' Willie gasped.

'It's in all the papers so it is, all about how you fell in love and what a hero the lady is Willie.'

'Fuck, who told them? This is all that family need just now.' Lynne's warning came back into his head. In all honesty, he had intended speaking to Bernie but the medical emergency with Ally and the relief of her coming through alive, had taken it from his mind.

Brenda shrugged. 'Well it wasn't me to be sure, I didn't know. She's very pretty Willie. A blessed saint she must be, rescuing all those children so she did. Mother of god, what a good woman. What's she doing with you? Why did I not know there was a woman? They're saying that she's been with you since last year!'

'Oh, ha-ha. She's not with me, well not in the biblical sense. We're close friends that's all. Have you brought one of those tabloid rags into the house?' In response Brenda reached into her bag and tossed a newspaper across at him. The headline under the red banner screamed out. '**Hero Social Worker is Willog's**

New Girl.' Willie knew immediately the story was made up from a few photos taken at the fundraiser where they'd met; the photographs had been in the publicity from the event. The other photos were of him outside the hospital the night of the incident. There was one of him hugging Lynne in the coffee shop, and her wiping a tear from his eye with a tissue. He reached for his phone. Ignoring the missed call alerts on the screen, he called his agent. Bernie quickly agreed to issue a statement, acknowledging Willie and Ally were friends, that he was devastated by her injuries and would be supporting her through her recovery. He also had Bernie announce Willie would be putting together an event to raise money for the families of the victims. He replaced the telephone and began to make a list.

'Do you want coffee?' Brenda put down her duster and switched on the coffee machine. 'Are you alright Willie? You look tired fella.'

'I'm fine Brenda. I've been at the hospital a lot over the last few days. Ally's out of danger now, but she's been operated on twice since Tuesday.' He poured the coffee into two mugs and handed her one.

Brenda smiled at him. 'Do you know you are nothing like people think you are? She's an incredibly lucky lady to have you in her life my boy.'

Willie laughed. 'You're just a teeny-weeny bit biased Brenda. I've been a complete and utter bastard to women most of my life and you know it. You've cleaned up after me too many times to not think that.'

'Oh, for the love of god, you just have been going with the wrong women. To be sure you needed a good god-fearing woman to set you on the straight and narrow and instead you went for bimbos, sluts and nutters.'

'That's not fair Brenda. My behaviour probably caused most of their problems. I do know what I am,' Willie sighed and looked at his housekeeper. 'Most of my problems are my own making, and I've realised I hurt a lot of people. There is no excuse Brenda. Too much wine, women and song!'

Brenda put down her coffee mug and folded her arms under her considerable breasts. 'No, too much wine maybe, a good song never hurt no one. You didn't pick real women, you picked gold-digger wannabes who used you for your money and publicity. You're a good time Charlie, Willie! Maybe you're just ready to settle down with the right woman now. God knows you're old enough to be ready.'

The door opened, and Danny appeared in the kitchen. 'Sorry Willie, I can't believe I slept as long.' He smiled at Brenda. 'Is this your mum?'

Brenda laughed out loud. 'If himself was my boy, I'd have kicked his arse up and down the street. I'm Brenda, his house-keeper-come-slave. To be sure lad, it's a real pleasure to meet you. Your mother sounds like a lovely woman. She is a real saint by the sound of it.'

'I'm Danny. It's good to meet you Brenda.'

Brenda picked up the coffee pot and got out a mug. 'You look like you need breakfast fella.'

'Danny's diabetic, Brenda, so don't go making your famous Irish breakfast for him.'

'So is my man diabetic, but he got it through the drinking, so he did.'

'I have type one,' Danny said, smiling. 'I've had it since I was two, I'm insulin dependent. My Pancreas doesn't work, my body doesn't make insulin, sounds as though your husband's pancreas makes some insulin or doesn't use it properly, that's type two. An Irish breakfast sounds good to me if it's on offer.'

Brenda began opening the fridge and freezer, bustling around the kitchen. 'Well, do you want breakfast or not William?'

Willie nodded. 'I'll go and get dressed while you make it.'

110

After a shower whilst they waited for breakfast, Danny called the hospital. He smiled as the sister on the ward told him his mother had had a good night and was doing well. He put down the telephone. 'All her signs are good. Mr Ruthven will be back at eleven to see us,' he told Willie, grinning. 'They say she's stable and out of the woods.'

'That's fantastic,' Willie said, tears gathering at the corners of his eyes.

The intercom buzzer went off suddenly and Willie pressed the speaker. 'It's me Wull, Davie's here too.' Frankie's voice came through. 'Buzz us in pal, it's cold enough to freeze the baws off a brass monkey out here.' Minutes later, the lift doors slid open and Frankie and David came into the room.

'Alright Davie?'

'I'm fine mate, but Lesley is after your blood. You really upset Gemma.'

'I know, I know. I've sent the wean some flowers. I was in a bad place pal.'

David shrugged. 'Probably did the little princess some good to be honest. Nobody ever says no to her.'

'She wasn't in the wrong mate! He was behaving like a lunatic.' Frankie looked over Willie's shoulder at Danny who was sitting at the breakfast bar checking his blood sugar.

'This is Danny, he's Ally's son. She had to have emergency surgery yesterday, and it was late, so he stayed here. Danny, meet Frankie Dastis and Davie Gibson.' Frankie watched as Danny put away his testing kit.

'I'm diabetic mate,' Danny said, taking out a small case from his jacket pocket and removing an insulin pen from it.

'You don't need to explain to him,' Willie said, laughing. 'He's probably tried insulin. He's smoked, snorted and swallowed every other drug known to man and some that don't even have a name.'

'I have never jagged myself though!' Frankie said, shaking his head and screwing up his face. 'Scary stuff, needles!'

'You actually get used to the jagging,' Danny said seriously. 'I've been doing it myself since before I started school.'

Brenda entered the room and glared at Frankie. 'He's not coming out to play today.'

'Oh, the lovely Brenda!' Frankie said, slapping her large bottom. 'How do men resist you?'

Brenda smiled warmly and clipped him around the ear.

'Ouch!'

'Grow up Francis or go to confession.'

'Oh, the chapel would come down around him if he did Brenda,' David said, lifting the coffee pot. 'We hadn't heard from you Willie and you don't answer your phone. When we saw the news this morning, we thought we'd better come and look for you. You'd better call your kids too. It's all over the papers bud.'

Willie looked at Danny who had raised an eyebrow. 'Brenda, show him, will you?' He said wearily. Brenda pulled the now crumpled paper from her bag and handed it to Danny.

'How did they find out?' he asked, looking annoyed.

Willie shook his head. 'They didn't find out, they made it up based on the fact I was at the hospital. Then they did some digging and found the charity event where we met, so they would link me to your mum through that. We were pretty drunk Danny, we posed for a couple of pictures. No harm done, I've issued a statement through my agent already, admitting we are close friends. I've suggested I organise an event to raise money for the victims, hopefully that'll deflect it a bit.'

Danny looked up from the story. 'What kind of event?'

'Well I thought a football game, you know like a testimonial and maybe a concert. Frankie here has loads of contacts. He's done promotional stuff before. He knows everyone who's anyone in Scottish show business and arty farty circles and he sleeps most nights with Lynne Lockhead, who knows all the serious news people. That, Franco, is your mission should you choose to accept it.'

Frankie nodded. 'Sounds good to me. How soon?'

'Start organising and we'll see. We'll get the match arranged first, strike whilst the iron is hot, I would say.'

'Okay, cool. I'll get to it, but why stop at Scottish bands? This awful thing affects everyone.'

'Oh Christ, Saint Francis of the Calton himself,' Brenda laughed.

'Any chance of breakfast then Brenda? I haven't had one of your full Irish's for a long time. I'll need strength to get working.' Frankie grinned at Brenda.

'Oh, sit down and I'll get to you after these two have eaten,' Brenda put two full plates onto the breakfast bar, she nodded at Willie. 'Right get that into you two, Frankie, do you want fried or scrambled eggs?'

***

Willie put his empty plate in the dishwasher and took the last drink of coffee from the white porcelain mug, he looked at his silver Rolex. 'Danny we'd better go if we want to speak to the good doctor. Davie, I'll come into the club on Monday with my accounts. Brenda, I'll leave these two in your capable hands. Oh, can you collect my dry-cleaning tomorrow for me?' He kissed Brenda on the cheek as he left.

'Any new freebies?' Frankie asked.

Willie smiled. 'Ask Brenda, I haven't been here.'

Willie put his key in the lift and Danny lifted his jacket and followed him in. 'This is pretty cool having a lift straight to your flat,' Danny said.

'Well it is eight floors up Danny. Even in my playing days that would have been hard going.'

'Do you miss it?'

'Playing? Yeah, sometimes. I miss the buzz, but it's something that as a professional player you accept. There are always younger, fitter men coming through the ranks. Trick is to retire before you become a has-been. I was lucky the assistant manager job for Scotland was opened to me then the big Scotland job came up at the right time. Because I had the stake in the clubs and hotels, I didn't need the money from a club job and could take it. I needed to work though. I'd five kids to support and two very high-maintenance ex-wives.'

'I thought you had three ex-wives?'

Willie grinned, 'I have, but Corinna, my first wife, has never accepted a penny for herself from me since the day we parted. She went back to university. She's a lawyer now and married to one of my old friends. I gave her away at the wedding. Bernie her husband, he's my agent. Very incestuous I know. Corinna and I get on better now than we did when we were married which is amazing, considering how badly I treated her.'

'Who's Gemma by the way? Why is she upset with you?'

'She's my goddaughter, she works for the company. She's a student. I was very rude to her a couple of nights ago and needed to apologise. She's a little madam, real diva but I love her to bits. I have always spoiled her. She's David's daughter, David's my cousin. Frankie has a twin, Alfie, they're my three business partners. Lesley is David's wife. We all grew up in the same area of Glasgow and were all at school together. Lesley's my first wife Corinna's best friend, she holds more of a grudge than Corinna does. Anyway Danny, all my problems in life are of my own making so I pay the price for being, as Frankie would say, a Bawbag. In reality, I am or have been a selfish prick. There have been many casualties in my wake.'

'What about my mum Willie? She's going to need someone who's there for her after this. You heard what the doctor said Willie. How can you know if you're ready for that?'

'I don't if I'm honest. How I felt when Ally . . . your mum, dumped me was a complete and utter shock to me. After I started seeing her, I cut down on the partying and I spent a lot of time with her. At first, well I suppose she was a challenge, but well . . . very quickly I realised how special she is. I wanted to be with her. I've been married three times, and for the first time, the phrase 'forsaking all others' meant something.' Willie smiled and shook his head. 'I'm not sure if I've ever been in love before. I've loved a lot of women, but in love? Not this boy.'

Danny, watching him intently as he spoke, knew he was either the sincerest person he'd ever met, or the world's biggest liar. He couldn't help liking Willie, which was not how he's expected to feel about him. 'You're what, forty-seven? And you've never been in love?'

Willie shook his head. 'Not until now. It's not pity either. I know how strong-willed your mother is, she won't need me to get better. Ally is the most incredible woman I've ever met. She'll most likely do that herself. If she lets me, I'll be by her side through it all, whether she needs me or not. I don't know why I feel like this, I'm not even sure she'll forgive me, because I'm not exactly clear on what I did wrong. But I know one thing Danny. I'll spend the rest of my life looking after her if she lets me.'

CHAPTER

FOURTEEN

The hospital was bustling with cleaners scrubbing everywhere, and staff were being briefed in the glass-walled rooms. Jimmy and Scott had arrived ahead of Willie and Danny and were sitting outside Ally's room. Willie smiled sheepishly when he saw the copy of the newspaper with the headline of his supposed relationship with Ally on the front of it. 'Someone from the royal family is visiting later today,' Jimmy told them. 'They won't go in to see Ally, but they've asked if one of us will meet them.'

You're used to that kind of stuff Willie. Can you do it?' Scott asked. 'Or at least be with one of us?'

Willie nodded. 'Sure, if that's what you all want. They're only people Scott, and you are all pretty articulate. You don't need me to be a spokesman, just be yourself.' The door of the room next to Ally's opened and a wheelchair was pushed through it. Willie turned to look at the man in the chair and smiled. He would have known this was Stevie Marshall even if Kiera wasn't pushing the chair. Willie approached and put out his hand. Stevie looked suspicious for a few seconds and then took it and gripped it. Neither man said anything, but both knew what the other was thinking.

'You alright Stevie?' Danny asked.

Stevie released Willie's hand and smiled, showing his white, even teeth. 'I'm just peachy Danny. How're you holding up? Are your bloods okay? You know stress makes things worse.'

'Stevie's diabetic too so he's been my mentor and coach for a lot of years now,' Danny told Willie.

Stevie smiled, 'I'm sure one of the reasons I got the job with the team was because of my diabetes. Danny had just been diagnosed when I was interviewed. Ralph, his dad, was on the interview panel, we actually became best mates,' he looked Willie in the eye before continuing, 'he was a great guy.'

Clive Ruthven came out of the room smiling; he was wearing a tweed suit, a fetching green colour with a bright pink thread through it. The colourful ensemble was finished with a pink bow tie and pink patent brogue shoes. 'She's definitely on the mend boys. Oh, and young lady!' he said catching sight of Kiera. 'You need a shave Steven, facial bruising is no excuse for being scruffy.'

'He's always been scruffy,' Kiera laughed. 'That suit Mr Ruthven, those shoes, wow!'

Clive chuckled, 'The suit? It's Harris Tweed, I had it specially woven. The shoes I had made in Hong Kong last year to match. I can't stand the chief executive here. Let just say, it annoys him because he needs me more than I need him.' Clive winked at Stevie, 'there's more than one way to be non-conformist.' Clive poured coffee into a mug and leaned back on the worktop. 'Okay, so here's the deal. Over the next forty-eight hours we're going to gradually bring Alyson out of the coma. She'll be monitored very carefully whilst this happens, but it is unlikely that there'll be any major setbacks now. One thing though, there's likely to be a degree of memory loss and until she is fully conscious, we have no way of knowing how much. It could be that she can't remember the incident, or at the furthest end of the spectrum she could wake up with years missing. You'll need to be patient with her, it'll take time.'

'If she has memory loss Clive, is it likely to be permanent? She had no memory loss after the accident, other than the actual impact. They thought she would have.' Jimmy shivered, remembering a very traumatic time.

Clive Ruthven shrugged. 'Who knows Jimmy? I can't see any major brain trauma. To be honest two head injuries would normally mean we would be expecting acquired brain injury, but I can't see any real scarring on the scans, so that's unlikely to be a problem. The back of the brain where she was hurt this time is where coordination and balance are, between that and her limb injuries she is more likely to have mobility issues, she could have to relearn walking. Over the years, I've stopped guessing as it's impossible to predict. We won't know what we have to work on until she's fully conscious.'

'So, she may not have any memory loss then?' Stevie asked looking around at the other people in the room.

'The thing about memory loss is it's not always a medical issue, sometimes it's emotional. The mind has no way to process awful things, so it shuts down. Let's just worry about the next few days. Now, when she comes around, I know you are all worried about her, but no crowding her and take it in turns to go in. You need to think about her needs over the next few days not your own.' He looked directly at Willie as he spoke. 'One last thing though,' he said, putting down the mug and turning to leave. 'Whoever is with her when she wakes, if she asks what happened, ask her what the last thing she remembers is. That may assist us ascertain whether any memory loss is physical or emotional.'

Over the next twenty-four hours they took turns sitting with her. Monday night came around; Willie had gone back to his flat with Danny and Scott. Unable to settle, he tried having a drink, but couldn't sleep. Leaving a note for the boys and his car keys, he called a cab and returned to the hospital.

***

Stevie was sitting beside Ally chatting to her still form; Stan was writing up notes. Ally lay on the bed, the bruising on her face after six days was turning yellow at the edges; she looked fragile and tiny in the big bed. 'You can't sleep either then?' Willie asked. 'You're going to have to be careful. You need to look after yourself.' Stevie said nothing, he looked up at Willie and then back at Ally.

Stan stood up. 'I'm going to take a quick comfort break. Julie and Tricia are outside at the station; if you need them just call.'

'He obviously senses the friction in the air!' Willie said, his voice calm. 'What is your problem with me, Stevie?'

Stevie sighed. 'I've no problem with you as a person Willie! I just care about Ally. I don't want to see her get hurt. You're all over the papers already, what is that going to be like for her? You court the press and put on a show, but she's been landed in the public eye for something that wasn't her doing. How do I know you're in this for the long haul? When we were trapped, she told me she had finished with you, and she told me why pal. That's what's eating away at me. You might have fooled Jimmy and the kids, but you don't fool me, and Ally is nobody's fool either. So, if you're not in this for the right reasons, go now before she wakes up.'

Willie stared at him. 'Have you always loved her Stevie?' he asked. 'That's what this is about! You're in love with her. She thinks you're her friend, she was anxious about telling you about me, but you're a rival for me, aren't you?'

'Ally was my best mates wife, she's my friend!' Stevie cried, his face reddening. 'I would never compromise that friendship.'

'No, no, Stevie?' Willie said, his voice steady and calm, a smile playing on his lips. 'Never try to kid a kidder mate. You didn't have the bottle to tell her how you felt about her, that's a different thing from friendship. Ally doesn't know, does she? Look Stevie, I'm not the jealous type, so I don't mind; but I'm going to go all out to win her back now, and I will look after her. Ally changed me Stevie, and I'm going to make her love me. So, you might as well give me the standard 'if you hurt her' speech. Just because no one believes I'm serious, doesn't mean I'm not.'

Stevie moved his wheelchair, shook his head and rested his plastered leg on the floor. 'Why do you think that is? Clive was speaking to you when he spoke about Ally's needs not our own. As far as I can see, everyone else in that room had Ally's best interests at heart before she got hurt except you. Good luck Willog. I'll be waiting in the wings though.' He patted Willie's arm as he wheeled himself out of the room.

Willie sat down and took Ally's hand; to his amazement she gripped it again. He began to cry, the emotions of the last week catching up with him. Willie knew that whatever happened from now on, this woman would come first for him. 'Ally, I love you, I didn't realise how much until I nearly lost you,' he whispered. 'I want to do things properly now; get to know you and make you trust me. I don't care how long it takes. They all think that I'm not sincere but I am.' Tears began to fall. He rested his head on the bed and wept. Suddenly he was aware of a hand touching his head.

A croaking whisper from above him cut through the silence around Willie. 'What a big girl's blouse you are Ogilvy, crying like a baby,'

'Ally! You're awake!' he cried. 'Thank God you're back with us.'

She looked into his eyes. 'What happened to me? Was I in an accident?' Her voice barely a whisper, she gripped his hand and looked up at him.

'Ally, can't you remember?' Willie kissed her face as his tears dropped onto her. He grabbed a pile of tissues from the box on the bedside locker, tearing them in his haste; tiny pieces of tissue rained down on the floor. Remembering what Clive had said, he asked, 'What's the last thing that you did? What do you remember?'

Ally sighed and shook her head, her brow furrowed as she tried to concentrate. 'I was at work then I was meeting you for dinner last night. Or was it last night? I feel so tired Willie,' she whispered. 'My throat is so sore.' She closed her eyes again and drifted back into sleep. Willie looked at his watch it was 4.30 a.m. He knew he should ring Scott and Danny, but he really wanted to be alone with Ally. Suddenly he was aware that was what the old selfish Willie would do. He kissed her forehead, laid her hand down and went out into the waiting area. Stan stood talking to another nurse.

'Stan, Tricia, she's awake, she's spoken to me.'

Tricia stood up and followed Stan into the room. 'We better go in and check on her then.' Stan said smiling.

Willie dialled his home number, eventually Scott answered. 'Scott, I came back to the hospital because I couldn't sleep. She's awake, she spoke to me. She's gone back to sleep. She called me a big girls blouse first though.'

'Sounds like Mum! I'll go wake Danny and come to the hospital Willie. See you in about twenty minutes.'

Willie smiled to himself. 'Scott mate, I've left the keys for my Porche on the coffee table, its insured through the company for any driver. Frankie has the Range Rover. Be careful with my car, please? It's my other love.'

When he returned to the room Ally lay awake, watching him. 'Are you going to tell me what happened?'

'No Ally, not yet. You were hurt, you've been extremely ill. I think we need to wait until your doctors have seen you before we start telling you all the details.'

Ally looked into his eyes; she took his hand. 'I had the weirdest dream Willie! I was with my mum and Ralph in a stadium and was watching you and the boys playing football. Dad was there too; he was standing watching. Then I was in an operating theatre, they had the back of back of my head opened. They started saying my heart had stopped, then they shocked me. Willie you've gone white!' She stared at him trying to remember. 'That was a dream, wasn't it?'

Before Willie could speak, Clive Ruthven came into the room, his large frame blocking out the light. 'What was a dream Mrs Campbell? Did you dream a dashing, devilishly handsome doctor saved your life? I'm Clive Ruthven, your consultant.'

Ally looked at him. 'It was you! You were doing something with the back of my head, and I was lying on my side. You had to turn me over, you held your hands out in front of you and a woman used a defibrillator. It was you, wasn't it?'

Clive smiled and nodded. 'I do believe it was dear lady.'

'You don't look surprised,' Willie gasped, looking at Clive.

'No Willie, I'm not, it's happened before. We think it's some sort of conscious brain activity thing that allows some people to see what is happening to them when they are in cardiac arrest. More common is folk hear what's happening. The visuals are rare but not unheard of.'

Ally looked up at him, 'My dead mother and husband were there. They told me that you would save me.'

Clive smiled at her. 'That part might have been a dream.' Clive took her wrist, his fingers on her pulse, then he put his hand on her forehead. 'Well, save you I did and you're going to be alright now.'

Willie took Ally's hand. 'She doesn't remember what happened to her Clive.'

'Well, best leave it like that for now. She's had enough excitement for the moment I would think Willie.' He sat down on the edge of the bed and adjusted the drip on Ally's hand. 'You need rest more than you need explanations Ally. May I call you Ally?'

'Of course,' Ally sighed. 'I'm so tired doctor, I just need to sleep.'

'Everything will become clear in time. Now I need you to get some rest. You've a long, difficult fight back to full health ahead of you my dear, you need to start now.' The big doctor rested his hand on Ally's forehead again. 'Now I'm going to send this man home. He has been here almost constantly since you came in.'

'Mum, Mum, I'm so glad you are awake.' Danny burst into the room closely followed by his brother. 'Mum we were so scared we were going to lose you.'

The door opened again, and Stevie wheeled himself into the room. 'Ally, you're back with us!' he cried. 'I heard the commotion. I would think the whole floor heard it.'

'Stevie, you're in a wheelchair?'

Stevie grinned and pretended to look surprised. 'Really, I hadn't noticed.'

Ally looked around the room. 'Someone needs to tell me what happened? Were we in an accident?'

Clive Ruthven stood up. 'Alyson, if you don't get some rest, I'm going to put you out again. Stevie please? You need to rest too. You can talk tomorrow. Now, all of you who're not patients, please go home and those of you who are, please get some sleep.'

One by one, they kissed Ally and left the room.

At last only Willie remained in the room; he gently kissed her lips. As her eyes became heavy, he whispered 'I love you Ally.'

Ally smiled and closed her eyes. Willie watched her for a few seconds then crept out of the room. Stevie had gone to his room, Clive, Ally's sons and Stan stood outside in the waiting area.

'She really doesn't remember, does she?' Scott asked Clive. 'What should we do?'

'Well she'll sleep a lot over the next few days. She needs a great deal of medication for the pain now, that'll sedate her somewhat. So, it might be better to wait, see what she remembers first. Keep all the newspapers so she can read about what happened at the school, that way she will have visuals of it and third-party information. Remember, she'll be hearing it all for the first time when you tell her, she may go into shock and disbelief. It all needs to be relayed to her when she is physically strong enough to deal with it. Stan, you're licenced to prescribe, aren't you?'

'I am.'

'Can you increase Mrs Campbell's pain relief if she needs it?'

Stan nodded. 'Sure, I'll call you if that happens,' he smiled, 'I hear you hadn't left the hospital anyway, Clive.'

Clive raised an eyebrow at the nurse then turned to the others. 'We'll increase the morphine drip now because she'll be in considerable pain. She's going to be immobilised for several weeks because of her injuries, particularly the broken pelvis. The orthopaedic surgeon will see her again now she's awake. The x-rays showed the break was clean and may heal itself, but with Alyson being awake she will be trying to move, this could affect recovery. However, there's a truss on her just now, and that may be enough. Her shattered thigh will definitely need more surgery to adjust the plate and remove some of the pins.' He looked at Willie. 'Have you done anything about a private hospital?'

Willie shook his head. 'You advised against it.'

'Yes, I did. I would stand by that just now. She'll get excellent care whilst she is in high dependency. There's too much media interest in her though, I think she needs to be in a place where we can control who has access to her. I've links with a private hospital on the South Side. I'd recommend she go there. I can continue to care for her. I'd say start organising it now, and I'll tell you when I think she should go.'

'What about Stevie?' Willie asked. 'Should he be going to a private hospital too? I can pay for it.'

'You're going to pay for Stevie's care? Danny asked.

'Why not? Your mum is probably alive because of him and it'll be better for them to be together. I mean, if she is going to talk to anyone about what happened, it's going to be him isn't it?'

Clive shook his head. 'Stevie's injuries are responding well. He will be able to go home soon and have care at home. His daughter has taken time away from her studies to care for him. With his GP and the practice nurse, he should be fine.'

'When will Mum go home? Surely once she is on the mend, we could do that for her?' Scott asked, looking around him.

Clive sighed. 'Alyson's injuries are much worse than Stevie's. She'll struggle to care for herself. I understand that there are no female relatives to help her if she needs assistance with personal care.'

Willie looked thoughtful. 'I hadn't thought of that, but I can hire a nurse for her if I need to, can't I?'

Clive shrugged, 'we're quite a bit away from her going home. Alyson will be in hospital for at least eight weeks, possibly longer. Now, all of you go home or from whence you came. I have a poker game to return to, and I was winning.' He winked at Stan, 'I'm way ahead of them all just now, so if you disturb me again it better be something extraordinary.'

'Do you ever sleep Clive?' Willie asked, shaking his head, 'I thought I was hyperactive!'

'Not when there is a poker game on the go. You best get home and sleep Willie.' He looked Willie in the eye. 'Or do you want to join us in the game?'

Willie smiled. 'Tempting as that is Doc, I think I need sleep more just now. Ready boys?'

CHAPTER
FIFTEEN

A lly lay looking at Stevie sitting in the chair at her bedside, his good leg resting on the bed. Three and a half weeks had passed since she had wakened, and for the past week Ally had continually badgered everyone, asking them all to tell her what she could not remember.

She was now well enough to watch television. Clive had decided it was time to tell her the details of the incident.

'Ally don't you remember anything at all?' Stevie asked. She shook her head slowly, 'it must be bad though, because everyone talks in whispers, and they won't let me have television.'

'You've slept most of the time for the last three weeks Ally, so you wouldn't have been able to watch the TV anyhow.'

Stevie looked up as Willie came into the room. They'd agreed that he would be the one to show Ally the newspaper reports; Stevie would fill in the missing hours for her. An uneasy truce and mutual respect existed now between the two men. Both loved Ally, neither wanted to force her to choose between them. In truth, they were unsure as to who would be the winner if they did. Willie sat down and handed Ally the newspaper from the day after the incident. The headlines screamed out at her. Ally looked at the two men, Stevie sitting on the chair beside

127

the bed, Willie perched on the bed beside her. Ally put on her reading glasses and began to read, as Willie and Stevie talked her through what had happened on that awful day. When they finished, Ally stared at them, her face white and shocked.

'Oh my God, I can't believe this!' Ally cried, 'this is horrific. Why can't I feel anything? There's something wrong with me. They must have done something to my brain during the operation. There's people dead, children I knew . . . all those little kids.' Ally looked from Stevie to Willie and shook her head in disbelief. 'Sally and three of her children. Poor little Alexis, left with no one, and I can't even cry!'

Willie wrapped his arms around her trying to calm her, wanting to protect her from the information he had just imparted. She looked him in the eye, 'Oh my God Willie, that bastard is still alive.' She thrashed around the bed, distressed. 'I can't cry. All those people wiped out . . . ' She became quieter. Looking from Stevie to Willie she asked, 'Why can't I feel something? Why can't I remember the hours before it? The last thing I remember is leaving work to go and meet you. That must have been on the Friday, so I have three days before missing too.'

Stevie met Willie's eye. Willie shifted uncomfortably. 'Ally, thing is . . . a couple of nights before it happened, we fell out and you dumped me.'

'I did? Why?'

'Because I'm a stupid arsehole,' Willie said smiling.

Stevie stood up and lifted his crutches. 'I've told you all I'm going to today. You've seen all the pictures and newspapers, perhaps your memory is best gone Ally. It was awful. You really are a hero though. They are talking of giving us medals, fancy that. I wonder if I should get a suit for the ceremony. Will a smart suit go with trainers?' Stevie asked. 'I could probably borrow one of Clive's suits, but I might shave too and get a haircut!' He pointed to the pile of get-well cards Stan had brought in for her to read.

'Look at the number of people wishing you well. You've touched a lot of lives in your twenty-odd years in social work Ally.'

'I'll miss you when you go home Stevie,' she whispered as he bent to kiss her.

'You'll have daytime television and Willie here to fuss over you. I'll come up as often as I can. I won't be able to drive for a while, but I need to let Kiera get back to university soon, or her grades will suffer.'

'I can arrange transport every other day if you want?' Willie said looking at him.

Stevie looked annoyed and said sharply, 'I can manage to get to the station, Willie. Ally, I'll catch you later.' With that he quickly left the room.

Willie followed Stevie into his room. 'What is it with you? Why can't you just accept what Ally and I have? Why do you have to refuse everything I do to try to help? I'm not just doing for you mate, I'm doing it for her too.' He motioned through the wall. 'I can afford it. It's not about the cost anyway. It's about you not being fit to get a train and two buses to get here and being too pig-headed to admit it. It'll be even worse when they move her to the private hospital on Monday. It's further away.'

Stevie looked angry. He stared at Willie, his face dark and brooding. 'Why do you need to try to play Mr Nice Guy, Willie? Can't you just leave it, concentrate on Ally? Just leave me alone will you. I was there Willie, you are trying to get her to remember, but I was fucking there. You have no idea how fucking awful it was.'

Stevie sat down on the bed and shook his head, anger and pain flashing in his eyes. 'We saw a child get her head shot open. He was using bullets with explosives in them. It exploded like a fucking melon Willie,' Stevie cried, tears building in his eyes, he shook his head as though trying to shake away a memory. 'I see it when I close my eyes. Ally was holding her hand, so she

129

saw it close up. She had bits of her brain on her clothes. We saw Gabby, the head teacher, with a bullet through her forehead and her eyes just staring at us. She was thirty-one years old; she was about to get married. Children were falling like fucking skittles. He was shooting as we ran for our lives then he came back and pointed the gun at Ally just before the explosion.' Stevie angrily wiped away tears falling now down his face. 'The bullet that caused the explosion was meant for Ally. If she remembers, she'll know that. Then we lay in the rubble, pinned to the ground with bodies all around us and we thought that we were going to die. We saw things that no one should ever witness. If she doesn't want to or can't remember, leave it the fuck alone!' He lay back on the bed and threw his crutches across the room, narrowly missing Clive Ruthven who had obviously heard the commotion and come to the door. 'I was there Willie and I don't want to keep going over it all. I don't fucking want counselling either Clive before you start bringing that up again! The sooner I get out of here the better.'

'Stevie, I didn't mean to upset you mate. I didn't think.'

'No, you never fucking do Willie. It's all about you. You were not there; you didn't lose anyone. You can't sort this for her. Let her forget for fuck sake, because what she'll remember is not going to do you or her any good. Clive, will you please just discharge me? I need to get home and start living again.'

The door was knocked lightly, Ruby entered the room. 'Do you think you could keep it down boys? Ally can hear you; she's distressed enough. She can't get away from it, the way you two can. She has to lie there and try to think.'

Stevie buried his face in his hands. 'Clive, can't I just go home today? Ruby can take me. I need to get out of here. I'll just rest. I'll be in my own home; I can get better quicker.'

Ruby looked at him, 'Stevie, you need help with this.'

Stevie looked sadly from Ruby to Willie then Clive. 'I need to share it with someone who was there. Ally can't or won't remember what happened and you know what? I don't want her to remember either, because it is so hard to have these pictures and memories in your head. Please, can we talk about something else?'

Ruby sighed. 'I've just come from the children's wing. I went to see wee Alexis; she's going to foster care. We're looking to keep her in Scotland just now but safely away from the public eye.'

'How did she take it Ruby?' Stevie asked quietly, calming down. 'Poor wee soul, it can't be easy to deal with all she witnessed. She saw him shoot kids beside her. Her last memory of her brother and sister is them terrified. Then she lay trapped all those hours. Now she has to go live with strangers, it's not fair, look what the care system did to her mother. I want to go and see her Ruby.'

Ruby sighed and shook her head. 'I don't think you're emotionally secure enough to deal with it, Stevie. She needs adults to be strong, you know that. Put your professional head on and separate from it. She knows how badly injured you and Ally are, she gets what happened. They make a big fuss of her at the hospital, and she's beginning to smile again. She's seven years old Stevie, she's been through so much. She's pretty resilient though.'

Willie stood up. 'I'd better get back to Ally.' He put his hand out to Stevie who took it and shook it. 'I'm sorry mate.'

Stevie sighed, looking sheepish. 'I just need to go home, and it's better that you're here with Ally. Willie, when we were buried in the rubble, she thought she was going to die. She told me what happened between you and her. She'd got scared about how she felt about you, asked me to tell you she was sorry, and it was nothing you'd done.' He looked sadly at the other man. 'She loves you . . . and you were right. What you said about me and her, you were spot on Willie!'

Ruby looked from Stevie to Willie, 'she has some issues with intimacy, I'll talk to you about it later Willie. It's not about you, it's her. She is oh . . . conscious and a little paranoid about her body. She came to my house that Saturday after she left you. Look maybe if you speak to her about it, she may tell you herself what her problem is, she might have forgotten what happened, but she won't have forgotten why.'

When Willie returned to Ally's room, Ally was watching the door. 'Is Stevie okay?' she asked, a look of concern on her face.

Willie shook his head. 'I don't know him well enough to say Ally, but I do know that what you both witnessed was horrific. If you've lost the memory of it that may not be a bad thing.'

Ally looked at him. 'I need to remember Willie, but I just can't. Now, I think you better tell me why I fell out with you before I got hurt,' she sighed and looked away. 'I think I can guess why.'

Willie sighed and sat down on the chair next to the bed. 'I made a move on you too fast and you got really mad at me. I was such a prick. It's hard to believe it's only just four weeks ago. So much has happened. You apparently told Stevie about it when you were buried under the rubble. You also spoke to Ruby, so maybe you will need to ask one of them what you felt like. I just know you were really angry at me. I'm not sure what happened Ally. It was the Saturday night; we were lying on the couch in my flat kind of messing about. I got a bit amorous I suppose. I was really turned on, I thought you were responding.' He looked sadly at her and shook his head, 'I tried to make love to you. Suddenly you went ape shit at me and left. You accused me of trying to force myself on you. I said some things and you said some things, then you left. You wouldn't answer the phone, then on the Tuesday the shooting happened.' He sat down beside her and reached for her hand. 'None of it matters right now Ally, we can sort things out later.'

No longer attached to a drip, Ally could move her fingers again. She gripped his hand then looked up at him. 'Willie you've been fantastic over the last couple of weeks,' she whispered. 'Willie, I don't remember that night, but . . . I've got some . . . some problems and I . . . I.'

Willie bent forward and kissed her. 'It's okay, we can talk about it all another time. It really doesn't matter to me. Whatever it is we can face it together. I'm in love with you Ally, one hundred percent, you have to believe me.'

***

Stevie sighed and looked at Ruby, he had calmed down. She handed him a mug of coffee. 'Ruby, I want to offer to foster Alexis when I'm back on my feet. Who better to take her on and care for her? I have experience of trauma. I know what she's been through. She trusts me Ruby, and I can care for her in a way no one else can.'

Ruby shook her head. 'You know it's not that simple. You've been severely injured, and you're emotionally involved with all this.'

'Well surely that's better than a stranger Ruby? The kid needs someone who she can connect with emotionally. I need her too, as much as she needs me.'

'What would Kiera think?' Ruby asked quietly.

'My daughter would be fine with it Ruby; you know she would. Besides, she has her own life and I suspect there's a boy she's involved with anyway.'

Ruby sighed, put her hand on Stevie's arm and looked him in the eye. 'Stevie, I've already applied to adopt Alexis. I wasn't going to tell you yet, but one of us had to after what she's gone through. Alexis doesn't know because I'm waiting for the panel to decide. I'm hoping to foster her in the short-term, with a view to making an application to the court to adopt. Hopefully, when she leaves the hospital it will be with me. It'll be a long, drawn-out process because we'll need to free her for adoption as her father is unlikely to consent. You know what that will mean, court cases and appeals.'

Stevie shook his head. 'Surely they won't drag it out? He sexually abused all of his kids, including Alexis. He raped and killed her fucking mother and sister in cold blood. Then murdered and maimed scores of people, mostly children. Surely, they won't listen to him or let him stop an adoption? You know the people who make these policy and laws, they just don't get fucking evil, do they? The fucking processes make it so hard to do what's right for kids.'

'Stevie, we don't get to make that decision. We just have to do the best we can in the process. Most of the time it's right that we must prove why someone shouldn't have access to a child. The law can't account for every situation. This one is a bit unique.'

'It's what Alexis wants that's important Ruby! We both know there could be major problem's later, Adverse Childhood Experiences.'

'Yes, I know. But for now, she needs to know that there is no way he can force her to see him.' Ruby sighed, 'I've been going in every day to the hospital. She managed to ask the question, could he take her away. I said no, we wouldn't let him . . . She said . . . *what if he comes with a gun?* I thought what the fuck do you say to that given what she experienced. As long as that man is alive that wee girl will never have a moments peace.' Ruby wiped away a tear. 'Folk like you and me, we understand ACE'S and we can be prepared for it if and when it happens, it will mean you and Ally can see her and help with the aftermath.'

***

134

Monday morning came around and Ally prepared to move to the private hospital. Before she left the Queen Elizabeth, Stevie came through to speak to her.

'Ally, I'm going home. It may be a few days before I can get up to see you. I'm doing okay now, feeling much better.'

'What about emotionally, Stevie?'

Stevie shrugged. 'It's the usual I think, flashbacks and dreams. I'm fine Ally, I'm making plans. I'm going to be off work for a while, so I might do something creative, paint or write a screenplay about what happened.' He grinned. 'Who could I get to play me in it? Do you think Keanu Reeves could do a west of Scotland accent?'

Ally sighed and looked sadly at her friend. 'I want to remember Stevie, feel something, but I don't. I just can't. It's like I know it happened to me, but I feel it happened to someone else. It's a really weird sensation.'

'Ally maybe it's better that you don't remember just now, or at all. It was horrific. Maybe Clive is right, your brain is protecting you by not letting you remember it all.'

Ally thought about this and shook her head. 'No, it's like there is a jigsaw with a piece missing. I just want to feel something Stevie. My head feels like I'm wrapped in bubble wrap.'

'That's the pain medication, it kind of makes you feel woolly.' Stevie sat down by her side as she turned her head to look at him. 'Ally, you and I, we're still who we were before. We're still friends, still there for each other. I'm just a bit more distinguished-looking with my scars now!'

Ally smiled and nudged him. 'You're a scruffy bugger Stevie. Keanu Reeves? Dream on. She shut one eye and studied him, yeah I can see him a bit, maybe if you tidy yourself up. Look at your hair, it's even longer than usual, and when did you last shave?'

Stevie smirked. 'I'm ruggedly handsome, Ally, you know that. Hey guess what? Not that I'm changing the subject or anything, but I think Gerry and Ruby have got together whilst we have been in here. You know, a bit of rumpy pumpy!'

'Nooo!' Ally cried; her eyes wide. 'She wouldn't do that. Gerry! You have to be kidding?' Ally thought about it for a moment. 'He's been in to see me several times Stevie, she's been with him each time now I come to think of it. There's something, he does seem different somehow, less anal. I thought it was just because he was feeling guilty.' Ally made a face and stuck her tongue out. 'No, not him and Ruby! She wouldn't, would she? What makes you think there is something Stevie, maybe it's just all this?'

'He was in with Ruby whilst you were in the coma, the day the Royals were here. Cammy O'Sullivan and his chief constable came in too. They weren't allowed in to see you because you were so ill. They were all in my room. There was just something about him and her together, it was kind of intimate.' Stevie smiled. 'He came in another day last week, again with Ruby. The day you were in theatre. Played chess with me. He didn't mention the H word once. Unlike some I can name.'

'Stevie, you really do need to have a haircut.'

'Can't because of the stitches in my head Ally.'

'Stevie, you don't have stitches in your head. They've been out for weeks.'

'I'll get one soon.'

Ally lay back on the pillow and laughed. 'Stitches or a haircut?'

Stevie turned serious. 'Ally, if you need me, you know I'll be on the other side of the phone any time of night or day, don't you? If you remember ... or just want to ask questions.'

'I will Stevie. I want to remember how I felt then forget what I saw.' She looked at him, reached out and took his hand. 'Was it awful Stevie?'

He nodded slowly. 'It was like nothing I have ever experienced Ally. I have no words to describe how it felt.'

'Was it . . . Was it frightening? Was I scared? Were you scared? Was it frightening at the time?'

'No, it was terrifying.' Stevie looked at Ally. 'When it was going off, we didn't have time to think. I suppose we did things instinctively. It was whilst we were trapped it became real. I did think we were going to die there trapped in the rubble. You did too Ally, you thought you were dying. You asked me to take care of the boys, you were so sure you were going to die.' Stevie looked her in the eye. 'You also asked me to say you were sorry to Willie for how you had behaved. You told me that you had feelings for him. Honey, you also told me you wanted to be with him and had panicked when he tried to make love to you!'

'Oh Stevie, I'm such an idiot about that.' She blushed, and he smiled.

'Want me to change the subject?'

Ally nodded, her face scarlet. 'I think I've worked out what happened with Willie. I need to know about what happened at the school, Stevie, how I felt, what it was like.'

Stevie sighed. 'In terms of what happened, we saw a lot of bad stuff then lay buried for seven hours.' He reached over and took her hand in his, his voice cracking with emotion. 'Ally, I never realised that there was that kind of evil in the world. I still can't believe it happened to us. We live in the most boring town in the world and this happens.'

Ally looked at her friend and gripped his hand. 'Stevie thanks. I know this is hard for you to talk about. I'll be there for you too.'

137

Stevie nodded. 'Ruby is going to take me home. Her and Keira are going to look after me for a few days.' Stevie smiled, then kissed Ally's cheek. 'You just sit back and get better now. They tell me that this hospital you are going to is like a high-class hotel.'

'Stevie, you're still my best man friend, you know that don't you?' He nodded, and with a wave of his hand he was gone. Ally lay back on the pillow and looked around. All her belongings were packed into a case which lay at the door; she was wearing wide palazzo pants and a baggy t-shirt ready to move to the private clinic Willie and Clive had arranged for her.

Ally looked up as Stan came in the door. 'Ready then?' he said, picking up Ally's case. 'I'll come down to the door with you. The hospital you're going to is amazing by the way, I cycle past it, it's on my route to work.'

Ally settled in the private ambulance she looked at the nurse as he walked backwards back onto the street, tears building in her eyes. 'Stan, you've been wonderful. Will you come in and see me if you are passing, seeing as you live over that way?'

The nurse nodded, 'sure will Ally, if it's okay.' Ally smiled at him and waved as the ambulance doors closed on her.

***

'No Willie?' Ruby asked as she put her head around the door. 'Wow! This is a hospital room? The boys said it was amazing, but this is unbelievable. It's like Gleneagles. You're out of bed too.'

Ally smiled. 'Willie has stuff on today, big game. They lift me out and sit me in the chair for physiotherapy every day, and today they said I could stay in the chair for a while. They're going to take me out onto the balcony to sit in the fresh air when the rain goes off.'

Ruby smiled and looked out of the window. 'I don't think it will happen today Ally, the rain is cold and torrential. Anyway, I brought you a visitor, some light entertainment!' She pulled the door opened and Cammy O'Sullivan looked around.

'Hi Ally. I knew I would get you in a bedroom someday.'

'You wish!' Ally laughed, hugging him. She kissed him on the cheek, and he pretended to swoon. 'Cammy, it's great to see you.'

Cameron smiled slyly. 'I came up a couple of times when you were first in hospital, but you were always sleeping.' His eyes twinkled. 'Lazy cow.'

Ally gasped. 'I was in a coma Cammy!'

'Whatever! Anyway, I'm glad you're doing better Ally. Hey congratulations on your award. I hear it's going to be presented by the Queen herself.'

Ally nodded. 'I heard you got a promotion? I'll miss you.'

'Aye right! You'll be glad to see the back of me and you know it. I start next week based in Glasgow, head of major events and incidents. Can I come back in and see you? I brought you flowers by the way, but the nurse took them off me at the door. I just popped in for a minute. I'm off to the Scotland game. All the proceeds are going to the fund. Your man invited all the incident team from the school to be his guests.' He smiled and shook his head. 'By god you're a dark horse Ally. Willog! What's he got that I don't by the way?'

'I couldn't possibly comment Cammy.'

'Well I'm going to have to start looking for a woman now you are off the market. I was saving myself for you.' He laughed and kissed her cheek. 'You look great by the way, love the scar, very distinguished.'

'Piss off.' She raised her hand. 'Cammy, thanks for everything.'

'Anytime, beautiful lady, hope we can stay friends. I'll come in next week if that's okay?'

'I'd like that Cammy, daytime telly is shit, once loose women is finished there isn't much entertainment till night-time!'

After he left, Ruby sat by the side of the bed, looked at Ally and smiled. 'How's it going with Willie then?' She asked. 'He's nothing like I thought he would be Ally. It's all a bit weird. The things they say about him, yet he has hardly left your side for a month now. He really is a nice guy; it would be hard not to like him.'

Ally nodded and sighed. 'I keep telling him that he doesn't have to be here every day. To be honest I'm struggling a bit with the whole relationship thing.' She looked at Ruby.

Ruby nodded and made a face. 'You were before. I take it you remember that?'

Ally grimaced. 'I remember everything up to the weekend before it happened Ruby. The last thing I remember clearly is meeting Willie after work on the Friday night before. Every detail, what we ate, where we were, what we talked about, I remember it all so clearly as though it was yesterday.'

'Then you'll remember what you were struggling with Ally? I take it he thinks it's his past and reliability?'

Ally nodded and looked at the floor. 'He thinks he has to prove he's serious about me. I don't know how to discuss the real issue.'

'S.E.X.' Ruby smiled. 'Would you believe that I am kind of in the same situation?' She blushed and looked at Ally. 'It's hard to think about it when you haven't done it for a while, isn't it?'

'Gerry?' Ally asked, looking her friend in the eye and smiling at the shock on her face.

'How did you . . . how do you know?' Ruby gasped. 'I didn't even know myself until after you were injured. It began the night after the shootings. Christ! You didn't see that too? When you were unconscious? Did you?'

Ally laughed at the look of horror on her friend's face and shook her head. 'No but from the look on your face it would have been something! So,' Ally asked, her eyes twinkling with mirth, 'tell me how *that* happened Ruby.'

Ruby sighed, her face became serious. 'When we came back from Glasgow the night of the shootings we went to the office. We were in a right state. Gerry said he had a bottle of whisky in his room, unopened. We ended up drinking it then . . . you know, we kind of did it!'

'In the office!' Ally squealed. 'Where?'

'In his room, on top of the desk.' Ruby giggled, blushing bright red now. 'It was bloody uncomfortable, but the sex was good. Actually, it was amazing. We got a taxi back to mine, did it again. We wakened up together sober and have been seeing each other since. How did you know Ally?'

'A little bird told me . . . Actually, truth is, it was a big scruffy bird.'

'Stevie knows?'

Ally nodded, smiled and giggled. 'You know Stevie, he misses nothing. I don't normally either. Between us we used to have all the office gossip sewn up. Ruby, far be it for me to criticise but . . . Gerry? What on earth were you thinking?' she gasped, 'and he's married! What about Ann?'

'Ally it's not what you think. He and Ann have not had a physical relationship for years.' She smiled. 'Ann's a lesbian, she knows all about us. They've just stayed together out of habit, but they lead separate lives. He's not like you think he is either, he's just a bit rigid and set in his ways. He's actually really sweet.' She blushed again. 'He is also a really good lover and you know . . . hung like a . . . you know what. He is everything I would want in a man, considerate and loving.'

'Grateful, I would think Ruby. You are so out of his league.'

Ruby looked at Ally over her glasses, which Ally knew was what she did when about to give her a telling off.

'Anyway . . . Mrs Campbell! Willie Ogilvy might be handsome and charming, but what about his reputation? Let's agree, you say nothing about me and Gerry, I'll say nothing about your choices?'

'Touché, Mrs Weir. That makes sense to me.'

Ruby looked serious for a moment. She looked away, her eyes misting over. 'Ally, all of us came out of that day changed. There were moments when we all came together in worry when you were missing, in pain thinking you and Stevie were dead. Then the joy and worry when they got you out. We watched little broken bodies being carried out and told people that their children were dead. Then that evening, knowing you were hanging to life by a thread. Something like that, well it changes you and makes you look for something. You were oblivious to most of it Ally, you can't remember even now.' She tailed off. 'I felt so alone. Your family were all gathered around and supporting each other. Stevie had Kiera and his parents worrying about him, even Laura turned up at the hospital. I just felt I had no one of my own.'

'You have always been there for me Ruby, whatever you choose, I'll be there for you. It's funny, I've just always thought you were part of my family. I never considered that you needed something, or someone, of your own. Does that make me selfish?'

No Ally, I was never lonely. I love you and your kids like they are my own.' Ruby smiled, 'that will always be the case. I haven't told anyone except Stevie, but I've been cleared to adopt Alexis. She has no one now either. It was murder with the fostering and adoption panel, you know what it's like, well meaning amateurs who've read a book on attachment. Oh, I'm being malevolent they are not all like that, just councillor Racy, and Mrs Smedley-Jones. They gave me a hard time. He had concerned about me being a single parent, he is a total misogynist as you well know, he's obviously not over the complaint into him I handled. She's a malicious cow with too much time on her hands and little knowledge of real life, she went on about boundaries, however, I got through it and managed to argue for her to come to me.'

Ally laughed, yeah you and I have a history with those two, don't we? He came on to me in the car park one day and I sent him away with a flee in his ear. He has never liked me since. I did a report on her boy, he is just like her, an entitled bully, weirdly her daughter is lovely. Anyway, you and Gerry? Are you going to be a couple, bring her up together?'

'The situation with Gerry is that I think I have strong feelings for him. Believe me, no one is more surprised than me Ally.' She smiled. 'It's early days, but we have spoken about being a family. But enough of me. You my friend, are deflecting from what you told me before you were hurt.'

Ally sighed. 'The fact that I've not been intimate with a man for fifteen years. I never actually wanted to until I met Willie. Now I'm not sure if I'm ready to show anyone my body.' She looked down at her chest. 'You know how bad the scars from the accident are!'

'Ally! You're so wrong about your body. How many times do you need to be told? I honestly think you have some type of body dysmorphia. Possibly wrapped up with Post Traumatic Stress. I told you years ago you needed counselling before it became a phobia.'

Ally shook her head. 'I don't know Ruby perhaps you're right. Either that or it's psychological about getting into a new relationship. It might even be worse now given all the new scars I'll have. I don't know what happened that night when I fell out with Willie, Ruby. He says I told you and Stevie about it. Stevie insists I didn't tell him any details when we were trapped, other than I wanted to have sex with Willie but couldn't. He said I told him I called you. I don't know why I can't remember! I can understand not remembering after the explosion, but why can't I remember the days before? I've read the minutes of the case conference, yet I don't have any memory of it either. Ruby what did I tell you? Did I phone you?'

Ruby shook her head. 'Actually, you came to my house. You were really distressed and angry, but I'm not sure now whether I understood at the time. I'm afraid you and I did what we always do when there's an issue, got really drunk. You implied he'd tried to force himself on you. I wondered if you were upset because you were afraid of being intimate with a man, had led him on and then panicked. You'd told me you were going to have sex with him that night! You were going to meet him for a meal in Glasgow, go back to his place. Ally, you even bought new underwear. You need to speak to Willie about it, ask him. He's another person who is not what he first appears to be. You're a beautiful woman with the most amazing figure. You work out, I've seen you naked. The scarring is not bad, Ally, it's all in your head. I think it's all tied up with Ralph dying and you having had the difficult birth. A few new scars are not going to make a difference. You're definitely a tiger who has earned her stripes.'

Ally shook her head. 'Know what I'm more worried about now? I'm worried about sex hurting.'

'Because of your broken pelvis?' Ruby asked.

Ally shook her head, 'Not entirely, I was worried before. I googled him after we met Ruby. There are several stories saying he is well endowed. What if it hurts? What if he is too big? The pain from my pelvis was bad, worse than the other injuries. I broke the other side in the accident. I need to ask someone about it, but I'm embarrassed. I haven't had intercourse since I was twenty-eight. It's been over fifteen years. How can I admit to that? The orthopaedic surgeon, well he's so young and good-looking, I just couldn't say it.'

'Why don't you ask Clive? You get on well with him. He's older and a brain surgeon, bound to know much more than the other guy.'

Ally looked thoughtful. 'I could probably ask Clive if I didn't look at him. You're right, he probably will know more.'

'Ask Clive what?' Clive's booming voice came from the doorway. 'I was just coming in to check on you and see how you had settled, when I heard you say you needed to ask me but were embarrassed.'

Ruby stood up. 'I think I'll go and get us a coffee and come back up.' She winked at Ally and made a sharp exit, closing the door behind her.

'Okay Alyson, what's the problem? Does it have something to do with your injuries?' He smiled at her then sat down on the bed. 'Let me make it easier for you. You are wondering about resuming a sexual relationship and whether the pelvic injury will be a problem.'

Ally nodded. 'You heard?'

He smiled and nodded. 'I was outside when you said you were afraid sex would hurt. I'm ashamed to admit I sometimes eavesdrop on my patients; it makes it easier to broach difficult subjects.'

Ally inclined her head and smiled back at Clive, 'Stevie and I both do that too, at work. It helps us to know what's going on.' Ally looked down at her lap and studied her hands. 'Oh Clive, I don't know what to do. Sex is the last thing I should be thinking about just now. I'm afraid it will hurt or do more damage. The pain down there has been bad at times, even worse than the gunshot wounds. I also had a fracture there fifteen years ago, from the car crash.'

'Ally, I'm kind of thinking that the only problems you are going to have are emotional, yes you've been through a lot of trauma. Yes, there will be some sexual positions you should avoid for a time. Gentle lovemaking and mutual caressing should not have any detrimental effect. In fact, it might be good for you emotionally. Why don't you try masturbating first if you are afraid of the physical side?'

Ally looked at him, for the first time they made eye contact. She realised his eyes were kind and serious, not teasing. 'Clive,' she said, blushing furiously, 'I've not had intercourse since my husband died fifteen years ago.'

'Well, all the more reason why you should when you feel physically healed,' he replied, smiling. 'I'm surprised Ally. You're a beautiful, vibrant woman. I should think any straight man would find you attractive. There's really been no one?'

'Oh, I've dated a few men over the years, but I just never met anyone I wanted to be with that way. I've messed about and done stuff, but not intercourse. I was only twenty-eight when Ralph died, I'd just come through a pregnancy and a difficult premature birth. I was gravely injured; I think I have some sort of phobia now.'

Clive nodded. 'It could also be emotional, a reaction to losing half your family. Losing Ralph, losing your mother and baby. Everyone reacts in different ways to the same process when they are grieving. You were never able to replace those especially important people. Maybe now you are ready and that can be a frightening thing.'

'I suppose it's a very individual thing, grief, you might be right.' Ally sighed considering what Clive had just said. 'One of our team lost her husband a few years ago. She was frumpy and ordinary before, a real plain Jane we thought. She turned into some kind of sex siren. Totally changed, got a boob job, dyed her hair, started taking drugs and became promiscuous. It was sad. She ended up getting dismissed for sleeping with one of her care leaver clients. Me, I went the opposite way, just couldn't bear the thought of someone else. I met Ralph the first week at uni. I was a virgin, so he was all I knew.'

He looked at her over the top of his glasses. 'Would you like me to talk to Willie? I would imagine if half what they write about him is true, he'll be very experienced in these things. He'll know how to pleasure you without hurting you. I needn't tell him about this conversation, I could just do it from a medical perspective.'

Ally nodded, her face beetroot red. 'Thank you, Clive. Even before I got hurt, I was keeping him at arm's length because I was afraid. As I said, it's not just the injuries it's more ... it's like a phobia. The other reason is I have so much scarring on my body. I know it's silly, but I suppose I'm kind of vain.'

Clive smiled. 'You are a beautiful woman Ally. If he loves you, he won't care about scars. Do you want to be intimate with him?'

She nodded, 'I think I do.'

'Well, just relax then and let it happen my dear.' Clive smiled. 'He's an incredibly lucky man!'

The door was tapped, and Ruby came back in carrying two coffee mugs; Clive took his leave. He walked back down the corridor. *'Fifteen years without intercourse,'* he said to himself, *'how strange. She is such an attractive woman as well. You would think that someone would have had the curiosity.'* He shook his head, then went off to see his other patients.

'Well?' Ruby asked.

'Do you know, Clive is easy to talk to. I think it's because he's gay Ruby.'

Ruby shook her head and sighed.

'What?'

Ruby laughed. 'About the sex?'

Clive doesn't think there would be a problem if we're careful about the position. He is going to speak to Willie for me.'

'Did he tell you he's gay? Clive, I mean?'

'Kind of, he said something about straight men finding me attractive.' Ally smiled and looked at Ruby. 'What's up with you? You look nervous.'

Ruby moved closer to Ally and put her hand on her arm. 'There's something else I need to speak to you about Ally.' She took a deep breath and looked at her friend. 'Scott has asked me to talk to you. He's in a relationship with a young lady, they're in love. He's not sure you'll approve Ally. He wants me to sound you out.'

'Why on earth would I not approve? If he's happy, I'm happy, he knows that. He's twenty-one years old after all.' Ally felt mildly annoyed at Scott talking to Ruby first. 'Is it someone older, or someone I know from work?'

Ruby sighed. 'His girlfriend is pregnant Ally, she's much the same age as him. He didn't know how to tell you. It was an accident, but neither of them wishes to terminate the pregnancy.'

Ally stared at her friend. 'It's not the end of the world though! I would have thought he could tell me anything Ruby, he knows that I was pregnant with him when Ralph and I married. I'm kind of hurt that he felt he couldn't tell me. What about her family?'

'Oh, they told her mother and she went off on one. But her father, he's going to be supportive but surprised.' Ruby took a deep breath. 'Ally, Scott is in a relationship with Kiera.'

'Kiera! She's like his sister. They have known each other since they were kids! Why did I not know?'

'It's been going on for about a year Ally. I think since before that other girl moved out of the flat. They just felt they didn't want you and Stevie to know. They were about to tell you then you both got hurt.'

'Does Danny know?'

Ruby nodded. 'Of course, he does, you know how close Scott and Danny are. Keira is really close to him too. I would imagine Danny would have been the first person they told. Apparently, they discovered that they were attracted to each other and tried to avoid it for a while. But they're lovely together Ally. They aren't just sharing the flat Ally; they share a bed.' Ruby smiled, 'apparently they have to do major reshuffling whenever you, Stevie or Laura stayover. When you speak to them, you'll realise that they're good together. If it is any consolation, I had to tell Stevie too.'

'How did he take it?'

'Much the same as you!'

'We are going to have to have a conversation with them. I can understand why Laura would be upset though Ruby. Keira is so young and just beginning her career. I'll ring Laura tomorrow Ruby; I haven't seen her for a while, but we are still friends, she sent me a lovely card a couple of weeks ago.'

***

The telephone beside the bed rang, Ally looked at the clock, it was almost ten oclock. She sighed as she heard Stevie speak. 'Well what do you think?' he asked.

'I tried to call you earlier, but your phone was off. I'm not sure how I feel Stevie. I'm still in shock about being a grandmother, without thinking about them deceiving us.'

Stevie laughed. 'I was livid they went to Ruby, Ally, were you?'

'I was annoyed, let's just leave it at that. She's so young Stevie, not even halfway through her degree. He's at least has only got this year to go.'

'They're not much younger than you were when you were pregnant with Scott, Ally! They've already sorted it all out. Despite that fact that in this day and age, they have managed to get pregnant, they're quite sensible. She'll finish her second year, have the baby then go back for the third year. Scott will have his degree by then so if need be, he'll take a gap year. The university are keen to support them, so hopefully they'll get him some research work. Hey, it's not the end of the world Ally. I can't think of anyone I would rather my daughter was with than Scott. He is such a lovely boy and I know he'll treat her well. And we are going to be grandparents! It's a new life. After what we've all been through, how can it be bad? Laura's not too pleased, so I get to be the supportive parent. That makes me feel good.'

'Stevie, that's horrible. Laura just wants what's best for Keira.'

'What!' Stevie laughed. 'Don't go all superior on me Ally! She left me for another man. Can't you allow me some smug, ego stuff? Did Ruby tell you about her plans to adopt Alexis?'

'Yes, I hope she is doing the right thing for the wee soul, Stevie, Ally pursed her lips. 'I'm worried about Ayrshire having so many bad memories for Alexis. She'll always be branded as his daughter too. Then there are other concerns Stevie, I mean, Ruby is great with kids, but is it for the right reasons?'

'If she hadn't, I would have done it Ally. I had discussed it with her.' Ally heard Stevie sigh before he continued. 'She moves in with Ruby on Friday when she leaves hospital. I'm sure it's going to work out, even if Gerry ends up the father figure!'

'Well that's another weird thing, isn't it? Anyway, how are you coping being home Stevie?'

'Surprisingly well, all things considered. Scott's here with Kiera by the way. He's helping. Given that he has impregnated my only child, he owes me big style.'

'I've not seen him yet, I decided this has to be face to face not on the phone even with facetime.'

'He'll be up to see you tomorrow. I went to the school this morning and left some flowers.' Ally could hear the sadness in his voice. 'They've opened the new school early, so the kids are going to be back next week. Have the police been in to speak to you yet? Seamus is pleading not guilty would you believe? They've charged him now and moved him to the main prison he's in the protection wing obviously.'

'How can he plead not guilty? Everyone knows he did it. What does that mean for us Stevie?'

'Pleading not guilty means there will be a trial, Ally, he wants his day in court no doubt, he's a psychopath babe, its all about him. We'll be called as witnesses. According to Davie at the prison, he's just wanting to drag us all in, cause everyone more stress. I suppose he's got nothing to lose really, we live in a democracy Ally even psychopathic bastards get a fair hearing. It won't be for a while; they have set it for late November early December, but you know what the system is like it will get postponed likely. The Police are still taking statements.'

'I can't remember anything Stevie. I'll be no use to them anyway.'

'Still nothing?'

'Nope not a thing. I keep looking at the stuff, trying to remember but I just can't.'

'Ally it's probably a good thing hun. It wasn't nice. The shooting was horrific and then lying buried! You were out of it for a lot of the time, but you knew you had been shot and you saw some really bad stuff too. Leave it, it's for the best, honestly.' Sensing the need to change the subject he asked, 'did you see the football?'

'No. Why would I watch football?'

'Not even the national team? Not even to support your man?'

'Not even that Stevie. Did they win?'

'Yup we won, did well actually. Willie was interviewed after the game. It's all over the news. The boys, Kiera and I were at the match as his guests. We would have come in, but Scott was late getting over, possibly deliberately so we didn't have time to come in to see you. Anyway, when Willie was interviewed, he

151

was talking about the concert he is organising with his business partner to raise money for the appeal.'

Ally yawned. 'Excuse me!'

'Am I boring you Mrs?'

'Not at all Stevie, I'm just really tired. They're still giving me strong painkillers and that's what is knocking me out.

'Okay I'll go and let you get some rest. I'll see you tomorrow. Night, night, gorgeous granny.'

Ally lay back on the pillows, her eyes felt heavy and she knew that she was exhausted. It had been a long day and she had not had her now customary afternoon nap. As she closed her eyes, the door creaked open and Willie came in. Ally blinked and switched on the dimmed light. He wore a suit, shirt and tie, Ally looked at him and thought how good-looking he was. 'I thought you'd have been out celebrating,' she said, sitting up.

He kissed her and she could smell alcohol and cigarettes on his breath. I had a couple with the boys. I missed you, you've really tamed me Ally. I'd better just go; you look tired babe.

I am, I missed my nap today, I had extra visitors. Ruby came in just after lunch she brought in Cammy O'Sullivan, after he left, we got talking. Then Clive came in and we had a long talk. He's really easy to talk to.'

'I think Clive has a bit of a thing about you Ally.'

'No, he doesn't, he's too professional for that. In any case I'm fairly sure he's gay.'

'Really, what makes you think that?'

'He said he was sure that any straight man would find me attractive, so there. Why would a hetro man say something like that?' Ally yawned again and lay back.

'I just came in for a quick kiss and cuddle. You're tired, I'll go.'

'No, come here,' she said patting the bed beside her. 'I think I need to snuggle; I've missed you too.' Willie took off his jacket, kicked off his boots and loosened his tie before hopping up onto the bed. Ally lay back against his chest, and he put his left arm around her shoulder.

'You smell of whisky and smoke!' she whispered.

'You smell of soap and bedpans,' he whispered back.

When Ally woke, she was still in Willie's arms. She felt comfortable and warm. It was still dark outside, but she could see his face. She looked up at him and smiled, he looked so peaceful. He opened his eyes, looking around. 'Good morning my lovely lady. I can't believe I fell asleep here.' He looked at his watch. 'It's nearly seven a.m. Brenda will think I'm out on the town, I'll get slapped when I get in.' He kissed the top of Ally's head. 'I would rather just stay here though.' She looked up at him; he kissed her mouth and forehead before turning around to face her. 'You're unbelievably beautiful, especially when you have just wakened. You look like a young girl, but you're all woman.' She kissed him back; her hand reached up; she touched his face. He moved his hands through her hair kissing her gently. 'I love you Mrs Campbell,' he whispered into her hair.

'Hmm I think I might love you right back Mr Ogilvy,' Ally whispered looking up at him, even in the dim light of the hospital room, she could see the desire in his eyes. She moved slightly and began to kiss him.

Willie's right hand moved down to her breast, he cupped it and began to rub her nipple through the thin fabric of her nightie, still kissing her. A shiver ran through Ally's body and she relaxed, allowed herself to enjoy the sensation. He kissed her neck and shoulder, then unbuttoned her nightie and began to kiss around her breast, his lips closing on her nipple. Ally shivered and moaned. She put her hand on his head, running her fingers through his hair as she felt her body respond. Shivers ran down her spine and she moaned again. He stopped suddenly and pulled away. 'Fuck, I'm so sorry Ally, I was getting carried away. I know you're not ready physically or emotionally, to let

me make love to you. You should know I'll never pressure you
again for sex. I'll wait for as long as it takes for you to be ready
babe.' Willie, buttoned her nightie, sat up and moved away
from her. Ally shivered, she wanted to pull him back down. Her
nipple tingled, she could still feel the sensation of his mouth on
it and she had a warm feeling in her groin. He turned his back
as he spoke. 'Do you mind if I have a shower here? I also need
to use your toothpaste. I've got to go back to the SFA offices this
morning for a press conference. I don't have time to go home
first.' Without waiting for a reply, he went into the shower room
closing the door behind him.

Willie leaned back against the wall and gasped. His trousers
strained against his erection, he tried to think of things to make
it go away. His usual picture when he had an erection at an
inappropriate time was Brenda, who he loved dearly but as his
surrogate mother. This however was useless, he felt too far gone.
All he could think of was the curve of Ally's small firm breasts,
the hardness of her nipple. He could taste her on his lips, smell
her. He realised it was exactly the scenario from the last night
they were together. She responded then too, then suddenly got
upset. Willie undressed quickly, got into the shower cubicle and
turned on the cold tap. Eventually, when he still had an erection, he masturbated, it was over quickly. '*Fuck sake!*' he said to
himself. *'I really have got it bad. I can't even touch her tit without
getting into a state.'*

Ally watched from the bed as Willie, came out of the shower
room with a towel around his waist. He was rubbing his hair
casually with a second towel. Ally breathed in sharply at how
physically fit he was for a man of forty-seven. Willie appeared
to be oblivious to Ally looking at his body. 'Has Ruby spoken to
you by the way?' he asked as he put down the towel and ran his
fingers through his wet hair.

'Ruby?' Ally said, pulling her thoughts away from lust. 'About what?'

'Kiera and Scott?'

'You too! Did they tell everyone but me and Stevie?'

'What? No. Stevie told me last night, they were at the game. Granny Ally, imagine that!' He turned away from her and went back into the shower room, when he came back out, he was fully dressed. He sat on the chair by the bed and put on his boots.

'Won't they notice you're wearing the same shirt and tie you had on yesterday?'

'No, it's a Scotland tie, so no one will be any the wiser. I have a clean shirt in my office.' He grinned. 'There were a lot of nights I didn't go home.' He kissed her, patted her head and was gone, leaving Ally in a state of confusion.

Scott and Kiera came in that evening for a visit looking sheepish and uncomfortable. Ruby and Stevie accompanied them. They sat discussing the impending birth. Kiera admitted that she'd been more afraid of telling anyone than Scott. Ally smiled at her. 'You can't think that we would have been anything other than supportive.'

'Stevie already told us that,' Scott said. 'We didn't mean to deceive you. It was just that we were so surprised ourselves at the strength of our feelings.' He smiled, 'when we were about twelve and thirteen, we had a bit of a kiss and cuddle, but it didn't go anywhere, and we never really thought about it again. Then about a year ago, we kind of realised that there was something, and well, it just went from there.'

'It was really weird at first, being together, but it just felt right,' Kiera whispered. 'When Melissa moved out, we decided that we would try it. We didn't know how to tell you we were in a relationship, never mind that we had managed to get pregnant. I felt so silly, like a little kid. We thought we had been careful and were shocked when it turned out I was pregnant. When we told Mum the day you two got hurt, she went off on one at us. She's still not speaking to me, I didn't expect that, so I was really worried about telling you. We were on our way to tell you when we got the call about the incident. You both got so badly hurt we couldn't tell you. Ruby guessed there was something and asked. We're both such cowards, we left her to tell you. I'm twenty-two weeks Ally. It's a girl, we decided we wanted to know the sex. We couldn't wait any longer to tell you because of this.' She lifted her sweater to show off a piece of elastic holding her jeans together.

'Well the first thing we'd better do is get you some maternity clothes!' Ally laughed. 'Ruby, you need to take her shopping for us. Keira I'm sure Laura will come around, it's just not what she wanted for you. She will be worried about you, I tried to call her this morning, I've left a message.'

'No. I think we have stolen her thunder Ally; she is pregnant too and due around the same time.' Keira looked at Stevie, sorry dad I hope you are not too upset.'

Stevie laughed, 'not at all, it's just funny because she was the one who didn't want another baby.' He sat down on the edge of the bed. 'This place is amazing Ally. I wish I'd stayed now and come with you.'

She looked at him. 'You've had a haircut and shaved Stevie, you look great. And you are wearing a shirt, not a t-shirt and one of your old, scruffy fleeces.'

Kiera giggled. 'I threw them all out when he was in hospital. I had a clear out for him. He needs to start looking for a woman, Ally. He's been on his own too long. If you can do it, so can he.'

Ally smiled, but for some reason the thought of Stevie with a woman annoyed her slightly. She shook away the thought. 'Maybe we could help you join one of those dating websites or something?'

Stevie smiled. 'Nope, if I am going to find someone, I'll do it the traditional way.'

The door swung open, Willie came in and looked around. They were all laughing; he noted how comfortable they were. He felt irritated at how Ally was with Stevie, then pushed the thought away, realising for the first time he felt envious of their closeness. Jealously was yet another alien state for Willie Ogilvy.

CHAPTER

SIXTEEN

Willie put his head around the door of Clive Ruthven's office. 'Clive, can I take Ally out for the day?'

Clive raised his head from the report he was reading and motioned for Willie to sit down. 'To where?'

'Oh, just out on my boat.'

'No helicopters or flights?'

'No of course not! Why would I do that?'

Clive raised an eyebrow. 'I do read the tabloids Willie. They used to be full of stories about your nights out. It's just that she could be at risk from deep vein thrombosis, and she may need oxygen if she was to fly due to the broken ribs and collapsed lung. It's been ten weeks; she'll be going home soon. We need to do one more bit of surgery on her thigh, but after that she can be treated as an outpatient.'

'Can I take her abroad then? I've got a house in Majorca. It's a short flight, a couple of hours.'

'Willie, I've actually been meaning to have a chat with you.'

Willie looked at him. 'Sounds ominous Clive, you look like a disapproving father.'

'Well, I doubt if her father, nice as Jimmy is, would want to have this conversation. It's about sex.'

'Sex! Why? I didn't know you cared Clive, but I'm kind of spoken for.'

Clive ignored the humour and looked serious. 'You've never been intimate with Ally, Willie! She told me. When you do attempt a sexual relationship, you'll need to be careful. She's had so many injuries, her pelvis appears to be healing, but there will be things that she cannot do yet.'

Willie smiled then pursed his lips. 'I'm not planning to seduce her on this day out Clive. I just thought she might enjoy being away from the hospital. She mentioned she wanted to go onto Ailsa Craig. My boat is kept at Wemyss Bay, so I thought we could sail along the coast, around Ailsa Craig and then back. She's not on as much medication, so I wondered if it would be okay. The weather is so good just now.'

'She's having the plaster taken off her left wrist this morning. If you want to take her out, do it the day after tomorrow.' Clive smiled. 'You're a lucky man William Ogilvy. Alyson's a very desirable woman and so beautiful. In fact, I'm a little in love with her myself.'

Willie nodded. 'You're not having her, Clive. I am going to treat her like a princess.'

'She deserves that Willie. She deserves the best there is in life. Now, there is a poker game tonight and I'm finally able to be off duty. Fancy it?'

CHAPTER

SEVENTEEN

Willie threw his cards on the table and took a drink of whisky, 'you lot are either card sharps or I've played with the best tonight.' Willie looked at Clive who was also out of the game; they moved away from the group, and opened the patio doors, stepping outside Willie put a cigarette in his mouth and offered the packet to Clive who took one and accepted a light. 'So, you're not a poof then? Do I have to watch you with Ally?' Willie asked.

'No, of course not! She's my patient, I'd never cross that line. She is exquisite, in perfect proportion and beautiful. Not in an obvious way, but it's her personality isn't it.' He grinned. 'I can't believe she thinks I'm gay. Although, I reckon she could turn a gay man straight.'

Willie nodded and grinned back. 'Perhaps, but she is my woman. Don't you take some oath or something that means you can't sleep with a patient anyway?'

Clive sniggered. 'The Hippocratic Oath. What a bastard that is. The ancient Greeks were a weird lot. However, Willie, technically it's the GMC who would object to a relationship between patient and doctor. If she was an ex-patient and of sound mental capacity, there would be nothing they could do if it was consenting.' Seeing Willie's face change, Clive laughed. 'Willie, I can assure you my only interest in Ally is medical. As if I could compete with Willog!'

'I can't believe you haven't had a shag for five years Clive. What did your wife die of?'

'Ovarian cancer.' Clive's face clouded and Willie could see he was being remined of a painful time. 'She died ten years ago. She was ten years younger than me, only thirty-four, our son was twelve. It's a horrible illness, often like in her case no warning signals until its advanced. Worse when you are a doctor and can't do anything. I have dated women since, but I'm not in your league Willie.'

'Hope you're not going to tell Ally you're straight Clive, you might be competition for me.'

'I will if she asks me.'

'She won't, she's too nice, but she may try to matchmake for you. She has loads of gay friends Clive, so you'd better be careful.' Willie took a drink and studied the big doctor. 'I think it's the moustache, it actually makes you look gay. The public-school accent doesn't help either.'

'I can't exactly help that, can I? I was public school educated. I'm the second son of a lord too.' Clive grinned and took a drink of his whisky, making a face as he tasted it. 'My brother, the first son, actually is gay, so there's no issue. Which means I'll inherit the title one day. My brother Charles is twenty-eight years older than me. My mother was the second wife. Charles is 80 now.'

'Really? You're so normal too. Ally might fancy being Lady of the Manor!'

'Ally loves you Willie, no doubts there, but you need to live up to that love. Can you?'

'Fuck I hope so!' Willie sighed, draining his glass.

CHAPTER

EIGHTEEN

'Where are we going?' Ally asked. 'How much of a surprise will this be?' Ally sat on her bed wearing a long, white cotton dress. Ruby had brought it in the night before; Ally had called her when Willie had suggested the day out. 'Find something in my summer clothes that is cool, long, with no buttons or zips,' Ally had cried down the phone. 'Bring a cardigan or light jacket too, oh and some socks.'

'Where's he taking you?' Ruby had asked. 'There's a heat wave here!'

'Don't know!' Ally had said. 'He said although it is warm, to have a jacket or sweater to wear as it could get cold too.'

Willie smiled as he carefully pushed Ally in a wheelchair towards the door. Clive stood outside the nurse manager's office leaning on the door frame watching them. He shook his head and pointed at Willie. 'Make sure you have her back by eight and that she has a rest at some point in the day.' He turned his attention to Ally. 'Young lady!' Clive said sternly, 'no acrobatics or dare-devil activities.'

'Young lady?' Ally whispered as Willie pushed her into the lift. 'He can't be that much older than us Willie?'

Willie shrugged. 'Don't know Ally. He's one of those people where it's impossible to tell what age he is.'

'I wonder if he is in a relationship.'

'Why?'

'Why is he in a relationship?'

'No, why are you wondering?'

'He's so strong and able but also gentle and kind'

'Ooh, have you got a crush on the good doctor?'

'No silly. I told you he's gay, Willie. I'd need to be good.'

Willie shrugged. 'Is he? Interesting but irrelevant. You and I owe him your life Ally. Would you be interested in him if he wasn't gay?'

Ally laughed, her eyes sparkling. 'No, he's my doctor and he's Clive, a really nice man, but I couldn't think of him that way. I've never actually thought of anyone that way recently because I'm in love with you.'

Willie smiled and lifted her out of the chair. 'Right answer Mrs Campbell, you win a day out. Now let's get you into the car, it's right outside the door. That's the great thing about private hospitals, you don't have all those parking limitations. I brought the Range Rover, I thought it would be more comfortable. We're going along the coast towards Ayrshire.'

Within ten minutes of being in the car, Ally had nodded off. She wakened as they drove into the marina. 'We're going on a boat?' she asked, looking around.

'How did you know?'

'You have lifejackets in the back of the car, I saw them when you opened the door to put the chair in, and fishing rods. It kind of gives it away. We're also driving into a marina.'

'Okay, which boat then Inspector Clouseau?'

'Oh, I would like it to be that one!' she said pointing at a large luxury cruiser, 'but it's probably that one!' she laughed, nodding at a small sailing dingy.

Willie chuckled and pointed at a medium-sized cabin cruiser which was moored nearby.

'WOW! It's beautiful! Who does it belong to?'

'Oh, she's mine, called Jakole after my girls. I even sat exams in navigation and sailing. I bought it a few years ago, but to be honest I've never really done much with her. She's never even been out of the Firth of Clyde. Now let's get you on board. It's really comfortable. I lived in it for a few weeks to get away from the press after I split from Belinsa. Actually,' Willie said grinning, 'it was as much about staying away from her as the press. She did a real job on me, selling her story, playing on the wronged wife thing. She's as cunning as a fox is our Belinsa. People get her and her soap character mixed up. Still, I was a lousy husband Ally, I probably deserved everything I got.'

Ally said nothing; she had googled him and read the stories. None of it added up to the man she had come to know. 'It's a beautiful day!' Ally sighed as she sat beside Willie whilst he steered the boat out of the confines of the harbour. 'Can we head along the coast to Ailsa Craig? Can we go on to it?'

Willie nodded. 'Yes, I've permission to land. We can have our lunch there. How does that grab you?'

'Wow, sounds great.'

Ally watched the beautiful Ayrshire countryside roll by whilst they chatted happily, they passed the landmarks of the Firth of Clyde. They sailed past the small Isle of Cumbrae, with the little town of Largs on the mainland to their left. Passing the Arran ferry at Ardrossan, down the coast looking at the beautiful Culzean Castle. Then out from Girvan to the small rocky outcrop, famed for its making of curling stones.

Willie expertly steered the boat into harbour; above them seagulls flew around. 'Be careful Ally! Sit there until we dock,' Willie said as he tied the boat up. He moved onto the jetty and began to unload. 'Stay where you are until I put the sun beds out, then I'll come back for you.'

'What's the big bird for?' Ally asked, as she watched him lift a large model.

'It's an eagle owl!' Willie said holding it up. 'Hopefully, it will keep the seagulls away from our lunch. My mate Alfie uses them at his place in Majorca.'

Ally stared out at the Firth of Clyde; the sea was calm; the small island just as isolated and ruggedly beautiful as it looked from the Ayrshire shore. Above them sea birds squealed from the hundreds of nests on the rocky outcrop. 'I always meant to come out here. I've been in Girvan loads of times, both for work and pleasure, but never got around to it. It feels as though we're alone in the world Willie, just you and me.' She tightened her arms around his neck as he manoeuvred his way across the rocks. 'It feels safe,' she added.

'I hope it's not all too much for you. You're still very thin,' he said as he put her down on the sun bed he had set up. 'You weigh almost nothing, you look tired.'

'It's all the sea air and possibly the time of day. I'm used to having a nap around about now. My body is probably reacting to that.' She yawned and smiled. 'Don't know how I'm going to cope when I'm back at work. Can't see Gerry agreeing to me lying down in the staff room at lunch time.'

'You're planning to go back to work then? You could probably live comfortably on what you'll get in compensation, Ally. It's a dangerous job you do.'

She looked at him and smiled. 'It's who I am Willie. I already have plenty in the bank. Because Ralph died so young, we were really well insured. Then there was compensation. I started trust funds for the boys, paid off the mortgage then didn't really spend much, so the interest added up. I'm, how is it they say it on those dating pages in the papers? Financially solvent!'

165

'Ally, I know it is way too early to discuss this, but I need you to think about us being together too. I want to be with you.'

Ally looked slyly at him from under her dark lashes, her eyes sparkled. 'Hope you're not after my money Willie?'

'Nearly losing you babe, it made me so sure you're what I want, I can't tell you what to do with your life. I'll be there whatever you decide . . . but I'm scared for you . . . what happened to you . . . it was awful.'

'Willie, lighten up, I don't know what the future holds for you and me. I hope it's us as a couple, but I will go back to work, I'll do it all again.' Her eyes clouded over. 'What happened was an isolated incident one in a million thing, you know that. God, I feel exhausted Willie, as if I swam here.'

'That's why I've lugged the bed onto the shore. Clive said you would need a rest. Let's have something to eat, then you can have a nap.' He began to lay out the picnic.

'Looks lovely Willie, did you do it yourself? Or do you have someone for that?' Ally asked as she took a plate from him. She sat up on the bed and tried to look as though she was eating.

'You don't eat much these days do you Ally?' Willie couldn't help remembering the night they met, her enthusiasm for the chips they had shared. Then there were the meals at his home when they had been hiding from the world. Ally sighed and put a forkful of salad in her mouth and chewed. Willie noticed that she had been moving the food around her plate for the last few minutes.

'This is lovely, and you have gone to lots of trouble, but I never seem to be hungry these days Willie. I think it might be the drugs I'm on. They are opiate-based, so that can affect your desire for food.' She sipped from a bottle of water. 'God Willie, the sun is strong.' She took off her cardigan, put it behind her head and lay back on the sunbed.

'Have you got sunscreen on?'

Ally shook her head, 'I never thought there would be so much sun.' Willie rummaged in the picnic bag and produced a bottle of suntan lotion. 'How responsible Willie, I am so impressed!'

'Oh, after Tommy Burns died from skin cancer, we all got a fright. I always have it, especially on the boat.

Ally raised an eyebrow. 'Who was Tommy Burns?'

'Ally, do you know anything about Scottish football?'

'No, and up until now I've never needed to know anything. It's not really about the game. I just hate the sectarianism that goes with football here.'

'It's not like that within the game, we actually mostly all get on and I have always socialised with both sides of that argument. I think it's mainly a west coast of Scotland thing Ally, I never really noticed it anywhere else.'

'So, who is was this Tommy Burns?'

'He was a footballer, ended up a manager, he even was a care-taker manager of Scotland once. He died a few years ago, great guy. Both your boys follow football.'

'My dad and Stevie saw to that. I never even watched them play, oh I just don't really like macho sports, I guess. I tried to make them do ballet or gymnastics but they kind of voted with their feet so to speak and loved football.' Ally smiled and looked at Willie, 'Ralph loved football too, he came from Paisley originally, so it was St Mirren, see I do know a little bit about football.'

Willie watched Ally struggle to put the cream on her upper arm. 'Here I'll help you,' he said, taking the bottle from her.

'Thanks, I don't have a lot of movement or strength back in my arm yet. It feels weird to have the plaster off. I'm afraid to move it too much.'

'Budge up a bit,' Willie said, laughing. Ally's hair was held back by a band in a high ponytail. Willie straddled the bed behind her and began to rub cream onto her shoulders. He untied the thin straps of her dress. He could smell the freshness of her newly washed hair and he breathed in her unique scent. Ally could feel his body close to her and unwittingly she moved back slightly, her bottom touching his groin. Willie immediately felt his penis rising; he wondered if Ally was aware of this. He began to move his hands down her shoulders and up her neck. Ally realised she liked him touching her. She moaned softly as he began to kiss her neck and earlobes, his hands expertly massaged her shoulders and the top of her chest. The front of her dress moved down and slid over her breasts; Willie began running his hands over them. She did not stop him, instead she pressed back against his chest as he pushed her dress down to her waist and continued to massage her breasts. Ally shivered and leaned back further, his lips brushed her neck and cheek. She turned her head, their lips met as he slid his free hand under the skirt of her dress and into her panties. Ally gasped; she made eye contact with Willie then closed her eyes. He felt her relax. He began to rub around her groin, he gently pushed with his finger and stroked, all the time kissing her neck and shoulders. Willie smiled to himself when he heard her gasp, cry out, and push herself against his hand as an orgasm ripped through her body. He wrapped his free arm tightly around her and held her, still kissing her neck.

Spent, she lay back against him and closed her eyes. 'God Willie,' she gasped, her body still trembling from the intensity of her climax, 'you are amazing. Where did you learn to do that? I've never . . . I don't know what to say. How . . . did you?'

'I've had a lot of practice Ally.'

'It's been a long time since anyone touched me there.' She was amazed she didn't feel embarrassed or uncomfortable. It was the most natural thing in the world right now. Her breasts exposed and to have this man, his hand still inside her knickers, touching her.

He moved away and came around to face her. He adjusted her dress and re-tied the thin straps. 'I really want to make love to you, but you need to know I won't rush you. I'll wait until you're ready for me. That was just a little taster of what I can do. There has to be some benefits from my wasted life.'

'I don't think it was wasted Willie,' Ally whispered looking into his eyes. 'Not when you can do that.'

'I think everything I did in life was leading me to this Ally, I have never felt as content and happy.' He sat on the ground next to her, stroking her hair; she felt her eyes grow heavy and sleep overtook her. Sitting watching her sleep, he thought how beautiful she looked. Willie smiled and adjusted his still throbbing manhood. He stood up and after washing his hands in a rock pool, he packed away the food and carried the cool box and table back to the boat then returned and lay on the other bed watching the sea, feeling relaxed and happy. He didn't sleep but he felt more at ease than he had in a long time. Looking at his watch he decided to waken her, worried about her getting burned. 'Ally wake up! Come let's get you back on board so you can have a proper sleep.' He kissed her; her lips twitched.

Her eyelids flickered then opened, she looked up at him and smiled. 'I'm so tired Willie.' She said, her voice husky.

'I know sweetheart.' He lifted her off the bed; she rested her head against his shoulder and closed her eyes. He carried her across the rocks on to the boat. 'There we are now!' He turned her around, so she was over his shoulder in a fireman's lift and took her down the narrow steps into the galley; he laid her down on the double bed.

'Oh sir, I hope you aren't going to try to seduce me.' She sighed. 'I'm sorry I'm spoiling your lovely day. I've had a fantastic time Willie. I'm just so much more tired than I realised.'

He smiled and touched her cheek. 'You've been so ill Ally. You were bound to be a bit weak. I'll go get our things. You just lie there and rest. I told you our day will come when you are ready.'

'I think I'm ready now, Willie.'

'Well I'm not, I'm afraid I'll hurt you.' Ally lay back on the bed and finding it was surprisingly comfortable, she closed her eyes. Willie returned a few moments later after stowing the sunbeds. He tiptoed into the galley. She was lying on the bed, her eyes closed. He looked at her heavily plastered legs and right arm and the now fading scar above her eye. He took a blanket from the drawer beside the bed and gently covered her. He kissed her forehead; she did not move. Standing for a few moments watching her sleeping, remembering the sensation of pleasuring her made him feel good. His penis began to rise at the memory. He smiled. 'Down boy,' he said out loud.

CHAPTER
NINETEEN

Willie guided the boat into its mooring. Given that it was a weekday, the marina was full of boats but deserted of people. The area where he kept the boat was reserved for weekend sailors. After securing the vessel to its mooring, he tiptoed down the stairs and put the kettle on the hob. Willie looked at his watch again; he didn't want to waken her because then he would need to take her back to the hospital. On board the boat, Ally was his and his alone. She looked so peaceful lying on the bed, her face free from pain.

Willie lay down beside her, pulling her towards him and holding her gently. She moaned and moved closer to him. He registered how good it made him feel just to be close to her. He untied her dress straps again and moved down. His lips found her nipple and he played with his tongue around it before beginning to suck gently. He could taste the sunscreen, but he carried on. After a few seconds Ally opened her eyes, moaned and blinked. He moved back, so his face was level with hers.

'Is it time to go?' she asked.

'Ally, we're in Wemyss Bay, you slept the whole way back.'

'You're joking? What a wimp I've turned into. So much for going on a booze cruise.' She sat up and rubbed her eyes. 'I guess I'm not as recovered as I thought I was.'

'You've been through a lot darling; your mind and body need time to heal. When you're discharged, I'd like to take you to my villa in Majorca for a few weeks. It would give you a chance to get away. It's pretty chilled there, but because I bought it during my Spanish playing days the security is really good. It'll also allow me to look after you properly and give us some space and time as a couple.'

Ally smiled. 'I'd like that Willie, I really would.' They began to kiss again. Ally took a deep breath and put her hand to his groin. She tried to undo his belt and couldn't.

'Ally!' he groaned. 'Please don't, I'm really struggling to keep myself from making love to you. I don't think your body is healed enough for me. I want our first time to be special.' He groaned. 'I'm a walking bloody hard-on when I'm around you.'

'Willie, shut up. Help me, loosen your belt. There are other ways.' He did as he was asked; she slid her left hand inside his jeans and boxer shorts. His penis was erect, and she gently rubbed. Much to her relief he was not as large as she had feared. He moaned and pulled away from her, rolling from the bed and standing up. Ally sat up and moved to the edge of the bed. 'Willie please, just let me do something for you.' He turned, she pulled him to her and began to massage. 'Come closer,' she whispered, smiling up at him. She pushed his jeans over his hips and began to kiss around his groin. Her lips closed around his penis; he reached down; his hands holding her breasts. He shut his eyes, enjoying the sensation of her mouth and tongue exploring his manhood.

Willie realised that he was about to reach climax. His hands moved to hold her head, his body shuddered, he gasped, his legs began to shake. 'Oh god! Ally!' He cried, as she put her hands on his buttocks and held him to her. She felt him expand in her mouth, grow harder, he exploded; she quickly swallowed.

'There, there, there,' she said, wiping her mouth with the back of her hand.

'Fuck sake Ally! Where did *you* learn to do that? He grinned. 'You swallow too!'

She giggled. 'I'm no saint Willie, you really need to take me off that pedestal you have me on. I've never slept with anyone since Ralph and never wanted to until now, but I haven't been a nun either!'

He pulled up his jeans, lay back down beside her and wrapped his arms around her. 'I need to get you back to the hospital honey before I decide to kidnap you and keep you as my sex slave on the boat.'

'I like it here.' She sighed. 'It's like nothing else exists.'

'Want to run away to an island with me Ally?'

'Hmm, maybe later, when I have had the last op on my thigh and can actually run.' She looked up at him. 'Do my scars not bother you Willie?'

'God no, it makes you interesting actually. You're a beautiful woman Ally, with or without scars. Who are you going to believe sweetheart, your own paranoia, or me? Look at the state I'm in Ally, I can't think of anything except how much I want you.' He pulled her closer, kissing her. 'Ally, I honestly have never felt this way before. The only thing that worries me is how thin you are now my love, because you need so much strength to recover, you look so delicate. I'd like you to recuperate at my house on Loch Lomond. You know I have a gym. I could be your personal trainer. Ally, I want us to live together. I don't care where we live, I'll buy somewhere in Ayrshire if I need to.'

Ally smiled and snuggled against him. 'Tell me about your house on Majorca. That sounds much more enticing.'

He looked at her and raised an eyebrow. 'I used to go out at the end of June, soon as the school holidays started. Since Euan started school, I go the last two weeks in July and the first two weeks in August because of the difference in the English school holidays. The kids all come the first two weeks then I stay on for another two.' He kissed her and looked into her eyes, 'why don't you come with us?'

'No, not yet. I won't come between you and your children. The holiday is their time with you. I've got surgery scheduled for the beginning of July anyway, so you go with the kids, and if Clive agrees I'll come over to spend the end of the holiday with you.' Ally laughed. 'If it works out, after we come back from Majorca we could move out to the house on the loch for a while. I've already thought about it. There's no problem with it whilst I'm still off work. I have a perfectly good house in Ayrshire we can live in too. We need to fit into each other's lives Willie, we need to compromise a bit just now, no drastic changes.'

Willie kissed her and held her gently against him; he kissed the tip of her nose then her head. 'Ally, I promise you, you'll not regret this! Now come on!' He laughed pulling her to her feet, 'I'd better get you back to your hospital bed before Clive sends out a search party.'

Ally slept most of the way back to Glasgow. When they reached the hospital, he put her into the chair and pushed her up to her room. Willie helped her undress and get back into bed. As he prepared to leave, she reached up, kissed him and put her arms around his neck. 'Thank you for today.'

Willie returned her kisses; her lips were soft, and he again felt his body respond to kissing her. He broke away. 'Get some more sleep sweetheart. I'll come in tomorrow to see you when I have finished training.' Ally nodded sleepily and closed her eyes, a smile playing on her lips.

TWENTY

'Willie! I was beginning to think you were dead, and I had missed the funeral,' Frankie cried, as Willie walked into the club. He and Lynne were sitting on one of the sofa's at the back of the club which was empty of people.

'How's Ally?' Lynne asked.

'Doing well. I took her out today, we went along the coast.'

Frankie smiled and shook his head. 'You really need to fuck her and get over this you know. Ouch!' he cried as Lynne slapped the back of his head. 'What?' Frankie stood up and motioned to Chris standing behind the bar to bring them a drink.

'Frankie, I know why you think that way about me. This really is different.'

'Have you slept with her yet?'

'No, but when I do, nothing will change.'

'Well tell me you love her after you have pumped her. Lynne! Stop looking at me like that. He's always the same, you know that. He gets horny at the thrill of the chase.' Frankie shook his head.

'Boss.' Chris acknowledged Willie, putting down the tray with six glasses on it. 'I brought you two each.'

'That's very thoughtful of you Chris, thank you,' Willie said, taking the whisky from the tray. Frankie waited until Chris had gone back to the bar before he spoke to Lynne.

'After he fucks them, he changes his mind, and everyone else has to clear up after him. Lynne, you know it's true.' He looked at Willie and sighed. 'The whole world will hate you Wull if you mess this woman about! The papers are running polls on how long it will take you to fuck up.' Frankie looked serious. 'They're giving her the George Cross! Do you know it's the highest award for bravery that anyone who's not in the military can be given? They're giving her it because there was a public outcry about them not. She is a fucking national treasure.'

'What a loss you were to the Diplomatic Corps, Frankie,' Lynne said, shaking her head. She looked over at Willie. 'He does have a point though Willie. Are you sure you're serious about her?'

Willie sighed and lay back on the couch looking up at the mirrored ceiling. 'Don't ask me why, but I know, this really is till death do us part. I've never felt like this before. I kind of knew she was special before she got hurt, but I didn't want to accept it. I love her. It's as pure and simple as that.'

Lynne stood up and stretched. 'Fascinating as this is, I have to go to bed. I'm doing the breakfast news.' She kissed Frankie and then her lips brushed Willie's cheek. 'You smell nice, kind of salty and perfume combined.'

'I've been out on the boat, doon the watter! I took Ally out for the day, went out to Ailsa Craig actually.'

'Nice! On the boat! Has anyone ever been allowed on it before? Ooh Willie, it will be your man cave next!' Lynne drained one glass of its contents and took the other with her.

After Lynne left, the two men continued to drink. 'Willie, I know I was kind of explicit in my choice of words mate, but fuck me, you really do need to be careful here. What I was trying to say is, she's not like your normal birds, you can't treat her like one.'

'Frankie, I'm serious about Ally.'

'Have you pumped her?'

'No, but it won't change anything when I do. Today on the boat we got a bit, well, intimate, and it felt . . . I don't know . . . incredible. She has only ever slept with her husband, which was fifteen years ago.'

'Do you believe her?'

'I've no reason not to.'

'Oh well, she's as near a virgin as you're going to get Willie. What you going to do about your annual jaunt with the weans?'

'Oh, I'm still going. I asked her today to come with me, but she won't. She thinks I need to spend my time alone with the kids. She'll come over after they come back. Are you going over to Alfie's in July?'

'Yeah for three weeks whilst Lynne's off. We go on the 18th. We all need to meet her Willie. If she's important to you, we need to get to know her.'

'You will, probably in Majorca. Her first week will run into the end of your second.'

CHAPTER

TWENTY-ONE

Ally packed up her belongings. She looked around the room that had been her home for the last eleven weeks. She was scared but excited about the next stage in the process of recovery. Still with only hazy memories of the hours before and after the atrocious incident that had changed her life forever, she was now not sure what she truly remembered and which memories came from what she had learned. All her plaster casts had been removed and she had been helped by the physiotherapists to walk again. She lifted her crutches and stood up.

'You ready to face the real world?' Clive Ruthven asked, looking kindly at her. 'You're doing great now Ally. I know you're still tired, but that will take time. I hear you are heading to Majorca?'

'In two weeks, Clive. Willie is there just now with his kids; he left this morning. I'm not ready to meet them yet. He needs to talk to them about me first, help them through it. When they come home, I'll go out and meet Willie there. He has a beautiful villa near Valldemossa. He sent me pictures.'

'You'll be travelling alone then Ally?' Clive asked frowning, 'you need to be careful not to over tax yourself.

'Don't worry Clive, Willie has sorted it all out. There's a housekeeper for me at home, his housekeeper is moving in with me for a couple of weeks. He's also arranged a nurse, in case I need medical help on the flight, but I'm sure it'll be alright.' Ally looked at her doctor. 'You don't think I should put it off?'

Clive shook his head. 'No. No, you're well enough healed physically now, if its two weeks till you fly, you'll be fine. I am, however, worried about your emotional state. The change of scene should do you the world of good. Ally, you are aware that your sleep is disturbed? The staff tell me that you're very restless, crying out in your sleep. You could be beginning to have sub-conscious thoughts. I'd like you to see someone when you come back from your holiday, hopefully rested and ready to deal with things.'

'A shrink Clive?'

'No, the psych's didn't think you needed anything yet. I meant a post-traumatic stress specialist Ally.'

'I'll think about it. Is this the same person you spoke to Stevie about?'

Clive nodded. 'He's good Ally, and no matter what you think, it will help to discuss what happened.'

'Even if I can't remember?'

'Especially as you can't remember. The sleep disturbance may be a sign that you're beginning to re-experience the event. These things usually come to one of four things. A. You never remember. B. You remember gradually, bits and pieces until it's complete. C. You remember suddenly.'

'Why do you look so worried Clive? I know everything now. I just don't have the feelings that must have gone with it at the time. Surely it can't be any more traumatic if I already know what happened?'

'The last option can be dangerous ... then there is the fourth option. D. You begin to remember subconsciously, in dreams for example, then suddenly it all returns.' Clive put his hand on her shoulder and looked at her. 'That, Ally, is what could be happening to you. Are you aware of the content of the dreams?'

Ally shook her head. 'Little bits, but mostly I just wake up tired.' She sighed and looked sad. 'I actually don't know what I dream and what I've been told. It is confusing me Clive, but I'm okay. Maybe the holiday will do me some good.'

'Well, please be careful Ally. You do look tired, as though you're not getting quality of sleep. You're also still very thin, so you need to make sure you're eating properly. You have the build-up drinks I suggested?'

'Yes but ... well they taste horrible.' Ally sighed, 'I'll try okay?'

'Yes, please do, or try to eat more. I do hope you enjoy the holiday and come back rested though.' He smiled at Ally. 'What about intimacy? How are you feeling about that? It's none of my business, but I take it a holiday alone will be an opportunity for you to begin an intimate relationship?'

'I'm kind of nervous and kind of excited Clive.' Ally blushed a little as she spoke, but Clive could see that she was anticipating something good. 'Willie has been great and really supportive.'

Clive looked at her. 'I spoke to him about a sexual relationship but to be honest Ally, I don't think there will be a physical problem.'

Ally nodded. 'He told me. I'm still finding it hard to discuss it with him, but it's better than it was. He knows I've not slept with anyone since Ralph died. I'm a bit scared, but I was scared before I got hurt, so it's not all about my injuries. I'm a born-again virgin, Clive! It's been nearly sixteen years since I had intercourse. What if I don't remember what to do?'

Clive smiled. 'Oh, I would think it's like riding a bike Ally, once you get back in the saddle and all that. If you believe the tabloids, Willie is an experienced lover. Hopefully, he'll press the right buttons so to speak.'

Ally looked up at him and blushed again. 'There has been some heavy petting I think you would call it, and so far, so good. You are so right, he can push button, ones I'd forgotten I had, makes my eyes water.'

Clive smiled and shook his head. 'Mrs Campbell, you'll make me blush.'

'Are you in a relationship Clive?'

'No, not at the moment. I'm a bit odd, not too good at relationships.' He smiled, I'm a bit like you, been a while … Anyway, enough of me, it's you we need to talk about.'

Ally nodded. 'Sorry, none of my business Clive. You've been amazing. I can't thank you enough for all you have done for me. Physically and emotionally, I know you've gone beyond the boundaries of the patient doctor relationship with me and Willie. I really appreciate all your help and not just the surgery and the fact you saved my life. I don't think I've ever met anyone as easy to talk to, you made me believe I could get better. I just wish I could remember. I think I need it for closure.'

'Ally your mind may just be protecting you from the pain. There is no physical reason for your memory loss that I can see, so it is most likely emotional. Look, speak to George.' Seeing Ally's blank look, he added, 'the trauma specialist! He implied he thought hypnotherapy might help you remember. Think about it whilst you're away, and I'll sort it out when you get back.'

Ally stood up and embraced this man who had become a friend to her. She knew he was a very clever man; a neurosurgeon who specialised in trauma injuries yet combined his skills with the friendly and loveable nature of a family doctor. Ally was not sure what she would do without their daily chats. They had some interesting conversations, discussing politics, society, they had found a lot of things in common during the months Ally had been hospitalised, particularly in the early days when she was in traction. Many sleepless nights had been spent with

Clive, who always appeared to have time for her. She was aware though that Clive had never shared any personal details with her. Ally had never asked him anything either, respecting his privacy. As a professional herself she knew how important it was to have boundaries. 'I'll call you when I get back Clive, I hope that's okay? I feel as though I still need your guidance.'

Clive nodded. 'No worries Ally. I'll miss you too. It has been an honour to know you and to see you getting your life together. But don't do too much too quickly, you need time now to mentally heal. I've taken you as far as we can physically. I'll see you at the outpatient's clinic from time to time. The orthapods think you might need some further surgery on your thigh but it's not major now. The pins on the plate might need adjusting.'

'Are you going back to London then?'

'No not yet, I'd got a bit restless there, this incident made me realise I needed something different. I've accepted a teaching post at the university. I'll continue to work here in Glasgow because they need me. What the Whitefield's incident has shown is that there is a lack in the North of specialised services for trauma injuries. So, in some ways your misery, led to a career opportunity for me. I'll still be practicing neurosurgery though, so it will keep my hand in. Tumours and aneurisms are my bread and butter.'

She looked away and smiled as Scott and Kiera came into the room. 'All ready?' Kiera asked.

'Yes, present and correct. It seems like years since I've been home.' She smiled and hugged Clive again. Taking a gift bag from her son she handed it to him. 'Clive, this is from me, Willie and the boys.'

Clive opened the bag and lifted out the bottle of malt whisky. 'Oh Ally. You shouldn't have folks, but I shall enjoy tasting this. I'll be taking a holiday for a couple of weeks before the term starts, I shall take this with me.'

'You should come over to Majorca, Willie wouldn't mind.'

'Oh, I think he might Ally. You certainly don't need me playing gooseberry my dear lady. Actually, I'm going to spend some time with a friend who has a yacht, cruising the Med.'

'Well if you reach Majorca, give us a call.'

Clive nodded and smiled. 'You have my mobile number if you need me Ally.'

CHAPTER
TWENTY-TWO

Ally waited as the nurse accompanying her collected her case from the baggage area in Palma airport. After many hours of delays, it had had an uneventful flight and although she felt tired, Ally was also looking forward to seeing Willie. She had missed him. Although they had spoken via the internet and phone, she had now not seen him for three weeks.

Willie stood in the airport outside arrivals; it was late, and he'd endured an exceptionally long day. He had waved his family off on their flight earlier, thinking that he had an hour to wait for Ally's flight, but had then been informed that her flight had been delayed for several hours. He'd wandered around Palma, done some shopping whilst he waited rather than return to his house. He too was looking forward to some quiet time with Ally. Much of the previous three weeks had been spent with Alfie and his family. Although he loved spending time with his children and Alfie was one of his closest friends, he had missed Ally dreadfully. Frankie and Lynne had cancelled at the last minute, giving no excuse. Willie was not too bothered; Frankie had made it clear he did not believe Willie was genuine in his feelings about Ally. Willie and Frankie's relationship had been strained recently.

Willie watched as Ally came through the door, accompanied by the nurse who was carrying her bag; Ally was still using crutches. He took in her white, skinny jeans and black tee shirt and was struck by the weight she had lost. Willie waved, making a mental note to feed her up, help her to gain some weight. She was small before, but she was positively waif-like now he thought to himself. Willie wanted to hold her, protect her. He realised she looked more tired now than before he left. He swept her into a hug; she shivered and held tightly to him. He felt her bones through her clothes but said nothing. He realised that this needed to be dealt with diplomatically. They parted from the nurse, who was heading back to Glasgow, and walked towards the exit. 'You look tired darling. What do you want to do just now? Are you hungry?'

She shook her head. 'No, I'm fine. I'm still struggling to eat, Clive got me some build up drinks with like a million calories in them, they taste horrible, but I had one on the flight. I'm just exhausted Willie, really worn out, but can't wait to start our holiday. I'm excited about seeing your house, it looks brilliant in the photos.'

Settling her into the car, he kissed her lightly and put her bags in the boot. Willie was worried, she looked pale and ill. Not only had her weight plummeted in the three weeks since he had last seen her, he was also shocked at her gaunt, exhausted, nervous appearance. They had only gone a few miles when he realised, she had fallen asleep.

He was carrying her into the villa when she opened her eyes; he took her straight through without putting her down and placed her on a bed. 'This is your room Ally,' Willie said smiling. 'Hope you like it.'

'It looks beautiful,' Ally said sleepily. She looked around. It was a large room with an ornately carved four poster bed as the centrepiece, the drapes were fine material and Ally thought they looked like mosquito nets and quickly realised that is exactly what they were. Willie softly kissed her forehead and suggested that she get some sleep.

He held her close. 'You look really tired Ally,' he whispered.

She leaned against him. 'I am exhausted Willie. I think I'll feel much better after a night's sleep. A family came up to me at the airport and asked if I was Alyson Campbell. They told me their niece had died at the school and thanked me for all I had done. The woman obviously needed to speak about it, but I couldn't tell her anything because I don't know what's a memory and what I've dreamt or been told. Then on the flight the captain welcomed me on board and the other passengers burst into a round of applause.' Tears welled in her eyes. 'I want to feel as though it happened, Willie. I just feel as though there is a big black hole and I'm falling into it. I think I'm having flashbacks, but I don't know if they are real or not. The flight being delayed for five hours didn't help. I was just sitting there trying not to think. The nurse, Evie, wasn't very talkative, so there was no distraction.'

'Well we'll definitely be chartering a plane to go home now Ally. I wish you had let me do it to get you over here. I told you those delays happen a lot. It was the last thing you needed. You need to relax. Come on, get into bed and I'll go get you a hot drink.'

'Willie I'm sleeping but wakening up tired. They said in the hospital I was restless. My dad and the boys are saying they hear me moving around and talking in my sleep, but I don't remember it all. I dream but I don't know if I'm reliving it or it's just what people have told me. The last couple of days though, I have been seeing pictures in my mind when I'm wakened and think it might be flashbacks. It's like a film running in my head or something.' Ally looked into Willie's eyes. 'Willie, can we leave it for now? I'll try to do some mindfulness before I sleep to try to steer the thoughts away. Brenda has been amazing by the way. She just looks after everything. She is a bit bossy not letting me do anything, but apart from that it's been great. She calls you 'himself' all the time though, that's a bit weird. She is getting on well with Dad too which is good. He's been looking for a flat Willie, I've told him he doesn't have to move out, but he says its time he had his own place. Brenda told him about a place she saw in Prestwick from the train. She really does get herself involved in everything.'

'She's a bit bossy Ally, but her heart's in the right place. Anyway, get into bed. I'll go get you a drink babe.' Willie walked through to the kitchen. They'd not discussed where they would sleep, so after a great deal of thought he had decided to offer her a room of her own but hoped they would share a bed by the end of the holiday. Willie was desperately worried now. She looked so fragile, and she was clearly stressed. He wondered if he should have brought her out here. When Willie returned five minutes later, she had undressed and put on a baggy t-shirt; he put the mug by the side of the bed and sat down beside her. She took a few sips of the hot milky drink and laid back her head on his chest. 'Willie, this is not how I planned our first night together being.'

He gently stroked her hair and whispered in her ear. 'We have all the time in the world Ally. Just rest now babe, I'll be here. Is it okay to sleep here with you?'

She smiled and nodded, 'I think I'd like that Willie. I hope I don't disturb you too much though.'

Within a few minutes, he felt her relax. When he looked down again, she was asleep. He moved her head on to the pillow. Kissing her softly and pulling the traditional Spanish bedspread over her. He lifted the half full mug and went back through to the kitchen. Willie poured himself a large whisky and wandered through to the open plan living area. Lying on the sofa he turned on the television, he suddenly felt very tired himself but unable to settle, he eventually dozed off. Willie wakened suddenly, startled; a howl broke through the silence of the room, lit only by the television. He could hear screaming and crying, he couldn't think where he was. Was he dreaming? 'Shit, Ally!' he cried, rushing through to the bedroom where he had left her. She thrashed on the bed, her arms and legs jerking, her screams loud and sounding like an animal in pain. He rushed to her side and tried to hold her to him.

Her eyes were closed but when they snapped open the terror in them was evident. She began to sob loudly. 'They're dropping around me. They're dying! Help them! Stop him!' she screamed.

'Ally, you're dreaming, honey! Ally, you're safe. I won't let anyone hurt you darling. Please, you need to hear me!' he cried. In desperation he pressed his lips to hers. 'You're safe my darling, it's alright.'

Ally stared at him, trying to focus. She saw his face and relaxed slightly. Still shaking she cried, 'Willie hold me, please hold me. I can't do this. I can't go through this. I don't want these pictures in my head. Please take away the pictures.' She kissed him, he responded, she began pulling at his shirt. He pulled it off and pulled her t-shirt over her head and held her, hoping the skin-to-skin contact would calm her. He could feel heat of her body; she responded with a passion that overwhelmed him as she began to kiss and caress him.

'Darling I love you; I want you! But we can't! I can't do it like this, you are distressed. Ally lie still, let me just hold you. I won't leave you alone, I promise I'll stay here with you!' he whispered. 'Please try to sleep Ally.'

'Willie, love me, make the bad things go away. Help me Willie!' She pushed herself against him; when he didn't respond, she slid her hands inside his jogging trousers cupping his manhood.

'Ally, we should wait babe, just until you are stronger. It's not that I don't want you, it's just . . . not like this.'

'No, please Willie. I want you to love me, I need you to take the pictures away.'

Willie began to kiss down her body; her face, neck, breast, his own body responding to her touch. She pushed herself against him crying out as he entered her; for a split second he thought that he had misjudged the situation. She began to kiss him passionately, holding on to him as he moved gently against her. She clung to him, her body shaking. He joined her as his climax reached the point of explosion. Gasping, he held her, kissing her head, face and lips. He looked at her, and in that split-second Willie knew for sure. He would never want another woman.

Ally looked up at him, 'I love you,' she whispered moving closer, her head nestled against his chest.

She fell asleep almost immediately, and he lay awake stroking her hair. He watched her, not sure what had happened but hoping she was out of pain. Willie sighed; he had never before felt the intensity of pleasure he had with Ally. He wanted to take her again and again. He was terrified though that he had done the wrong thing, taken advantage of her vulnerability for his own satisfaction. He was satisfied, he realised. He wanted to explore every inch of her but knew that he had to take his time and make sure he was careful. Still holding her as she slept peacefully in his arms, he drifted off to sleep himself.

When Willie wakened, it was light outside and she was gone. He jumped up and looked out of the French windows. Hearing a splash, he glanced at the pool and saw Ally swimming towards the deep end. He walked out onto the patio; naked, he dived into the pool and swam towards her. When he reached her, he wrapped his arms around her and guided her to the side of the pool.

She looked into his eyes. 'I am so sorry about last night; I don't know what happened. I wakened up reliving the shooting and the explosion. I've remembered it all Willie, all my feelings about the situation. I have to learn to live with it now. I've spent four months trying to recall it, and I suddenly remember now!' She groaned, 'I've been desperately trying to remember but I wanted to have this time with you, without problems.'

Willie kissed her gently and held her. 'How do you feel darling? You were pretty distressed last night. I hope you don't think I took advantage of you? I wanted our first time to be memorable and planned a real seduction. When it happened though, I just wanted you, so much.'

'No. You were wonderful, incredible actually. It felt good to be making love with you. It felt kind of ... I don't know, natural. I know it was over really quickly, but it was such a release Willie. You're pretty amazing. Do you excel at everything you do?'

He smiled and kissed her. 'I was so scared I would hurt you, break something or really upset you. I love you so much Ally. I just want to do it right. I have made so many mistakes in my life. I want it to be perfect with you.'

'I love you Willie, how did that happen? Do you think you can put up with my craziness? I remember things that you and Stevie didn't tell me, I ... I don't know if it's better or worse. I do know that I'm not afraid of making love with you, I just want to keep doing it.' She moved against him and looked up into his eyes.

He felt his penis rise and he began to kiss her, gently at first and then with more and more passion. The water splashed over them. He groaned. 'I just want to keep touching you.'

Ally giggled, 'Me too, I want you to touch me. I don't know if it was you and I making love, or my memory coming back, but I have had the best sleep since I wakened from the coma.'

He lifted her up and sat her on the edge of the pool before clambering out and pulling her to her feet. He led her back into the house. Inside the room, he sat her on the bed and kneeled in front of her. Peeling off her wet swimsuit, he gently began to touch her. He kissed his way across her breasts to take her nipple in his mouth, softly nibbling as he pushed her back on to the bed. His lips made their way down her body until he made contact with her groin. Ally began to shudder as he pushed her towards a climax, her hands pressed down on his head as she held him to her. Willie waited until she stopped trembling and gasping. She moved on top of him and he watched her face as they moved together. Within a few minutes, simultaneous climax came overpowering them.

Afterwards she lay in his arms and any doubts either of them had evaporated. 'Ally, I want you to marry me.'

'Is that a proposal?'

'Do you want me to do it on live TV or at a football match over the tannoy? Because I will Ally. I've actually never proposed to anyone before.'

She rolled over and looked at him. 'Willie you've been married three times!'

He sighed and pulled the bedspread up to cover them, he kissed her wet hair. 'I never wanted to get married Ally. I just didn't know what else to do. With Corinna I was only fifteen when she got pregnant, the priest and our families said we had to, she's a couple of months older than me. So, we did, the day after my sixteenth birthday. Love? No not really. I had kind of made my bed and had to lie in it. With Hailey, she suggested it because she did not want to be painted as a scarlet woman. I thought, why not? I had abandoned my wife and three children, so I suppose I wanted it to be for something. We had been going out for about six years although we didn't live together. I was never faithful to her either, but she was pregnant with Jade.

Then with Belinsa, she proposed to me on Valentine's Day. I actually had no intention of marrying her, but again I just went along with it all mainly because of Euan.'

'Oh Willie!' She looked into his eyes. 'Let's not rush things, just enjoy what we have and see where it goes. Marriage is just a piece of paper. I know how I feel and so do you. To be honest, the feminist view of marriage is . . . its slavery. I've never considered getting married again, Ralph was a bit of a traditionalist and my parents would have been horrified if we had just lived together. You and me? Do we need to? I'm not saying I wouldn't, but it just doesn't matter to me.'

'Ally, I have no doubts.'

'I actually don't either Willie, but this is not just about me and you. We have our kids to consider. Yours have been through all your failed relationships. Mine have never had to share me. They need to be able to accept us first.' Ally smiled, 'we can talk about it another time.'

'Okay, but I won't change my mind Ally! Did you have a look around the villa?' he asked, changing the subject.

Ally shook her head. 'No, it didn't seem right somehow.'

'Well, go and have a good snoop. Hailey decorated it all. She is bonkers, but she does have quite good taste. Luckily Belinsa hates Majorca, too common for her. She preferred Marbella, so she never came here, or it would have been pink with leopard skin and sparkles.'

'Meow!' Ally said, stretching her fingers in a claw-like manner.

He grinned. 'Oh, I know. She irritated me from the day I met her, but most of the time I was too drunk to care. I was mostly drunk the whole relationship. I'm really ashamed of myself now.' He looked into her eyes. 'With you Ally, I want to stay sober, so I don't miss anything.'

CHAPTER
TWENTY-THREE

Whilst Willie made breakfast, Ally wandered around the three-storey building, peeking into the five bedrooms, each decorated and furnished in traditional Spanish décor. The villa was modern, spacious and airy. She walked through the open plan living area and onto the terrace. The views were tremendous; she leaned over the terrace's wooden railings, and he came to stand beside her.

'Well?'

'It's beautiful. The view is terrific. The top floor bedroom is amazing.'

'I would have put you there, it's my favourite, but it's three flights of stairs up to it. I thought you might struggle with that.'

'You could carry me up at night, ravish me.'

'I could ravish you right here.'

'Ravish, in a point of law Willie, is when a man carries a woman away with sexual intent.'

'Well I have sexual intent all the time when you are around. What did you think of the rest of the house?'

'I love the bathroom on the second floor.'

'The spa one? Want to try it out then?'

She kissed him. 'Oh, yes!'

***

They lay in the bath, her head resting on his chest, both feeling happy and relaxed. Willie kissed her and then stood up. 'We'd better get out of here and get dressed, I've got loads to show you.' He lifted her from the tub, wrapped her in a bath sheet and carried her through to the bedroom and laid her on the bed. 'While you are lying here naked, I'll massage you.'

'What?' she gasped. He could see the panic on her face.

He smiled and held up a bottle of suntan lotion. 'You really need it here, especially walking in the sun.'

Ally rolled over on to her front. 'Okay go for it.'

Willie smiled. Ruby had told him in confidence about Ally's problems with her scarring and body image. She suggested that the more Ally felt she was exposing Willie to, the more she might relax and accept that she was not disfigured in the way she thought she was.

'Do you fancy a walk around the village Ally?' Willie said as he rubbed the cream into her legs. He was talking to try to forget about his ever-growing erection but didn't want to tell her this in case she thought he was some kind of sex maniac. Three times in eight hours was a lot even for him, yet he knew he could do it again.

Ally smiled. 'I can't actually walk far. It's all a bit weird; when I'm lying or moving on the bed with you.' She blushed slightly, 'making love there's no real pain. When I try to walk then the thigh starts playing up. It gets really painful. So, walking might be an issue, although the physio said I must move more each day, it's still just a bit much to walk far.'

'You don't need to, I got a chair for you, and Clive reckoned that you should get as much fresh air as possible. Roll over so I can do your front.'

Ally sat up, put on a pair of knickers then did as she was asked.

'You spoke to Clive? When?'

'Before I left Scotland, I had a long conversation with him. Okay actually . . . I played poker with him and his mates again, they put us out pretty quickly, so we had a drink and a chat. He reckoned the fresh air and sun would be good for you. I'll push you around. It's a lovely little village.' He smiled at her. 'Ally, I'm so turned on again right now, just touching you makes me hard. Don't think that's ever happened to me before. You're so beautiful darling; I could just do this all day. I need to get you out of here before we spend all our time in bed. Hopefully, no members of the press know you are here with me yet, so we might get a few days peace. I've been coming here for seventeen years now, so the locals all know me and will not give anything away.'

'How come?'

'I played for Spanish teams and am a bit of a local hero. The villa is ideally suited for privacy. There is nothing in view on two sides because it sits out from the rest of the village. There are steps up to the back gate, but you really have to have been in here to know how to find them. I want to take you up to the hotel we own here in the village for lunch, the chef is amazing. There, all done.' he said, putting down the lotion bottle, 'sit there for a minute and let it dry.' He sat down on the bed and handed Ally the suntan lotion bottle. 'Can you do my back for me babe?'

'Do you and your friends have a lot of business interests here Willie?' Ally asked as she rubbed the lotion into his back. She could feel a stirring in her groin now too. Willie, watching her in the mirror, nodded, wondering if she was talking to avoid thinking about sex. He looked up into her eyes. Even in the mirror, he could see the confusion on her face.

'We own nine properties on the island and another six on Ibiza. It's mainly hotels here, and clubs on Ibiza. Supply and demand. When Alfie moved here, he just kept buying stuff and it's paid off. Davie used to panic because he thought Alfie was going to bankrupt the firm. It has made us so much money though. Alfie, David and Frankie are very astute businessmen and know when to invest and when to walk away. We employ local people too. The Spanish like us because we pay well, and they have good conditions. The Brits like coming to our clubs and hotels because they are safe and English-speaking. Alfie is fluent in Spanish too, so it helps, one of the only benefits of a 1970's and 1980's Catholic education. All of us speak Spanish to some extent, which is lucky, the twin's dad is Spanish, and their mum is of Italian descent, but they grew up in Glasgow. So perhaps languages come naturally to them. I can understand more than I can speak it, but I get by.'

'Wow I learn something new about you every day. Spanish . . . amazing.'

As I said I get by, I can order food and coffee, converse with the barman. Alfie and Betty are amazing, people don't realise it's not their first language. They speak it at home, so the kids are all bilingual. You'll meet Alfie and Betty in a couple of days, they want us to go over. Some of my other friends are there too. I wanted a day or two just us first.'

'There, all done!' Ally wiped her hands on a towel and sat down beside Willie. 'What's that in Spanish?'

'Todo listo,' He kissed her and brushed her hair from her face. 'Gracias, te amo. All dry now? Let's get dressed and go out, mujer sexy.' He grinned and stood up, adjusting his manhood.

Ally giggled, 'you speak Spanish with a Glasgow accent.'

'I know, come on get your sexy arse in that chair.'

***

Willie cooked dinner that evening, and they sat outside eating on the patio by the pool. 'Paella! It's fantastic Willie. I can't believe you cooked this yourself from scratch. You're full of surprises Mr

196

Ogilvy. Although it doesn't take much to impress me, I don't cook if I can help it.'

'I find cooking therapeutic Ally. Those meals at my house, Brenda didn't make them, I did. I don't know why I didn't tell you. I thought you might think it was weird or something.'

Ally put her fork into the rice mixture and stirred it a little. 'I'll try to do it justice, but after that wonderful lunch . . . I'm not sure. I'm also really tired too.'

'We could eat dinner in bed if you want babe.' He walked through to the kitchen and she heard the fridge open. When he returned, he was holding one of the build-up drinks and a straw. 'It's that or this,' he said pointing to the plate.

Later she lay in his arms. The room was dark and cool; she felt desperately tired and he guessed she was fighting sleep. 'I'm afraid to sleep Willie,' she admitted. 'I keep seeing the shootings. It's as though I'm seeing it in freeze frame, then all the memories come back. I remember the feelings when I was trapped now, the fear. I was so sure I was dying, and I was going to die without doing all the things I wanted to do.' Ally took a deep breath and moved closer to him. 'Willie, one of the biggest regrets was that you and I did not make love that night. I was so embarrassed I freaked out. It was a total overreaction.'

'Ally, my darling, it doesn't matter now. Please try to sleep.'

'Willie, I need to tell you what happened. It's better I explain it in the dark, because I can't see you, and you can't see my red face.'

'I can feel the heat from it on my chest, sweetheart.'

Ally took a deep breath. 'Willie, when I came to your flat that night, I had every intention of sleeping with you. I'd even bought new underwear. It was such a big thing for me. You see, the accident left me with a lot of scars and I've always been self-conscious about them. I was so glad when you dimmed the lights. When we were on the couch you were lying against me, you started touching me and I just couldn't relax. I felt your erection through your jeans. I thought you were too big, I just panicked. I'd googled you when I first met you, there were loads of scandal stories about your behaviour with women. There was a story about you with a model, a kiss-and-tell thing, where she said you were so well-endowed that it was only halfway in.'

Willie laughed. 'I remember that one. She was a wannabe WAG and trying to make me like her by saying that I was ... what was it? The largest man she had ever seen outside of porn films. It did me a lot of good at the time, made women curious and men jealous. God, I can't believe you were afraid of that, I thought it was my womanising.'

'I'm physically small, Willie. I'd not had sex for so long. I was afraid.'

'Are you disappointed that I'm normal size?'

'I'm relieved that you are not over-endowed Willie. I'm not sure what normal size is. I haven't exactly got much experience in these things, but it fits, and you really know how to use it. That's the main thing, isn't it?'

'The media love scandal Ally, they jump on whatever sensational story they can, and it didn't do my reputation any real harm at the time. Watch the tabloids. They will rehash that story and lots of other ones now. They're so interested in you and me at the moment. You learn to say nothing to the press because they will jump on any little detail and embellish it. People like me, and now you, sell papers.'

'Willie, I am still worried about my scars, they're really bad. I don't want to sound superficial, but they aren't nice. When I was in the accident all those years ago, they had to remove my spleen and I had all sorts of injuries. Now there are new scars. It's kind of stupid and vain, but I think I avoided being with men because I was embarrassed. You're the first man since Ralph died, apart from my doctors, who has seen me naked.'

'I saw them today, the scars. I love the thigh one especially, all those stitch marks, and there are not many women with bullet wound scars. Makes me feel you're tough.' He laughed and kissed her, looking into her eyes. 'Ally, I wouldn't care if you looked like Fiona from Shrek. I love you for who you are. You're beautiful, your body is beautiful. Ally, all my adult life, my sex life has been played out in the press. I won't lie to you; I've slept with some very beautiful women.' He sighed and kissed her gently. 'Thing is, all I thought about was superficial things which I now realise didn't matter, I didn't know then what was important. It took nearly losing you to make me see. I want you more than I have ever wanted anyone. Look!' He took her hand and put it on his groin. 'Thinking about you and your body does this to me. Ally, I love you and I love being with you. The sex is great, but it doesn't matter. I like the way we can talk. I love that you're funny, special and clever. I love everything about you.' Willie kissed Ally and sighed. 'Right now, though, we both need to sleep babe so put it all to the back of your mind and relax.'

'I'm afraid to sleep Willie, but I'm so tired.'

'I'll be here with you, holding you,' he whispered into her ear. 'You're safe now. I'll never let anyone hurt you again, I can promise you that. You can stop being strong babe, you can let go, let me look after you, please?' Ally drifted off, but the dream came back; she shuddered and gasped as she kept wakening up. Tears poured down her face as she sobbed into Willie's chest. Eventually she slipped into an exhausted slumber. When he was sure she was in a deep sleep Willie got up and tiptoed through to the living room. He telephoned Clive Ruthven, not sure who else to speak to.

'Willie, old boy! Are you having a good holiday?' Clive's voice boomed across the line. 'I was in one of your clubs in Ibiza tonight, and I'm rather drunk my friend.'

'I need some advice Clive. If you are pished and having a good time, I don't feel so bad about asking. It's Ally, she's remembered and is distressed. I don't know what to do. She didn't sleep much last night, and she's very restless tonight. I took your advice and got her out in the fresh air. My bloody legs are aching from pushing that chair uphill. Clive, she is about six stones if she is lucky, she looks like something out of a concentration camp.'

'Do you have access to a computer Willie?'

'Yes, I have an iPad, an iPhone . . . the usual.'

'Okay, I'll try to get the psychologist to contact you using FaceTime or Skype. Are you okay Willie? You'll need to be really supportive.'

Willie was instantly annoyed. 'Why does everyone think I'll be selfish now? Clive, I love her. I'll do anything I can to support her.'

Willie heard Clive take a sharp intake of breath before continuing. 'Just let her talk about it Willie. She's an intelligent woman, she'll sort it out in her head. She'll get better quicker with your help, and she'll overcome this and learn to live with the memories. Willie, I could get the ferry across in the morning. Or I could ask my friend to turn around, we just left Majorca. I thought about contacting you both but didn't want to intrude.'

'No, I'll manage Clive thanks. It's a six-hour round trip on the ferry. This sounds selfish, but I want her to see me as supportive and helpful. If you come over, you're the one who is helping her. You saved her life Clive and I'll always be in your debt and in awe of you. This, however, is my time.' Willie walked back through to the bedroom. Ally was still asleep, looking calmer than she had earlier. He lay down beside her and took her into his arms. She moaned softly and nestled her head into the space between his shoulder and chest. Willie looked down at her and was suddenly overcome with doubts. *What if I let her down?*

What if I'm not strong enough to support her? What have I done? I love her so much.'

'What are you crying for?' Ally whispered, opening her eyes, seeing the tears running down his face.

'I'm scared Ally, scared I'll let you down. I'm such a wanker at times. I don't know why, I just am. I love you so much, I can't face life without you. I worry that I'll fuck it all up. I'm not good at relationships, but it's never mattered before. I've never loved anyone this much. You could do so much better than me Ally.'

'Willie, I love you. I knew your past when we got together. I have to say that you're not what I thought you would be, and I fought falling for you. You can't help who you love Willie.' She smiled up at him. 'When we were making love, I realised that I haven't felt that good for a long, long time, if ever. We'd better get some sleep because I want to get up tomorrow and try to do something. I haven't been on Majorca for years and would quite like to see some more of the island. What about your places here? Can we visit more of them?'

Willie smiled. 'You're amazing Ally. The way you are so resourceful and brave.'

'I'm not brave Willie! I'm terrified most of the time now. I don't know if remembering might help eventually. Not being able to remember made me really scared. I'm probably a bit of a control freak if I'm honest. Stevie is doing a lot better than me, he appears to be moving on, sorting his life out. He's already back at work on light duties whereas I just don't know if I can now.' Ally shook her head and looked up at Willie. 'Danny took me to the school to leave flowers at the memorial, I had a panic attack. We went to my office, I froze at the front door Willie, I just couldn't go in. It may be worse now I can remember what actually happened.'

'You'll get through all this Ally, I'll help you. I thought we might do some visiting soon. My mate Frankie and his girlfriend are here now with Alfie and Betty, as I said. I really want you to meet them. It's like my inner circle I suppose. Frankie is more like my brother than my friend. He's being a bit weird just now, but we'll sort that out soon.'

'Frankie? He's the one who's with Lynne Lockhead?'

Willie nodded. 'Why she puts up with him is anybody's guess, but yes, Frankie and Lynne are an item.'

'Alfie is Frankie's twin?'

Willie nodded and smiled. 'They're identical, like two peas in a pod. Nature wise they couldn't be more different. Alfie's a real family man and he and Betty have four girls ranging from two to ten. He dotes on Betty, she's a former model, gorgeous, so are their girls. They live in a huge farmhouse outside Palma, with loads of animals and land. It's a fucking madhouse Ally. I spend a lot of my time with them when my kids are here. The last time I was here Becky, their oldest, had a piglet in her room. It was actually sleeping in her bed. This time Andi, the second eldest, had decided she was a horse and they allowed her to live in the stables for a week. When Frankie is there as well it's even worse. He's a bigger kid than his nieces.'

'What about your kids Willie? They know about me now. How did they take it?'

Willie sighed. 'It would have been better if they had heard it from me. Lynne had warned me to tell them before the press found out. Then you had that scare, and I didn't get around to it. They're worried of course, it was that *'oh not again Dad'* thing. It's not about you though, it's because of my past behaviours. I think the older three realise you're special to me, so hopefully they'll accept us as a couple. Jade will be more difficult, I'm afraid she is a bit territorial where I'm concerned. Euan is just a lovely wee boy, he's really easy to get on with.' Willie smiled thinking about his youngest, 'if you can do video games, he'll like you. I do want you to meet them all as soon as we get back!'

202

Ally lay back against Willie's chest and closed her eyes. 'We'll help them to get used to us,' she mumbled. Willie kissed the top of her head and gently rolled Ally over, wrapping his arms around her.

CHAPTER
TWENTY-FOUR

They ate breakfast by the pool. Ally ate slowly, but did manage to finish, more to please Willie than from hunger. Willie smiled. 'See, it's sun, sea and sex, it's giving you an appetite.'

Ally got to her feet. 'Come on, let's swim. They said I should exercise my leg and do breaststroke for my pelvis.'

Willie moved towards her and pulled her into his arms. He unwrapped her sarong and kissed her, running his hands over her neck and shoulders. His lips followed. 'Your skin is so soft Ally.' They were interrupted by the loud comedic ring of Willie's iPhone; he moved to answer it. 'Alfie! How are you mate? Yeah we should be able to do that.' Willie sat at the table watching as Ally balanced on the edge of the pool. He laughed as she took a deep breath and dropped into the cold water; the shock made her squeal. A few minutes later he joined her in the water. 'That was Alfie, asking when we would come over. If it is okay with you honey, I'd like to go this afternoon.'

Ally smiled. 'Of course, I'd love to meet your friends. You spent weeks with mine.'

'You'll like them once you get used to them, Frankie especially. You'll see his good points.'

'I'm a bit worried about meeting your friends Willie.'

'They'll love you Ally, just wait. If they don't, it's their problem babe. They'll be nervous about meeting you too. You *are* about to be given a George Cross.'

Ally shrugged. 'I truthfully don't feel that I did anything that anyone in my shoes would not have done. Stevie's the real hero. He rugby-tackled a man with a gun! But it would be rude to refuse an invitation from the Queen wouldn't it? What time do we need to be with your friends, and how long does it take?'

'Chez Dastis? It's about twenty-five minutes from here. Oh, early afternoon babes, it'll give you time to rest up. Now, if it's too much for you and you get tired, just say, Ally. I'll bring you home again.'

She nodded and wrapped her arms around his neck. 'Okay, but for now though I want you, right here right now.' She pushed him into the corner of the pool and pulled his shorts down over his hips. He grabbed the ladder with one hand and used it to steady himself. She wrapped herself around him, as he removed her bikini top and his mouth found her nipple.

Willie pulled her bikini bottoms down and Ally leaned forward as he entered her. 'Ally, you need to be careful babe, you'll hurt yourself. Oh, if you knew how much I want you.' When he looked up, he realised Ally was lost in her orgasm; her eyes rolled upwards. Willie felt his own climax begin and he gasped as it took hold. He closed his eyes. When he opened them again, he watched their costumes float across the pool.

***

'It's beautiful!' Ally gasped as they drove through electric gates into a large estate. The area was surprisingly green, and colourful flowers peeped out of flower beds along the driveway.

'Betty comes from a family who owned a nursery, so she knows a lot about growing things. She stopped modelling a few years ago and designs clothes now, so she has a very artistic eye for detail. Perhaps she could design your outfit for you meeting the Queen?' They reached the house and Ally could see people sitting around a large table. Two small children played on bicycles around the driveway and Willie carefully parked the car away from the house to avoid them. He helped Ally down from the jeep and handed her the crutches.

Her first thoughts were panic as Willie, his hand on her waist, led her across the garden onto the raised decking area around a pool where his friends sat. 'Everyone, this is Ally,' he said, smiling as the two men stood up. 'Ally, this is Frankie.'

'You're thinking, how does he know who's who?' Frankie stood up and walked around the table. 'He knows because I'm better-looking than Alfie. Actually it's because of this.' He pointed to his left eye, above his brow there was a small scar. 'He did that with a catapult when we were kids. That's why he can tell us apart, it's just guilt.'

'I have one too!' Ally said, smiling. 'A scar above my eye, not a twin.'

'Ally, it's good to meet the woman who tamed Willog.' Frankie leaned over and kissed her cheek. 'Christ you're tiny, sweetheart, like a little doll.' Alfie came over, followed by three women.

The older of the women rushed to Willie, he hugged her tightly, kissing her cheek. 'I didn't know you were here Yvonne. Is Hughie with you?'

'No Willie, he's in Glasgow. I'll fill you in later.'

Alfie shook Ally's hand and kissed her cheek. 'Ally it's really lovely to meet you at last darling. Obviously, I'm Alfie, and this is my wife Betty.'

The tall, beautiful woman with striking titian hair smiled. She greeted Ally warmly. 'It's great to meet you at last Ally, welcome to our home.' She kissed Willie. 'You're looking happier Wull.'

'Hi I'm Lynne. It's good to meet you Ally.'

Ally smiled. 'I knew who you were of course. I've seen you so many times on TV.'

Lynne nodded, 'I interviewed some of the children you saved that day. You're a real hero. I hear you have been awarded a medal for bravery. You so deserve it.' She looked at Ally, her eyes sad. 'It must have been tough?'

'I've had better days, Lynne, but a lot of people did a lot of things that day which have gone unrewarded. My two boys were there. They were digging people out, helping the emergency services. They were exposed to so much. Me? I was oblivious to anything most of the time.'

The third woman who was still standing with Willie's arm around her, came forward. 'I'm Yvonne, Ally, Willie's sister. Betty and I are close friends, so I stay with her when I am here. I knew my brother was on the island, but I thought you two might need some time alone. I wasn't being rude by not visiting.'

'Yvonne, hello, it's good to meet you. Willie has told me loads about you. You're a nurse, aren't you?'

Yvonne smiled and nodded. Ally realised she looked a lot like Willie. Her dark hair was cut into a neat bob and although Ally knew she was several years older than her brother she looked younger, with smooth, pale skin and the same twinkling blue eyes. 'I work at The Children's Hospital Ally, orthopaedics, so I've nursed a lot of the children who were hurt at the school. Including Alexis Driske, so I've met your friend Ruby. She's lovely Ally.'

Ally smiled and nodded. Another couple appeared from the house. 'David, Lesley, you made it!' Willie cried. Ally looked up at them. The man was tall and thin with red receding hair and a pale, freckled face. Ally was startled by his blue eyes and knew instantly that he was related to Willie.

David followed his wife, who was small and curvy with blonde hair and large brown eyes. She smiled, and Ally instantly liked her. 'We came in with Yvonne the day before yesterday.'

Willie grinned at her. 'That's brilliant, we're all together now.' He draped his arm around his sister's shoulder. 'Ally, meet Lesley and David, two of my oldest friends. David is also my cousin. Lesley is my conscience!'

Lesley rushed over and swept Ally into a hug. 'Sorry Ally, I'm a hugger, can't help myself. God, you're skin and bones, hen. We really need to feed her up Willie. I know you're not normally as thin, because I saw your pictures on the news and in the papers.'

David smiled and shook his head. 'Lesley is about as subtle as a brick, Ally. It's a bit like that catchword programme on the telly with my wife, you know? Say it as you see!'

'It's okay, I like honest people. She's stating the obvious. I *have* lost quite a bit of weight recently. I think it's got something to do with the painkillers they've been giving me. Willie is already feeding me up.'

Yvonne nodded. 'It's because the painkillers are opiate-based Ally, they'll do that. It'll pass though.'

Willie untangled himself from his sister and put his arm protectively around Ally. 'David is the quiet, brainy one of our crowd.' Ally smiled as David, who appeared a lot quieter than his gregarious wife, kissed her cheek.

Ally relaxed and began to enjoy the company. She did feel very tired, but it was nice to be out and socialising. The others drank several bottles of wine as they chatted. Willie remained sober with soft drinks. Ally, because she had been reducing her medication and did not want to overdo things, was sipping lager.

Willie refused alcohol because he said he wanted to be able to drive them home; he appeared uncomfortable with his friends. Given what he had told her about them, Ally made a mental note to ask him why later. Frankie was loud and boisterous;

he ran around the garden with the children, winding them up. He pulled Willie to his feet and suggested a game of rounders, making the adults join in with them.

David, pleading a sore foot, excused himself to sit with Ally as the others spread out in the garden. 'Willie is really happy Ally; I have never seen him this relaxed and calm with a woman before. He loves you a lot. He's not the bad guy the press paints him to be you know.'

Ally nodded. 'I'm learning something about Willie everyday David.'

David lifted the wine bottle from the cooler and poured himself a generous glass. 'You're so tiny,' he said smiling, 'you're smaller than Becky,' nodding towards Alfie and Betty's ten-year-old daughter who was running backwards to try to catch the ball Frankie had just hit.

'Alfie and Betty are both tall though,' Ally said, smiling broadly at the little girl's antics. 'Their children are bound to have height too. My sons are both quite tall. Their father was over six foot. They have both taken their height from him, luckily.'

'Are you divorced?'

'No, I'm a widow actually.'

'I'm sorry Ally. How did he die? Your husband?'

'He was killed in a car crash, my mother died too. He was driving, and I was in the back with my baby. I was severely injured, my baby girl died. She was only six weeks old. It was fifteen years ago.' Her eyes clouded over, and she looked away.

'Oh God Ally, how awful. I didn't know, I'm sorry! I can't even start to imagine how that must feel to lose so many people together. You must have been really tough to have survived it.'

'You never really get over a loss like that David, but you just have to get on with life. I had two young children, so it was a case of carry on and get through! You get to a point though where you can discuss it and it's like it happened to someone else. My mother got in the front of the car, so I could be in the back with the baby to feed her. We swapped seats and I lived. I don't remember much about it, I was unconscious. We had put my sons into nursery and school and were heading for Glasgow, Christmas shopping. A lorry crashed through the central reservation and took the front of the car and them with it. Ralph was only thirty, my boys were three and five at the time. I was twenty-eight and a widow, just like that.'

'So, you brought your boys up yourself?'

'My dad helped. He took over as the male role model and still lives with us.'

'Your father lives with you? What're you and Willie going to do?'

'We've not really discussed much about that. I'm going to be off work for a few months yet anyway. I've a couple more surgical procedures to get through. My eldest son is at university in Glasgow and lives there. My younger son will join him in September. My dad and I always said that he would live with us until the boys grew up, but we kind of got into a routine I suppose, there was never any reason for him to move out.' Ally smiled, 'he is looking for a flat now, but I will miss him when he moves. We are closer than a lot of fathers and adult daughters.'

'It must have been really scary, the shooting and then the explosion?'

Ally sighed. 'Actually, I have had difficulty remembering what happened. My head injury affected my memory. I'm only just starting to recall it. If you don't mind David, I don't want to be rude, but I would rather not talk about it.'

'I'm really sorry Ally, I never thought,' David gasped. 'I've been living with Lesley too long; I'm forgetting my manners.'

'It's okay. It's all come back suddenly over the last few days so it's still very raw. I'm trying to make sense of it all.' She looked up and smiled as Willie came across the lawn towards them.

Willie pulled a deckchair over, sat down beside Ally and put his arm around her shoulder. 'Well I'm out for now, those kids are lethal. Davie, what do you think of my girl?'

David looked Willie in the eye. 'I think that you have hit the jackpot Wull. Just see you appreciate her.' Changing the subject quickly, they began to talk about the island and the different sights.

A short while later the others drifted over as the game ended. Alfie and Betty excused themselves to prepare the barbeque. The others continued to drink. The children splashed around in the pool. Frankie became loud and animated, ignoring Lynne's attempts to silence him. 'Stop it, I'm on holiday! I'm allowed to drink. Since he's joined the bloody temperance league,' he cried nodding at Willie, 'I have no one who is fun to drink with.'

'I'm drinking with you,' David snorted.

'I said *fun* Davie.'

'Oh diddum's!' Lesley said. 'Did the bad lady break up your bromance?' She turned to Ally. 'Those two are toxic when Willie's drinking too. Willie, I think you look better. David and I are really proud of you.'

Lynne smiled. 'Don't pay any attention to Frankie, he is like a little spoilt boy, needs to be the centre of attention when he's drinking.' She turned to Ally. 'I don't want to pry, but you really do look so frail. I know I don't know you, but I saw a picture of you before the shooting and you looked athletic and healthy. One of the things your doctors said to the press was it was because you were so fit and healthy that you survived. My sister's a personal trainer and nutritionist, I could ask her to help.'

Frankie took a swig from his glass and leered at her. 'Yeah, maybe you should get Maggie involved. I mean, you're a good-looking woman Ally, but you really are way too skinny. You look like a twelve-year-old. Willie must think he is riding a bag of spanners.'

'I don't think he is complaining, Frankie,' Ally replied.

There was a moment of stunned silence before Willie stood up. Ignoring Frankie, he looked down at Ally. 'I think we should hit the road soon; I don't want you tired out.'

'I don't want to take you away from your friends Willie. I'll be okay, honestly. Betty and Alfie have gone to a lot of trouble organising the barbeque, I don't want to spoil things.'

'I can't believe you're not drinking Wull!' Frankie said, sitting down in Willie's vacated chair. 'You really are pussy-whipped these days.' Willie looked at Frankie and then without saying anything turned away.

Lynne shook her head. 'Don't be so bloody rude Frankie.'

Still ignoring Frankie, Willie pulled Ally to her feet; his arm around her waist he guided her towards Betty and Alfie who were preparing food next to the barbeque. 'Betty, Alfie, we're not going to wait for the food.'

'Oh Willie, no! Please stay, we really want to get to know Ally,' Betty cried.

'There will be other days, plenty of time to get to know her, just not today.' He looked Alfie in the eye and grimaced. 'Frankie is being an obnoxious prick and trying to provoke me.'

Alfie looked at Ally. 'What's he said this time? He's just drunk Ally. No one pays any attention to him when he's like that. I suppose we're all used to him though.'

'Ally is really tired,' Willie said, pulling Ally closer and kissing the top of her head. 'She's recuperating and not back to full strength yet.' He looked at Alfie, 'and your brother just insulted her, joking of course!'

'I'm fine Willie, you fuss too much. I've been a social worker for over twenty years. I've developed a thick skin to insults and have probably heard them all.' She grinned. 'Can't recall I've ever been compared to a bag of spanners though.'

Alfie raised his eyebrow. 'I hope Frankie hasn't upset you Ally. He's just a rent-a-gub. He's a prick at the best of times, but ten times worse when he is drinking like that. He's been worse than normal this week, but he and Lynne have had personal problems.'

'Is that why they only came over this week?' Willie looked at his friends, 'he said it was to do with Lynne. I assumed it was work.'

Alfie shook his head and glanced over at the group on the patio, then at his wife. 'No doubt he'll tell you what's happened when he's ready.'

'I know he's your brother, but he is a wanker at times,' Betty put in. They turned as voices rose behind them, in time to see Lynne throw her glass of red wine in Frankie's face.

'Oh dear! Here we go again,' Betty hissed, nudging her husband. 'They've been fighting since they got here!' She looked at Willie and Ally, her eyes pleading. 'Willie, could you and Ally take Lynne with you? I'll come get her in the morning.'

Willie looked at Ally and grimaced.

Ally smiled. 'Of course, we can. But is that the best thing?'

'Yes!' they all said at once.

'They end up fighting. He just should never drink spirits. Lynne is really feisty; she can give as good as she gets. I don't want the girls exposed to it again,' Betty added. 'It's been murder this week with them both in the mood they are in. They don't realise the impact on us, never mind what the girls think.'

Ally watched as Frankie stormed off in the direction of the stables. Alfie put down the spatula he was turning the meat with and went off after him. 'Alfie!' Willie called. 'Keep your hands off him.'

Alfie nodded and grimaced. 'I'll try.'

CHAPTER

TWENTY-FIVE

'I'm so, so sorry Ally, what an introduction to our little gang,' Lynne cried, as Willie drove along the highway. 'Thank you so much for doing this. He's a nightmare when he's like that. He just should stick to wine or beer. Ally, he was very rude to you. I hope you don't think that he meant any of that. He thinks he is being funny. He can be hilarious, but when he drinks like that, he takes it too far.'

'I am too skinny!' Ally said, smiling. 'He was just stating the obvious, and I know my bones are sticking out. I look like someone who has been starved. Sex with me might . . . feel.'

'No, Ally, it does not feel like a bag of spanners. You have beautiful soft skin,' Willie said, smiling. 'I can't get enough of you.'

'You're a beautiful woman,' Lynne added. 'He'll be mortified in the morning Ally. He always is.'

Willie looked in the mirror catching Lynne's eyes. 'I don't know what's wrong with him, he's a royal pain in the arse.'

'You can talk,' Lynne sighed. 'You've been worse than him many times. Anyway, thank you for not reacting. You would have been justified in kicking his head in for what he did.'

'Ally, are you okay?' Lynne asked, realising Ally had stopped speaking.

'She's asleep Lynne. She's really tired all the time, having really bad flashbacks and sleep disturbance. That's why she's looking so delicate.' When they reached the villa, Lynne held the doors open for Willie, who put Ally straight to bed. She watched in silence as he carried Ally through the doorway and laid her on the bed, then made her way back downstairs. Willie helped Ally undress, then held her as she curled up and went back to sleep. He kissed her gently and tucked her in, before returning to the lounge where Lynne was pouring wine into two glasses. 'Not for me, I'm going to have whisky. I've a good malt in the cupboard, do you want one?'

'No, I'll stick with the wine thanks.'

Willie sat down and took a sip from his glass. 'Are you going to enlighten me to what's going on?

'Are you really mad at him Willie?'

Willie nodded. 'You're fucking right I am. How dare he insult her? Fuck sake even he must realise she has had enough to cope with over the last few months. You might hear her during the night, she cries out in her sleep a lot.'

Lynne looked at him and sighed. 'Poor wee thing, she's been through so much. I'm impressed by your devotion to her Willie. Changed days!'

Willie looked at Lynne over the top of his glass. 'What the hell is wrong with Frankie, Lynne? I could cheerfully strangle him. I've never known him to be so rude, unprovoked, and especially to a woman, that wasn't him trying to be funny, it was an attack on me, using Ally.'

Lynne looked at him, tears gathering in her eyes. 'There's actually no excuse for the way he behaved tonight, or me fighting with him Willie. We've had a bit of a major life event. We are not coping. You might as well know the whole story. I was pregnant, I had a miscarriage a few weeks ago. I asked him not to tell you. I know he probably needed to talk, but I just felt that you had enough on your plate. Anyway, he has Alfie, and Davie too. Difference between you and Alfie is he doesn't take Frankie's shit; he tells him like it is. Davie just lets the insults roll over his head.' Tears ran down Lynne's face. 'I'm thirty-five, I feel time is running out, my biological clock is ticking. Frankie didn't want the baby anyway. He doesn't want to change Willie; he's scared of commitment. I want the whole works, marriage, kids . . . and he doesn't. The baby was a bit of an accident, I was changing from one pill to another. I can't work him out Willie. He says he loves me and wants to be with me, but. I saw the relief on his face when they told me I'd lost the baby. Why doesn't he want to be with me?'

'I don't think it's that he doesn't. I think he's just as you say, scared. We had a lot of shit happen in our childhood Lynne, and it affects him.'

Lynne shook her head and sighed. 'You all keep saying that, but I don't know what that shit is! His parents are fantastic, and he has always had you three.'

'You need to ask him about that Lynne, not me.'

'I have, but he just says you are all talking shite.'

'He's actually good with kids,' Willie said, changing the subject. 'He's always been great with mine. Lynne, he does love you. Yes, he is a bit of an arsehole, loud and parties a lot, but there are never any other women you know. He is not like me in that way, he has not chased women for a long time. There is no one else for him but you. There hasn't been since he met you.'

'Unlike me you mean Willie?' She looked him in the eye.

Willie stared at her and shook his head in disbelief. 'Lynne, it was a long time ago, we were fucking drunk and coked up. I never meant to, neither did you. No one else knows. Let's keep it like that, especially now. What the hell made you bring that up now after all this time?'

'I'm sorry Wull, it's been on my mind a lot recently! I guess I'm a bit jealous. Not of Ally being with you, I love Frankie . . . but just the way you've changed for her.' Willie put his arm around her and pulled her close, she rested her head on his shoulder and began to sob. 'I have been with him twelve years now Willie, I'm tired of waiting for him to change and grow up. Getting pregnant made me realise I want to have a family and a proper home. He's forty-seven Willie. He can't live above the club forever. Anyway, enough of me,' Lynne said, wiping her face with the back of her hand. Willie passed her a box of tissues, she took it and smiled at him through her tears. 'How are you doing?'

Willie sighed; he took a long drink then rested his head on the back of the sofa and looked up at the ceiling. 'I'm okay I guess Lynne. It's hard you know, when she's so fragile, I just want to make her better. I spoke to her consultant and he's going to try to arrange for her to speak to someone. She's an extraordinarily strong character normally Lynne, a bit like you, but she's just so frail right now. It's been a long time since somebody really looked after her. I think she struggles with not being well. I'm finding being unselfish surprisingly easy. I just want to help her.'

Lynne smiled, 'you have never been selfish Willie. You have been thoughtless and reckless, but you have always been generous with your support. Joe McCann is at the hotel Dastis, Willie. Maybe you should talk to him about Ally?'

'What is *he*, doing here?'

'Oh, Frankie invited him to come over with us, but I insisted he stay at the hotel, not with Alfie and Betty. Yvonne is there without Hughie and Joe is chasing her as usual. Anyway, he might be able to advise you on how to help Ally.'

'He's a sports psychologist Lynne. Not to mention he's an arsehole when he's drinking, worse than me actually.'

'Yes, but he does work for Help the Heroes, servicemen who have post-traumatic stress! That's what Ally has Willie. He might be able to suggest something.' Willie took Lynne's glass from her and poured them both a drink. 'You're so different with Ally, Willie. Do you think the change is permanent?'

'God, I hope so Lynne. I love her,' he said simply, 'I really do. I don't ever want to hurt her. I hate seeing her suffering and looking so ill. I think, however, it might be useful to talk to Joe, even if it is just to get advice. I'm way out of my depth here.'

Willie sat up for a while after Lynne went to bed. He eventually went upstairs but still did not feel sleepy; Ally appeared to be sleeping peacefully. He crept into the en-suite and turned on the shower. He stood under the water. He had eventually calmed down over Frankie's behaviour. As Lynne had pointed out, they had all put up with his own behaviour over the years.

The cabinet door opened, and Ally got into the cubicle with him. She grinned and kissed him; water rained down on them. Willie immediately began to respond to her. Lifting her up, kissing her, he gently pushed her against the back of the cabinet. She moaned and moved against him. His legs trembled as he held her tightly, the water rushing down onto their bodies. Afterwards, Willie draped a large bath sheet over them both and carried her through to the bedroom where he gently laid her on the bed. She smiled up at him. 'I woke up horny Willie, I wanted you. Can't believe we managed that, and it didn't hurt.'

'Oh sweetheart, you can do that anytime you like. I don't believe how quick it was though.'

Ally shut her eyes and smiled. 'Me neither, I'm still quivering down below!' she said sleepily. 'Think my pelvis is mended, don't you?'

'I told you I can't get enough of you. You will tell me if I hurt you? I'm still wary, believe it or not.' He looked down at

Ally and smiled, she was already asleep. Willie, still damp from the shower, lay beside her and wrapped his arms around her as she breathed evenly and relaxed, her wet hair against his chest.

CHAPTER

TWENTY-SIX

Willie opened the door to a very sheepish-looking Frankie. 'Willie mate, I'm mortified. My mouth just runs away with me.'

Willie shrugged. 'It's not me you need to worry about apologising to Frankie.' He looked his friend in the eye. 'But if you ever do that again, I'll take you apart. Don't fucking mess with her!'

Frankie nodded and put out his hand, Willie took it and Frankie gripped it then embraced his friend. 'I deserve that now bud. Is Lynne still here?' Willie stood back and pushed the door opened. Frankie lifted two large bouquets of flowers from the side of the door. He walked through to the kitchen. Ally and Lynne sat at the breakfast bar drinking coffee. 'I'm here wearing sackcloth and ashes,' he muttered. Willie watched from the doorway with his arms folded, saying nothing. Frankie put one bouquet down in front of Lynne and stood looking at Ally, holding out the other. 'Ally, I'm so sorry. What I said was unforgivable. You're a beautiful woman, and Willie is a lucky man. Me? I'm just a prick. You have every right to be angry at me.'

Ally nodded and took the flowers. 'Apology accepted. They're beautiful, thank you Frankie.' She stood up and lifted her mug.

'Willie, can you put these in the sink please? We'd better leave these two to talk.'

An hour later, Lynne came out to the pool. Her face was wet with tears. 'Willie, could you possibly take me to the airport? I've booked a flight home. Betty will bring my case to the airport.' She began to cry quietly. 'I can't do it anymore. I think this is the end for me and Frankie.'

Ally stood up. 'Look, I feel as though I'm intruding. You need to talk. I'll go and attempt a walk to the shops.'

'Ally, I'm so sorry. What must you think of me?'

'I think it's sad that your relationship is ending Lynne, and I think you need your friends. I hope that we can be friends too.' Ally moved around the table and hugged the other woman.

Lynne looked up at her. 'Can I call you to meet for a coffee or something when you get back to Scotland?'

'Of course, Lynne, I'd really like that. Willie, I'm going to hobble down to the supermarket. I'll see you when you get back.' She kissed him gently. 'I'm so sorry about this Willie.'

'Why are you sorry? You haven't done anything.'

'I just feel me being here with you has changed something for you and your friends.'

Lynne watched as Ally walked away. 'She's lovely Willie.' He nodded, also watching Ally disappear into the house through the bedroom veranda.

'Are you sure this is what you want Lynne?'

'I don't think I want to wait any longer Willie. I told you last night I love him, but I've had enough of his behaviour. Funny thing, but Ally has it half right, it was seeing you with her that made me realise that I can't go on with him the way he is. Alfie and Betty, David and Lesley have always been different. But you! You were so much worse than him! Then I saw the way you look at Ally. I don't think Frankie will ever look at me like that.' She stood up. 'Willie he'll need support, but just don't let him spoil things for you. Now can you take me to the airport while I still feel strong enough to go?'

Ally walked through to the kitchen. Frankie was leaning against the worktop with a mug of coffee in his hand. 'Are you alright Frankie?' she asked.

He nodded. 'I'll live. I know it's my own fault. I do love her, but I just struggle with commitment. I'm going to take off now and work out how to win her back.'

'You could walk to the shops with me if you want? I struggle a bit with the cobbles, I could do with a strong arm to hang on to.' She looked him in the eye and smiled. 'I'd also like to get to know you Frankie. You're so important to Willie, and we kind of got off to a bad start.'

Frankie smiled. 'I'd like that Ally. Willie is important to me too.'

Ally took his arm and lifted her bag from the table. 'Okay, come on.'

As they walked Frankie watched her out of the corner of his eye. He could see the determination on her face as she moved. 'Are you in a lot of pain Ally?' he asked. 'Do you want to go back to the house for pills or something?'

She looked up and shook her head. 'It's not too bad now, actually. It's mainly just when I'm walking. I'm reducing the painkillers gradually. I've been on them so long I was becoming dependent, so I have to wean myself off them.' She looked up at him, 'I'm sorry about you and Lynn, Frankie. She seems like a really nice person.'

'Oh, she is, she's much too good for me actually. I put her through a whole load of shit. She had a miscarriage three weeks ago, and she's devastated.'

'Are you?'

'No not really, I think I'm relieved. I didn't want the baby. I don't want to be a father.'

'Why not?'

'Oh, I just don't think that I would be good at it, and I don't want the responsibility.'

'Did you have a bad childhood? Sorry Frankie, I don't want to pry if you don't want to say.' Ally looked up at him, 'it's just, with my background, I'm always interested in why people make those kinds of decisions. Professionally, given the shit I clear up, I think it's better if someone doesn't have kids they don't want. However, I just think that you and Lynne would make good parents. I watched you yesterday with your nieces. That makes me think that it's something from childhood.'

'You are very intuitive Mrs Campbell, it wasn't good. My parents were and still are great, much better than Willie or Davie's. Their parents were weird, strict and religious. Alfie and I had a much better family life. We were the youngest. There were six boys, five now, our older brother Vernon died twenty-five years ago. He was married to Yvonne.'

'Willie told me that. What happened to you then Frankie, to make you so commitment phobic? You appear to love Lynne and have been together a long time now I hear.' She staggered a little and cried out in pain.

'Are you alright Ally? Do you need to sit down?' Frankie asked, concern on his face.

She nodded. 'Sorry Frankie, I can't walk too far without a rest. It's actually doing my head in. I can't do the things I want to do.'

'Come and we'll sit in this bar and have a coffee.' He guided Ally into the outdoor seating area of a café bar. 'Dos café por favor,' he called to a waiter. The waiter quickly brought over the drinks.

Frankie stirred his coffee and stared out to sea; Ally looked at him. 'Do you want to talk about what's causing the problems between you and Lynne? I might be able to help.'

Frankie shook his head and smiled sadly. 'Thanks Ally but it's too far gone for that. Besides, you have enough problems of your own.'

'I'm a good listener and have a bad memory Frankie. It's also easier to help sort out other people's shit than it is to work on your own.'

'I'll remember that Ally,' Frankie sighed. 'But to win her back I must make decisions, change my lifestyle. I don't know if I can change. I think I have to sort it all out in my head before I speak about it.'

CHAPTER
TWENTY-SEVEN

'Ally, this is Joe McCann, Dr Joe McCann.'

Ally smiled at the tall, blond, good-looking man standing in their lounge. 'Thank you for coming over Joe, we really appreciate it.'

'Do you want a drink?' Willie asked.

'No, just coffee please Willie, I've drank enough the last few days to start worrying about my liver.'

'You've been with Frankie then?' Willie asked. 'I was with him myself last night. He's really angry at Lynne, but she has put up with so much from him. You can't really blame her for taking a stand now.'

'Oh, he'll be fine Willie, he just needs to lick his wounds and get over it,' Joe said, a serious expression on his face.

'That's not very sympathetic Joe. He's supposed to be your mate,' Willie gasped.

Joe smiled and shook his head. 'Oh, he is, but he's giving himself so much sympathy now that he doesn't need anyone else's. You are too soft with him Willie. You let him wallow in it. Now let's leave Frankie out of the equation just now, we need to discuss you two. Ally, I hope you don't mind, but after Willie involved me, I took the liberty of speaking to Clive Ruthven.

225

He's in Ibiza just now with a mutual friend. I've worked with Clive a few times over the years. He's a fantastic, talented surgeon. I jumped over there on the ferry yesterday and had lunch with him. Ally, how bad are the symptoms?'

She looked him in the eye. 'Pretty bad. I trained as a counsellor too Joe, and I know all the signs and symptoms of PTS. I think it may be better when there's some closure. The trial's not until February though. What I possibly need now, is for someone to help me understand what was going through my mind that day.'

Joe nodded. 'What about your friend Stevie? He must be the one person who knows exactly what you are going through. Have you spoken to him about it?'

Ally shook her head. 'Not since he and Willie told me about the shootings and the explosion. He really doesn't want to discuss it. Stevie is very laid-back Joe; he's been mainly okay. He says he gets some flashbacks, but he is back at work now and doing fine. He never really lost consciousness during the time we were trapped, and although his skull was fractured, he had no other head injuries. He had no memory loss either. Stevie got a bit cranky for a bit while he was in the hospital but once he got home, he says he's been mainly fine.'

'Do you think he is telling the truth?'

'I don't know but he looks okay. I had dinner with him the night before I came out here. I talk to him every couple of days. I don't get the impression he is suffering too badly. I've known him for many years, I would know.'

'Have you told him how much you are struggling?'

'No, I didn't actually. Do you think I should have?'

'Do you think you should have?' Joe asked, looking directly into Ally's eyes.

'Don't do the counselling with me, Joe.'

'This is fascinating!' Willie said. 'It's like watching tennis.'

'How do you feel?' Joe asked, ignoring Willie.

Ally stood up, she stretched and walked over to the open patio doors. 'I don't need to talk about remembering the shootings. I need to talk about how I felt when little kids were falling around me. I'm a fucking professional, I should have been able to save them! I trained to look after people, and I couldn't do anything.'

'So, what could you have done?' Joe asked.

'I could have prevented it. I should have known how dangerous he was. I did the fucking interviews with his kids and his wife. Despite her having her back to them, both men could hear the emotion in her voice, they knew she was struggling to speak.' Willie stood up and made to move towards her, but Joe put his hand out and stopped him.

'How could you have known what he was going to do Ally?' Joe asked quietly.

Ally spun around. 'I don't know! But I should have been able to do something.'

Willie looked at her. 'Ally, there was a man with a gun, shooting. How could you have done anything?'

Joe put his hand up again. 'Willie please, just sit and listen. She knows that don't you Ally? This is about how she felt and feels now.' He looked at Ally. 'Do something now.'

'How can I? I can't go backwards in time!'

'Take part in Willie's benefit thing.'

'Doing what?'

Joe shrugged. 'You choose. Take the tickets at the desk, lap dance, you do something that you are comfortable with. As a social worker, you trained to help people change, not rescue them Ally. Once you get it through your head and heart that there was nothing you could do at the time, and put your energies into doing something positive, you'll be able to start to put the ghosts to rest. Ally, you were exposed to a terrible, tragic atrocity and one that should never have happened. The fallout for the people in Whitefield's will go on for many, many years and should never be forgotten but they, and you, need to move on. We can discuss this further Ally, another time. I know this is not the orthodox way to do trauma counselling, but you need to discuss your feelings. Let's look at what we can do for now to channel your thoughts consciously, and it might influence your unconscious thoughts. How long are you over here for?'

'Another two weeks,' Ally said quietly.

'Then I would like to meet with you another few times this week and then by Skype a couple of times. We can continue when you come back to Scotland. Willie, do you mind if I see Ally alone a couple of times before I go home? It may be better if she doesn't feel she is worrying you.' Ally looked at the ground, saying nothing, and Willie realised that Joe had hit on something important.

'That's Ally's decision, I would think. But no, I've no objection to her doing anything that she thinks will help her.' Willie looked at Ally and then moved towards her. 'Babe, I want to help.'

Joe smiled, 'Okay we can start tomorrow!'

'Joe, you're on holiday!' Ally gasped.

'Well I think we all have a role to play in helping with recovery. I think I can help you. I would also be interested in meeting with your colleague too, as I'd be able to help you piece things together by speaking to him if he's willing. Will you ask him?'

Ally nodded.

'Ally, for now I'll take you both through some breathing exercises which are designed for PTS sufferers. You'll have delivered similar before but like most professionals you do the giving, not the taking. Willie you're so laid back you probably never needed to learn relaxation techniques. You normally get it from a bottle. Just watch and learn mate.'

'She's fallen asleep!' Willie whispered ten minutes later. 'That was amazing Joe.' He took a throw from the back of the sofa put it over Ally then kissed her forehead. 'Do you want a proper drink now?'

Joe nodded. 'My usual Willie. Can we go somewhere else to talk? It would be good for her to get a rest. Let her sleep when she needs to, her mind and body need it.'

Willie sat by the pool with Joe. 'How are you coping Willie? You must be right out of your comfort zone with this?'

Willie nodded. 'Everyone keeps saying that. I don't like hearing it said. But if I'm honest . . . I would normally have run a mile.'

'She's a special lady Willie, you really don't want to let her get away. She's so not your normal type though. You're a clever guy but you just drink too much, and your relationships are normally about sex. No depth, one-dimensional, but I sense this is different. How did that happen?'

Willie nodded and sighed, 'I'm not sure Joe, but from the first night I met her she was a challenge. Then I don't know what happened, I've never felt like this about a woman before and it all got a bit scary.' He looked Joe in the eye. 'Then she got hurt, I realised . . . I realised I didn't want to lose her. Can she get over it Joe?'

Joe smiled and nodded; he took a drink from his glass of brandy and put the glass down on the table in front of him. 'Yes, I think she can. Your Mrs Campbell is a very strong-willed lady. She needs to work her way through her feelings, but my guess is that she will recover and without too much help. It will always be there Willie, will rear its ugly head from time to time, so it's important you both know how to work through it. Clive Ruthven filled me in on a lot of it. He likes her Willie. I don't know a great deal about him personally, but he warned me that if I tried anything with her, he would break my fucking neck.'

Joe smiled. 'He's a big man Willie, I wouldn't like to get on the wrong side of him. I always thought he was a bit unusual for a brain surgeon. Have you seen the size of his hands?'

Willie laughed. 'I think he's a little in love with her Joe, but he is an honourable man and won't do anything about it. Strange as it may seem, she loves me.'

Joe took a drink and nodded. 'She's special Willie. There's a real chemistry between you two that doesn't happen every day.'

Willie sighed. 'She has been through so much. She was in a near fatal accident years ago and lost her husband, mother and baby.'

Joe sighed. 'I read that in the newspapers. She'll have suffered then and possibly put all her efforts into her remaining children and work. Clive said she refused counselling at the time. There's probably what we call unresolved conflict, which will be affecting her. You do need to look after her just now Willie, but I'm sure that in a few months she'll be looking after you. Have you slept with her yet?'

'Why? Will that have an impact on her recovery?'

'No, but Frankie doesn't think you have. He reckons that once you have, you'll lose interest. He put money on it with me. I think my money is safe. How was it?' he grinned. 'I'm a man too.'

Willie smiled. 'Fucking incredible. I'm hooked.'

'You know, I think that Frankie is afraid of the way you have changed.'

'What is wrong with him Joe? You're the shrink. Right from the start, he tried to put a spanner in the works with me and Ally. You know, making me doubt I could be sincere.'

'He's jealous Willie.'

'Of me and Ally?'

'Sort of, strange as it sounds. I think your miracle transformation has shaken him up. I don't want to breach his trust

Willie, but believe it or not, I've been helping him with his feelings! He'll get over it. Right now, he is feeling like a prick.'

'He is a prick!' Willie said, smiling.

Suddenly screams cut through the quiet evening air, both men ran back through to the lounge. Ally was screaming and writhing on the sofa. Joe looked at Willie, 'Let me deal with this,' he said, gently moving Willie aside. Willie watched as Joe sat down beside her. 'Ally wake up. Ally you're safe. Ally, it's all over.'

She opened her eyes. Willie winced at the expression of terror on her face.

Joe, however, kept talking calmly to her, 'I want you to breathe. Now take deep breaths. Breathe in for a count of seven . . . hold it . . . now out for a count of seven. Count it Ally, one Mississippi, two Mississippi. Feel your heartbeat slowing, your mind clearing. Breathe Ally. Everything is going to be fine. Make your thoughts still, make your body still. Let your breath take the pictures in your head away and replace them with good ones.' He put his hand on her forehead, continuing to talk to her in a calm voice. She gradually began to respond and eventually she slept.

The two men tiptoed out of the lounge and onto the patio. 'Willie, you really need to look after her. When she gets like that in her sleep, do what I did there, keep saying her name and reassure her.'

'The first time she did it, I ended up making love to her, then I was really scared I had taken advantage of her.'

'If it works, and it's consensual, do it. Sex can be a release Willie, for women and for men.'

Willie grinned. 'Fuck, it was a release. I thought I was coming from my toes.'

'Not for you, you prick, for her!'

Back outside, as Willie poured whisky into their glasses, the gate creaked open and Frankie appeared in the backyard. 'Oh, there you are Joe. The hotel said you were up here.'

Willie stood up. 'Frankie, have a beer? I hear you are off spirits.'

Frankie smiled. 'Oh, ha-ha Willie, very droll. I have been speaking to Lynne by Skype. I am going to have to . . . **Willie, what's wrong? Joe!**'

Willie was on the ground, his eyes rolling, his body jerking unnaturally. He stopped and opened his eyes, he tried to get to his feet, Frankie and Joe helped him onto a chair. 'What the fuck just happened Willie?' Frankie asked.

Willie stared at them. 'I don't know. I just probably stood up too quickly and fainted.'

'Has that happened before?' Joe asked. 'That was a seizure Willie. Have you had one before? You really should go up to the hospital and get checked out you could have bumped your head when you fitted.'

'It wasn't a fit Joe. I've fainted a couple of times. I have had a viral thing for a few weeks, an ear infection, but it's not responding to any treatment and the flight over made it worse.'

'Have you seen a doctor?'

'Just pour me a drink Joe and shut the fuck up. Do you think I prescribed myself antibiotics?'

'You can buy them over the counter here in the chemist Willie.' Joe said, shaking his head and taking a drink from his glass.

'Okay so I lied, but I'll see my own doctor when I get back. I'm sure it's nothing to worry about.'

'Fuck sake Willie!' Frankie gasped. 'You're doing too much. That's what happens when you go from naughty to nice. It looked like a whitey to me.'

232

'It would look like a whitey to you Frankie. I've had no drugs, only this.' he said, lifting his glass.

'You do know you shouldn't drink while you're taking antibiotics Willie?' Joe said taking a drink from his own glass.

'Of course, I do,' Willie replied, taking a gulp of whisky. 'That's why I'm not taking them anymore. That's probably all it was.'

'Oh well, as long as you know.' Frankie pulled open the ring on his can of beer and sat down. 'Where's Ally?'

'Asleep on the couch.'

'Have you fucked her yet?'

'Subtle Frankie, say it like it is. We've made love several times, not that it's any of your business, but she's the best I've ever had. I plan to be doing it for the rest of my life Frankie. I proposed too, but she said no.'

'Well that's a first for you, one of your women saying no to marriage. Oh well Joe, you'll need to be my new best friend, mate. He is right under the thumb now.'

'Piss off Frankie,' Joe smiled. 'I can't keep up with you these days. Fuck sake, we're nearly fifty.'

Frankie took a drink from the can. 'Okay, how can I get Lynne back?'

'Get a personality transplant,' Joe said, smiling at his friend.

'Oh great, do they do them now?'

'You can have mine. According to you lot, I don't use it much,' David said as he came through the gate, followed by Alfie.

'Hey just think what you could do with David's personality bro.' Alfie laughed, taking a can from the cool box.

Willie grinned. 'That's two words I never thought I would hear in the same sentence, Davie and personality.' He took a can from the cool box at his feet and tossed it to David. 'Where are your women?'

'Out in town. They'll end up back here, they were already drunk when we left them. You've plenty of space anyway,' Alfie said, taking a drink from his beer can. 'We've got an all-night babysitter.'

'I have a sick woman to look after,' Willie laughed.

'You always have a sick woman to look after. At least you didn't make this one sick,' Frankie said, grinning at his friends. 'I had a long chat with her when you were helping my missus to run away. She's alright Willie, I like her. She might just be what you need. We had a drink and sat out at the harbour for a while. If it doesn't work out with Lynne, I could go for her myself.'

'After what you said to her? Ally will be heartened to hear that.'

'Is Yvonne with them too? I hear Hughie stayed at home.' Joe grinned.

'You stay away from my sister Joe!' Willie slapped him on the back of the head. 'You need to find a free woman.' He stood up and pushed Frankie, 'and you, don't even think about making a move on Ally. I'm just going to check she's okay.'

As he disappeared into the villa, Frankie looked at Joe. 'Could an ear infection, antibiotics and drink, do that?' he asked the other man, 'his eyes were rolling in his head.' They quickly filled the other two men in.

Joe shrugged. 'I'm a psychologist not a medic. I actually don't know. I suppose it's all about balance, so it could. Why don't I ask Yvonne? She might know.'

'You'd better stay away from Yvonne. Willie will go mental if you go near her again. She's married to Hughie now.' David sighed.

'She's wild in bed,' Frankie said, smiling.

'You too?' Joe raised an eyebrow then smiled.

'Just the once, years ago.'

'David shook his head. 'Sometimes I think I must have spent my teenage years with my eyes closed. What the fuck?

234

'Does Willie know?' Joe asked looking around.

'Of course, he does. Thing is, she was the big girl when we were teenagers Joe, the one all our mates wanted to nail.'

Alfie nodded in agreement, saying nothing. Davie smiled, silently remembering. Frankie looked around at his friends, 'by god she was good. She dumped me for an older guy, our Vernon.'

Willie came through the doors and back to the table. He laughed and slapped Frankie on the back of the head. 'I've got ears Frankie, and she is my sister.'

'What's a sister between friends Willie? Technically, she is my sister-in-law. Is Ally okay?'

'Yeah, she's awake and calm. She's freshening up. You might be a steamer and a letch, but you are good with that relaxation stuff Joe.'

In response Joe grinned and raised his glass. 'She's a beautiful woman Wull, I might try hypnotherapy with her next.'

'You're not hypnotising my woman McCann, no chance.'

'I can't believe you let him anywhere near Ally, Wull. You didn't leave him alone with her?' David gasped.

Joe smiled and took a drink, swallowing before he spoke again. 'I never mix business and pleasure boys.'

'I'm really glad you don't, it could get confusing.' Ally came up behind them. Willie pulled her over and she sat on his knee, he wrapped his arms around her.

'You're feeling a bit more rested?' Joe asked.

She nodded. 'Yes thanks. You are a bit of a miracle worker Mr McCann.'

Joe grinned back at her and nudged Willie. 'I have been told that before, but never from a woman sitting in another man's lap.'

'Do you want a beer Ally?' Frankie held up a can.

Ally took it from him. She leaned back against Willie. 'I'm not interrupting, am I?'

'Not at all, Frankie was just discussing how he is going to win Lynne back. Maybe you could advise him, give him an unbiased female perspective?' Alfie grinned. 'All our women are saying Lynne is better off without him.'

'I don't think I could be any help where relationships are concerned. I do think if you want the same things though, you are halfway there,' Ally said, smiling at Alfie.

'What do you and Willie want?' Alfie asked.

'Peace and harmony,' Willie said, quietly playing with her hair.

They were interrupted by the sound of female voices.

Willie laughed. 'They didn't stay out very long.'

The gate opened and Yvonne, Lesley and Betty came into the garden, giggling and walking unsteadily. 'Ally I hope you don't feel left out. We phoned earlier to see if you wanted to come out with us tonight, but Willie wouldn't let me speak to you,' Lesley said, lifting a beer from the cool box.

'She was asleep,' Willie laughed.

'He did tell me, but I'm not quite ready for a girlie night out yet. I didn't want to spoil your night by being a wimp. When I'm better I'll be right there with you.' Ally was aware of a tension between Willie and his sister. They sat around the table outside as darkness fell. Yvonne was an attractive woman; both Frankie and Joe were paying her a lot of attention. She told the group her marriage had ended. 'How many is that now?' Alfie asked.

'It's only four. Just one more than him,' she said, pointing at Willie.

Frankie laughed. 'Ally, did he tell you about his brothers and sisters?'

Willie smiled, but Ally realised he was annoyed. He glanced over at Frankie. 'You know I don't speak about the black sheep, they just let the side down.'

Yvonne sipped her drink. 'Ally, we have two brothers. John and Benny are priests and our sister Catherine is a nun. What can I say? We're a family of saints and sinners. Our parents stopped talking to Willie after he left his first wife, and to me, when after my first husband died, I married a protestant.'

'They always hated me anyway. I mean what staunch Catholic family in Glasgow call their son William?' Willie laughed, but Ally noted the pain in his eyes.

'You were a surprise baby Wull. You were not supposed to happen. She told me once that she sat in the bath drinking gin with both of us, trying to bring on a miscarriage. We interfered with the time she could spend in the church probably.' Yvonne looked at Ally. 'Our Cath, who is seven years older than me and twelve years older than Willie, brought both of us up.'

CHAPTER
TWENTY-EIGHT

'It must hurt you a lot, what your family did to you?' Ally sat up in bed, watching Willie undressing.

He shrugged. 'I made choices they just did not agree with. My mother was very narrow-minded, and my father was a bigoted bully. We used to hear him beating her up. As a young kid,' Willie's face clouded over, 'I learned to stay out of his way.'

'Are they both dead?'

He nodded. 'They were to me, years before they actually did die. I didn't even go to the funerals. Yvonne did, but it bothers her more than me I suppose. My brothers and sister still speak to us. In their profession, the God Squad, they must be more forgiving. To be honest they are alright, especially our Cath. They're the only true Christians I've ever met. At school, we were mostly bullied by the priests and nuns.' Willie sighed and looked away, his face reflecting pain. 'I know there are mostly good people out there in religions, but my experience of it wasn't great. I had it beaten into me, so did Davie, his dad was my mum's brother. Alfie and Frankie are much the same about the religion, but they have a brilliant family. Their mother became my mother. Their dad's a great guy. He's my role model for what a father should be. Six boys, only a year between each of them, all a bit wild, but he was there for them, still is actually. He's eighty-five but still there for them and Davie and me.'

'So why does Frankie say his childhood wasn't good Willie?'

Willie sighed; his eyes clouded over. 'Frankie was sexually abused by a priest when he was a boy. Not many people know. He doesn't broadcast it, I shouldn't be telling you, but I think he needs to deal with it Ally.'

'I knew there was something pretty sinister from his behaviour Willie. I thought it might be something like that. Does Lynne know?'

Willie shook his head. 'Men see being abused as a slight on their masculinity. You must know about these things Ally; with the job you do.'

Ally moved closer to Willie. 'I've met quite a few adult survivors of abuse. A lot of the extra familial stuff was done by people in a position of power. Some of the religious stuff is the worst because they use the religion to do it and then hide behind it. Leaves you really messed up.' Willie said nothing. He raised an eyebrow, then lay back. Ally wrapped her arms around him and gently kissed the top of his head. 'It makes you forget there are thousands of genuine, good people in the Church though. Did anything happen to you?'

'I took a few beatings, got touched up a few times.' He looked over at the window and sighed. 'I was forced to give a dirty old bastard a blow job once. I've never told anyone this. I was still primary school age maybe ten or eleven. I was so scared I bit his cock. Got the shit kicked out of me, but he never tried me again.'

'Willie that's awful,' Ally gasped. 'You never told anyone?'

He shrugged and brought his knees up, as though protecting himself. Leaning back against her chest, he looked up at her, then away. Ally tightened her arms around him, and he brought his hands around, resting them on hers. 'The football saved me from the worst of it, I think. They couldn't risk it because by the time I was about ten they knew I had talent, and the big clubs were interested. Incidentally, when I moved to the boys club, I was touched up by a coach once, but I told the boss of the club and he moved him. Not sacked but moved to the older teams. Better than nothing. There was a lot of it went on in the football circle. We were kids from poor backgrounds, sport was a way out, so a lot of guys . . . well, let's just say it wasn't nice. I think what was worse though, was the adults, they knew it happened.'

'Didn't you ever tell anyone?' Ally repeated.

'Mostly there was no one to tell, but guys don't talk about this do they? I think we are programmed to believe *the boys don't cry thing*. Then there was the religious connotation for me as well. I was brought up to do as the Church said. Are you religious Ally? I never asked you. I avoid religion and politics in most conversations.'

'Not particularly. It doesn't just happen in the Catholic Church. Willie people get involved in all sorts of things to gain access to kids. My parents weren't particularly religious, and I think in my job I saw too many bad things to believe. Now though, after that strange dream, near death experience or whatever it was when I was in surgery, I don't know.'

Willie sighed and tightened his grip on her hands. 'I think that's why I became such a sinner Ally. The religion was literally shoved down my throat until I couldn't see any good in it. I want to believe in something, but I just can't believe the atrocities that are carried out in the name of religion.'

Ally nodded, gently stroking his hair. 'The meeting we had with the workers from Belfast on the day of the shootings. That's what they said about religion. They spoke about the things that happened during the Troubles and after. That was mainly a religious divide, wasn't it? Then there's all the stuff in the Middle East.'

240

'Ally, we can't save the world!'

'I know! But we can make our wee bit a little better. What you've just told me helps me understand Frankie a bit better though, if he was let down and hurt by people who were supposed to protect him. Couldn't his parents help if they were a close family?' Ally asked, her lips brushed the top of Willie's head as she spoke.

Willie sighed loudly and looked up at the ceiling. 'I don't think it ever occurred to him to tell them. We were all from a background where the Church was the centre of the community at that time. We only found out about Frankie when Alfie and Betty were getting married. Frankie was supposed to be best man. Betty decided she wanted to get married in the chapel which was next to the school we went to. Frankie was I think abused in that holy place as an altar boy and had vowed never to set foot in it when he grew up. We were very drunk, and he lost the plot at the stag night. I ended up being best man because he fell out with Alfie and refused to go. Alfie didn't want to choose between his other three brothers. The only reason Frankie told us at all was because of how hurt Alfie was. We wanted him to go to the police and report it, but he wouldn't. He didn't want his parents to know because of what it would do to them. Alfie was never touched. Strange isn't it with them being identical? I think it might have been because Alfie was, even as a boy, always more assertive than Frankie. He and Davie were also very clever and in the top streams at school, so they had the good teachers. I had the sports talent.'

'Has he had help with it?'

Willie shook his head, 'I doubt it. Since the wedding we've never spoken about it. It's out there though, and certainly a big thing for Frankie. He's never discussed it with Lynne either. She knows there is something from his past, we've told her that much. I think when she asks, he fobs her off. I have thought about telling her, but I don't know if he'd forgive me if I did. He may have talked to Joe, they're such good mates. Frankie brought Joe into our circle, not me. I knew him from my playing days, but it was Frankie who initiated the friendship. He was a regular in our first pub.'

'Joe is good at what he does Willie.' Ally sighed. 'I feel more rested than I've done since the accident.'

'Hmm I suppose so, but just be careful. He's a wanker when he's drinking. Frankie and him, they've done some crazy stuff. They do quite a lot of drugs together. I don't know who leads who into trouble but Christ they can get into some mess. I can't really talk, I never really got into drugs. But I didn't need to, I drank. When I drink, I don't always know when to stop and I have been every bit as bad. The three of us have done some weird shit. Some of it made the papers, some didn't. Because of Lynne and the clubs, Frankie has a lot of journalist friends, so he sometimes manages to keep it out of the media.'

'Do you regret any of it?' Ally asked, kissing the top of Willie's head.

'If I'm honest…no not really, apart from the things I've done to people I was supposed to love. There are women I have treated like shit. Apart from Corinna, they all knew what they were getting into. I never lied to them. I regret what I did to Corinna. That was bad. I had three young kids, I just walked away.'

'Did you never love Hailey? She's unbelievably beautiful.'

'Hailey was a nutter. She used to kick the shit out of me, I probably deserved it. Honestly, she's a beautiful woman, but she has no real talent or anything. She can't cope with getting older, or not looking a million dollars. I think she spends most of her alimony on plastic surgery, and stuff. I didn't love her; I suppose I was at the height of my career when we met and fickle enough to think that a woman didn't need to have a personality if she was beautiful.' Willie sighed. 'She rationed sex with me because it messed her hair up. She actually was stupid enough to think I would care. She's not good to Jade either. She resents her but uses her like a weapon to get at me. Jade is fifteen now and is going through a Goth period. Hailey acts as though she should be sectioned. The kid has had to put up with some really fucked up behaviour. Hailey's pregnant again, and Jade says she's finding it difficult. She's living with my oldest daughter Leah at the moment. Hailey kicked her out. She can't live with me full time because of the way Hailey reacts. She once reported me to social work you know?'

'Really, you never said.'

'Yeah a couple of years ago, two social workers knocked the door saying she had reported me as being drunk with Jade and Euan in my care.'

'Were you?'

'Not that day.' He smiled, 'I shouldn't be telling you this because you will be shocked. I ended up sleeping with one of them, she was married, safe, she won't ever say anything. Not while the investigation was going on. I gave them complimentary tickets for the club when it was all finished. I don't even remember her name Ally.'

'What about Belinsa?' Ally asked shaking her head.

'Belinsa, she's a nasty piece of work where I'm concerned. She just wanted to be a WAG. It went along with the whole soap actress thing. I was at the end of my playing career. She's a good mum to Euan though and puts his needs first. She's clever, very devious, nothing like her soap character. People don't get that; she plays a lovely person. I really was bad to her though Ally, a total bastard. I was rolling in drunk when I did roll in at all. She got a better offer. I was relieved when she left me. Anyway, how the hell did we get onto my fuckups? That's just the highlights Ally, the former wives club! I've been a total wanker. Fortunately, after Euan I had the good sense to have a vasectomy. I was often

243

so drunk that I did not even know who I had slept with. Just for the record, I have not looked at another woman since I met you!' He looked her in the eye. 'I've had myself tested for all sexually transmitted diseases and got a note from my doctor just in case you didn't believe me.'

Ally sighed. 'Do you know something Willie? I never even gave that a thought, pretty irresponsible of me I suppose. I'm glad you don't have anything though, amazing with the life you've led.'

He sighed, 'I'd never have slept with you if I hadn't been checked first.'

'I trust you Willie, but you have had a charmed life really.'

Willie looked thoughtful, 'in terms of my lifestyle, I was lucky I was always able to play football. I would most likely have been dead otherwise. Football gave me the status I needed. It gave me boundaries most of the time. I never physically abused a woman. I am not big on mental torment either, I don't lie, although I know sometimes the truth hurts. Most of the time I just neglected them which probably is worse than, or as bad at times as physical abuse. It's emotional abuse, isn't it? I knew they all thought they could change me, bring me out of my darkness. Truth is, I didn't want to be anywhere else.' He rolled around to face Ally. 'Until now, I'm so happy with you darling, you're truly the best thing that ever happened to me. I hate that you are having all these difficulties. I wish I'd met you sooner.'

Ally shook her head. 'I suspect that this is our time. You would never have looked twice at me years ago Willie, and I certainly would not have been attracted to you.'

'Do you believe Ralph had something to do with it?'

'I don't know, but in the dream or whatever it was, he said me loving you and being loved by you would lead to the next love of my life.'

'You're the love of mine Ally.' He looked straight into her eyes. 'God sweetheart, I find it so strange to be feeling that. I've never said it to anyone who wasn't related to me before either. The only person I've really loved apart from my kids was me. Know what I think? I think you're a witch.'

'Yeah well, you had better be careful I don't turn you into toad.'

He smiled. 'I think I've already been one! In fact, right now I'm a horny toad. Come here, I'll show you.'

'Willie, we have a houseful of people. Don't . . . '

'Shh, I'll be quiet.'

***

Next morning the group assembled by the pool. Willie served up breakfast. As he sat down to eat his own beside his sister, Betty looked over at him and smiled. 'Can we just stay here?' she asked. 'No cooking. No kids, no potty training. No crying and fighting. Honestly, girls are such little bitches to their sisters.'

'Oh yes,' Willie laughed. 'To their brothers too.' He nudged Yvonne.

'What?'

'Do you know she gave me my first cigarette when I was eight. I caught her smoking and said I would tell Mum and Dad! I hadn't worked out that they didn't like me. At the time, I thought they would actually be interested. She made me smoke till I was sick then said she would tell Mum I smoked too.'

'I was only twelve or thirteen Willie.'

Later, as everyone lay by the pool, Ally went for her daily walk. As she walked through the olive grove at the side of the house, Frankie caught up with her. 'Mind if I walk with you?'

'No of course not. It's good to have company.'

'Is it still painful to walk?' Frankie asked, seeing the concentration on her face.

245

'Yes sometimes. The crutches help, but I'm determined to be back on my feet properly by the end of the summer. The physios didn't want me to come away so soon after getting the casts off. Willie wanted to hire someone here, but I just feel that there have been so many people involved in my care that I want to do something for myself. So, we agreed on a set of exercises and a walk that I add distance to every day. Willie usually comes with me, but he needs to talk to Belinsa by Skype. There's a problem with Euan which apparently is Willie's fault.'

Frankie sighed. 'She's a pure cow Ally, a real nasty piece of work. Willie doesn't say much. He blames himself for the way she behaves, but she never loved him. She was with him because it brought her publicity. Euan is a smashing wee fellow, but he was conceived deliberately to trap Willie.' They walked through the grove, coming out on a secluded cove with a sandy beach. Ally sat down on a rock and spread her legs out in front of her. 'Why do you keep covering yourself up Ally?' Frankie asked, nodding at her cropped trousers and long-sleeved top.

Ally sighed. 'Scars! I'm working on it. It's just vanity really.'

He raised an eyebrow. 'You're a beautiful woman Ally. Willie's a lucky man.'

'I'm human Frankie.' Ally sighed and looked out to sea. 'I passed a woman on the beach yesterday. She had had obviously had a mastectomy and she was sunbathing topless. I think it was very brave of her, but people were staring too. I want to be like that, not care, but it bothers me, and I hate exposing myself. Willie is really good about it. He says that they are part of me, and he loves my scars.' She looked up at Frankie. 'Most of my scars are visible ones. I'm working through the emotional ones; everyone expects me to have them. It's not like yours, no one can see hidden ones Frankie.'

'What did Willie tell you?'

'He told me he was sexually and physically abused in school. He said you suffered worse though. I told you I could listen Frankie, I meant it. I'm used to these things. Willie reckons you're really affected by some of the stuff that happened to you. Do you want to talk about it?'

Frankie picked up a stone and threw it into the sea. He nodded. 'It's pretty bad stuff, Ally.'

'I doubt it will be anything I haven't come across before Frankie. It won't go any further. Were you abused?'

He picked up another stone and threw it, then looked away and took a deep breath before he spoke. 'You could call it that! I was raped on a weekly basis by a smelly old priest for over two years for a start. Sometimes I couldn't walk because of the pain. I still have problems now with my arse, because of the damage they did to me.' Tears rolled down his face. 'Fuck Ally, I'm sorry. I didn't mean to blurt it out like that.'

'It's okay Frankie. Let me help? I know you don't know me well, but honestly; I might be able to. When did it start? There was more than one? You said they.'

'The first time it happened I was eleven, the age Becky is now. When I look at her, I think I was just a baby.'

'Do you want to talk about it?'

He stared out to sea. 'I don't know! I used to be able to control the feelings, but recently I started to feel angry again. I don't want to have kids because I'm scared that I won't be able to protect them. But now I'm losing the woman I love because of how I feel, and I can't tell her because I don't know how to try to explain it to Lynne.'

'Tell me about it Frankie,' Ally said, touching his arm lightly.

Frankie sighed and looked away. 'It started out as the priest being nice to me. None of the other teachers in the school were. Alfie was clever, so was Davie. And Willie, well, he could run rings around us on the football pitch. So, I suppose it was something I craved, the attention I mean.' Frankie sighed, and Ally could see the pain in his face. 'Joe reckons I probably have ADHD, so I would imagine that I was quite difficult to teach.'

'Have you spoken to Joe about the abuse?'

'God no, I don't think I could tell another man about it. I managed to tell Davie, Willie and Alfie a little. Their faces, they were so shocked. I couldn't do it . . . tell them . . . tell them what it was like.'

'Try to begin at the beginning Frankie! Tell me what you can, and we can fill in the rest later. I think you need to talk. If it helps don't look at me when you are saying it.'

'Father Gerard, he was really good to me. Nothing happened for a long time then he started to make suggestions, play games. It began with him touching me. I didn't like it at first, then he gave me a blow job and I came. Fuck Ally!' he gasped. 'I . . . I got.'

Ally reached out and took his hand. 'You got confused because you liked it, the sensation?'

He nodded. 'I mean, I thought if I'm not gay, how could I like that?'

'Because it's a sexual function Frankie, not a feeling thing. If I took your penis just now and started touching it, you would probably come. If Willie did it, you would eventually react. That's what a lot of people who abuse children do, it's part of the grooming process. Doing something that the child enjoys and then making them feel some gratitude to the abuser. This way the abuser's perverted need to justify their abuse is satisfied, and the victim is easier to control. This works especially well in a religious context because there is the guilt thing as well.'

Frankie nodded, 'I can understand that Ally, but I had never thought of it that way before. The first time he took it further, he sent for me and took me to his flat in the school. I had just come from gym and hadn't showered. He put me in a bath and was really gentle with me, almost loving. I was embarrassed being

248

naked in front of him. I was twelve, and well . . . you know? Then he made me kneel on the bed and oiled me up then he . . . I remember he kept stopping and putting objects in me.' Frankie stared out to sea saying nothing for a few minutes. Ally could see this was difficult for him. She waited, saying nothing until he composed himself. 'The brothers all carried a truncheon to beat us with, in their belts. He lifted his from the chair and put it in me. It really hurt, and I started to cry. He took it out and hit me with it and made me wank him.

He sent for me a couple of days later this time he made me give him a blow job. I was really sick Ally, spewed my ring. Even now what? 35 years later . . . I can still remember the taste, even the thought of it makes me boak.' He shook his head and wiped his eyes with the back of his hand. 'I learned pretty quickly to swallow, I also became a total hypochondriac, inventing illnesses to stay off school.'

'Oh Frankie, I'm so sorry. That must have been awful.' Ally could see the little boy he had been in her mind's eye and feel the pain and confusion, but she knew that she had to let him continue to speak for as long as he needed to.

'It got worse Ally; he told my parents he would help me catch up when I missed school. For a while he just made me touch him and give him oral, then one day he raped me. He was praying all the time he was doing it and made me pray too. Afterwards I was in shock, I was so sore I could hardly walk, and bleeding. I couldn't tell anyone because he told me that god would punish people I loved if I did.

Didn't you try to tell someone?'

Frankie sighed. 'Who would have believed me over a priest in those days. Then he pulled me in every week and did it. He was never gentle with me again, he just abused me. He used to talk to god and pray whilst he buggered me Ally, asking God to forgive me for making him sin. It went on for about two years where he did everything imaginable to me.'

'How did it end?'

'Just before I turned fourteen, he sent for me and there were two other men there. One I knew, Brother Matthew, and another monk. They made me give the one I didn't know a blow job while they watched, and then he and Brother Matthew spit roasted me. You know what that is?'

Ally nodded, saying nothing.

'It didn't hurt as much by then; sadly, I was used to it. But the humiliation of these dirty bastards using me like that was the end for me. I had just had my first sexual experience with a girl and realised that I probably wasn't gay. I thought about killing myself for a few days then I went back and told him that if he ever touched me again, I would tell someone. He tried to hit me, and I decked him, I was so angry that I had to walk away before I killed him. I went to my geography teacher, who wasn't a priest, and told him ... not all of it ... just enough. The next thing he was gone, the priest I mean, and it was over. The geography teacher also disappeared, but I was safe. Fuck Ally, I've never told anyone most of that. I just put my head down and got through school. Didn't draw attention to myself.'

'Frankie, I think you're just ready to deal with it now. If you really do love Lynne, you need to tell her all you've told me.'

He wiped away tears from his eyes. 'I don't know if I can. How do you explain that you let someone abuse your body for years and did nothing?'

'Frankie, you were a child, Lynne's a journalist, she'll have come across abuse. I think she'll be more likely to be hurt you didn't tell her. She loves you Frankie. She thinks you don't love her enough to have a baby with her when it's all about trust. You were abused by people in a position of trust, you are bound to have difficulties. You should also look at counselling, from someone who you don't know personally. It's easier to off-load this stuff if you're not afraid of shocking the person listening. I think that you've only given me the highlights.' She reached over and wiped away his tears with her fingers. You are probably ready to start counselling Frankie; I can put you in touch with someone who can help.'

'You're a very clever lady Ally Campbell. I actually feel a bit better having said it all, like I said I've never told anyone the details. I think you are a bit of a miracle worker.'

Ally put her arm around Frankie, he leaned his head on her shoulder. 'No, it's my bread and butter, being able to get people to tell me things. I quite often take statements from historical abuse sufferers, so I've learned the questions to ask and how to ask them. It's common for it all to come out like that. You're just ready to deal with it. I also know just from what you have told me that a prosecution could be possible. You have such a good detailed memory of it all. If any of these men are still alive, there's a distinct possibility that the procurator fiscal would proceed with a case, then it would be up to a court to decide.'

'Do you think I would be believed? It would be made public too wouldn't it? I don't know if I could do it, it's been a secret so long that it's become part of who I am I suppose.'

Ally looked around at Frankie. There is a point of law called the Moorov Doctrine, unique to Scottish law. Basically, it's used when there is evidence of similar patterns of abuse. With some of the religious abuse especially, these men were creatures of habit so there's often real similarities in what they did and the way they did it. There is the possibility there's someone else on file who's come forward and the police might be sitting with evidence. It can be like that with historical abuse. Not enough to start proceedings, but the doubt is there so they log the statement and keep it on file. There is also the teacher you told; he can verify you told him.

'Where do I start Ally if I wanted to do it? I'm not sure if I do, but . . . well I will think about it.'

'When you feel ready, go to the police and tell them as much as you can. You know there have been other survivors of this kind of thing who have managed to get the perpetrators jailed. Police are keen to follow allegations of historical abuse.'

'If I did it . . . went to the police. Would you go with me Ally?'

'If you want, but you need to talk to Lynne about it too. I don't think she'll think any less of you for it, but she might get upset if you haven't trusted her enough to tell her.' Frankie helped Ally to her feet, they embraced.

'You're something else Ally, thanks for listening. It was really easy to talk to you about it.'

'I haven't done anything Frankie. You were just ready to talk. Probably that's why you have had all the relationship difficulties recently. You've let what these men did ruin half your life. Frankie don't allow them to stop you and Lynne being happy. Pushing people you love away well it's a symptom of what you've been through. The fear of not being able to protect your own children is also part of most parents psyche. Some people are afraid that they will be abusers too because they are so confused. I think that you'll be a better parent because of it, Frankie. You'll bring children up, able to talk to you about things.'

'Ally, could you do me a favour?'

'If I can.'

'Could you tell Alfie, Willie and Davie the whole story. I told them it happened once, and I played that down, I didn't tell them what happened. I don't know how to say to them I let him rape me once a week for two years. I've tried to tell them a couple of times, but I can't say the words. Could you ask them to keep it to themselves for now though? I know Father Gerrard once did something to Willie, because he told me, but I don't think it was just as extreme as what happened to me.'

Ally spoke to Willie later that day, without giving him any details. He arranged for Alfie and Davie to come to the villa. Frankie sat upstairs on the balcony whilst Ally told them the story. All three men were shocked at the level of the abuse. Alfie was upset that his brother had not told him the extent of his suffering.

'He's my twin Ally. I should have been able to feel his pain should I not?' he cried. 'When we were eight, I broke my leg, they had to give him painkillers too because he could feel it. When Wull split his eye with the catapult, I felt it. When he told us after his outburst before my wedding, he said the old bastard did things to him. That was bad enough. No wonder he is such a fucking prick at times, coping with all that shit on his own! Ally, is it right to be angry at him for not telling me?'

Ally shrugged, 'Alfie, it's taken him all these years to be able to talk about it. I knew because that's what I do for a living. As soon as Willie told me that he had disclosed abuse, it all fitted in with his behaviour.' She put her hand on Alfie's arm and spoke gently to him. 'Would it do either of you any good if you're angry at him for not telling you?' Ally said, looking him in the eye.

'No, I don't suppose it would, but I need to speak to him.' He looked around at the shocked faces of the other two men. 'We all do. We should have noticed at the time. The amount of times we've all had a go at him because of his behaviour and the way he has treated Lynne, he never said how bad it was.'

'He couldn't do it, tell you, especially you Alfie. It's the emotional part of it all.' Ally sighed, feeling emotional herself. 'He was groomed and abused over a long period of time. He is actually doing well to have coped and been as successful as he is. That's probably because of all of you. He just needs you all to understand, and not to treat him any different. He's still your brother, and your friend.'

'I thought he had been touched up, made to give oral, that was bad enough. But this? Two fucking years he suffered and we ...I never knew!' Alfie looked at Ally. 'He has known you five minutes and he told you all that!'

'He's ready to deal with it, that's all Alfie. I just asked the right questions and let him talk. You three need to just listen. Let him know that you don't think any less of him and will support him.'

Ally went upstairs and spoke to Frankie who returned with her to the group. Alfie stood up and embraced his brother; tears falling, the two men stood sobbing. 'You fucking daft prick!' Alfie sobbed. 'You could have told me how bad it was.' When Ally was sure they could speak calmly, she left them to discuss it all with a bottle of Willie's malt whisky and went to bed with her kindle.

When Willie came to bed several hours later, he was drunk, tearful and emotional. 'Ally how do you manage to do your job? Hearing things like that? Why don't you get fucking angry and want to get drunk and forget what you hear? Folk like you, Stevie and Ruby, you are all so normal, yet you deal with that kind of shit. Before I knew you, I had this view of social workers, but I never realised the kind of abuse you hear about and deal with. It must have some effect on you, do something, listing to all that stuff?'

Ally sighed then nodded, 'yeah it does sometimes, it's why it's important to talk about it, offload. You can't tell your loved ones. I mean when someone says, did you have a good day at work? What do you say? It's the same for anyone who works with trauma. I think it's always there. You learn to deal with it and shut it out, social workers mostly develop a black sense of humour too. Sometimes though, it gets to you wakes you up at three in the morning, or you get flashbacks when you're driving to work, sometimes you drink too much to forget.' Ally sighed and looked at him. 'It's called vicarious trauma Willie. It does affect you, but someone needs to be there to listen. I've been lucky, always had good managers who let me off load, and friends like Stevie and Ruby who gave me peer support. There is a lot of good stuff in our work too, and a lot of funny things happen. We try to make people's lives better, not worse. Sometimes we make tough choices, other times we hear real tragedy. I also get to see people come out from the most awful situations and go on. There are happy and sad endings. If you let it get you down, the bad guys win.'

***

Over the next few weeks Willie watched with pride as Ally grew stronger. She gained weight, slept better and returned to the strong, confident woman she had been before. The dreams and the night terrors still came but she could control her responses to them. They remained in Majorca longer than first intended as Ally was making good, steady progress.

Despite Willie's reservations, Joe McCann had proved to be a godsend to Ally. He had remained in contact by video link with her and continued to counsel her through her recovery. There was also the beginning of a wonderful friendship with Betty and Alfie; the two couples spent a lot of time together. A few nights before they returned to Scotland, Willie and Ally had them over for dinner.

'I'm dreading going back to Scotland, my sons tell me it is really cold and wet just now. You're so lucky to live here.'

'Hmm, Betty might not agree with you Ally. She wants to go back to Scotland,' Alfie said, smiling at his beautiful wife.

'You do?' Ally asked.

Betty nodded. 'I'm worried about the girls' education. Becky is now approaching the age for secondary school, and Andi is doing so well academically, that I worry about neglecting their education. The international school here is good, but it's not the same as the education they would get in Scotland. We have considered boarding school, them staying with our parents and being educated in Scotland. We're a family though, and it just isn't right to split the girls from their sisters. Just now we're looking into me and the girls coming back and Alfie staying, here having just weekends and holidays together.' She looked at Willie. 'We want for Alfie to come back to Scotland permanently eventually, though.'

'We have a board meeting next month,' Alfie said quietly. 'I was going to discuss it with you, Frankie and David then. We'd not want to move right away, but I'd rather be with them.'

Ally looked at Willie, then at Alfie and Betty. 'You have obviously put a lot of thought into this.'

'When we came over permanently, Becky was four and Andi two. Amy and Billie were born here. I've loved it Ally, but it was never to be forever. Real life and real issues take over,' Betty said, smiling and taking her husband's hand in hers. 'I would definitely retire over here though. I love the relaxed lifestyle.'

CHAPTER
TWENTY-NINE

'Ally, you look wonderful, what a tan you have. Did you just lie in the sun for six weeks?'

'No, it's just the lifestyle there, it agrees with me. I wish you had come out for a week when we were there. I've never known you to knock back the chance of a holiday.'

Stevie smiled and lifted the coffee from his kitchen worktop. Ally took the mug from him. They were sitting at the kitchen table in Stevie's house.

'How are you Stevie? I know you didn't take up Joe's offer of counselling but thank you for talking to him about my missing hours. Are you sure you are alright, don't need counselling?'

'Ally, I haven't felt the need for counselling. I've been surprisingly alright so far. I get occasional flashbacks, but nothing too serious. Unconscious thoughts yeah, I suppose so. When I get the nightmares, I get up and write until I'm able to sleep. You know we always try to make people take counselling if they experience trauma, one size doesn't fit all though. I guess people all cope differently. Doesn't make them weaker or stronger, it's just different coping mechanisms, who knows? I might need help later, but I think I will know when, and how to ask for it.' He sighed and looked at Ally, 'I'll tell you what I do hate though, the hero tag, you know the headlines *hero social worker goes back to work*. That annoys me and it's that kind of stuff that makes people scared to ask for help. I . . . we only did what most people would do in our situation, I was fucking scared Ally.'

'I think I feel survivor guilt Stevie, I know it's not logical I've been working through it, but it's there.'

Stevie pursed his lips, 'If I feel guilty about anything it's that you suffered so much during and after and I really didn't.' He took her hand in his across the table. 'You always did overthink things though Mrs Campbell. Still, I'm glad you're home. Are you coming back to work or does the WAG lifestyle suit you?'

'I had a meeting with the acting Service Manager this morning as it happens. But you knew that didn't you?'

He nodded. 'I should've been a detective.'

'I'm coming back next month, one day a week to start with.' She sighed. 'It'll be really strange without Gerry and Ruby though.'

Stevie nodded. 'Where you going to live?'

'In my house. Where else would I live?'

'What about Willie?'

'He'll live in Glasgow during the week when he needs to, and my house here when he doesn't. We'll be together at Loch Lomond for weekends when we can.'

'Is that what he wants?'

'No, it's what we both want. Stevie, you're one of my closest friends and we've shared so many things. Please be happy for me?'

Stevie sighed and put his hand over hers on the table. 'I am Ally, and I don't dislike Willie. I can see how happy you are. I'm just afraid for you.'

'Don't be Stevie, this is right for me. Stevie, do you think we can get back the friendship we had?'

'I wasn't aware we had lost it!'

'Stevie, please be my friend just now. We're about to be grand-parents. We've been friends all these years. Don't let us lose that.'

'I don't want to lose it either Ally, it's simply hard to share you with another man.'

'I feel the same about your new girlfriend.'

Stevie smiled and looked into his friend's eyes. 'Did Kiera tell you?'

'She did, but I wish you had Stevie. How hard could it have been to say to me that you had a secret love?'

'Like you can talk about keeping relationships secret Ally!'

'What's she like?'

Stevie smiled. 'Oh, she is a teacher at the academy, biology. Her name is Cathy, and it's a casual thing.

'Do I know her?'

'Doubt it she came back here after her divorce; she was living down south for years. She's back in Ayrshire living with her parents in Dalrymple whilst she looks for somewhere. Stevie smiled, 'I think you'll like her she's lovely. She's a bit younger than me actually, but really sensible and worldly wise.'

'Why don't you bring Cathy casually over for dinner at the weekend with us? We're going to be here, I have a hospital appointment in Ayr on Friday for a pre-med thing, then surgery on Monday. Dad moves into his new flat in a fortnight, but he is playing snooker on Saturday in Glasgow and staying with a mate, it will just be me and Willie. I really want you and Willie to be friends.'

'Stevie smiled and nodded. 'Saturday, it is then.'

'Yes.'

'Sevenish? It will be Willie cooking and not you?' Stevie said grinning, 'I'd quite like Cathy not to have food poisoning.'

'Of course, Willie will be cooking, its either that or takeaway. I can get to know Cathy whilst you and Willie watch sports on

TV. Ally put down her coffee cup and stood up and hugged him. 'Stevie, you know I love you, don't you?'

'I love me too Ally. Oh, and you. Did you see the scan pictures?' Stevie asked.

Ally nodded and put down her coffee mug. 'I can't believe you paid all that money for the 3D ones.'

'Well she is my only child Ally. Hmm it's pretty amazing, isn't it?'

'Worth the money?'

'Absolutely.'

'You're looking good by the way Stevie. Everyone in the office is saying how much better you look these days. You suit your hair like that. Does Cathy like it?'

Stevie smiled and nodded, well I have a young thing, so I need to look a bit trendier, make an effort. She thinks I look like Keanu Reeves. I had met her just before we got hurt. I was at a meeting at the school, I never thought she would be interested in me, but I had arranged to meet her the weekend after and obviously that never happened. She sent me a nice card and when I got home she came and visited. Its early days but . . . I like her a lot.'

They heard the door slam, and Kiera and Scott came into the kitchen. Kiera waddled over and sat down, the baby bulge making her small frame look even more fragile. 'Well, was everything alright?' Ally asked.

'Yes, the baby is growing normally and no worries. Still three weeks to go though. I feel huge.'

'It's because you're so small Kiera. I was the same. The boys were both eight pounds and I was massive by the end.'

'What about Abby?' Scott asked.

'She was premature, only four pounds when she was born. She was so tiny.' Ally sighed remembering. Her face clouded over, then she smiled. 'I remember Danny thought she was a doll when your dad brought you to the hospital.'

Scott looked thoughtful. 'It's one of the only clear memories I have of Dad and Gran, Mum, going to the hospital. He took us to McDonald's. Gran gave him a ticking off for feeding us junk food because Danny was sick in the car on the way back. Then he was hyper and punched the baby.'

'He didn't punch her,' Ally said, shaking her head. 'We were really worried about how you would adapt to the baby. We bought you baby dolls to fuss over to get used to the idea of a baby. Danny's said mama, if you pressed its tummy. He thought Abby was a doll, so he pushed her in the tummy to make her speak.'

'Never could stop being social workers, we had to analyse it all.' Stevie smiled, remembering. 'A lesson we still pass on to all the pregnant mums we tell to try a doll when there is a toddler sibling. Don't buy one with a tummy squeak.'

'I remember looking at Abby, she was so tiny, and Dad saying, 'you have to look after her now.' Six weeks later our lives changed forever, yet I don't remember any of that. The next thing I remember is, I think, Christmas day and the adults all crying, but I didn't know why, because Heaven seemed like a really great place. It's also my first real memory of Kiera. Stevie came over with Ruby and brought her to play with us.'

Stevie smiled ruefully. 'That was probably the funeral, not Christmas Day Scott. And it wasn't Ruby, it was Laura. She looked after you, your mum was still in hospital. You did spend Christmas with us that year though, but you were at ours.'

Kiera looked at Scott and then at Ally. 'Does it hurt to talk about Abby?'

'Sometimes, but I learned to live with the pain. It seemed so unfair then and still does now. I lost my mother, my husband and my child that day. Half our family wiped out in an instant.

By the time I came around from the coma, the funerals had been held, so it was a long time before it felt real. I don't think you ever really get over it, the death of a child. There's always that 'what would she be like now' thing, and the regret can be like a physical pain. My mum I miss every day, her and I were close, me being an only one. Ralph . . . oh he was an amazing man, wasn't he Stevie?'

Stevie nodded sadly. 'We were great mates; I still miss him. I knew at the interview we would get on. He told me later he was only asked to be on it because someone was sick. The team at the time was mainly women, and I think the two things that sold me to him in the interview were my diabetes and the fact that I was a man. When the accident happened, we were all shocked to the core though.' Stevie looked at Ally and put his hand over hers on the table. 'Your mother, despite her pain and grief, pulled herself together quickly and just got on with it. Amazing woman.'

'I was angry for such a long time. I had two small children who needed me though, so I just had to go on. It's always there though. The pain becomes part of who you are. You can either lie in a dark room saying, *'why me?'* or you can make the people you lost proud of you. Doesn't make it hurt less.' Ally stood up, wiped away a stray tear and smiled. 'Anyway, I had better get going. Willie is taking me out to dinner for my birthday.' She picked up her walking stick.

'Where's he taking you?' Stevie asked.

Ally shrugged. 'Big surprise.' She smiled. 'He's like a big kid when he's planning something. He wants me to get dressed up, said I had to wear bling!'

'Do you actually have any bling?' Kiera asked, smiling. 'You're not really a bling, person, are you?'

'No but I'll improvise. Little black dress! All this having to socialise in a formal setting regularly is new to me. I'm used to a pie and a pint on a Friday night after work and getting dressed up once a year for the Christmas do.' She hugged them, and then made for the door.

At five o'clock she was sitting in Willie's car as he drove down the A77 turning on the M8, she asked. 'Where are we going?'

'No, wait just a little longer.' Willie took the slip road for Glasgow Airport. He turned and looked at Ally, 'just a wee trip!'

'The airport? What have you done? I have a hospital appointment the day after tomorrow, and I've asked Stevie and his new girlfriend to dinner on Saturday and you are cooking.'

'We're flying to Paris by private jet for dinner. Then dancing.' He patted her knee, 'well, shuffling around the dance floor on your gammy leg in our case.' He grinned at her. 'Then one night in a posh hotel, so you can thank me properly. You'll be back in plenty of time for your appointment.'

'I don't have anything with me Willie!'

'You do, I got your kids to raid your wardrobe. Well, Kiera did actually. Scott and Danny didn't want to rummage in your underwear drawer.'

***

'That was beautiful Willie,' Ally said, putting down her fork. 'What a wonderful restaurant. The view is tremendous. You can see the whole of Paris from up here. You're bloody mad Willie, this must have cost a fortune. It's not even a special birthday.'

'It is Ally, it's the first one we're spending officially together. Last year we had only just started going out, I was fighting with my feelings, so didn't make a fuss.'

'Willie, you bought me diamond earrings!'

'Which you returned to me. You said in the note, *'diamonds won't get you into my knickers.'* I was just being nice too. Spent ages picking them.'

'Willie, you got your secretary to buy them. It was on the delivery note! Are you going to deny you were trying to lay me?'

Willie shook his head, 'no you were spot on. I was. I couldn't work out how do impress you, you were a bit of an enigma, I had never met anyone like you. Penny only did the order, I picked them.' He smiled at the waiter who disappeared into the kitchen, returning a few minutes later with a cake complete with sparklers and candles. Ally bent her head to blow the candles out and gasped. On the top was the most exquisite ring she had ever seen. It was a large square-cut emerald surrounded by diamonds. Willie got down on one knee in front of her. 'Ally I love you, please marry me?'

'Willie, I don't know what to say?' Ally spluttered. 'I was so not expecting this.'

'Then say yes,' he said, looking into her eyes. 'You know you want to. I picked the ring and bought it myself. Argyle Arcade, I'll show you the receipt if you want. I know how you feel about marriage, but this is important to me Ally. I want the whole world to know how much I love you. I'll take your surname if you want. Please Ally say yes, look at me I'm shaking with fear.'

'Yes. I'll marry you. I do believe I love you too Mr Ogilvy, and I want to be Mrs Ogilvy if we do it.' Suddenly the room burst into applause, as the staff and the other diners clapped and cheered.

The waiter appeared with a bottle of champagne. Willie wrapped his arms around her and kissed her. 'I love you so much Ally. I'll make you happy, you wait and see. Now let's see if it fits.' He took the ring from the cake and slid it onto Ally's finger. It fitted perfectly.

'You're amazing, you guessed my ring size perfectly!'

Willie pursed his lips, 'Danny borrowed your engagement ring for me, and we got it sized.'

'Did you involve everyone I know in this Willie?'

'Pretty much. It should be a family affair.' He took her hand and kissed it, stood up and sat back down beside her as the restaurant returned to normal. 'Ally I don't want to wait to get married. At our age there doesn't seem much point in a long engagement.'

CHAPTER

THIRTY

'Christmas Eve? Mum! That's only what? eight weeks away!' Scott Campbell looked at his mother and shook his head. Are you mad, what happened to marriage is slavery and all your feminist ideals? Shocking Mother, double standards.' Scott grinned, 'will be an amazing wedding though all of his showbiz and sports pals. Wow.'

Ally shrugged. 'That's not what we want. We are going to have a small winter-themed wedding, just us and a few close friends, then have Christmas with you all before going on honeymoon. Kiera you will have had the baby and we can all be there. It'll be good to have something positive to think about at Christmas. I agree with Willie on that.'

'How did Willie's kids take it Mum?' Danny asked.

Ally smiled. 'Not as badly as we thought they would. We've arranged a dinner at Willie's house next Saturday night for you all to meet up and start getting to know each other. It's Willie's weekend for having Euan, his youngest. Keira are you alright? You look as though you're in pain.'

Keira gasped; she was sitting on Ally's couch, and her face reddened.

Scott moved to sit beside her, 'are you alright babe?' Keira whispered something in his ear and Ally, watching intently, realised the young girl was embarrassed.

'Mum, Keira's water has just broken. We think she's in labour.'

'Ally, I'm so sorry, I know this is not a good day for this to happen, with it being Abby's birthday! Your new sofa is all wet too.' Keira began to cry.

'It's only a sofa, and I'll cope with the date. Now, come on let's get this show on the road. Scott, you'd better phone the hospital then call her mum and Stevie. Willie's on his way here. I'll wait for him and come up to the hospital later.' Ally kissed the young couple. 'It's all good. Keira, stop crying and breathe. How far apart are your contractions?'

***

'Oh God, she is so beautiful Kiera!' Ally gasped, looking down at her four-hour-old granddaughter.

'All six-pound six ounce of her,' Stevie said, smiling.

'Dad she's three kilos,' Kiera gasped. 'You need to think kilos.'

'She looks like that picture of Abby you have in your bedroom,' Danny said quietly.

'I noticed that too Mum, as soon as she was born,' Scott said, looking sadly at his mother and brother. 'I held her and thought *she looks like Mum!* Then she opened her eyes and it was, *oh my god. It's like the same baby!*'

'She's just the first baby girl to be born in the family since Abby, and there was bound to be a likeness. I think she looks like you Keira, but yes, I can see us in her too.' Ally kissed the top of the baby's head and smiled through tears. 'Abby was very like you Scott. You favour my side of the family that's all. Thea will be her own person with her own personality. Thank you for putting Abigail in her name Kiera, I'm very touched.'

267

Willie, knowing how much Ally was struggling, put his arm protectively around her and kissed her cheek. Willie had come to the house to find Ally in floods of tears; she was over the moon about the baby, glad Keira and the baby were safe. However, the grief of losing her husband, mother and especially her child was always there. Some moments, Willie knew, she found harder than others. He had held her, cried with her, then drove her to the hospital to visit. Laura, Keira's mum, who was also heavily pregnant, had been in the delivery room with Scott and her daughter, and she had left to allow Stevie and Ally some time with the young couple and their new granddaughter.

'You'll be able to get a dress fitting now Keira. Willie and I would like you to be my bridesmaid, along with his daughters. Although we are keeping it small, we want you all involved.' Ally smiled at the young mum, who grinned back.

'There's still two months to go. I plan to be back in my own clothes.'

'Now you'll be able to go too baby Thea,' Scott said, kissing his daughter's head.

'I can't believe I'm marrying a granny,' Willie laughed.

'The ring is beautiful Ally!' Keira sighed, twirling it on her own finger. 'Why an emerald? That's quite an unusual stone for an engagement ring.'

'Could be controversial in Glasgow Willie, you buying a green stone!' Danny laughed.

'Well, Ralph bought me a ruby one when we got engaged, and Willie has been engaged a few times and has never bought an emerald for anyone. He also says it matches my eyes.'

'No wonder you have had so many women Willie,' Scott laughed, nudging him. 'You're a real smoothie.'

Ally smiled and took a box out of her pocket. 'I'd like you to have this Kiera.'

Kiera opened the box; inside Ally's ruby engagement ring sparkled back at her. She gasped, 'I can't take this. It's yours.'

'Kiera, my daughter died, but if she'd lived, I would have wanted her to be like you. She would be sixteen today, and I often wonder what she would have been like. Ralph is Thea's grandfather; I think if there's a heaven he'll approve. In time you can pass it on to your daughter.'

'Why don't I just put it on you, and we can get engaged too? If it was good enough for Kate to wear Diana's ring then it's good enough for us,' Scott said.

'You old romantic! I think I will marry you Scott Campbell.'

Willie laughed and slapped Scott on the back. 'No wonder you think I'm a smoothie. That is possibly the most unromantic proposal anyone has ever made.'

'I was thinking cheapskate,' Danny said, grinning.

Scott looked around. 'I actually asked you if I could propose, didn't I Stevie?'

'I said I would give him a thousand pounds and a ladder,' Stevie cried, winking at Ally. 'Did you ask Jimmy if you could marry Ally, Willie?'

'Of course, I did, right after I asked Danny!'

CHAPTER

THIRTY-ONE

'I'm much too old for a hen party!' Ally protested.

Betty smiled. 'No, you're not. You needed to have something. The girls all thought that you should.'

'Frankie's even picking up the bar bill and he's given us the VIP area at the club. He's so grateful to you for talking me into meeting him for dinner,' Lynne said, smiling and putting her arm around Ally. 'Thank you,' she said.

Ally winced.

'Are you still sore?' Yvonne asked. 'Did the drugs not work?'

'I actually didn't take them today, so I can drink. My recovery consultant says it's the dampness here in Scotland, it makes the pain worse. Its mainly just the shoulder and one hip now that are bad, but they are looking at surgery options, which I really don't want. We're going to spend more time abroad next winter to see if it makes a difference.' She looked over at Betty Dastis. 'We are kind of thinking Betty, we might swap places with you and let Alfie come back and work here. Willie's Scotland contract is up at the end of next season, he's going to stand down. He'll need to do something, so that might be the answer.'

Betty smiled happily, 'that would solve several problems Ally. Have a drink, see if that helps the pain. If it doesn't, you can just get too drunk to notice.'

Ruby looked concerned. 'Ally, is it awful?'

'No, it's bearable. I had so many injuries some of it is because arthritis has set in now. I might have got it anyway. They reckon some of it is from the car smash, now coming back to bite me on the bum . . . and the arm and leg and shoulder and ribs. Alcohol and heat help.'

Ally had been building a relationship with Willie's children, and his three daughters were here with them. Ally realised that the elder ones had been through three marriage breakups with their dad, and they were understandably concerned about Willie's impending marriage to her. She knew better than to try to force them to accept her, and she was touched that Leah, Korrie and Jade had come to the hen party. Ruby had brought Kiera with her, but they didn't stay long as Kiera had to get home to feed baby Thea. Ally was glad, however, that they had made the effort, especially as Ruby and Gerry were now living in the South of France with Alexis.

After the other guests had gone Ally sat upstairs in Frankie's flat with Lynne, Lesley, Yvonne and Betty. The women had become good friends to her over the last few months. They were taking Ally for a spa day as a present in the morning. Frankie had gone to stay with Willie, leaving them his flat. They had drunk a lot, and they huddled on the sofa in their PJs giggling about the night they had just spent in the club. Ally had learned she could trust these four women; they had embraced her into their tight little group, she was relaxed in their company. They began to discuss their first sexual experiences with their respective partners.

'I was really drunk the first time with Frankie,' Lynne said. 'It actually happened here in this room. It wasn't that great cos he was as drunk as me. Afterwards we ended up in the bathroom with him holding my hair out of the way while I was sick. I'd only met him that night too. I was celebrating my first TV news broadcast. I meant it to be a one-night stand, a bit of rough, but he grew on me. Next morning, we did it again sober. Took me a few weeks to accept how I felt about him, and believe me I fought it, but within a month I knew I was hooked.'

'Tart,' Lesley laughed. 'I had to almost rape David. We've been together since we were fifteen. We didn't have sex until we were seventeen. It wasn't for want of me trying, he was just so shy. When you look at the difference between him and Willie, with them being family, it's absolutely amazing. He's good at it now. I taught him everything he knows.'

Yvonne nodded, 'he definitely has a lot more confidence. It's kind of weird, the twins and Willie, they make fun of him, but if anyone else does they get angry. Davie used to be nervy and lacked confidence, but you've been good for him Lesley, he's so laid back now. Him and Alfie were always dead brainy at school.' She looked at Betty, 'talking of tarts, tell Ally how you met Alfie!'

Betty smiled, remembering. 'Alfie kind of wooed me, he says it was love at first sight for him. I was doing a fashion show in Edinburgh and he was there with his girlfriend. He kept watching me on the catwalk. I noticed him of course, how could I miss him? He came backstage. He told me she was his sister, and I agreed to go out with him next night. He admitted over dinner that he was in a relationship, but that he had just ended it the night we met. I would normally have walked away, but a bit like you Lynne, I thought what the hell, just do it! They're so good-looking, the twins. Then that weekend we went out in Glasgow. We got wasted and did it on every surface in the flat.'

'The one Willie lives in now?' Ally gasped.

Betty nodded and grinned. 'It saw some action that night. But the girlfriend let herself in, she had come to collect some stuff and return the key for the lift. We were naked on the floor in the lounge, no hiding place. I was mortified. I knew though that what I felt for him was special. Alfie said the relationship had been going downhill and when he saw me, felt what he felt, he knew it was over. She saw him looking at me, and they had a row. Karen stormed off, so he came backstage.' Betty smiled and looked around. 'From the moment I met him, I never wanted to be with anyone else.'

Yvonne smiled sadly, tears filling her eyes. 'I was a bit of a wild child and had been with a few guys before I settled with Vernon. I'd known him all my life, we were friends first. It stared because we had both fallen out with partners and went out for a drink. The first time we did it was in the back of one of those old tenement closes in Parker Street. He dared me to do it. We'd gone to a nightclub, supposedly to pull but we didn't. Mainly because we were flirting all night, we walked home. We were drunk, and we did it. I can remember afterwards, we both looked at each other in amazement. He looked like the twins but was just special, and the sex was great, memorable. I have been divorced twice, widowed once and now separated. I think if Vernon had lived, I would still be married. He was *the* one.' She looked thoughtful. 'You know, I really think that's what went wrong with all my subsequent relationships . . . no one ever lived up to the memory.'

Betty smiled and put her arm around Yvonne. 'He was a great guy I hear Yvonne. Alfie worshipped him.'

Yvonne nodded and took the tissue Ally held out to her. 'I still have nightmares about the police coming to the door that night to tell me he was dead. Twenty years, and my feelings are still as raw sometimes as they were that night.'

Ally nodded. 'An accident is a strange one isn't it? I wakened up after the car accident, I was too ill to understand, it was New Year's Day when Dad had to tell me that half my family were dead and buried. I didn't think I would ever be whole again.'

She put her hand out and touched Yvonne's arm, 'you get used to the pain though, don't you? You just end up living with it, but you have had no time to say goodbye, and you have so many regrets. It took me years to think about another relationship.' She smiled, 'my first time was with Ralph. We met at uni, Fresher's Week. I was a good girl, a virgin. Took me ages to sleep with him, and I thought I'd been careful. I got pregnant in my last year of my degree, managed to finish it before I had the baby. We had to get married though, our parents were shamed. I'd still have married him though, even if I hadn't been pregnant, maybe just not as quick.'

'What was he like Ally? Ralph?' Lynne asked.

'He was, I suppose he was a bit like Stevie, very laid back but gentle and kind. Him and Stevie became friends straight away he was more Ralph's friend than mine at that time.'

'Have you and Stevie never been you know? Had a thing? You are so close?' Yvonne asked.

Ally shook her head, 'god no, we are close but not that way. Don't know why, because he probably is the type of man I would have gone for before . . . well, before I met Willie. I suppose sometimes you are too close to be intimate.'

'What was Ralph like? Was it the same as Willie? Do you feel the same?' Yvonne persisted

'Ralph was . . . oh, he was special. Sex was good. He was one of these guys though, who needed to know you were satisfied, or he couldn't do it. You know how sometimes you just want,' she blushed, before continuing, 'you just want a shag, scratch an itch. He didn't do spontaneity. He was, perhaps, too considerate if that makes sense? That would be my only complaint I suppose. He was a great husband and a fantastic father though.'

'What about you and Willie, Ally?' Yvonne asked.

'It's actually quite boring ladies,' Ally said, smiling. 'Not the sex!' She rolled her eyes, 'that's amazing. Just how we got together, it took a while. The first time we slept together we were in Majorca. I met him in July last year started seeing him seriously at the beginning of September, so I'd known him more than a year before we had sex.'

'You were ill for a lot of it though,' Lynne said, do you think if you hadn't got hurt you would have done it sooner?'

Ally sighed, 'I don't even know if we would still be together. We'd had a big row just before I got hurt, I'd been keeping him at arm's length. He thought it was because of his reputation, but it was because I'd not had sex for fifteen years. I kind of flipped out when he tried to make love to me.' Seeing the other women's surprised looks, she added, 'I've some real hang-ups about my body and was terrified of him, well any man, seeing me naked.' Ally put her hands over her face and looked at the others through her fingers. 'I also had googled him. A story came up where a model was saying he was very well endowed. I was terrified. Luckily, after I got hurt, I didn't have any memory of falling out with him. When I was in the hospital, we kind of mucked around. He kept thinking he was giving me space, but I was like *just touch me again please!* He took me out on the boat for the day when I was in hospital. That was the first time he touched me intimately.' Ally blushed. 'He brought me to the most intense orgasm I had ever experienced with one hand. I was left wanting more.'

'Is he as good as they say, Ally?' Betty asked. 'I've always wondered.'

'Hey, you,' Yvonne said laughing, 'that's my baby brother you are talking about. Well Ally, is he?'

'I've no complaints,' Ally smiled slyly. 'Willie is a very considerate lover and a very experienced one, but I don't want to think about how many women he has slept with before me. Crikey, it must be like one of those AIDS posters you used to get in pub toilets. You know, there am I with my one partner and hundreds of other people because of Willie. He was aware of it though, he went and got tested for everything before he slept with me. Still he's worth it.' She giggled. 'He knows what buttons to push and boy, he pushes them. I was really scared at first because of my injuries. I had a broken pelvis and my thigh was shattered but he was gentle and careful. To be honest, I get tingles in my gut just thinking about what he does to me.' Ally glanced over at Lynne and realised that she was looking at her intently.

'Lynne, what's the story with you and Frankie?' Yvonne asked.

'Oh, it's back on again. He has told me a whole load of stuff about his childhood and it explains a lot of things about him.'

'What about his childhood?' Betty asked. 'Their parents were fantastic, still are. We have a real close family.'

'Some stuff happened that deeply affected him.'

'He'll be spinning you a line!' Lesley said, laughing. 'He's such a bull-shitter, he just wants you back. Frankie went through his childhood as the joker in the pack. Never cared about anything.'

Lynne shook her head. 'No, it's pretty bad. But he doesn't want you to know yet. I think your men know. Willie knows, and he wouldn't lie for Frankie.' Lynne looked at Ally. 'Would he?'

Ally shrugged, 'no I don't believe he would. Willie has a knack of not actually telling you anything he thinks you don't need to know but if you ask him outright, he won't lie.'

Yvonne nodded in agreement. 'Yeah, with Willie it's knowing the right questions to ask. He was always the same. Our mother used to say, 'tell the truth and shame the devil,' but if she didn't ask Willie if something happened, he never volunteered it.' Yvonne giggled. 'For being such a fucking bastard with women, he is remarkably honest and trustworthy. He is also very loyal though. If Frankie had secrets and asked him not to tell anyone, then he won't. In fact, the four of them are like that about each other. You won't get anything from them that one of them has asked the others not to repeat.'

Lynne sighed. 'He just said several times that that there was a reason for Frankie's behaviour and to ask him. Frankie always laughed it off. This time though, he told me. I know I've you to thank for that too Ally. He told me what you did.'

'Oh, come on! You can't leave it like that,' Betty cried, looking at Ally.

Ally shook her head. 'Not our tale to tell Betty.'

CHAPTER

THIRTY-TWO

'Ally, you look gorgeous. What a beautiful gown. The cape's lovely too. You look like one of those Russian princesses.'

Ally smiled at her father, who was wiping away tears. 'Thank you dad, my friend Betty designed it for me. I wasn't sure about the whole dress and veil thing at my age, so she suggested the cape. I must admit I was hoping for a white Christmas and its happened so it's perfect. Anyway, you said you wanted to speak to me before we went?'

'Darling, I'm so proud of you the way you have coped with all the bad things that have happened. I've something to tell you, I hope you will be pleased.' He smiled and took her hand. 'I've met someone and have been seeing her when you think I'm playing snooker. I didn't want to say anything until I was sure. Her name's Margaret. I'll introduce you to her after your honeymoon.'

'Oh, Dad, I'm so happy for you. I'm sure I'll love her.'

'Well it's one less thing for you and Willie to worry about when you start your new life.' He kissed her and held her close.

The door was tapped, and Ruby came in. 'Ally, how beautiful you look. Jimmy, you must be so proud of her?' Jimmy Jackson smiled and nodded.

Ally smoothed down her dress. 'I was just telling dad, Ruby. I wasn't sure about the whole wedding dress thing, but then Betty showed me this in a drawing, her friend made it for us.' Ally lifted the bottle-green velvet cape. It had cream fur trimming around the hood and a cream satin ribbon which matched her satin long-sleeved column dress which had green velvet panels making up the bodice matching the cape. Her hair was piled on top of her head with tiny pearls threaded through it.

'Ally thank you for including Alexis, she's never been a flower girl before. She is so excited.' Ruby hugged her friend, kissed her cheek then left.

Kiera came through from the bedroom wearing her dress, which was the same bottle-green velvet as Ally's cape, carrying her cream velvet cape trimmed with green fur. 'You look beautiful Kiera,' Ally said smiling, 'you'd never guess you've just had a baby.'

Leah, Korrie and Jade followed Kiera into the room. 'You look like a princess Ally!' Jade breathed.

Ally hugged her. 'A very ancient princess, Jade, but thank you.'

Caitlin, Leah's daughter ran into the room with Alexis. Jade scooped her up.

'Come here Lexi. Turn around, your bow needs tied,' Leah called. 'Don't you look beautiful Miss Lexi Weir.'

Ally looked at the four young women in front of her. 'Thank you for agreeing to be bridesmaids. It means a lot to us. Did Thea's dress and shoes fit, Kiera?'

Kiera smiled. 'She looks lovely. Dad's just bringing her up. The little lady decided to fill her nappy as soon as she was dressed. We're leaving in a few minutes. I wanted to make sure you didn't need anything.'

Ally shook her head. 'No, I'm fine and just about ready to face the world.'

Kiera kissed her cheek. 'Ally, you look gorgeous. The dress really works.'

The door was tapped lightly, and Stevie came in holding Thea. He looked at Ally and whistled. He handed the baby to Jade, who was holding out her arms. 'You look fantastic Ally. Girls, you do too.' The four young women filed out, giggling and talking. The two younger ones followed. 'Jimmy, can I have five minutes with Ally?'

'Of course, I'll wait downstairs.'

Ally looked at Stevie as he put his arms around her and held her close. 'Stevie please be happy for me?'

'I am Ally,' he said, letting her go and sitting down on the bed. 'I just wish it was me.'

'You want to get married?'

'No Ally, I wish I was marrying you.'

'Stevie you're kidding?' Ally gasped. Looking into his eyes though, she realised he was serious.

He shook his head and smiled. 'Ally, I loved you for years, even before I split from Laura . . . but I chose to settle for your friendship rather than tell you and lose it. I know now it was the right choice. What you and I have is special. When I saw how quickly you fell for Willie, I realised that you would never have gradually learned to love me, not the way you love him. Ally, I truly am happy for you. I want you to know that I'll always be there for you, no matter what. When we were lying buried in the school, I vowed I would tell you how I felt if we lived. Willie knew I loved you. He guessed right away; he could see it. He loved you enough though, to want you to be happy. He told me to go for it, never did the whole 'she's my woman thing.' I thought at the time it was his ego, but it's not. He's a great guy

Ally. I'm sure that this it the right path for you darling, I just wanted you to know.'

Ally looked at Stevie and smiled, 'I'm really flattered Stevie. I love you so much, it's special, the friendship we have. I think it's as special as being in love because it will always be there. Your friendship means the world to me.' She hugged him and kissed his cheek, then wiped the lipstick away with her finger. 'You are a special man Stephen Marshall. Cathy is a lucky woman.'

***

The guests were already in their seats. Ally and Willie had decided against a religious ceremony, but they did not want to be married at a register office either. They had in the end been rescued by Frankie who suggested they use their luxury Ayrshire spa hotel which was usually closed at Christmas. Snow had been falling all the night before; a white Christmas made it all more special. The hotel grounds looked beautiful and a carpet of white covered the gardens outside the large windows of the Doon Water Hotel. 'Are you nervous?' Yvonne asked her brother as they stood in the hotel foyer.

Before he could answer Frankie butted in, 'Nervous! Why would he be? He has done this more times than the registrar.'

Yvonne slapped Frankie playfully. 'At least he has had the guts to try Dastis, unlike some. When are you going to make an honest woman of Lynne?' Without waiting for Frankie to answer, Yvonne kissed her brother. 'She's wonderful Wull, you're a lucky guy. But she's a lucky lady too.'

The Celebrant appeared beside them and smiled. 'All set William?'

Frankie winked at Billy. 'Are you ready young Mr Ogilvy?'

Billy laughed. 'Yes, I think I am, now that I've sorted out the speech, I'm ready to do this Uncle Frankie.' He looked at his father and grinned. 'You should have maybe filed the speeches from your other weddings Dad and saved us all a lot of work.'

'Oh, you're a real comedian. You didn't let him write your speech, did you?' He nodded at Frankie, who was grinning back as he disappeared through the double doors.

Billy smirked. 'Oh, no Dad, it's all my own work. Frankie is master of ceremonies, so you get two for the price of one.'

The Celebrant led them downstairs and through the large banqueting hall to the table in front of the glass doors leading out to the gardens and the beautiful River Doon setting. Fresh snow was falling outside, it looked like a winter wonderland, she looked at the assembled guests and spoke into the microphone in front of her. 'Could I ask everyone to take their seats, as we are just about to begin!'

At the top of the stairs, Ally held onto her father's arm tightly; he kissed her cheek, and Kiera handed Ally her bouquet. As they descended the stairs cameras flashed and Ally could hear whispers of 'Aww, how lovely! She's beautiful.' She looked over at her sons, Scott smiled broadly, and Danny was wiping away a tear from his eye. They stood next to Stevie who was holding sleeping Thea. Stevie winked at his friend as she passed; beside him stood the lovely Cathy. As Ally reached the front of the room, Willie turned to look at her. Her father kissed her gently on the cheek and placed her hand in Willie's. Willie turned and kissed her on the lips whispering, 'you look stunning babe.'

The Celebrant smiled at Ally, 'are you ready?'

Ally nodded. 'I am!'

'Willie?'

'Oh yes!'

The Celebrant began to speak. 'I have been asked to conduct many weddings, they are all special to the people who are being married and their families. When Willie and Ally came to see me, I was a bit worried that I would not be able to do them justice. They are two incredibly special people as you all know. However, they were adamant that they wanted a small, quiet, simple, non-religious ceremony their loved ones could take part in. All of you here witnessing this union have a special place in their hearts. They wanted to share their love and promises to each other with you. They have asked me to say to you all, they are not going to tug at your heart strings. They're going to exchange their vows, then they want everyone to celebrate with them.'

Despite them trying to marry in a simple, tasteful ceremony, when it came to the part for them to exchange vows, both Ally and Willie were overcome and tearful as they spoke. As Billy took the rings from the little cushion that Caitlyn was holding out, he too looked emotional. Most of their guests were dabbing their eyes with hankies by the time they were pronounced husband and wife.

***

'Are you in pain darling?' Willie asked, as they sat at the head of the banqueting table. 'You haven't eaten much.'

Ally nodded. 'A little. I didn't sleep well last night, I missed you. I didn't want to be out of my face at our wedding, so I didn't take the painkillers. I'm okay though Willie. It was a lovely ceremony wasn't it?'

'Hmm, my best wedding yet Ally.'

She slapped him playfully. 'Your last wedding mister; if I have anything to do with it.'

Willie looked into his new wife's eyes, nodded, smiled and kissed her gently. 'Oh no, here we go,' he hissed as Frankie got to his feet and called for quiet, hitting a glass with a spoon. 'Hope he's sober.'

Frankie had, however, been well warned by Lynne that he had better remain tee-total until after the speeches. In his eagerness to please her, he'd done as he'd been asked. Silence fell over the banqueting suite. 'For those of you who don't know me, I'm Frankie Dastis, and I've known Willie Ogilvy all of my life. I'm your master of ceremonies for today. I was going to make some quip about Willie collecting wedding rings as a hobby, or him getting a new wife each new decade. He does love wedding cake.' Frankie looked around the room and smiled. 'Or my personal favourite, Willie you don't need to marry every woman you sleep with more than once!' He looked over at the table where Corina sat, her eyebrow raised. 'Sorry Cor, you can slap me later. In all honesty, everyone close to Willie is delighted that he has found Ally and I can't think of anything to say other than I am in awe of this couple, who have been through so much to be here today. So, that's it. No jokes, no wisecracks Wull and Ally, only good wishes and much love. I really believe, as he does, that this is forever. I would now like to introduce the father of the bride Mr Jimmy Jackson.'

Jimmy stood up; he looked at his daughter and her new husband and smiled. 'I have walked with my daughter today to marry a really great man. When you give your precious only child away at her wedding you need to know that it is the right man. I know that they wanted this day to be happy and without tears, but I fear that I'll struggle to say everything I need to say about this union, without emotion getting the better of me. I apologise now if I make anyone cry, but I hope you will share the joy that my grandsons and I feel. I'd like to take everyone back to an exceedingly difficult night last February, when my two grandsons and I were told four bits of news. My daughter had been one of the victims in a terrible and tragic atrocity. She was badly hurt, in a coma, clinging to life. But she was a hero who had saved so many children! Then I was told she was in a relationship with a man who I had only seen on the football field and on the pages of newspapers. It would be difficult to say what the strangest piece of news was that night. The fact that she was brave and fearless did not actually come as a shock. As her father, I lived with that fearlessness and knew that this was true. The strangest bit of the news was the fact that she had been in a relationship with this man here. They had been seeing each other in secret for months. To say I was stunned would be an understatement, but she was clinging to life and I wouldn't have cared who she was with if she lived.' He looked over at Willie, 'the boys and I decided to give him the benefit of the doubt. I made many vows that night and said a lot of silent prayers. Within hours, however, I realised that Willie Ogilvy was nothing like the media image I'd known. I came to know how much he loved my daughter. He barely left her side for days, he held us all together when it was touch and go as to whether she would survive. He truly is a tremendous man, a sincere man and a great man.'

'Thank you, Jimmy,' Willie said, smiling at his new father-in-law and then at Ally, 'not sure I deserve it though.'

Jimmy nodded and continued. 'We have, as a family, suffered a great deal of tragedy. As most of you know, sixteen years ago, Ally lost her mother, husband and child in an accident, where she was seriously injured. She recovered and is the lynch pin in our family. She is a wonderful daughter, brilliant mother, and now a loving wife. I don't know about obedient Willie, but you can't have it all. I'm immensely proud of my girl, and when I see her and Willie together, I know that although there is no man alive who could love her more than me, he runs a close second. I'm immensely proud of the woman she is and delighted to welcome Willie into our family. I ask you to raise your glasses to the bride and groom.'

Frankie stood up. 'Jimmy, that sums it up nicely. I think we all know how special this couple are. Now before we all start greetin into our drinks, I would like to introduce the man of the hour, the one and only Groomzilla! Ladies and Gentlemen, Mr William Ogilvy senior! Over to you Wull.'

Willie stood up; he looked around him and smiled. 'I have a lot of people to thank for the fact we are here today. Firstly, to Jimmy and his late wife Ella, thank you for Ally. To Ally, for agreeing to go out with me in the first place, despite my reputation. To Stevie Marshall, Ally's friend, who kept her alive when they were buried in the rubble of the school. To the amazing surgeon Mr Clive Ruthven and his team, especially nurse manager, Stan Morton, without them my wife would not be here. I can never repay them for what they gave me.' Clive smiled and nodded, sitting at a table with the team who had looked after Ally both in The Queen Elizabeth and the private hospital.

'To my five amazing and resilient kids; Leah, Korrie, Billy, Jade and Euan, and my beautiful granddaughter Caitlin, who have supported me even when I have hurt them. To Ally's brilliant sons, Scott and Danny, thank you for hearing me out and giving me a chance that awful February night in Glasgow.' He looked over at his stepsons and then back to the gathered guests. 'Can you imagine how they must have felt? The last person any son wants their mother to be seeing is a well-known womaniser who has been married three times. My mate Frankie here describes her as the woman who tamed Willog.'

Frankie smiled and held up his hand, his thumb pushing down; he made a whipping sound.

Willie nodded and continued. 'As for Ally, not a lot of people know this but Jimmy, Scott, Danny and I sat by her bedside watching her in a coma for days, through hours of surgery, ups and downs. We didn't know at times whether she would live or die.' Willie's face clouded, 'I was terrified, and I kept thinking, give me a chance to love this woman the way she deserves. She was literally seconds away from death several times and as I said before, but for brilliant hospital staff she wouldn't be here today. Finally, Clive told us she was out of danger and we sat around waiting for her to wake up. The first thing she said to me when she opened her eyes was . . . *'Ogilvy, you're a big girl's blouse.'* Where Ally is concerned, I am afraid this is an accurate description. I wake up and pinch myself to make sure that I'm not dreaming, and that this woman loves me. I know how soppy that sounds, but it's true.'

'I've had a lot of good stuff in my life and the bad stuff has been mostly my own fault.' He looked over at Corinna and Bernie, 'I have, as my mate here said, done this four times now. I've been blessed with a lot of lucky breaks in my life and known a lot of beautiful women, but I honestly feel that the best has been saved for last. If I died tomorrow, I would die happy in the knowledge that this woman loves me. Ally, I'm in awe of you and promise you that however long or short the rest of my life is I will give you the life you deserve.' He raised his glass. 'To my beautiful wife, the love of my life . . . to Ally.'

'To Ally!' the assembled group repeated.

'The other thing I want to say today is I'm a very lucky man. I have an inner circle of special people around me who love and protect me.' He smiled at the table nearest him, 'no matter what I have done they've always been there for me. They're the people who are not afraid to tell me I have been a 'baw-bag.' Frankie, Alfie, David and their families who, whatever daft thing I have done, have been there for me. They've taken Ally into that circle. The dictionary says family are a group of people who are related by blood or marriage. The real definition is those three guys who, along with Ally, my kids and my siblings, are my family. Please raise your glasses folks to Frankie, Alfie and David.'

'My main task though, is to raise a toast to the beautiful brides-maids. Kiera, who was with us through that awful time, sharing the fear and pain. Kiera is a remarkable young woman who has recently become a mother to our beautiful granddaughter Thea.

Beautiful Alexis, the bravest little girl I have ever met. She also is now the daughter of Ruby, Ally's best friend, her adoption having gone through just three days ago.'

'I'm Lexie Weir now!' Alexis, sitting between Ruby and Gerry, called out.

Willie smiled. 'Finally, my four girls. Leah, who is not only beautiful like her mother but also like her mother, wise beyond her years. Korrie, gorgeous and a talented singer who you'll hear later, she's a chip off the old block. I'm sure she will keep the gossip columns in business in my absence. My baby girl Jade, who is becoming a beautiful and talented young woman, she's just been picked for the Scotland ladies under 16's. I'm so proud of the young women they have become despite having me as a father. And, of course, the wonderful Caitlin. It was hard for me to be a granddad. It meant I was getting old for a start. But Caitlin is just the centre of our family and along with new baby Thea, makes Ally and I very proud grandparents. I have raised a glass to many beautiful women, but nothing gives me more pride than this toast. I raise my glass and invite you to join me now in a toast to the beautiful bridesmaids. You'll all be relieved now that I've nothing else to say, but thank you for sharing this day with my wife and I.'

Frankie stood up again. 'That was lovely Wull, and so true, even if half of us grew beards listening. You're a very lucky man. Now folks, I would like to introduce another Ogilvy, who has all the talent his dad had and more. Last year's UK Young Player of the Year, best man here today, the one and only Billy Ogilvie.'

Billy stood up, grinned and began to speak. 'I think I'm here today because Dad's three closest friends, Frankie, Alfie and David have all done this before for him, so there is no one left.' There was an outburst of laughter from the guests. 'Okay, part of my job today is to thank the groom for his toast to the bridesmaids. Three of them are my sisters. They scrub up well, don't they? Kiera, who had a baby just ten weeks ago, doesn't she look radiant? My stepbrother Scott is a very lucky guy. Alexis, what can I say that my dad didn't? Such a beautiful, resilient and brave wee girl, well done Lexie Weir. Lastly Caitlin, my beautiful little niece.' Caitlin, who had climbed onto Willie's lap, waved to him.

'Now I want to tell you a bit about my dad. Some of you here today will know him well enough to know that what they say about him in the press is not always accurate. Some of you will still be wondering what on earth Ally is thinking, wondering how bad the bump on the head was!' Ally laughed and held Willie's hand under the table. 'My dad is, without a doubt, a very lucky man. I'm not going to say anything about his history with women, but it would be fair to say my dad has until now not been well known for chastity. However, he is, and has always been, a great Dad. At first, like Frankie and everyone who knows my dad, I was thinking 'oh no, not again!' then I saw them together. I knew, as did everyone who loves him, including my mum.' He looked over at Corina, 'she asked me to say that, by the way. We all realised what he had with Ally was the real thing. I got to know Ally. I'm so in awe of her. Her bravery is not in question, she has a George Cross for God's sake, and she has taken on my dad. My sisters, brother and I have grown very quickly to love her for the amazing person she is. But also, it's obvious that Dad loves her and with good reason. My Dad is a great guy. Most of my life I have strived to be as good a football player as him, and when you follow your father into any profession there will always be comparisons. Over the last ten months, I've learned about my dad the man. Today, I want to be as good a man as him. However, it is a mountain that I have to climb.' Ally held Willie's hand as he wiped away tears from his eyes.

Billy lifted his glass and turned to face his father and his new wife. 'Now he has Ally beside him you will all see the real Willie, the man we know. As he said, our family is not just related by blood. Family are the people who love you unconditionally. Now I turn to Ally, Dr Alyson Campbell now Alyson Ogilvie, which makes them Dr and Mr Ogilvie. How did he manage to pull her? She's so beautiful inside and out and obviously had her children when she was twelve. Ally, my brother, sisters and I are deeply honoured to welcome you to our family. I would like you all to join me as I raise my glass to the bride and groom.'

'Thank you, Billy,' Frankie said. 'That was a lovely speech. He wouldn't let me write it for him folks. I offered, but he was adamant that he didn't trust me. Now we have the other best man, the effervescent Euan Ogilvy.' Frankie lifted Euan onto a chair and held the microphone to him.

'My dad has got a new wife and she's lovely. She gives me sweets, and she tells Dad to let me watch the TV. She makes Dad give me back my Xbox games and tells him to let me win when we play my games.' He looked at his sister Leah, who mouthed *nice*. 'Oh, and Ally is nice, and we all love her.'

Frankie smiled. 'Now folks, Willie and Ally want you to have a good night. It's a free bar, so enjoy yourselves. Thank you.'

Later, when everyone was dancing, Ally and Willie slipped away and upstairs to the bridal suite. 'This is such a beautiful room Willie. What a great day it was.'

'You look tired babe.'

'Willie I'm truly shattered. I'm glad we're all staying here tonight and will wake up on Christmas morning all together. I'm sorry that Belinsa wouldn't let Euan stay, but as a mother I can understand that she wants her child with her on Christmas morning. It was good of her to come and pick him up, especially when you didn't invite her and she has had to drive back to Manchester.'

Willie shook his head and rolled his eyes. 'Oh, I am sure that Belinsa will get maximum press coverage of her sacrifice.'

Ally decided not to comment further. 'It was really good of Clive to come too, wasn't it?'

Willie nodded and looked thoughtful. 'It was good of him to make the effort. I think the gay boy is a bit in love with you Ally!'

Ally moved towards him. 'Oh well, what can I say? I'm irresistible. I pulled the most eligible straight man in Scotland. You really suit your kilt Willie. You do look like a real Scotsman.'

Willie sat on the edge of the bed and pulled her onto his knee. 'I *am* a real Scotsman, and if you didn't look so tired, I would show you how much of a Scotsman I am Mrs Ogilvy! Are you really going to change your name?'

'Of course, I am. I'm very traditional really, I'll be Ally Ogilvy now. Ruby got me a lovely swimsuit for the honeymoon with Mrs Ogilvy across the bum. It was a lovely day wasn't it? The speeches felt like they were from the heart. Frankie behaved impeccably Willie; I was impressed.'

'He's so keen to keep Lynne sweet Ally. Did she tell you their news?'

'Yes, she told me at the hen party.' Ally looked into his eyes and then away. 'Willie, when did you sleep with Lynne?'

'I have been done Ally. Definitely not me.'

'No of course not, it's Frankie's baby.' Ally looked her new husband in the eye. 'No, Willie, don't make light of this. What you did before you met me is none of my business. You have done some weird and wonderful things but Lynne? I need to know what happened Willie. Did you have an affair? Does Frankie know?'

Willie sighed. 'Ally, this is our wedding night. What good will asking something like that do?'

'Willie, you haven't denied it.'

'No Ally I haven't because I did it once. I vowed I would never lie to you. When I asked you to marry me, I told you that I would always answer you honestly, no matter how painful. This is one question I wish you hadn't asked.' He looked her in the eye, a sad expression on his face, his eyes bright with unshed tears. 'I am at times mortally ashamed of myself. There's no excuse for many of the things I did.'

'Willie, tell me what happened! I need to know. She is becoming a close friend and there's a barrier there.'

Willie pulled Ally close and spoke over her head. 'Story is that Frankie and I quite often shared women. Alfie too, before he met Betty. It was never anything dodgy and always consensual. I didn't know that he was serious about her. To be honest I don't think he did either then. Frankie has always done a lot of drugs, and I kind of thought I was missing something, so when he did a line of coke with Lynne the week they met, I tried it. It was years ago. I was still with Hailey, but it was going wrong. It was a difficult time. Sometimes I didn't bother to go home for weeks at a time. Off season, I used to stay with Frankie a lot.'

Willie sighed and held Ally closer. 'We were in the club and went upstairs. Frankie did his usual party piece when he is wasted and fucked off to bed leaving me with her. Don't even know who made the first move. I know it's not an excuse Ally, but I was high. It was once, and I swear I've never done it again. I think it meant more to her than to me, but we never discussed it. We both acted as though it never happened. She brought it up in Majorca, the night that she and Frankie fell out. She said that seeing you and I together made her realise that she couldn't carry on with Frankie unless he changed. I've never told anyone about what she and I did. To my knowledge neither has she. Ally, I have done loads of things I'm not proud of, but that was one of the lowest points of my misspent life. How did you know?'

'I'm a social worker Willie, trained to observe behaviour. We were having a girlie talk after my hen party. I shared something private about you and it was something about the way she looked at me, it said '*I've been there.*' Willie I'm sorry, but it's been bugging me since that night. I expect there are loads of women who you've slept with, and what you did before you met me shouldn't matter.' She moved slightly and looked up at him. Is there anyone else in our close circle I should know about?'

'No, only Lynne, I don't think Frankie knows and I really think its Lynne's choice to tell him or not.' Willie kissed Ally gently, 'you are amazing Ally. You didn't react to what I have just said.'

'There's really no point in reacting it was a long time ago, besides, you've been honest with me and not tried to be anything you're not or lie to me. I know you won't ever be unfaithful to me either.' Ally smiled and looked at him, wiping away his tears with her finger. 'Now are you going to tell me about the honeymoon?'

Willie smiled and slid his hand inside her dress; he cupped her breast and nuzzled her neck, kissing it gently. 'Picture this? A boat, just you and me. The Caribbean, white sands, blue sea. Just you and me. Hundreds of miles from anyone. Just you and me. Do you get the theme here?'

'Could it be just you and me?' she laughed.

'First though, a night in a luxury spa hotel in London. Ally, I don't know why I know that this is forever. I've never promised anything to anyone that I couldn't deliver. I was many things before I met you, but I know that I will never sleep with another woman.'

'What if you meet some really beautiful woman? I don't know, Angelina Jolly? Jennifer Aniston?'

'I have been on the other side Ally and the grass isn't greener sweetheart.' He kissed her; despite her tiredness Ally found herself responding. Standing up, she began to undress. He joined her, and his kilt fell to the floor.

'A real Scotsman!' she breathed as she put her hands on his manhood. He unzipped and removed her dress. Underneath, she wore a white lace basque and stockings; she and Ruby had shopped with Betty for the right underwear.

'Jesus, you're so beautiful. You need to keep this on.' Willie slid his hand inside Ally's panties and pulled them down over her knees. She stepped out of them. They moved onto the bed. Their lovemaking was slow and deliberate. Ally clung to him as she climaxed, crying out; his breath hot against her skin as he joined her. He whispered in her ear, 'you're mine darling. I'll never let you go; I'll treat you so good you'll never want to go.' Afterwards Ally slept soundly, wrapped in his arms. When she woke, he was watching her. 'Good morning Doctor Ogilvy.'

'Good morning Mrs Ogilvy's husband,' Ally said sleepily smiling up at him.

'Ally, did I tell you I love you?'

'Oh, I am not sure. Let me think.' Ally kissed him on the lips and smiled.

'Merry Christmas, my darling,' Willie whispered, nibbling on her ear as his hands moved over her body. After a leisurely bath, they dressed and went downstairs to have Christmas with their nearest and dearest. With everyone there for the wedding, it had been easy to arrange for them all to spend Christmas Day together before they left for their honeymoon on Boxing Day. It was a relaxed and happy day; the Ogilvy, Campbell, Dastis, Gibson and Marshall families together, celebrating.

CHAPTER

THIRTY-THREE

The Christmas Day party continued into the night; Willie drank too much. The flight to London on Boxing Day was marred by his massive hangover. 'Sorry babe, I should know better! I didn't realise I drank as much. It's a long time since I've had a hangover like this. Never mind though, the day after tomorrow we will be lying on a deck with blue sea and no one for miles.'

They checked into their hotel and were shown to the bridal suite. 'Ally, I feel fucking awful babe. I hope this is a hangover and not some bug. Maybe I just need to sleep it off? I'm so sorry.'

Ally looked at him. 'You're a funny colour Willie. Were you okay before? Before lunch yesterday? Perhaps it's food poisoning?'

He groaned. 'Wouldn't everyone have it?'

Ally was worried at how unwell Willie was. 'Perhaps we should get a doctor?'

Willie shook his head. 'No, leave it a few hours then see how it is. I'll go have a sleep; see how I feel then.'

'Perhaps we shouldn't go tomorrow. If you're ill abroad it could be dangerous.'

'No way Ally, we're going! I'm sure I'll be fine.'

***

Later Willie wakened; feeling a great deal better, he walked through to the lounge of the suite. He smiled; Ally lay on the sofa asleep. He put on the kettle and made himself coffee. Suddenly he heard her cry out and thrash around the on the sofa. He rushed to her side. The nightmares were rare now, but he knew what to do.

'Ally, please wake up! Babe you're dreaming. I'm here, it's all over. You're safe. You're my wife now, and you are safe.'

Her eyes snapped open and focused; she sighed. 'Each time I think it's gone it comes back,' she whispered. 'Willie, hold me please. I'm scared. I was dreaming I was back in the school. He was trying to kill Thea and Caitlin! I was trying to hide them. I lay on top of them and I crushed Thea, but it wasn't Thea, it was Abby. I don't know how I knew.' Ally looked up at her new husband and sighed, 'Willie I haven't had a nightmare in weeks. It was Frankie and Danny, going on about the bloody trial on Christmas night. I really did not want to think about it until we got back.' She looked at Willie. 'Are you feeling better?'

Willie smiled and nodded. 'Yes, my love, it must have been a hangover after all. I wakened up feeling much better. Never mind me, my sickness was self-inflicted Ally, I didn't think I had much though. I guess I can't drink the way I used to anymore, probably not a bad thing.'

'I didn't think you had much either Willie, but there was a lot going on. Everyone kept filling my glass, perhaps that's what caused the dream.'

'Ally, you're stressed with the trial coming up love. It will be over soon, and they will lock him up forever. You know he did it, everyone knows he did it. Do you want me to call Joe?'

'No, I want to fast forward until it's all over, he is convicted and locked away for good. Then you and I can get on with the rest of our lives. I believe he's dangerous. If I'm feeling like this, just think how the child witnesses feel! Ruby says Alexis has been really unsettled. I miss her so much but moving away was the best thing her and Gerry could do for Alexis. It was great to see them at the wedding, but sad knowing that she won't be just down the road anymore.'

Willie pulled her closer and kissed her. 'We'll get over to France to see her after the trial Ally, I promise.'

She moved away from him. 'I'm going to run a bath and soak up to my neck. Want to join me?'

'Not just yet babe, I need to call Belinsa, she has sent me a cryptic text about Euan.' Willie sighed, 'sorry babe, she is probably doing it deliberately to mar our honeymoon, but I know better than to ignore her. It ends with me on the front pages of a tabloid.'

Ally was getting out the bath when she heard a crash then a thud followed by a scraping noise. 'What have you dropped?' she called, going through to the room. Willie was lying on the floor, having some sort of fit. His eyes rolled, his body convulsed and jerked unnaturally. **'Willie!'** she screamed. She held him, and gradually he came around. His skin was the colour of putty and he shook as he tried to speak, his words making no sense. 'Willie, no, don't move. Please let me help you to get on to the couch. Thank god we're still in London. I'm going to call the emergency services.' Willie began to protest then passed out.'

The hospital accident and emergency department was busy, people sat around blood and bandages everywhere; Ally was shown into a room by a young doctor wearing black scrubs. He looked at her and shook his head. 'I'm so sorry Mrs Ogilvy. We think that your husband has a disturbance in his brain. We need to carry out some tests to see what is going on. He's recovered from the fit and is resting, his vitals are good. You can go in and see him in a few minutes, we are about to take him for a scan. Has this happened before?'

Ally shook her head. 'Not to my knowledge. He's very fit. He was a professional footballer.'

Ally was shown into Willie's room. He lay on the bed a drip attached to his hand; he looked pale and tired. She rushed over and hugged him, tears falling freely. 'Willie, I was so scared.'

'Ally it's nothing. From time to time I get these funny turns, but it goes away. I think it's migraine. I get a headache for a couple of days then after the funny turn the headache goes away.'

'This has happened before? Have you seen a doctor?'

He shook his head, 'no, I meant to, it's happened a couple of times. The last time was when we were in Spain. I kept thinking I'd need to get it checked out, but after I have the turn, I always feel better. That made me think it's some sort of migraine.'

'You never thought to tell me? Willie for Christ's sake! Why won't you trust me, share things with me? Why do I always have to ask before you tell the truth?'

'I'm sorry babe, I didn't want to worry you, and I really didn't think it was anything major.'

CHAPTER

THIRTY-FOUR

The young doctor sat looking at them, he shook his head. 'I am afraid that you have a mass on your brain, looks like a tumour Mr Ogilvie. It's quite large, and you will almost certainly need surgery.'

Willie looked at Ally and her eyes filled up with tears. 'No Ally, please don't cry.'

The doctor stood up and shook his hand and patted Ally's shoulder. 'I'm very sorry Mr and Mrs Ogilvie but without operating I can't tell you what the prognosis is. I don't want to operate unless it becomes imperative because once we do, you're stuck here. We've spoken to a specialist in Scotland and sent him the scan. Because of the seizures, we need to get you home for him to assess you as soon as possible. Mrs Ogilvie, can you come and sign some paperwork?'

Ally followed the doctor from the room. He motioned to her to follow him into the nurses room, he shut the door. 'How bad is it doctor?'

'On a scale of one to ten, where ten is bad Mrs Ogilvie, I think it's about a seven.'

'So, there is some hope?'

'It depends what they find when they open him up, but I think you need to prepare for the worst and anything else is a bonus. I'm sorry to be so blunt, but the chances of him surviving more than a year if it is what the specialist thinks it is are slim.'

'Is the specialist Clive Ruthven?' Ally asked quietly.

'Why yes! Do you know him?'

'He saved my life. Would it be okay if I speak to him?'

The doctor nodded. 'Do you have a number for him?'

'Yes.' She took out her phone and keyed in Clive. The doctor raised his hand in a silent wave and left the room.

Clive stared at the mobile in his hand; Ally's name came up on the screen. He'd been expecting her to contact him since the call from London the day before. Clive couldn't answer it; tears welled up in his eyes, he kept picturing the happy couple at their wedding. He put his phone, still ringing, into the top drawer of his big antique desk. He knew he had to speak to Ally. Clive realised that she would be scared and would look to him for help and a cure. All Clive's years in medicine combined with his experience and knowledge of the human brain, meant that he knew there would be only one outcome in this situation. He needed another drink before he could have any conversation with Ally.

Ally spoke to the answering machine. 'Clive, it's Ally Cam … sorry, Ogilvy. I don't know if you are aware of this, but you were asked to look at a scan from the London Teaching Hospital.' Ally's voice broke and she couldn't speak. 'Clive, it was Willie's scan and it's not good, I know.' She couldn't continue and began to cry, 'I need to speak to you.' Ally pressed the end call button and put the phone down; she buried her head in her hands and wept.

A few minutes later Ally's phone buzzed, Clive's name came up; Ally pressed the call button and raised the phone to her ear. When he spoke to her, she immediately realised he knew. 'Ally,

I'm so sorry my dear, I didn't get to the phone in time. Stupid question but . . . how are you?'

'Well I'm trying to be brave, but it's not easy Clive. This is so not fair! Clive, before this all kicks off, I need you to be honest with me. Is he going to die?'

There was a long pause before he answered her. 'Ally, I am booked on a flight and will be with you in a few hours. I'll travel back here with him.'

'Clive, you didn't answer me. Is there any hope?'

Clive took a deep breath. 'I don't think so Ally, but I'll do everything I can.'

'Thank you for your honesty Clive, I'm grateful, and I trust you.'

The door was tapped lightly, and Willie's doctor came back into the room carrying two cups of coffee. 'Did you speak to Mr Ruthven?'

Ally nodded. 'He's coming down tonight,' she said quietly.

'He's a bit of a god in neurosurgery. The best there is,' the doctor said, smiling, I was his student about fifteen years ago. I do defer to him a lot,' he smiled and rolled his eyes, 'what an experience it is working with him, I love it and look for any chance to do it, sorry that was insensitive of me Mrs Ogilvy.'

'Well, I'm living proof of his gift,' Ally said quietly.

The doctor nodded. 'I came up to Scotland after the tragedy, to help. Clive is amazing. His son's a medical student here just now. Lovely boy, he was working in accident and emergency before Christmas and Clive was here for a few days. We met up for a drink. He mentioned he was going to your wedding.'

'Clive has a son?'

'Sean Ruthven,' the doctor answered, 'he's just started, Clive's wife worked here too, she was a lovely woman it was so sad, she was so young.'

Ally went back to the room; Willie sat up in bed. 'Well, how long have I got?'

'Willie don't be a drama queen. You have to battle now.'

'Ally, I want you to know that if I die, I'll die a happy man. I would rather have a few months with you than a lifetime of what I had before.'

'Willie, Clive is going to be your surgeon. I have just spoken to him. We are sorting out a medical flight for you. He is going to fly here today to assess you and come back with us.'

***

Ally returned to her hotel; she knew everyone would assume they were away on honeymoon. She called Willie's children first. Unfortunately, only Korrie answered. Ally told her that there was something wrong with Willie but decided not to tell her everything yet. Korrie told Ally she would get her siblings and break the news. Next, she called Scott and Danny and told them the news. A few minutes later her phone rang, Stevie's name popped up on the screen. 'Ally, Scott just told me! Oh . . . fuck . . . Ally, I'm so sorry! How are you?'

'I'm okay. I have to hold it together. I wanted to scream and shout but there's no point. Stevie, I'm so scared. I don't know what to do. I have to tell people. I don't know what to say.'

'Ally, do you want me to fly down? I will if you need me.'

'No, they're stabilising him. Clive is on his way here. We're hoping to be bringing him back to Scotland tomorrow. Clive is the best neurosurgeon there is. You and I are living proof of that.'

When Ally returned to the hospital the next morning after a sleepless, tearful night, Willie was sitting up in bed looking as though there was nothing wrong. Clive was sitting by the bed talking to him. He nodded at Ally; Willie smiled. 'Hi babe, you look tired.'

'I think you're a big fraud Ogilvy,' she said quietly.

302

'Ally, I made it all up for attention, what can I say! Have you phoned Frankie, David and Alfie?'

She shook her head. 'I didn't know whether you wanted to tell them yourself when we had some news. I could only get Korrie when I called the older kids. Leah and Billy didn't answer their phones. I only told Korrie you had done something to your head and were having surgery. I told her to get the others and let them know that we will call them when there is news.'

'Ally, I need you to tell Frankie, Davie and Alfie for me.'

'I think you would be better doing it yourself, face-to-face Willie. The same with your kids and your sisters and brothers. You have to tell them.'

'I can't Ally. I need you to do it for me.' He looked at Clive, who shrugged and stood up.

'Ally my dear, the flight is booked for ten tonight. I'll do the biopsy as soon as we get back. Please excuse me, I have to do some paperwork.'

'Ally!' Willie said, as the door closed behind the big doctor, 'I need you to call people for me. I just can't do it babe.'

'You sure?'

'I can't do it,' Willie said quietly. 'I'm a coward Ally, I hate hurting people. Ally can you lie beside me please? I'm so sorry that this has happened when you have the trial coming up.'

'Oh, Willie please, don't even think about that, it's just not important,' Ally said, as she kicked off her shoes and climbed onto the bed beside her husband. She felt exhausted and fell asleep; his arms tightened around her and he too dozed off.

Clive Ruthven put his head around the door; his heart was filled with sadness as he looked at the sleeping couple. Ally, so small, curled up beside her husband of five days. Willie, so handsome, his face pale, his arms wrapped around his wife. Clive looked at the ceiling and shook his head. His work and his personal life had taught him that there was no real rhyme or reason to illness. He desperately hoped that he could do something to help this couple be together longer. In his heart, however, he knew that this was unlikely. He quietly closed the door on the sleeping couple. The flight was not for a few hours so there was no point in disturbing them. He walked along the corridor and entered the staff toilet, locked the door, sat down on the toilet and wept.

CHAPTER
THIRTY-FIVE

Clive, still in his operating greens, guided Ally into the office. He closed the door behind them. 'Ally sit down, I need to have a talk with you.'

'Clive, I can see by your face, this is not good.'

'I wanted to speak to you before I go in to see him.'

'How bad is it?'

'As bad as it gets Ally, I know just by looking at it my dear. His blood tests and needle biopsy all pointed to a very aggressive cancer, but I had hoped that there would be more I could do. I want to tell you that there's a cure, but I know that all I can do is buy him some time.'

'How long?'

'A year, maybe a little longer if I can operate. I need the results back from the biopsy first then it all depends on how much of the tumour I can remove.'

'Is there nothing at all Clive? Why now? Why has it happened so suddenly?'

Clive closed his eyes and sighed. 'Ally, he's known for a long time that there was something wrong. He must have, this type of tumour grows initially very slowly, then starts to show symptoms and the growth speeds up. I have to be honest with you it is treatable in its early and even mid stages.'

Ally looked at the doctor and shook her head. 'Why would he hide it from me?'

The big man shrugged, his face showing the pain he felt for this woman sitting in front of him trying to be brave. 'Ally you'll have to ask him that. I could kick myself too. Joe McCann told me he saw something in Majorca, Willie apparently said he had an ear infection. Joe asked me if that could cause a seizure. I asked Willie and he denied it. I'd no reason to believe that it was anything other than a faint. He said he had been drinking, taking antibiotics and painkillers. I thought he had just over-done things looking after you. Now, I'll go and speak to him myself Ally. I sometimes find that they say more if their loved ones aren't there. You go get a coffee or go outside and compose yourself.' He stood up and wrapped his arms around her. She reached to his chest and she could smell the sandalwood after-shave that she had found so comforting in the days when she was seriously ill. Now she also knew that he had a son and had been married. Not unusual, lots of gay men had families, and reached a point where they could come out, but she was now beginning to think she might have misunderstood him. He dropped a kiss on the top of her head and tilted her chin to look into her eyes. 'Now Mrs Ogilvie, I hope you don't think I do that with all my patients' wives. Just the ones whose brain I have been inside.'

Ally stood in the relatives area with a mug of coffee. She heard her name being called, 'Ally what the fuck happened? Did he have a fall? I just heard on the news he was having brain surgery!'

'Christ Frankie, I haven't even had time to call anyone other than his kids. Someone must have leaked it. I wanted . . . *we* wanted to do it face-to-face with you Frankie, I'm so sorry. It's a tumour, a massive one and it's not curable. I've just been with the doctor.'

'There must be something Ally. We can pay,' Frankie gasped, the shock evident on his face.

'Frankie, the surgeon, Clive Ruthven, wouldn't lie to me. He saved my life last year. Willie and I got to know him well.' Tears began to run down her face. Frankie pulled her to him and wrapped his arms around her, holding her close. They sobbed into each other's arms. Suddenly there was a flash and a photographer ran off down the corridor. A nurse came over and suggested they sit in the relatives' room in private.

Frankie put his arm around Ally's shoulder and led her along the corridor following the nurse.

Ally sat with her head in her hands. 'Frankie, I don't know what to do. Clive says Willie needs to know. I want to pretend he is going to get better. I need to talk to him. Frankie, this is not fair. I only just found him. It's not fucking fair, so not fair. They say he must have known something was wrong.'

Frankie slapped the side of his head. 'He passed out when we were in Majorca last July. I knew there was more to it, but he was adamant it was to do with an ear infection. Why didn't I make him see a doctor? Joe told him he needed to, and he said he would. All that stuff about me and talking about myself pushed it into the background Ally.'

'He's an adult Frankie,' Ally said sadly, 'he made choices, his choices. He never told me anything either. Not a bloody thing!'

When she walked through the door, Willie was watching her. 'Well, well, it doesn't look good does it Mrs Ogilvy?' He smiled at her and took her hand. 'Don't you crack up Ally! Sometimes life is just a bag of shite darling. I wouldn't change anything.' Catching sight of Frankie standing in the doorway he raised his hand. 'Frankie, how are you?'

'Better than you, daft prick, it would seem.'

'Hope you are not here hoping to pull Ally if I croak it now.'

Frankie's face crumbled. He tried to speak, but tears welling in his eyes, his voice was a whisper, 'fuck Willie, I don't know . . . I . . . I . . . don't know what to say.'

'Oh no Dastis, don't you dare feel sorry for me. I'm going to die mate, but we all are. I'll be a good-looking corpse, and you'll all remember how pretty I was. Ally, I need you and Frankie to be strong here. I want you to go get my kids and bring them in. There's a chance I won't survive the surgery, so I need to see them all. Clive reckons if I get through the op, I could have a year or more, so there is no hurry that way. I'll have time to plan. He tells me though that there's been a leak and the press have the story. Ally don't start crying please, you'll start me off. I can't waste time on tears and regrets just now babe. You've the trial to get through, and I'm aiming to be there with you for it. Clive says they'll try to remove most of the tumour. Although it'll just grow back, it should slow it down a bit. Frankie, we must look at the future of the company. Alfie needs to come over. Ask David to arrange a partners meeting with the lawyers when he gets here. If need be, we can have it here in the hospital.'

'Willie, this is so not fair!' Frankie wiped away tears with a tissue.

Willie smiled and shrugged. 'That's life mate. I've had a good life. There are babies lying up in the children's hospital dying who haven't had a life. Besides, it's not over yet. By the way Ally, Clive isn't gay!'

Ally stared at him. 'What kind of conversation did you have with him today?'

Willie laughed. 'He told me months ago when you were in here. I played poker with him and his cronies a few nights, fucking wiped me out too. I don't know, it was a wind up to start with, and then I forgot to tell you.'

'And the relevance of Clive's sexuality to this current situation is . . . Willie?'

'He thought Clive was competition, Ally.' Frankie laughed through tears. 'Oh, how fucking insecure. That's for us mortals, that kind of shit.'

'Oh, it's really not relevant to anything now, is it?' Willie laughed. 'Okay, I thought that you might like him a bit too much Ally. He did save your life. You are both clever and intellectual and all that.'

'Willie, he's a brain surgeon! I'm a fucking social worker. Hardly on the same intellectual level. I like him the way I like lots of people. I enjoyed our chats. He made me feel I could get better. Willie, I am now, and have always been, one hundred percent in love with you.'

'Hmm, he's in charge of my care now, he knows you think he's gay, I told him, so it might be better if you tell him you know. He is going to be inside my brain soon, he said he would tell you he wasn't if you asked him. Of course, I knew you were too polite to ask him about his love life.'

Frankie smiled and shook his head, he looked at Willie. 'I forgot what a fanny you can be. You have been so normal for the last while. Never known you to be jealous or insecure though mate.'

'I'm not jealous, nor am I insecure, I just thought that I would make sure that there was no competition.'

'You are a dick Ogilvy,' Frankie said shaking his head.

'I know.'

***

'Clive is there absolutely nothing you can do?' Ally asked. She sat looking at the big man in front of her. The oak desk separating them stretched out in front of him. Willie had fallen asleep, so Frankie had gone off to sort out some meetings, and Clive had asked to speak to Ally in his office.

Clive sighed and rested his hands on the leather blotter on the big desk. 'Ally there are some things we could try to prolong his life, but I'm afraid it is inevitable that this will end in death sooner rather than later. Some of the things we can try might buy him a couple of extra months, but the quality of his life could be less, so he needs to make that decision. Ally, I can get a second opinion for you?'

'What? No Clive, you've always been upfront with us. I trust you, we both do.'

'Ally, if I could make this any easier for you and Willie, or make it go away, I would. You need to know that. If I could recommend anywhere in the world you could go to treat this and the outcome would be any different, I would.'

CHAPTER

THIRTY-SIX

Seamus Driske sat in his cell; he was angry, very angry. He knew that everyone hated him. He truly did not care. Because everyone knew his name. He was infamous. Like Hitler or Charles Manson, the world would remember Seamus Driske. He lay back against the wall and took a deep breath. He knew he would have a visit today. He had specially asked for this, and he had a plan. He was not afraid, because if the plan worked then he would go down in history. If it didn't then he was not afraid to die. Seamus had watched lots of people die, some brave and defiant, some begging for their lives.

'What are you smiling at?' the guard asked as he brought in Seamus's evening meal. Seamus put down his book and took the tray from the guard.

'Oh, just amusing myself. This book is really funny.'

'Who's your visitor?

'My lawyer. I'm making a case for being a political prisoner.'

'You, a political prisoner! You are the lowest of the low Driske, a paedophile, rapist and murderer. You don't deserve to live, fucking tattie muncher. It's a pity they did away with hanging. Even that's too good for you. You should be put in a room with those kiddies' families.'

Maggie Parker

'Ah, but I'll be in the history books. Everyone will remember my name. Who'll remember you? Even your boyfriend probably won't remember your name. Oh, or is it your wife? Hard to tell, I heard. Any kids? Ha-ha, I heard the others talking about you. How you're a Jaffa, seedless, couldn't have kids. Just got a couple of wee dogs I hear, Bob. Heard they look better than your fucking ugly wife. Mind you, your mate Tommy's shagging your woman for you, so if she gets pregnant, you'll know it's not a miracle.'

The guard lunged at him and began to pummel. Seamus smiled; the pain was worth it. He knew the guard to do this with; the one who had so little self-control that he would react. The others talked about him behind his back, about his miserable nature, his wish for children that never came. He was known to have a personality disorder and lack of control. He was an inadequate man, touchy, arrogant and volatile. He hid this behind a joking, comedic front. He also had a nasty violent streak.

Seamus had heard the other prison officers talking about how the prison management hated him and were waiting for an opportunity to get rid of him. Seamus also knew that Bob was a gambler, had debts to pay and could not afford to lose his job. He knew he had a slight heart problem and was on medication. He was disliked by so many people in the prison, particularly his colleagues. 'Takes one to know one!' Seamus thought as he sank into unconsciousness.

CHAPTER
THIRTY-SEVEN

'Ally, the trial's been postponed apparently.' Stevie held the letter in his hand. 'Seamus has been hurt in prison. They think someone beat him up, but he says he fell down in his cell. He's pretty badly injured. It has been put off indefinitely.'

Ally gasped. 'That's all we need. We need closure.'

Stevie nodded. 'I know Ally, but it's probably a good thing for you. It means you can concentrate on looking after Willie.'

'It's not just about me though is it Stevie? All the people involved need closure. The families, they need to be able to move on. I really hoped that he would do the right thing and just plead guilty instead of putting everyone through this.' Ally and Stevie were sitting in Willie's loch side house; Willie was due out of hospital in a few days and Ally had moved in, helped by Stevie, Jimmy and her sons that morning. The others had gone home; Stevie had stayed on to have dinner with her.

'This really is a beautiful house Ally. How come if he has had it for years everything looks new?'

'He never really lived in it. He has the flat on Riverside Heights which he lived in when he was in Glasgow. He only used this when all the kids were staying with him. Do you want the tour? It's impressive. He had it built to his own design. It's the only one of his houses which none of his other women have been in. He started building it when he separated from Belinsa. He kind of vowed to keep it for him and his kids. The house is positioned so that it gets the best views possible. Being on the east side of the loch it's remote and private enough.' Stevie looked out at the loch through the bi-fold doors which made up the front wall of the kitchen where they sat. She led the way through to the lounge. The room was bright and airy with French windows opening on to a large raised decking area which had steps going down the garden to a dock where a small motorboat was moored. Ally smiled and nodded. 'Sometimes it's easier to use that to get out than driving around. He keeps one of his cars at Duck Bay, in the car park.'

Stevie took in the large, open, inglenook fireplace with a black stove burning brightly against one wall. The furniture was large and comfortable looking. The remaining wall was lined with a partially filled bookcase and display area. The polished wooden floors reflected the flames from the stove. Brightly coloured scatter rugs had been laid around the room. Upstairs, she led him into the master bedroom. 'Christ Ally, this room is bigger than my entire house. What a view from the balcony!' he said, opening the double doors.

'It's north facing, the veranda. You can see Ben Lomond, look at the top covered in snow. There's a basement too which houses a small pool and a gym. Fuck sake I sound like an estate agent.'

Stevie came back in and closed the doors, sitting back down beside her on the large ornate four poster bed. He put his arm around her shoulder. 'This is a beautiful room Ally, look at all the cupboard space. You can have all your shoes here.'

Ally smiled. 'Willie has more clothes than me Stevie. The corridor is just all cupboards, so we have enough storage. Have you seen the en-suite?'

'It's amazing Ally. The picture window looking over the loch and that great spa bath, you could just lie there and look out at the view. I take it the picture window is one way?'

'Yes, it's mirrored on the outside so that no one can see in.'

Stevie turned his head, so he was looking at her. 'Ally please let me be there for you. You don't need to be strong all the time hun!'

Ally rested her head on his shoulder. 'Thanks Stevie but I'm fine, honestly. I suppose I'm glad that the court case has been put back, but we also need the closure.'

'Did you get your criminal injuries offer?'

'I did, but Willie's lawyer has knocked it back and advised me to wait until after he is convicted.'

'Mine said much the same.'

'The offer from the council is substantial anyway. I've accepted their second one.'

'Me too. It feels good that I don't need to work Ally, although it's no fun now Gerry has gone. I have no one to wind up! But I still want to work.'

'They offered me his job Stevie!'

'Are you going to take it?'

'I don't know. I don't want to be knocking doors now. It's weird really, I could never imagine moving into management but suddenly I don't want to do the frontline stuff anymore. Do you?'

'No not really. They offered me Ruby's job.'

'Should we take the offers, work together again?'

'You'd be my boss Ally.'

'Ah, but there are pluses to that Stevie.'

'What?'

'I would be your boss. You'd have to manage the social work-ers, and you are better dressed these days. We both are financially secure. We have reasonable pensions to look forward to and with whatever the criminal injuries are, we'll have plenty in the bank.'

'Yeah you dream about this don't you? Money in the bank, not having to work. It's why we buy lottery tickets.' Stevie sighed, 'Just never thought I would be rich because someone else's misery. It means nothing really money, it can't buy you the things you would really want. I really do want to do something meaningful with it.'

'I'd give it all up to be able to bring all the kids and adults who died in the school back.' Ally's face clouded over, 'then there's Willie, he's forty-eight and dying. He can't do anything about it, even with millions in the bank.' Weeks of pent-up emotion rose to the surface Stevie's closeness helped Ally release some of it. She began to cry. 'It's not fair. It's just not right.' She stood up and kicked at the bed. 'It's not fucking fair. Why Stevie? Why didn't he tell me about the fits? Why didn't he trust me enough to tell me? Clive reckons that if they had got it when it started, then the outcome could have been different. He didn't tell me because I was so ill, and he didn't want to bother me. He took the first one just before the shootings, and then again when I was in the coma. He was in the fucking hospital with the one man in Britain who could have saved him, and he didn't say! I'm so fucking angry Stevie. I feel I'm being robbed. I love him so much and he is leaving me. Everyone I love leaves me.'

Stevie looked at her; she fell into his arms. He held her close, stroking her hair, kissing her head and not saying anything. Eventually her sobs subsided, she became quiet.

'Ally! I'm so sorry honey. You're right, it's not fair. Why don't we just blame Seamus for that as well? It might help if you can blame someone.'

'Other than me you mean.'

'Ally, this isn't your fault.'

'If he hadn't met me, he might have gone to a doctor.'

'Ally if he hadn't met you, he would probably have been too drunk to notice there was anything wrong.'

'That's what he said, he did know there was something wrong. He thought . . . he thought because so many of the players of his generation apparently end up with dementia from heading the ball . . . he says . . . well he says it is because the ball they used when he was a young player was heavier. He was a forward, so apparently more at risk. Clive isn't ruling out that his career has put him more at risk.' Ally looked sadly at Stevie, 'it doesn't really make much difference, he's still dying.'

Stevie kissed her cheek. 'How are his kids taking it?'

'Oh, Korrie, as usual, has gone off the wall. She's like Willie was at her age apparently, totally self-absorbed. She is a lovely girl, but there is only Korrie suffering. Leah's been great. She's been there for us, as has Billy. Their mum Corinna is lovely too, you met her at the wedding. She came with Leah yesterday just to say she is thinking about me. Jade is devastated of course. She's having to cope with her mother as well. Hailey has post-natal depression and Jade feels she should be there for her baby brother. The father has taken off, leaving the poor wee soul to take on the responsibility of both mother and baby. Willie and I try to be there for her, but Leah is great with her and no threat to Hailey. Jade loves being around Caitlin. Euan doesn't really understand, and we haven't told him much. Belinsa has given a big story to the newspapers about how devastated she is, how much she loved him and how badly she was treated. Willie reckons she is a good mum to Euan, but how can she not see that slagging off Willie in the papers will ultimately affect her boy.'

'How's Willie?'

'Willie is stoic, accepting of the inevitability of his death. However, Clive reckons that he could have longer than he first thought so that's good. They managed to get more of the tumour than they expected. Willie made a good recovery from the surgery. Clive thinks that with radiotherapy they could add another year. Willie wants to plan a big party for his, Davie and the twins fiftieth because he now thinks he'll see it. Do you know him and the twins, they were born a day apart in the same hospital? They were neighbours! Davie's only a month older than them. His father was Willie's mum's brother. How was the concert?'

'It was great Ally, amazing, we got to meet all the artists, Black Velvet did a song dedicated to Willie. They filmed a get-well message for him, it's a shame he couldn't be there.'

'We thought about postponing the surgery, but it was important it went ahead to allow us to buy some time. The concert had to be on the anniversary of the shootings, which was important too. In the end, Willie did that pre-recorded film as well. We've got the recording of it; we'll watch it once he is home. They made a lot of money for the fund, and it means that we can provide for the families and for the community. The press has been a nightmare this week though. They know he has had his surgery. They're trying to get pictures of him. They were out on a boat on the loch yesterday, taking pictures when Leah and Korrie were here.'

Stevie sighed. 'He's a public figure and so are you. They think you are public property.'

'Once he's recovered from the surgery we're going to go to Majorca for a couple of weeks in April. After he finishes the course of radiotherapy. All of us together, his kids and mine. He wants to do some family stuff while he's still fit.'

'Yeah Kiera said. She reckons that the only problem is Korrie.'

'She's a lovely girl really, Stevie.'

'Yes, you said, but you always see the best in people. All that internet sex stuff must have upset Willie?'

'Oh, he expects it from Korrie. She's such a beautiful, talented girl, a real free spirit. He blames himself for her being wild.

You know, leaving Corinna and treating her badly. Corinna and Willie believe she was targeted.'

'Was she?'

'Leah doesn't think so. She thinks Korrie staged it to help her singing career. Billy's upset because of the stuff the fans are shouting. Stevie don't repeat this, but Frankie thinks it was Korrie who tipped off the press about Willie's collapse then told them it was an incurable brain tumour. It would kill Willie if he knew, so we're not saying anything. Frankie says a reporter who Lynne knows told them.'

CHAPTER
THIRTY-EIGHT

'Welcome home Dad, you look great.'

'I feel good Leah, thank you for coming over. I really do feel good sweetheart. I'm going to rest up for a few days before we leave for Majorca.'

'How long will it take you by boat?'

'A couple of days or so. Chartering a boat is something I've actually always meant to do. Although I believe I'm fit enough to take my own boat, Ally said no.'

'Do the crew come with it, or are they an extra?'

'You hire the complete thing Leah. When are you lot flying out?'

'Caitlin and I are coming out with Jade, Euan and Danny on Friday. Scott, Kiera and Thea are coming Saturday. Billy and Korrie have Sunday flights. He has a game on Saturday.' Leah looked at her father and sighed. 'She's seeing Ramie Char again.'

'After what he did! He filmed them having sex! She'd better not ask to bring him Leah. There are limits to my patience with her.'

'No, he has a midweek cup tie Dad, so he couldn't. I don't think he would be brave enough to face you anyway. Billy played against him the other week and the crowd was egging them on to fight. Korrie is not the innocent abroad you and Mum think. She just doesn't think when she does things. Dad, she is selfish, reckless and stupid.'

Willie sighed and looked his eldest child in the eye. 'I know sweetheart, I really do. But she's your sister and my daughter. We all need to be there for each other even when we don't agree with each other's choices. Leah, I can always guess what she's going to do, because she is so like me, before . . . before I met Ally.'

'She's pretty special Dad, Ally, I do really like her. She was really nice to Mum too when she came in to see you.'

'Leah, that's my biggest regret in life, what I did to your mum. It was a young love her and me, first love, and would never have worked. But the way I did it. After I'm gone, remember how much I love you babe, not all the stupid things I did!'

'Dad, I'm seeing Archie again. I think I want to give it another try. I hope you will be happy for us. When he heard about you, he came up. I was upset and well, we got talking. Life is too short to fight with people you love, isn't it?'

After Leah left, Willie moved over to sit beside Ally on the big couch. He stared into the fire Ally had set. 'Ally, I've asked Brenda to come and work here, she's agreed. I want you to go back to work. You need to build a life for when I'm gone. I've got someone coming to convert the garage into a self-contained apartment for Brenda and her husband Dermot. He's good at repairs and such so he'll be a kind of handyman for us.' Seeing the pain on her face he put his arm around her. 'Ally, we have to discuss a lot of painful things over the next few days. My lawyer is coming over tomorrow. Frankie, Alfie and David will also be here. I'm going to sort out my will with them as witnesses. Once I've sorted out all the practical matters, then I can relax, enjoy the time I have left. Babe, I have to do these things. I need to feel that I'm leaving you with as little mess as possible. Come upstairs with me, I need to lie down for a couple of hours.' He winked at her, took her hand, leading the way.

Half an hour later they lay naked in the big bed and Ally rested her head against his chest. 'God Willie you're amazing, but you need to stop doing that, you'll tire yourself out.'

'Ally, I plan to be still making love to you until the day I die. If I can still do that then I have something to live for. You know what? I feel better than I have done for the last couple of years, no headache, no dizziness and Clive reckons, no more fits, because all the pressure is off my brain I can still perform. Luckily, the tumour is on the opposite side from the sexual workings according to Clive.'

Ally began to laugh, despite her pain. 'Only you could be told you have a terminal illness and ask about whether you could still have sex. You really have got your priorities right, haven't you?'

'Oh yes Ally. I'll be, to quote Frankie, pumping all the way to my grave, if I have anything to do with it.'

She looked at him. 'Are you afraid Willie?'

He shook his head. 'No, actually I'm not. I might be when it comes closer, but I just think that there's no point. I'm going to die. There are babies lying up in the children's hospital who haven't had a life. Look at all the little kids who died at the hands of Driske. I've had a good life. I have you darling. Everyone dies someday Ally, even you. You'll be ninety-nine and wrinkly. With me, it's live fast, die young and have a good-looking corpse.' He sighed and pulled her closer, kissing the top of her head. 'I have regrets sweetheart. I didn't get to be with you longer. I won't be there to give the girls away at their weddings. I won't see Euan, Caitlyn and Thea grow up or be there for other grandchildren.' He looked into Ally's eyes and smiled at her through his own tear-filled eyes. 'What was that soppy film we watched in Spain? The one with Julia Roberts dying because of her diabetes?'

'Steel Magnolias?' Ally sobbed.

He took her face in his hands and kissed the tip of her nose. 'Julia Robert's character says, 'I would rather have five minutes of wonderful than a lifetime of nothing special.' That's how I feel Ally. Before I met you, I thought my life was special, but it wasn't. Okay, I wanted us to be Darby and Joan, grow old together, still shagging at ninety. I'll be up there looking after you and the people I love.'

'You're sure you are going to heaven then?'

'Oh yes, I scored fifty-two goals for Scotland, I've got to be in with a shout. Ally, I need you to listen to me!' Turning serious he sighed. 'I don't want you to be alone darling. Don't mourn me for fifteen years. Six months is too long. I want you to be with someone who you love and who loves you.' Willie looked into her eyes, he smiled and kissed her. 'Ally, what if it wasn't a dream and what Ralph told you is true, and he did have something to do with us meeting? If it is then I'll send you a good man from the grave.'

'It was a dream Willie!'

'I don't think it was babe. How come you remembered that and nothing else? I've been thinking about what you said he told you. He said, 'nothing is forever and through loving Willie you will meet the next love of your life.' I think someone else is the next love of your life, and I've an idea who it could be too.'

'What? Don't be ridiculous Willie. I'll never love anyone the way I love you.'

'No maybe not. But the way you love me is different from the way you loved Ralph. Someone else is out there. You'll love him just as much, only it will be different again. I never loved anyone except myself and my kids before you Ally and that's the difference. You made me capable of loving a woman. I need you to promise me, when you realise you have feelings for this man you will follow them even if it's at my funeral.'

Ally gasped. 'You can't possibly want me to be with one of your friends.'

Willie grinned. 'No of course not, you're too good for those three. Besides, they're all settled now. Anyway, enough of this, you'll know when it happens!' He looked at her. 'I want to discuss the memoirs with Lynne. Now she's going on maternity leave it would be the perfect time to make a start. I just need you to ask her, she will do it if you ask. Now come here and let me release some more tension.' His began to kiss her neck and he moved down to her breast; his lips closed around them. Ally responded and rolled over on top. As she moved against him, she felt her eyes fill up with tears, and although her body moved towards climax, she began to sob silently. Her tears falling on to the pillow, trying to stop him seeing how upset she was.

Willie pulled her face towards him. He held her until she stopped crying and gently moved her hair, which was tangled and wet with sweat and tears, away from her face. 'Ally, you have to listen to me! I don't want you to have to hide how you feel babe. I don't know why I'm not frightened and crying too. Maybe the tumour has anesthetised my feelings about that or something? You can talk to me about how you feel, but I honestly do believe there is something after death. I'm not sure if it's the God and angels the priests used to beat into us, but it's there. It's all around us, I think I'll be there looking after you.' Willie kissed her and wrapped his arms around her. 'Now sleep beautiful lady, tomorrow's another day.'

Next morning Ally was up early and showered. Willie lounged on the couch watching football. Frankie and David arrived with Bernie and Kevin Willies lawyer. 'Ally stay here will you. I need you to hear this so that there will be no mistake in what I want to happen.'

Despite the serious nature of the visit, Frankie and Willie had the others in stitches as they recounted some of their adventures. Willie sat in his big chair; he pulled Ally onto his lap as he calmly discussed what he wanted to happen. Frankie, Alfie and David had already agreed to buy out some of Willie's shares in the clubs. This would provide substantial financial settlements for all five of his children; as well as some shares, they would hold seats on the board.

The remaining shares were to be Ally's to do with as she pleased, as well as the loch side house and the holiday home in Majorca. Ally protested but Willie silenced her. 'Ally, you've made me happier than I've ever been. Because of you, I will die a happy man. We still have loads of time honey; I'm not planning on going any time soon. I want to leave money in a trust fund for the people in Whitefield's, to give kids the opportunities that they would not have had, and a soccer school in Glasgow for deprived children. I'm still enough of an egocentric wanker to want my name to be remembered. I want to be cremated and my ashes to be scattered in Majorca. Remember when we walked along the beach in the moonlight? Scatter them there. This is the music I want to be played. No black, no priest and no fucking hymns please!' Ally began to cry, and Willie tightened his grip around her. 'Ally, I'm sorry but we have to do this. I have three ex-wives and two of them are likely to try to contest this will, I need to speak to my Korrie too, because she can be a loose cannon, I don't want my kids falling out over it all.' Frankie wiped away a tear from his cheek with the back of his hand and David buried his face in his hands.

'Oh, for fuck sake you two, liven up. Davie you've been telling me for years I was going to kill myself. Well now I'm dying and it's not even my fault. Look, please keep your tears until I'm gone the lot of you. I've had a good life, a lot of laughs. I need you two and Alfie when he gets here, to look after the other people I love. Apart from Ally, I trust you three more than anyone else in the world. I need you to witness what I want and to make sure that it is carried out. Then I've a good bottle of whisky and we can all get drunk together.'

'One last time Willie?' Frankie said, smiling sadly.

'Fuck that, I have at least two years. I think we can get drunk a few times in that space of time. You two have got to remember me for the next thirty-odd years. You have to keep me alive for my descendants. You also must try to keep my Korrie on the straight and narrow, and that gentlemen could be your hardest task ever. Frankie, you're her godfather, so good luck with that. Bernie, stepfather?'

Bernie smiled and nodded. 'She's just you with tits Willie.'

'Oh, and Frankie, if you let Joe make a move on Ally, I'll come back and haunt you. Same goes for you all, Ally is off limits. I'll make you suffer if you try.'

Frankie smiled and winked at Ally. 'Might be worth taking the risk Willie.'

'When's Alfie getting in?' Bernie asked.

Frankie looked at the gold Rolex on his wrist. 'Oh, about now, he's coming straight here. Shouldn't be too long, about an hour, I think. Lynne and Lesley are picking them up. They're going to Cameron House for a spa day with Betty after they drop him here. Ally why don't you join them honey? I know you said no,' Frankie said kindly. 'You need to get away from him for a while, they've booked it for four just in case.'

Willie laughed. 'It will do you good sweetheart, then we can party when you bring the girls back. We can go over my last will and testament.'

***

After the women, the agent and lawyer left, the four men sat around the table. The whisky bottle on the table between them. 'For fuck sake, don't look so fucking miserable. The wake is *after* I die. I want you three to look after my family. Euan especially, he's only nine and even if I get another two years, he is still going to be young and without a father. He is shaping up to be an even better player than Billy, so he'll need a guiding hand. Alfie, you have only girls so be his dad. Belinsa likes you. All my wives liked you more than they liked me, even Hailey.'

'Wull, I pumped Hailey while you were still married.'

Willie looked at Alfie and burst out laughing. 'You fucking dark horse. She wouldn't even let me after she had Jade.'

'I did Belinsa!'

'Christ, you too,' he said, slapping Frankie. 'What is this, confession time? Am I supposed to be angry?'

'I know about you and Lynne the week I started going out with her.'

Willie looked at Frankie, he made a face. Does Lynne know that you know?'

'She told me Wull, when you were diagnosed. She didn't want it coming between us. I told her what happened to me as well, so no more secrets. Well, actually, I didn't dare tell her about Belinsa, there was a bit of an overlap there, and I did tell her I had never slept with anyone when we were together . . . '

'You never said she had told you about our one-night stand!'

'Didn't want to fall out with you mate. I kind of thought I would need to punch you or something and didn't want to, seeing as you were so ill.'

'Well Davie, it looks like you are the only one that has never shared a woman with us.'

'I haven't done Betty or Lynne either. I did shag Annie Brown though. Took her virginity actually.'

'No . . . you didn't!' Alfie laughed. 'Tell him Frankie.'

'Davie, she told us all that. I came home one night, and it was the usual, climbed in the window and he was in bed.'

Alfie giggled remembering. 'He said to me, 'I broke in a lassie tonight, it was Annie Brown. I said, oh was she was crying and holding on to a lamp post afterwards saying it was so sore, and she had never done it before? He said 'aye, were you watching?' I said no, I had her last week and she did the same thing.'

Willie laughed out loud. 'Then I told you she did the same with me. Cried out loud and said it hurt and she had not done it before and asked me not to tell anyone. I was fourteen, how would I know?'

We were fifteen, so you were definitely first Wull, as usual.'

David smiled. 'No, you weren't, I did it when I was thirteen. She was my first, and she said I was hers. She didn't do any crying though. Maybe I am not as well-endowed as you three? But I've never told Lesley, so keep it to yourselves. She thinks she was first.'

Frankie shook his head sadly. 'Christ boys, we have treated women in a shocking way, haven't we? I can't imagine ever cheating on Lynne now. You would never do it to Betty. They are both too far out of our league for that. Lesley would never let you Davie.'

David smiled. 'You too Willie, you've never even noticed another woman since you met Ally. I did snog Corinna at the scout hall disco when we were twelve, does that count? Anyway Willie, you and Ally, are you still able to do it? Cos if you can't, I could oblige, I am feeling a bit left out here!'

'Yes, I am, thanks. Apparently, I got a tumour on the side that doesn't control sex.'

'Is there a bit in your head that controls sex?' Frankie asked.

Willie shrugged. 'I love Ally, and I want you all to remember that I have never been interested in anyone else since I clapped eyes on her. I need you all to promise me, until she takes up with her new man, you will look after her.'

They all looked at him. 'She took fifteen years to go with you, so it could be a long wait,' Alfie said quietly, taking a large gulp of his whisky.

'No Alfie, I hope that within a year she'll have begun a relationship with someone. I'm going to make sure she does.' Willie tapped the side of his nose. 'I have a cunning plan!'

Frankie took a deep breath; 'you really do have something wrong with your head.'

'Yeah, and I have the scans to prove it. Anyway, we are all now loved up and happy. We all treat women well Frankie, don't we? So, I think we have definitely all grown up at last boys.' Willie poured them all a whisky from a second bottle. 'Try this one boys.'

'This is good stuff,' Alfie said, taking a sip.

'Should be, it's eight hundred quid a bottle. It's a Chivas but a good limited edition. Well, you can't take it with you and I'm not fucking leaving any of you my whisky collection, I'm drinking it first.' He turned serious. 'Frankie, I also want you to do something about the Brothers and what they did to us. I'm going to give a statement to the police before I die, and I want you to think about it. Now you've told Lynne about it there is no reason not to. I discussed it with Ally because I needed to know what the process is for this kind of thing. They need people to say what they saw. Brother Matthew is still alive, so is Father Gerrard. I've had a private investigator looking into it. You need closure on this Frankie. That dirty old bastard needs to be punished too.'

David rested his hand on Frankie's shoulder. 'You should at least think about it mate. You were a wean. He was supposed to look after us.'

Alfie nodded. 'I told you years ago, you should do it. Now that I know what you went through, I think you need to speak to the police. These men are getting older, just like us.'

Frankie nodded. 'Ally has arranged for me to speak to someone she knows from the police, and she'll sit through it with me. That's a hell of a woman you have there Wull.'

'What about Ally after you go?' Alfie asked quietly. 'She'll be a wealthy widow!'

'She would be without my money Alfie. Her compensation from the council is seven figures. There's criminal injuries compensation to come too. I want her to stay here though. I've left it to her. When I bought this house, it was to be a family house.' He took a gulp of whisky. 'I need you lot to promise me that you'll stick to the agreement we made today. I need to be able to die, knowing that you'll be there for Ally.'

'You know we will. All that swapping women was years ago, and I'm not into it at all,' Frankie said. 'Lynne is enough for me.' The other two nodded. 'She's safe with us. We'll veto any men that come sniffing around. After what she did for me Willie, I'll always be grateful to her and will make sure when she does move on, it's with the right guy!'

'What about Joe?' Willie asked, looking around the table.

'He's pumping your Yvonne again Willie.' Frankie laughed. 'Sorry, but somebody had to tell you.'

CHAPTER
THIRTY-NINE

Ally lay on the massage table as the therapist worked on her neck, shoulders and back. 'Mrs Ogilvie, you're so tight with tension. You really do need to come over more often. We can book you in weekly or one of the girls could come over to you. My dad had cancer, and it helped my mum to get out for a few hours and have some pampering.'

After her massage, Ally got into the jacuzzi where the other three women sat. 'I'm so glad you decided to come Ally, it really is something you should do regularly. I can't believe Willie is dying. Oh Ally, it's so unfair, it's just not right.' Lynne put her arm out and pulled Ally closer. 'Is there anything that Frankie and I can do?'

'Lynne, just look after yourself and have a healthy baby.'

Tears began to run down Lynne's face as the jacuzzi bubbled away, she tried to blink them back. 'You're both being so brave.'

'We really don't have any choice, do we?' The water bubbled around the four of them, and Ally felt a strong bond with these three women who only a year ago, she'd never met. 'Look, Willie's philosophy is that there's no point in wallowing in self-pity when nothing can be done. He wants to enjoy what life he has left,' Ally said quietly.

'And you?' Betty asked.

'I'm devastated.' Ally's voice broke. 'I'm not angry, or bitter, just plain sad. I'm trying to do what he wants, be brave, but I want to go out and howl at the moon. I love him so much. I can't believe that this is happening!'

Lesley and Betty's names were called through the tannoy to go for their next treatment. Ally smiled through her tears. 'Go for heaven's sake, Lynne will keep me company. I'm fine, honestly, it's just hard to keep putting on a brave face.' She looked sadly at the other women. 'He won't let me be sad.' She began to sob. 'He talks as though he's going on a holiday or something.' Ally stood up; she grabbed a towel from the side and buried her face in it. 'Lynne, I don't think it's good for you to spend too long in the jacuzzi in your condition. Let's go through to the lounge and have a coffee.'

The lounge was empty; wrapped in aqua-coloured robes and slippers, the two women sat down in a corner. Lynne reached out and touched Ally's hand. 'Ally, is there anything I can do?'

'Actually, there is. Willie wants to write his memoirs and he wants someone to do it with him. He needs someone he can trust. You're a journalist Lynne.'

'I don't know what to say Ally.'

'Say that you will consider it. Willie wants to leave a warts and all account of his life Lynne.'

'What about you Ally, would it not be better being written by you? You have a PHD.'

Ally shook her head. 'My doctorate is in social work; I'd be too academic; this needs someone with a journalistic flair. It also has to be someone he trusts. Lynne, it has to be you. I'm committed to write an account of our experience of the shootings and explosion with Stevie now. Besides, I couldn't be objective telling Willie's story, I'd want to do an analysis of everything. We both want you to tell the story for us.

Ally you must be hurting so much, I . . . want to be there for you, you know you can talk to me about it. I want . . . to . . . help.

Willie will fight till the last you know Lynne. He's very determined to have as much quality of life as possible.' Ally wiped away a tear, 'I love him, and I love being with him, but he just . . . you know wants to be intimate and I just keep thinking that he won't be with me for much longer. He is making all these plans and they are all short term.'

'Are you still able to . . . have sex?'

'Oh yes, and it's every bit as good as it always was, better perhaps because we know it's precious. I . . . I just don't even want to contemplate life without Willie.'

Lynne moved over, put her arm around Ally's shoulder and held her close. 'We'll all be there for Willie and for you, before and after, Ally.'

'When I was in surgery, my heart stopped. I think I was hovering between life and death for a little while. Something happened.'

'Willie told us about the dream Ally.'

'I don't think it was a dream Lynne. I saw them operating on my head and my heart stopping. They were shocking me back. Ralph and my mother were there, and I keep remembering what they said. I asked my mother where Abby, my baby daughter, was and she said that she was preparing to return to me. Ralph told me to follow my heart with Willie and that he loved me. He said loving Willie and being loved by him would lead to the next love of my life. Then he said nothing is forever. I found out Kiera was pregnant. Thea's the spitting image of Abby. And now this with Willie. It's led me to believe that there is something after death Lynne. I think he'll be around me when he goes. Lynne, please say you'll do the book. There's a really good story there, and you have known him for what, twelve years?'

Lynne nodded.

'Well who better, you've been part of a lot of it.'

'Ally it's just . . . there's some of the stuff . . .'

'Lynne, I know that you and Willie slept together.'

Lynne stared at her, shock registering on her face. 'Oh, fuck, Ally, did he tell you that?'

'No, you did! You kind of look at me a certain way sometimes when I am talking about Willie. I just knew. I noticed it after my hen party. We were talking about our first time, and I looked at you and I knew. I asked him Lynne, he told me what happened. Willie doesn't lie if you ask him outright you know that. He doesn't volunteer information sometimes, but lying, no.'

'Do you mind Ally? It was a one-night thing, we were really wasted. I was young and stupid. I would say it didn't mean anything, but I'd be lying. It meant more to me than to him. Even wasted, he was a fantastic lover, so considerate. I never really thought about it until you and him got together, and Frankie and I began to have problems. At the time, I fell in love with Frankie pretty quickly and never wanted to sleep with anyone again. Frankie and Willie, I think used to share a lot of women Ally, which is probably why it happened. If it's any consolation, I have never touched drugs since. I can't believe you are okay about this!'

Ally smiled. 'Why wouldn't I be? It was before I met him, and you and Frankie, well, I can see how much you love each other. Will you tell Frankie?'

'He knows Ally. I told him a few weeks ago, when we found out about Willie being terminally ill. He was fine about it. It was over twelve years ago, he just said *'let's just put it in the past,'* he's not going to tell Willie he knows. I'm just a bit embarrassed about it now.'

'So, that's not why you are hesitant about the book?'

'It was part of it but I'm afraid I won't do him justice Ally. Ally, I just can't believe this is all happening.' She wiped away a tear.

'Lynne, there's no one who could do it better.'

'Ok, I'll talk to him when we go back.'

'Thank you!'

'Ally, I love you. You're the bravest person I've ever met.'

'I love you too Lynne. I'm not brave. I've never had any option but to try to survive. Promise me we will always be friends.'

'You bet; I want you to be this one's godmother.' Lynne rubbed her swollen stomach.

Ally reached out and patted Lynne's baby bump. 'At least Willie will get to meet him.'

'What makes you think it's a boy, Ally?'

'Just the way you are carrying it. A summer baby is nice Lynne. Roll on July!'

Lynne and Willie began working on his life story right away; she decided to use her maternity leave to write it. Lynne began to visit several times a week. Willie, and at times Frankie and David, talked and shared stories about their younger days. Willie wanted the story to be published after he died. They had publishers fighting over the rights.

CHAPTER

FORTY

'So, we can go on holiday Clive?'

'Of course, Ally, Willie is doing great. As I said, he responded well. We got most of the tumour, and the radiotherapy has slowed down the growth.'

Ally looked at him. 'Does that mean . . . you know?'

'Ally my dear, I know what you're thinking, but no, it doesn't mean he'll live. It'll grow again and could grow elsewhere too. There is the little secondary one deep in his brain already. It's not growing yet but it will. We've blasted it with the radiotherapy but it's not accessible to surgery, and eventually it will get bigger and become a problem. When that happens, we won't be able to do much except make him comfortable. However, given how much of the primary tumour we got, he may have longer than we first thought.' Clive reached over and touched Ally's arm. 'Ally, you have to know that if there was anything that could be done to stop this or cure him, then I would do it.'

'Miracles do happen Clive, until the worst happens I can still hope.' Ally gripped Clive's hand and gulped back tears as Willie returned to the room with a nurse.

'Everything present and correct Mr Ruthven.' The nurse handed the file to Clive and left the room.

'Okay, so I'm officially in remission then. How long Clive?'

'You're in what I would call abeyance. You should have two to three years of quality life now Willie, perhaps a little more. We don't really know until we see how the primary tumour grows, and we'll keep watching the secondary one. The radiotherapy has had the desired effect. Thing is Willie, it's not an exact science. From what you have told me about your symptoms, this tumour grew very slowly originally. So, the hope is that it does that again and buys you some time. The drugs you are taking will slow it down and give you a good quality of life.'

'Clive, can you tell me what will happen to me when it starts again? Will I have dementia? I've seen some other ex-players with it, I just don't want that to happen, I want to die with my faculties. Clive, I need to know the truth. I can handle it. Ally needs to know too; she's getting into the 'hoping for a miracle' saga.'

Clive looked from Willie to Ally and sighed. 'You will begin to have the headaches again. You may experience a change in personality, become aggressive and angry. The pressure will build up, the fits will begin again. There could also be a degree of memory loss and mild dementia. But when the primary tumour grows again it will, in all probability, invade the space where we removed it, then just expand. You'll slip into a coma and die fairly quickly Willie. Is that blunt enough for you?'

'It is, thank you Clive. I needed to know. I've been considering an assisted suicide abroad.'

'No Willie, I can't condone that.'

'I don't care what you condone Clive. I'm not asking you to refer me to do anything, just to make sure that I'm fit to travel when the time comes.'

After they left, Clive Ruthven opened his desk drawer and took out a bottle of whisky. He poured a measure into a glass and leaned back in his chair. He had given the worst news possible to people more times than he cared to remember. This couple were special to him though, it felt as bad as telling a member of his own family. Clive had gone through so much with Willie whilst Ally was ill. He had watched their relationship develop; he had come to see them as friends. He saw and admired the bravery Willie was showing. He smiled when he remembered Willie asking him early on if it would affect his virility. He had shared with Clive some of the intimate details of his sexual adventures before meeting Ally, and that since meeting Ally he had felt more fulfilled with her than he had at any other time in his life.

When Clive had first met Willie, and Ally was his patient, like everyone else in Scotland he had read the stories of Willog's adventures with interest. At that time, Clive had doubted that he had a genuine bone in his body where women were concerned. He had been amazed at the relationship as it developed, and he knew Willie loved this woman and would cherish her. Clive had watched the romance and knew the feelings they had were mutual. Ally adored Willie. He thought sadly of how distressed she was, he remembered his own experience with his wife and her illness and death. He opened Willie's file and held the scan picture up then put it on the screen. He peered at it and then put his glasses on and looked again. 'How extraordinary!' he said out loud. He picked up the telephone and dialled. 'Rajas, how are you? It's Clive Ruthven, I wonder if you could give me a second opinion on something.'

CHAPTER

FORTY-ONE

Ally sat by the side of the pool next to Danny, watching Willie fooling around in the water with Caitlin and Euan. 'It's hard to take in how ill he is Mum. Look at him!'

'I know Danny, but Clive's the best there is and even he doesn't know how long Willie has. He reckons that when the symptoms come back it will be over pretty quickly.'

'Mum, are you going to be okay? Are you coping?'

'I just have to, Danny.' She shot her son a withering glance.

Danny smiled; he had seen that look many times. He sighed. 'Mum, it's really weird. I never knew my dad; he was just a picture on the wall. I've no memories at all of him alive. I was so angry when I found out about Willie. Although I wanted you to be happy, I suppose I just thought that it would be with Stevie.' Danny looked at his mother, 'we all thought you two were an item you know? You're so close, and he was the father figure for me. Willie though, he's great, I really mean that Mum. When I see how you are together, I couldn't wish for better for you. The way he treats Scott and me, he is amazing. He loves you so much Mum.' Seeing Ally fighting tears Danny changed the subject quickly. 'How was your sail over? Wasn't it really long? Why couldn't he fly?'

Ally sighed. 'Clive did not want him to be subjected to the pressure of flying after the surgery. Willie really wanted to have this holiday though. It was a bit strange coming here by boat, and it took a long time, but it was quite nice. We have such a nice crew and the cook was amazing. Once we got into the Mediterranean it was great, and it was much more relaxing than flying. There was no waiting around, no anxiety. How are you Danny? I feel bad I've had to devote so much time to Willie lately, that's one of the reasons we were so keen to have this break while he is well. Caitlin is the same age as you were when your dad died,' Ally observed, watching Willie splash around the pool with her.

'It's her granddad though Mum. She still has Archie. When he and Leah are not together, he has loads of time with her. She was telling me on the way over they are seeing each other again. That's got to be good for wee Caitlin if they can sort their relationship out.'

Ally looked over to the side of the pool where Leah was rubbing sun cream into Jade's shoulders. All of Willie's children were dear to her but Leah had become a great friend to Ally and a support to Willie in his illness. 'She's a lovely girl Danny, so sensible and loving, I forget she's only thirty-two. I'm happy for her and Archie. Willie says it was Leah who ended it, not him. She didn't want to be away from Scotland, and he was playing down south. He's on the transfer list apparently and has agreed to come up here to live and play. So, we know he'll look after her and Caitlin, help them through what's coming.'

Danny smiled as he watched his stepfather encouraging Caitlin to jump into the pool. 'It's still someone who should be in her life, and like me she won't remember him. I have no memories and Scott, although he was older, really only remembers from photographs.' Danny looked at his mother and shook his head, tears building up. 'Life is shit sometimes Mum, isn't it? You have had some really bad breaks. Doesn't seem fair that one person can have all that happen to them.'

'That's just life Danny, but I have loved and lost some really great folk too. That gives me lots of great memories.' She pulled her younger son closer and kissed his cheek. 'Now enough sad stuff, what's happening in your life?'

Danny took a deep breath before speaking. 'Mum I've been seeing someone. It's getting serious, I wanted you to know. I don't want it to come as a shock the way it did with Scott and Kiera. I don't know where it's going but I really like this girl. I want you to meet her.'

'Don't we already know her Danny?' Ally said, smiling.

'You know?'

'About you and Gemma?' Ally nodded. 'Frankie told Willie. She's a nice girl Danny, and she's Willie's goddaughter.'

'She's a bit of a diva, but I get on well with her. We kind of hooked up at the wedding. She's worried you'll be upset. We told David and Lesley before I left. They were nice, and they think a lot of you. Gemma loves Willie too. We're kind of thinking that she could move into the flat with me, now Scott and Kiera are moving out.'

'I should say isn't it a bit early to do that, but I can hardly talk can I Danny? I've met and married a man in under two years. I suppose if it's right, it's right.'

Later, in their bedroom, Ally lay watching Willie sleeping, his face tanned and relaxed. He moved slightly and opened his eyes. 'That's creepy babe!' he whispered, pulling her closer.

'What?'

'Watching when I'm sleeping. It actually wakes me up. Come here, let me . . . make you purr.' He began to kiss her neck and shoulders.

'No Willie, not with all the kids here. These tiled floors, you hear every movement.'

'I'll be quiet babe, promise. We can do it really . . . really . . . re ally slowly, they won't hear us. God, I love you Mrs Ogilvie, you are one sexy lady, and I can't get enough of you.'

To Willie's horror Ally began to cry. She pushed him away and stood up, opening the patio doors onto the veranda of the large top floor bedroom. He followed her out onto the terrace, the lights in the valley below twinkled in the moonlight, and they could hear the sea rushing in, hitting the rocks on the other side of the house. Ally was holding the ornamental wrought iron balustrade, looking out over the garden. He could see her body shaking, no sound came out though until he touched her shoulder. 'Willie, I can't do this, I can't lose you now. I can't imagine what my life will be like without you! I want to scream and howl at the moon.'

Willie held her, kissing her, letting her sob. 'Let it out babe. Stop saying the word can't. You can, and you will. Darling, this isn't fair on you, but you should realise you have made me the happiest man alive. I'll be the happiest man in the cemetery too. Being here this week, with everyone I love, it's . . . I suppose bittersweet. Ally, this is life, you know that. Babe you need to start dealing with it. Ally talk to me, tell me how you are feeling?'

'When I wakened up all those years ago, they let me believe for a few days that everyone was okay. Oh, Dad thought he was doing the right thing. I was asking for Abbey, asking where she was. They told me she was with Ralph and my mum. It was New Year when they told me.' Ally shook her head sadness etched on her face at the memory. 'The shock was immense Willie. I thought a lot about death and loss. I thought the shock of a sudden death was worse than anything else. I thought about my own death, and that perhaps knowing you are dying is better. You can prepare yourself and those around you. You can get used to it.' Ally began to sob into Willie's chest. 'It's fucking not, Willie. It's worse in some ways. I keep watching you and I know what it's like, that emptiness after someone dies . . . the longing, the grief. This is dragging it out.' She looked at him in horror, 'Willie, I'm so sorry, that didn't come out right. I didn't mean it to sound like that. Oh God Willie, I'm turning into a fucking neurotic!'

'Babe, there is no right way to deal with this, no wrong way either I suppose. I just want to enjoy what I have left with you and with all of them.' He held her kissing her face and head. 'Maybe it's selfish but I just want to be with you every minute, let's just cherish what we have and as I said enjoy what we have left?'

'I know, and I'm ruining it, making it all about me. I'm as bad as Korrie. Fuck, there I go again.'

'Ally, knowing how much you love me and will miss me is special too, babe. I'll be here,' he touched her head, 'and I'll be here!' He rested his hand over her heart and looked into her eyes, tears in his own eyes he smiled. 'Ah ha, my old magic is still there. I thought I had lost the ability to turn every woman I get into a relationship with into a nutter. Davie asked me that one night when we were drunk. He said, *are they mad before you meet them, or do you turn them all into psychos?'* My work is complete,' Willie smiled. 'You are officially mad.'

'Willie, I can't stand that I'll never touch you again, never hear your voice. I close my eyes, listen to you speaking, try to focus on remembering what you sound like. I lie watching your face, trying to remember every line, contour. Maybe I'm a bit mad after all?'

'Is this about me? Or is it about Ralph babe? What do you remember about him?'

'I look at photos and I can't remember what he sounded like! I can remember what he looked like, what his skin felt like, even what he smelt like, but I can't remember his voice. When I had that dream, I heard him speak. That's why I know it was real, it happened. I love you so much Willie, I never thought I could, and now I'm losing you, what if I can't remember things about you?'

'No Ally, if what you say is true, I'm going to be there. With Ralph.' Willie smiled and kissed Ally's forehead. 'Might get a bit crowded when you are with someone else!'

'I'll not be able to Willie. How can I?'

'Oh, you will, and you will be loved, and love, again. You are too loving not to babe, I hope if nothing else, I have made you able to realise you can love again.' He began to kiss her, and she melted into his arms, returning his kisses, her face still wet. He lifted her off her feet and carried her back into the bedroom.

CHAPTER

FORTY-TWO

Ally stepped out of the shower; Willie stood brushing his teeth at the sink, his hair still wet from his own shower. Ally looked out of the window of the Riverside flat. She could see a pleasure boat winding its way up to start the day of taking tourists along the River Clyde. Willie looked at her and put his hand on the small of her back. 'Babe I think I should come with you and rearrange my appointments today.'

'No Willie, it's better you are not there because the press will just focus on you. What are you doing at the lawyer's office anyway Willie?' Ally stepped away and lifted a towel from the heated rail. 'How much bloody money do you have when it's taking this long to write up your will?'

Ally began to dry herself. Willie moved over and pulled her towards him; he began to kiss her gently at first then with more passion. 'We have loads of time before you have to leave Ally,' he said. His eyes had the usual wicked glint in them which told her he was aroused. 'Enough time for a full session actually.' He lifted her off her feet and carried her through to the bedroom. 'Brenda won't be here until later, I asked her to go to the supermarket this morning.' On the bed, Willie kissed his way down her body, using his tongue, making featherlike movements. She shivered and pulled him back up, so they were face to face. His lips met hers and they moved together on the bed. The intensity of their lovemaking meant Ally quickly forgot how anxious she was about the day's trial.

Afterwards she lay in his arms, and as he held her, she felt a moment of sadness as she realised that the days of her being able to do this were numbered. Her fear was that there may come a time when, due to the frailness of his body, Willie would be unable to make love and she knew it was important to him. She found it difficult to accept how ill he actually was. His body still toned and tanned, he looked like a man in his prime and in great physical shape. Just over six months ago she had promised to love this man until death parted them, believing that they could have many years in front of them to enjoy each other. Now she had no idea how long he would remain with her. They had been to visit the facility in Switzerland where Willie and she would go when the time came, travelling by boat and train from Majorca. It had been a beautiful trip despite the destination and purpose, although she didn't want to focus on what lay ahead next time they made that journey. It comforted her that as Willie moved from this world into the next, she would be lying beside him, holding him. Most of their friends thought this was weird. Ally would have too just a year ago. However, she now accepted this was what her husband wanted. Ally felt at peace with the world now, grateful for every minute she had with Willie.

CHAPTER

FORTY-THREE

The court was hushed as they brought Seamus into the witness box. Armed guards sat on either side of him. He looked around the court and grinned. 'You all wait and see!' he shouted, 'I've listened to your shite for a month now, bring it on . . . bring it fucking on.'

'Mr Driske could you please be quiet, or I will have you removed from the court,' the judge said, looking at Seamus then at his lawyers. 'Counsel please make sure your client refrains from any further outbursts.'

Ally and Stevie sat together in the witness room oblivious to the shouting in the court. Stevie held her hand and Ally tried hard to focus on remembering as much as she could. Stevie could feel her palm sweating and attempted to distract her. 'How's Willie?'

'He is doing okay, dealing with it all. He's actually much better than I am. He has an appointment with Clive today.'

'Ally, you know I'll be there for you, don't you?'

Ally nodded. 'Yes, but you need to concentrate on Cathy too. She's lovely Stevie, I could not have chosen better for you. Willie responded well to the radiotherapy and Clive has been fantastic.

He's been treating Willie as a private patient. Not many couples have had the same man inside their brain Stevie.'

'How was your trip Ally? Kiera said you went back to Majorca with Willie's friends? I really would like to see the villa. Sounds idyllic.'

'You could go Stevie, Willie wouldn't mind. I'd love to say we could go with you, but we really don't know how Willie's health is going to pan out. We had two great holidays, some bits were sad, but the weather was great. You know we went to Switzerland this time too?'

Stevie nodded, 'How was that?'

'Interesting! It's all set up to allow death with dignity that's denied people here. Willie wants it to just be me and him, but Alfie and Betty have agreed to be there for me after ... Stevie, can we change the subject please?'

'You're really starting to look like a WAG Ally, with the tan and the sunnies.'

'Piss off Stevie,' Ally said, dabbing her eyes and composing herself. 'I'll be back at work after the trial.'

'Is that wise Ally?'

'Willie is encouraging me to return. He wants me to have something when he ... when he's not here anymore. Fuck Stevie, all roads lead to Rome! He and Lynne have finished the first draft of the book too, so hopefully it will be ready to be published before ... I can't say it Stevie, it's too hard.'

'Before he dies,' Stevie said simply. Ally nodded. 'Let's change the subject sweetheart. What are you doing this weekend Ally?'

'Oh, we are going out on the boat. When I was ill Willie took me to Ailsa Craig, and we had a picnic.' She smiled and blushed. 'It was the first time we were intimate. We're going to do it again this weekend. We're staying at Willie's flat here for the next week or two while the court case is going on, to save the travelling in and out of Glasgow every day. I can walk here in ten minutes from the flat, it's good for my legs too. Saves me having to do my physio. Come for tea when we get finished today. Willie would love to see you. It's been a while Stevie.'

The tannoy creaked to life and the voice coming through it echoed across the room. 'Calling Doctor Alyson Ogilvie.' The trial had been going on for four weeks; finally, they were ready to start hearing evidence from Alyson and Stevie. Each day, apart from the five days she and Willie had been on Majorca, Ally had telephoned to be told they did not need her. Yesterday she had received the call to say that they were ready to hear from her and Stevie. This morning Ally had lain in Willie's arms crying after they made love, terrified of the day ahead. She knew that once this trial was over, she would be free to spend all her time with the man she loved. Willie would have accompanied her to court, but he had an appointment with Clive. Ally looked at Stevie and stood up. Stevie hugged her and said, 'be brave, gorgeous.' The children involved, including Alexis, had already given their evidence by video link, it had been decided that the adults should appear in person.

Ally was ushered into court; she looked at the man in the dock and he grinned at her. 'Ah, the Accidental WAG social worker!' he shouted. 'The woman who caused all this. Fucking frigid bitch! A year and a half I've waited to be face to face with you, fucking whore.'

'Mr Driske I will not tell you again.' the judge shouted, banging his fist on the ledge in front of him. 'Please be quiet! Or you will be removed from my court.'

Seamus continued to glare at Ally as she was sworn in. Ally began to be questioned by the prosecution team. Seamus continued to shout and threaten and eventually the judge ordered him to be removed from the court. As he was being ushered out of the dock Seamus clutched his chest and fell to the ground.

People began to run around; a defibrillator was produced. The judge ordered the public gallery to be emptied.

Ally watched in horror as the first aider tried to revive him on the floor of the court. The policeman handcuffed to Seamus produced a key and the handcuffs were taken off. An ambulance was on the scene in a few minutes and he was lifted on to a trolley unconscious being given oxygen. Reporters ran from the court switching on their mobile phones, each trying to make the first announcement of the collapse of the most hated man in Scotland. Ally was ushered from the court; she watched as the ambulance carrying Seamus Driske roared off, the siren loud as it made its way through the traffic. Stevie came out to stand beside her. 'What happened?'

'He collapsed in the Dock, Seamus. I think he's dead Stevie.'

'Best thing probably, saves us reliving it all Ally. Hope it was painful.'

'He just stood up, clutched his chest and hit the deck. He was shouting at me though, blaming me for his behaviour.'

Cameras began to flash as the press noticed them standing together. 'Stevie, Ally, what are your thoughts?'

'Do you think he's better dead?'

'Stevie come on? You must have an opinion.'

'Ally how does it feel?'

'Did seeing you give him a heart attack?'

'Please, we've been through enough guys,' Stevie said. 'Ally and I have no thoughts on Seamus Driske. He took ill and collapsed. We're not really in a position to comment.'

'Ally how is Willie doing?' one of the reporters asked.

'He is doing well thanks. He's recovering from radiotherapy and in good spirits. Now if you will excuse us, Stevie and I have a life to lead.'

'Ally are you relieved that you did not have to give evidence today?'

'A bit if I'm honest,' Ally admitted quietly. 'Reliving it all is not something I was looking forward to.'

'How will you feel if Seamus dies?'

'I will feel that the families of those murdered have been robbed of seeing justice done.'

'But there will be one less bad man in the world,' someone in the crowd shouted.

Stevie took Ally's hand and pushed her into a waiting taxi. 'Ally I'll take you up on that offer of tea tonight if you don't mind. I'd like to stick around in Glasgow for a few hours and find out what happens to that bastard. Although I do hope he's dead Ally. It's the only way wee Alexis and the other injured kids will ever feel safe.'

'Don't you think that if he has died, he'll have got off lightly?'

'No Ally, I think we all deserve him to be dead.'

'Ally, the press, they're at the flat too!' Stevie said as the taxi drew up. Ally got out and Stevie followed her into the building. He smiled when the driver refused to take any money from them.

'We'll issue a statement through our lawyer later, when we know what Seamus's condition is,' Ally responded to their questions. Ally got in the lift and turned her key in the lock. The lift moved up. She looked at Stevie and smiled. 'It's good to be with you Stevie. I'm sorry, I meant to call you when I got back, but with Willie's treatment I'd just been so caught up in everything before we went then had to play catch up when we got back here, we've had some issues with the kids, well Korrie actually, she is such hard work.'

CHAPTER

FORTY-FOUR

'You're looking well Willie,' Stevie said, smiling as he shook hands with his friend's husband.

'Thanks Stevie, we had a good time in Majorca, got to go twice in a month. It was great having all the kids there.'

'Thea loved the pool I hear!'

'Yes, she's a little star, she was so good.' Willie looked at his wife. 'I heard about Driske collapsing on the news. I've unplugged the phone too, it kept ringing, Ally, are you alright babe? I wish I'd come with you.'

'Willie, we discussed this. I know you wanted to support me, but the press would have jumped on your story. If you'd been seen in public since the news about your illness being terminal broke, it might have been okay. Besides, you had your appointment with Clive today. How did that go?'

'Oh, fine, same as same as. I'll tell you later.'

'Willie, it's freezing in here.'

Willie grimaced. 'The air conditioning is jammed on Ally. It's broken. Brenda did it this morning after you left. I'm waiting for the engineer to come, they said it might be early evening now. There's press downstairs so perhaps we should go out for a while.

Fancy coming to the flagship with us Stevie? You could stay here tonight.'

Stevie smiled. 'Why don't we go out for dinner? I have to go home.' He shook his car keys. 'I've some work I need to finish.'

'Coffee Stevie?' Ally asked.

'Yes please, I'll have one just now. Hopefully, the press will get fed up and we can get out without being followed.'

'We could just go around to the Vine Leaf for dinner,' Willie said. 'I'll phone and book. Charlie on the ground floor will let us go through her house and out over the veranda if we ask. Where's your car Stevie?'

'It's still at the court. We just jumped in a passing taxi.'

'Well it's walking distance then, anyway the restaurant is just along the street.' Willie lifted the telephone and dialled; he walked through to the lounge to talk to the restaurant. Coming back through, he sat down. 'I've got reservations for five o'clock Stevie, that means you can eat and get down the road early. We can leave the keys with the concierge for the air conditioning guy. It's wee Sid who is on nights this week. It's a pity Cathy isn't here Stevie. It would have been nice to see her.'

'She'd have liked to have been there to support us, but she doesn't want to be all over the press by being with me. So, I felt that it would be better if she stayed at home. Speaking of which, I'd better phone her and tell her I'm here.'

As he finished speaking to Cathy, Ally handed him his coffee. 'You make such great coffee Ally.'

Ally smiled. 'It's a bean to cup machine Stevie, you can't do much wrong.'

Willie stood up, he pushed back the stool from the breakfast bar. 'You two catch up. I'm going for a shower and to get tidied up. I've a reputation to uphold.'

Stevie followed Ally out on to the roof terrace. 'Ally, it's warmer out here than in the flat.'

353

'The air conditioning is brilliant, and Brenda is brilliant, but put them together . . . She's menopausal but just will not slow down. She's having hot flushes, so keeps it turned up as high as it will go when she's working. Willie loves her, she is more of a surrogate mother than an employee, but she drives us mad. She's been worse since he's been ill. She also thinks I'm some kind of saint. I told her just to stay at the loch this week, but she insisted on coming once a week. She's gone home now, thank God.'

'Willie looks great.'

'Yes, he's feeling better. He says he had forgotten how he used to feel. They think he must have had the tumour for a long time, and it had been putting pressure on his brain. I just wish he had done something about it though.' Tears welled up. 'He could've had a better chance of remission or cure if he had. They think he could have a couple of years now.'

'Well that's something Ally. It's still awful though.'

'It's not fair Stevie, just not fair.' He moved over and sat beside her and put his arm around her shoulder as she sobbed her heart out. 'It's not fair. Everyone I love dies, it's not fair. It's my fault, I'm sure I'm a fucking jinx.'

'No Ally, it's not your fault babe, it's just life.' Neither of them saw Willie watching from the kitchen.

When Willie walked back through ten minutes later, Ally had composed herself. 'It's quarter to five, will we stroll around? Des will have our table ready.'

'There's still no news on Seamus!' Ally told him. 'Know what though? It doesn't matter.'

Stevie smiled. 'Yeah, we'll know soon enough. If he lives, the trial will be off for him to recover, and if he dies it's all over. Fuck it, I'll have tea and then just go home. If they want me, they'll find me.'

'Des said he has the chef making your usual Al,' Willie said.

Ally smiled and nudged Stevie. 'Des is a character. He's Frankie and Alfie's cousin, it must be in the genes.'

Willie laughed and nodded in agreement. 'They're all as mad as a box of frogs in that family, both sides. It's an unusual mix; Spanish, Italian, Scottish. Des is from the Scottish-Italian side.'

The mood during the meal was light-hearted, and Ally and Willie drank a bottle of wine. Stevie drank mineral water. They had just ordered their sweet when Willie's phone rang. He glanced at it. 'Oh, it's only Bernie my agent, he'll want to do a press statement about the trial likely. We can do it later; I really can't be bothered about it now.' He switched the phone off and put it in his shirt pocket.

As they left the restaurant, Stevie turned to say goodbye. 'I might as well go back to the car from here,' he said, putting on his jacket.

Ally hugged him, and Willie shook his hand. 'Let's do this again soon with Cathy, mate.'

'Sure Willie.'

They walked slowly back along the river, Willie with his arm around Ally's shoulder. Ally leaned into him. What the illness had taught them both was to savour every waking moment. A young couple sitting on a bench shouted to them and asked if they would mind them having a photograph taken with them. Ally and Willie agreed, and they posed happily for the selfie. As Willie and Ally approached the flat Willie sighed. 'Well the press have not lost interest anyway. Oh look, the air condition-ing guy is here!' he said catching sight of the van parked outside the block. 'Come on, let's try Charlie's patio again. She said she would leave it open for us when she went to work.'

They entered through their neighbour's unlocked patio door and then, locking it carefully behind them, went out through her front door. There was no one in the foyer. Willie pulled Ally to him as they entered the lift. 'At least I won't need my thermals to make love to you tonight babe!' he said as he kissed her lips.

'Don't you ever feel you have enough sex Willie? You were fantastic this morning by the way, and how do you manage to learn all those new tricks?'

'Oh, they're not new darling, I just have a great big repertoire. It comes from all my years of messing around.' Willie grinned. 'Got to say, I have never had such a fulfilling sex life as I do now. It's as though I was made for you, or you were made for me.' He nuzzled Ally's neck. 'I never want to get back out of bed with you when we do it.' Willie began to kiss her passionately. 'We have never done it here in the lift.' He whispered sliding his hands inside the front of her top. I could just jam it between floors and go for it.'

'Why? We have a perfectly good bed and couch in the flat.'

'And the air conditioning man babe, live dangerously Ally.' Willie said laughing. He turned the key and the lift shuddered and stopped between the seventh and the eighth floor. He pushed her up against the wall and they kissed.

'This is madness!' Ally breathed, as he removed her trousers and his own then lifted her up against the wall of the lift. 'The camera! We'll be seen!'

'No, it cuts off after the sixth-floor babe. It's for the lower floors.'

'Willie, no! Stop it, this is madness.'

'You love it really!' he gasped. 'Come on, we are like fucking teenagers again and you feel hot.' He pulled her top up and unfastened her bra with his free hand. His mouth moved to her breast. Ally held on to him, grinding her hips against him as her body gave way to the enormous tidal wave they both knew was coming. Neither of them noticed the light flashing on the security camera mounted on the ceiling of the elevator.

'I can't believe we just did that when there's a workman in the flat,' Ally said, as they both dressed. 'You're incredible Ogilvie. You've been so horny lately.'

'Oh, I spoke to Clive about that. He thinks that the drugs are helping, there's an element of hormone in them. He's thinking of trying them himself. He hasn't been laid in a while.'

Ally stared at him, 'you discussed our sex life with your doctor, with Clive? I'll never be able to look him at him again. What's more, he discussed his sex life with you?'

Willie grinned and kissed her. 'I think it's the only charge he gets. He's more like a mate than my doctor now! Christ sake Ally, we don't actually have many things he doesn't know about. He's been inside both our brains. That must count for something.'

'Willie, these hormones, are they dangerous?'

'Yeah they could kill you.' He laughed and kissed her head. 'Who cares babe?' He looked into her eyes as he kissed her and nuzzled her neck. 'If I can perform like that I don't care what's in them. It's not as though I have to worry about the long-term effects now is it?' They got out of the lift and realised there was no sign of the workman. 'There must have been more than us with problems Ally, he'll be in someone else's flat first. Stevie looked good, didn't he?' Willie said, smiling.

'It's amazing what a haircut and a shave can do. I think it's Cathy's influence.'

'Did you and him never ever even snog Ally?'

'No never! We were close but not that kind of close.'

'Do you think you will, after I go?'

'Willie what on earth? He's with Cathy, and I think he is happy.'

'He has been in love with you for years.'

'He isn't in love with me Willie. He loves me, and I love him, but I don't fancy him, I don't think he actually fancies me either.

357

We both know it's not that kind of thing. It would be like sleeping with my brother or something.'

'Whatever.' Willie lifted the remote control and pressed. 'That's odd, it's not working.' He looked at the Sky box. 'It's off too. Must have been a power cut or something.'

He heard a phone ringing and walked through to the kitchen. 'Stevie has left his mobile Ally,' he called. He heard the lift ping as he walked through. 'Ally, what are you doing?' There was no answer. 'Ally, where are you?' Ally stood in the middle of the living room staring. 'Ally what is . . . going? Jesus, how did you get up here?'

Seamus Driske was standing at the lift with a gun pointing at Ally, who appeared frozen to the spot. 'Oh, you have every right to be surprised. Did you think I was dead? You hoped I was, didn't you? You fucking wanker.'

Willie moved towards him. 'Get back in that lift, now and just go.'

'Make one move and I will shoot her now instead of waiting till we've had a chat. Make a move Willog, and I will take her out.' Still pointing the gun, he walked towards Ally and pulled her roughly towards him. 'You are quite fine Mrs Ogilvy!' He touched her breast. Ally cringed and moved away from him. 'What's up Mrs Ogilvy? You forgotten what it's like to be felt up by a mere mortal? Do I repel you? Ha-ha. We will see whether I still do after I have fucked you. Then I am going to cut off his cock and ram it down your throat. That was quite a performance in the lift, for someone who's dying. Ally, the social worker, you're not my normal type but you are do-able!'

'Don't you touch her! Take your filthy hands off her. Don't fucking dare!' Willie cried.

'What you going to do Willog, kick me? You haven't got the bottle? You're a fucking dying man.' He pulled at Ally's top and she closed her eyes as he ripped the front from it exposing her white lacy bra. 'Nice tits for an old bird,' Seamus grinned. He slid his free hand inside her bra, still holding the gun to Ally's head. Willie lunged at him. '**Bang!**' Ally closed her eyes as the gun went off. When she opened them Willie was on the floor.

'**Willie, no!**' Ally screamed. '**You bastard!**' she cried, '**he has done nothing to you. He wasn't even involved.**'

'Shame, I wasn't going to kill him yet Mrs Social Worker, just stop him being silly.' He kicked Willie's body. Ally tried to get to him. She fell to her knees and tears blinding her, crawled towards his body. Seamus laughed loudly and pulled Ally up by the hair. 'You're right, he has done nothing to me. I've done him a favour, so I have, he was going to die anyway. You and I are going to have some fun then I'm going to kill you too. You can be together. I was going to let him watch while I fucked his wife, so he died knowing how a real man does it. None of that romantic stuff with me Alyson, just a good old-fashioned man-fuck.' Ally felt her head spin; Seamus pushed her towards the veranda door. 'Feck sake, it's cold in here,' he said. 'You should get that air conditioning sorted. Oh dear, you can't because I killed the repair guy. Ha ha-ha, Mrs Social Worker, oh of course, it's Dr Ogilvie now! You are not as smart as me though, now are you? There I was wondering how I was going to get in when I saw you climb over the balcony downstairs. Good old Charlie, going off to work and leaving the door open for you. What a good neighbour. Do you want to beg me to let you live?'

Ally looked at him. 'Do what you like to me, but you will still be an insignificant little man.' She kept looking at Willie's body lying on the floor, a pool of blood spreading out over the cream lounge carpet. Her heart was breaking; she wanted to lie beside him, die with him. 'You're an insignificant nobody Mr Driske. You'll always be a nobody!'

'Oh, how nice, how brave and noble! I'll tell you what I'll do, after I have fucked you up and down the house, I'll kill you slowly. I put your man out of his fucking misery, so I did.'

'You bastard! I hope you rot in hell,' Ally screamed as she tried to get to Willie. She wanted to hold him just one more time; he lay face down on the carpet, and she just wanted to look at him.

Seamus pushed Ally out onto the terrace. 'Fuck me, a hot tub! Well maybe I won't shoot you, I might fucking drown you instead. Now get them off!'

'No,' Ally screamed!

He hit her head with the butt of the gun, she fell to the ground. 'Get up you fucking tart.' He pulled her to her feet by her hair. 'I would kill you first, but I want you to feel it, I want to be the last thing you see and feel.' Pulling her face towards him he forced his lips on hers, pushing his tongue into her mouth. Ally could taste his foul breath and she gagged, her head hurt, and she couldn't see straight, she tried to speak but nothing came out.

'I'll just fuck you once, and then I think I will have a shot of your arse. It's your best feature so it is, and I've been banged up for over a year, got a lot of fucking in me. Have you been buggered before by a man? Get them off!' Pushing her backwards, Ally fell against the tub banging her head; she struggled to focus as he got down on his knees beside her. He pulled at her trousers. Ally, dazed from the bumps to her head, was powerless to fight him as he ripped them from her legs and threw her into the hot tub. Her head smashed off the side. The pain was excruciating, her head spun, and she fought to remain conscious. She knew that if she passed out, she would die.

From somewhere Ally heard voices and a buzzing. Suddenly she felt herself being pulled from behind out of the water and heard the noise of a gun going off. She struggled to focus through the mist in front of her. 'Stevie? How did you get here?' she cried. Suddenly she was aware of Willie, on his feet and struggling with Seamus. Willie was punching him as the two men fought. 'Stevie, leave me! Stop them!' Stevie moved towards the two men, the gun in his hand. Just as Willie pushed Seamus he stumbled, pulling Willie towards him. She heard the noise of the gun going off, a loud crash, a scream and then nothing. Ally staggered to her feet, then fell; the glass wall on the balcony balustrade was gone and Ally tried to make sense of it. '**Willie!**' she screamed. '**Willie!**' She crawled on her hands and knees towards the gaping hole.

Stevie grabbed her and held her, stopping her from moving. 'Ally don't look. Please don't darling, it's no use.'

'Willie! Willie! No, Stevie! No, not like this! Not Willie too! Not yet! It's too soon. Please god no! I'm not ready for him to die!' She began to scream. Stevie held her as she passed out. He was crying himself, holding her to his chest.

CHAPTER

FORTY-FIVE

'How is she?' Danny cried, running into the waiting area where Stevie sat staring into the cup of milky tea in his hands.

'I'll leave you to talk,' the nurse sitting with him whispered. She put her hand on his shoulder as she stood up.

'They've sedated her Danny; she has a skull fracture.'

'Stevie how could this happen? How did Seamus get out?' Danny stood staring at Stevie whose eyes were raw and red from crying.

'Danny, they think he faked a heart attack, might have been using drugs that stopped his heart and then when they shocked him back, he got away.'

'How did he know where they were?'

Stevie shrugged. 'He probably knew where your mum and Willie lived when they were in Glasgow, because of the press coverage of the trial. There was that interview Korrie did about her dad and Ally, she gave them photos of herself on the terrace and you could see the view. Or it could just have been stuff that was in the media when they found out about your mum and Willie. Remember they were camped out there for days. It would be easy to find this place. I don't know how he got in to the flat though. Your mum was so dazed she was not making sense in the ambulance, and then they sedated her.'

'You've saved her life again by the sound of it. How did you know, Stevie?'

'I didn't.' Stevie pursed his lips and looked at Danny. 'Believe it or not it was down to chance. I lifted your mum's keys instead of mine when I was at the flat earlier. Then when we went out for dinner, I left the two of them at the restaurant. It was a nice evening, so I walked back to the car, it took about twenty minutes. Then I realised I had your mum's keys. I also left my phone. I got to the flat and went to look for the concierge to ask if I could just go up. Instead I found his and the repair man's bodies. Of course, I called the police. They told me about Seamus escaping. They had tried to warn us, but they didn't know where we were. We were in the restaurant down the road, but Willie had switched his phone off. Your mum never carries her mobile when she is not working as we both know. I realised I had the lift key on her keys, so I got straight up. He thought he'd killed Willie. He'd been shot but was on his knees in the living room. I managed to get Seamus away from your mum by shooting at him. He had put the gun down to . . . well, he was about to sexually assault her. I missed him though. Willie dived at him and they started fighting. I fired the gun again and it went off twice. I was shaking so much I shot through the glass panel then they fell through it.' Stevie began to cry, remembering the horror of the moment. 'Oh, dear God Danny,' he sobbed, 'it was horrible. It's my fault Willie died. I was just trying to stop them. I've never fired a gun before.'

'Stevie, it's not your fault. No one will see it like that.' Danny looked at Stevie. 'What about Mum? Did she see it happen? Did she see him, Willie I mean?

'She is in shock, but she didn't see it. She has a nasty head wound. The ambulance man thinks that he hit her with the butt of the gun.' Stevie sat with his head in his hands.

'How are we going to tell her he is dead Stevie?' Danny cried.

'She knows,' Stevie said quietly. 'She knew he was gone straight away. She has another head injury too there was some blood and bruising on her. She passed out, she was still breathing and everything. But she knew he was dead. Danny it's so not fair.'

'Mums tough Stevie, you know that better than anyone, she will deal with it. I'm worried about another head injury. Has anyone let Clive Ruthven know? I'd want him to be treating her now. We need the best, don't we?

***

Clive Ruthven saw the news and cried out in despair. 'Dear god, no!' he gasped. He rushed from the staff room. Pushing through the hospital corridors towards accident and emergency.

They were sitting in the corridor. 'Stevie, Danny.'

'Clive! You heard then?'

'I saw it on the news. Where is she?'

Stevie pointed in the direction of the room.

Clive opened the door. Ally lay sleeping in the bed, her head was heavily bandaged, her face deathly white. The young doctor tending to her looked up. 'Mr Ruthven, what brings you here?'

'Ally, Mrs Ogilvy, is a friend of mine. How is she?'

'She has a small skull fracture but it's not too bad. She appears to be stable.'

'Scan results please?'

'But Mr Ruthven, she is Mr Phillips patient.'

'No, she is mine now. Scan results!'

A small, grey-haired man entered the room. 'Ah Clive, I thought you might be here.' He stood, dwarfed by the big man in front of him.

'Mr Phillips, is this alright?' The student stammered.

'Of course. Leave us please, the woman in room 404 needs you to change her drain.'

'Sorry about that Clive, fourth year student, got him terrified. Anyway, my friend, I knew you treated Mrs Ogilvy before. Poor soul, she appears to have been through so much.'

'You know I operated on her last year Terry, missed aneurism. She almost died.'

'Nothing there this time though Clive, I double checked.'

Clive nodded. 'Could I take over her care?'

'Of course. Bloody awful news about her man. Willog, was a fantastic player in his day and the best manager Scotland has ever had. I take it you were involved with his care too? They're saying he would have had a few years although he had the tumour.'

Clive shook his head. 'We thought he had about two years, but he had a secondary tumour. It had not responded to the treatment. He would only have had a few months at best, but it's irrelevant now.'

'Did he know, Clive?'

'Actually, I spoke to him just today. I had advised him that it might have been the case a couple of weeks ago, but after his scan today I realised it was growing fast . . . but he didn't want his wife to know yet. He was keeping well, so he felt he wanted to just carry on that way and not tell anyone right away. They'd been on holiday, had a great time, and she had the trial to attend.'

'At least he took that evil bastard with him.'

Clive nodded and sighed. 'I operated on Seamus Driske too. If only I'd had the balls to let him die when I'd had the chance!'

'Well old boy, the world is a much safer place tonight.'

Clive looked at the sleeping form on the bed. 'A much sadder place too!' he said quietly.

When Terry Phillips left, Clive sat down beside Ally and took her hand. 'You poor little thing!' he whispered. 'This is just not fair.'

Ally stirred; her eyelids flickered as she tried to focus. 'Willie, I had the most awful dream!' She looked at Clive and closed her eyes, then opened them again, pain unrelated to her physical injuries evident on her face. 'It wasn't a dream?' she mumbled.

'No Ally, it wasn't a dream,' he looked sadly at her. 'I'm afraid Willie died at the scene, along with that animal Driske.'

Ally struggled to pull herself up to a sitting position. 'Clive, I need to see him to believe that he's gone.'

'Ally what you need is to stay calm. You have a nasty head wound and a fracture to your skull. Because of your history I need to make sure everything is in order.'

'Clive, he's dead, Willie's dead! How can I be calm?'

He stroked her face gently. 'Ally please? You need to try to just relax. Willie died trying to save you. If you die too, he died in vain.'

'Clive, I need to see him!'

'Ok, Stevie and Danny are outside. Scott and your dad are on their way here I understand. I'll go get them to sit with you, see what I can find out. But you need to promise me you'll lie there and rest.'

Ally nodded, turned away and faced the wall.

***

'He looks asleep!' Ally was beyond tears. Willie looked peaceful and calm. His face was pale but showed no sign of strain or pain. His long dark lashes touched his cheek and Ally would have thought he was asleep if she had not known.

'Ally he didn't feel anything. He would have died instantly when he hit the ground. He's at peace now,' Clive whispered as she moved towards the bed, towards the lifeless body of the man she loved.

She kissed his lips, they were cold; the texture was of marble. She touched his bandaged head, kissed his forehead then laid her head on his chest. 'We really didn't get much time together, just a very traumatic two years. It's a drop in the ocean really, but it feels like a lifetime.' She lay there for a few minutes before standing up, kissing him again and turning away. She looked up at the ceiling wondering where he was, she knew he could see her. She knew he was there, could sense his presence, Ally blew a kiss at the ceiling.

Clive ushered her out into the corridor, his arm around her shoulder. Frankie and David stood weeping, both rushed to her. Ally sobbed into Frankie's shoulder; he held her tightly, kissing her head, his own tears falling unchecked onto her hair. 'Go in and see him boys, it'll set your minds at rest. He looks peaceful,' she whispered, her voice hoarse. She moved away and embraced David.

'Ally, you need to know, no matter what happens now, we'll be there for you.' David Gibson touched her face gently. 'We promised Willie months ago, when he knew about the tumour, that we would do certain things, and we'll all make sure we do Ally. Alfie is on his way over.'

CHAPTER
FORTY-SIX

'How did he get out? When he did, why did no one think to go and find Alyson Campbell? It should have been obvious he would target her. She was in the public eye because of her relationship with Willie Ogilvy being common knowledge. How could this happen?' the Justice Secretary roared at the assembled group of senior police officers, his senior staff and Scottish Prison Service heads.

'The medics say he took some heart pill or other and it can cause a surge, which resembles a heart attack, but the person recovers quickly,' the chief constable said, looking around. 'He appears to have got it from someone inside the prison. We've done a check of people prescribed it, and one of the prison officers was taking it. Looks as though he has given Seamus the drug. It could have killed him instantly so it's a hell of a chance to take. He didn't have much to lose, though did he?'

The prison governor sighed. 'We put this particular officer with Seamus because he is such a miserable bastard, we thought he could not be compromised. There'll be a public outcry as well now. They have to feel safe, and everyone wanted Seamus to be punished. They'll be glad he is dead, but he has taken Willie Ogilvy with him.'

The chief constable swallowed hard. 'I knew Willie quite well. He was a great guy, for all his reputation. I got to know Ally and her family too, after Whitefield. Her and Willie, well it was a shock, but they were a great couple. I hear that he would have died anyway from the brain tumour.'

'That's not the point is it?' the Justice Minister cried.

The chief constable shrugged, 'Oh I don't know, he died saving the woman he loved sir, and that's maybe what he would have wanted. For years he has been in the papers for the way he treated women. Then he dies heroically, trying to save one who everyone thinks is a saint. I hear there is a book about to come out about him, the real story of his life.'

CHAPTER
FORTY-SEVEN

'You ready Mum?'

Ally nodded. She smoothed down her black linen dress and put her feet into her black patent court shoes. Fumbling in her bag, she pulled out a pair of Ray-Bans and put them on. 'You look nice Scott. It's funny to see you looking so smart.'

'Well, after being a student for five years, I need to get used to wearing a suit. I'm so lucky. Imagine Willie thinking I could work for the media side of Olgida Leisure.'

Ally smiled. 'He knew that you could do it. Now, with a first-class masters, in business studies, you can look after my shares. You won't need many suits though, working in Spain with Frankie and Lynne. It was a good time to make the switch with the baby coming, them getting married, and Alfie and Betty wanting to come back to Scotland. Lynne's new job with Sky means she can live in Spain most of the time. Who has Thea?'

Kiera stood up and put down her coffee mug. 'Mum has her for a couple of days. Now I'm not breastfeeding it's a lot easier, she's pretty great coping with her and wee Matthew.'

'Is Laura upset about you going to Spain?'

'No not really, she realises it's less than three hours on a flight. I think she had hoped that we would stay in Ayr and the babies would grow up together. I expect she will come over a lot and we'll be back and forward. She did say that If this hadn't happened and we had gone down south as planned, it would have taken longer for her to visit. Dad's upset about me not finishing my degree though.'

'Well, Stevie and I discussed that, you could transfer to an Open University course. Maybe not in social work right away, but if you do social sciences or social policy, you could pick up your social work postgrad later.'

Keira smiled and looked at Scott, she turned her gaze back to Ally. 'For now, Ally, I'm just enjoying being a mum, and being a mum in Majorca might be quite good, Betty has put me in touch with a mother and toddlers group and Scott and I are learning Spanish.'

'You and Stevie paying off our student loans has meant we can enjoy life and letting us live in your villa until we find something of our own has left us no real worries.' Scott said quietly. 'Thank you.'

Ally picked up the Order of Service from the table. Willie's smiling face looked back at her. 'It's the right one isn't it? Alfie took it at our wedding, and he just looks so relaxed and happy. It's how he would want to be remembered. I put the one he chose on the back. I know he wanted it to be one of him and I, but it was just too weird seeing my face on his Order of Service. It's his life we are remembering not mine. I was only part of it for two years.'

Ally walked through to the living room. Willie's children, his siblings and his closest friends were all there, along with her father and Margaret, who had quickly become a good friend to Ally. They had their own private service for Willie before they headed out to face the public funeral they had decided that

Willie needed to have. The decision to have a public service at Hampden, followed by a private cremation, had been taken after discussion by them all. This again, was not strictly what Willie had asked for, but the outpouring of grief at his violent death had led to them deciding to share the service of remembrance with the public. There would be a charity football match after the service between Scotland and Northern Ireland. Whilst only those closest to Willie would attend his cremation.

As the three black cars followed the hearse carrying her husband, Ally, sitting in the back of the first car, a stretch limousine, with Willie's four eldest children, Alfie, Frankie and David, looked out at the crowds. Belinsa, who appeared to have no shame and had insisted that she accompany her son when he really wanted to be with his siblings. Frankie had put her in the second car with the partners of the occupants of the first car, Willie's siblings and Ally's sons. Never one to miss an opportunity for publicity, Belinsa was dressed entirely in black with a black veil covering her face. Hailey had stayed away; Corinna was attending with Bernie. They were not part of the cortege, having chosen to go directly to the crematorium.

Alfie put his arm around Ally as they left the car to flash-bulbs and under the gaze of the silent crowds. Willie was a public figure and Ally knew she had to share this with them. Willie's coffin, draped with the national flag, was carried onto the pitch by some the Scotland football squad, many of them openly weeping as they proudly carried him on their shoulders.

CHAPTER

FORTY-EIGHT

One year later . . .

'Ally, you better hurry or you'll miss the flight.'

'Thanks for doing this Stevie. You, my darling, be a good girl for Gramps.'

Thea toddled around the table. 'Gana!' she called, 'Gana.'

'She knows you're going; she's seen the case. She's a smart cookie.'

'Thanks again Stevie, Cathy.'

'Hey, we get a free holiday!' Stevie said smiling, 'and we get in some practice before our own baby is here. He patted Cathy's very obvious baby bump.

'Kiera and Scott should be here the day after tomorrow. They've had a great honeymoon by the looks of it.'

Frankie came out of the kitchen, a coffee mug in his hand. 'You ready sweetheart?'

'Hmm, as ready as I will ever be.' He kissed her on the forehead and put his arm around her shoulder.

'You look great Ally. Living in Majorca really suits you,' Cathy said, scooping up Thea.

'Well, I'll be going back to Scotland soon Cathy. I'm looking forward to going back to work. It was the right decision to take the Glasgow job. I just needed to step away from the limelight, but I also needed to come back to something different too.'

Frankie put his arm around Ally's shoulder and kissed her cheek. 'Lynne is really grateful you are doing this Ally. We all know how hard it must be.'

'No Frankie, the book is great, exactly what Willie and I wanted, warts and all. He worried about how he would be remembered, and she has got a balance. I know it wasn't finished when he died, but they had finished the interviews and discussions, so he knew what would be in it. I'm glad we waited for the anniversary of his death to release it.'

Frankie leaned over the pram in the corner and kissed his sleeping son. 'Okay William Ogilvy Dastis, you be good for Uncle Stevie and Auntie Cathy.'

Ally smiled as they arrived at the bookshop; a life-size cardboard cut -out of her late husband stood by the door. The small assembled crowd cheered when Ally and Frankie got out the car. Ally reached over, kissed her fingers and touched Willie's face on the cardboard cut-out. Cameras flashed all around her. 'How do you feel Ally?' a reporter called out.

'Sad but proud!'

Lynne appeared beside her. Ally turned and hugged her friend. 'You look great Ally,' Lynne whispered. 'How are you feeling today? Is this too much?'

'No, I'm fine Lynne. I loved it so much. Although I thought I knew the story, I couldn't put it down. I told you it needed to be written. Willie knew you had to be the person to write it.'

Ally watched as the face of her late husband came up on a huge screen. This was no surprise for her; Willie had left a memory stick marked 'Book Launch'. After Willie's death, his lawyer had produced several recordings on these sticks. Willie had made them when he knew he was dying, which Ally realised now was why he had spent so much time supposedly writing his will. There was one recording for each of his children and one for Ally, telling them how much he loved them and that he wanted them to remember him with laughter and joy, not sadness. He had said to Ally in hers that he realised that with this she could remember his voice and how he looked. Ally had watched it a lot in the dark days after his death when she could not accept he was gone and felt angry and sad. He also left similar ones for his three childhood friends. Alfie, Frankie and David had never divulged to her what he said in these recordings, but she knew, like herself, it had brought them a lot of comfort in the days after Willie's tragic death.

Willie began to speak, and Ally dabbed her eyes with a tissue as she heard his voice. 'If you're seeing this, then I'm dead. I hope I died in bed with my beautiful wife Ally, the love of my life, by my side. But if I didn't, then there must have been a good reason for it. This book is going to open a lot of doors and a lot of wounds. My friends and my wife have been brave letting me tell their stories along with mine.

The book is a journey from my earliest memories of a dysfunctional family, through a very abusive school regime, and my terrible treatment of some of the most beautiful women in Scotland. I hope the people I have hurt in my life can find it in their hearts to forgive me. Particularly my first love Corinna, she forgave me and became my friend, and is a fantastic mother to my elder kids, and Bernie her husband is a very lucky man. The other thing I perhaps won't see but hope for is that the people who hurt me, and my friends will be held to account.'

Willie smiled and continued; Ally took a deep breath seeing his blue eyes sparkling. 'My three mates Alfie and Frankie Dastis and Davie Gibson have been there with me sharing my life and my death. We even planned my funeral. I'm truly the luckiest man who ever lived. I've had a fantastic career, a lot of fun and been very lucky to have people who love me around. My beautiful children, and grandchildren are the centre of my life. Although I didn't always behave in an acceptable way. I hope they carry the fact that I loved them all their lives. My two wonderful stepsons, and my father-in-law who accepted me into their lives and showed me nothing but respect. Then there's my fourth wife Ally. I was only with her for a short time I know, but she truly was the light of my life, the woman who made me believe in love and taught me more about it than I ever thought was possible. Neither of us knows why we have this chemistry, but it was there for me from the start. I hope that she's able to share the love she has to give with someone else, and if not, then get a move on Ally. He's out there. You know who he is. I told you.'

Lastly to the wonderful Lynne Lockhead who agreed to write this book with me. Without her there would be no book. I don't even have an O-Level. She bravely gave up her maternity leave to sort out my ramblings and put them into an order that would be readable. My mate, Frankie Dastis, is almost as lucky with his woman as I am with my lovely lady. I don't want tears. I hope the book helps all of you who love me to carry on and have great, fulfilling lives. For everyone else, I hope you will enjoy the book and it will lead you to understand not just me, but the people closest to me. It is their story too.'

***

Afterwards, Ally joined Lynne, Frankie, Alfie and David for a photograph. As she walked away, she heard a familiar voice. 'Ally, it's great to see you!'

'Clive, I'm so glad you came. How are you? You've shaved off your moustache too, very macho. Thank you for your emails. It's become part of my daily routine checking to see what you are saying each day.'

'Clive Ruthven smiled, less gay looking?'

She blushed, 'I can't believe I thought you were gay.'

'Understandable mistake Ally.' He smiled, and his eyes twinkled.

'Not that I'd have had any problem with you being gay of course, but I'm glad you're not.'

'Me too!' he said, bending to kiss her cheek. 'I so enjoy your emails too Ally.'

'What you asked me last night Clive? The answer is yes. I think because we've been apart and have just been communicating by email, I know you so well!'

'I'd rather hoped that would be your answer Ally. I was afraid, as I said, to see you today in case I was reading it all wrong.'

Ally looked up at Clive and smiled. 'Oh no, you got it exactly right. I was wondering how to bring it up.' Her face turned serious, 'Clive, can I ask you something? I needed to be face to face with you to ask this.'

'Yes of course you can.'

'The post-mortem report said that Willie only had weeks to live. You told Lynne he didn't want me to know.'

Clive nodded. 'We only found out for sure the day he died, and he wanted to have some quality time with you before he told you. He loved you Ally.'

'I know.'

'You must miss him?'

'I do, but I promised him that I wouldn't be alone. I'm ready to move on Clive, and I hope you will be a part of that.'

He looked down at her and smiled. 'I was surprised he told Lynne that if I agreed she could put it in the book. Lynne asked me before it was published.'

'Me too,' she admitted.

'He said that you and I would be perfect for each other and admitted he hadn't told you I was not gay because he was worried I would snatch you away.'

Ally smiled and looked him in the eye. 'I wouldn't have let you then. I hope you do now Clive. Let's just take our time and see where this goes.'

Clive shook his head. 'No Ally, I think we should rush this. I have it on good authority you are worth it. Dinner tonight?'

Ally smiled and nodded. 'Do you know what I think Clive?'

'What?'

'Somewhere, there is a poker table with a large bottle of malt, and Ralph and Willie are discussing football and arguing about who found you for me!'

Other Books by Maggie Parker

Black Velvet: Living the Dream
ISBN: 978-1-910757-69-7

The Rock band, Black Velvet, are living the dream. Five musically talented childhood friends from a small Scottish town, they are catapulted to international stardom under the direction of their controlling manager Tony Gorman.

Black Velvet Out of the Ashes
ISBN: 978-1-910757-78-9

The Story of Black Velvet continues, as the band carry on with Simon Forsyth as their new manager. They continue to live as a family at Brickstead manor, and move on to a new chapter in their careers.

The Politician
ISBN: 978-1-910757-82-6

When MP Caoimhe Black attends a wedding in her native Ayrshire, she runs into Tony Carter. Many years earlier Tony and Caoimhe had a secret affair which resulted in tragedy, they have not seen each other since their relationship ended. Neither have been able to forget the feelings they once shared.

The Lighthouse
ISBN: 978-1-910757-94-9

When Social Worker Stephanie Wilson attends a conference, and meets a former colleague, she has no idea her life is about to change. Grieving from the death of her policeman husband four years previously, Steph has thrown all her energies into her growing family, the business she and her late husband developed and renovating a disused lighthouse.

The Doctor
ISBN: 978-1-79674-000-4

When family doctor Carrie-Anne meets Calvin a handsome oil rig worker, on a North Sea Ferry during a storm, they quickly become friends. He travels with her to her Shetland holiday home, and a relationship develops as he waits to be returned to his oil rig. When her daughter and son-in-law find her in a compromising situation, Carrie-Anne discovers that Calvin has been pretending to be an ordinary person, he is in fact a Hollywood Actor. Carrie-Anne hurt and angry, sends Calvin away but she is forced by her feelings, to examine her life, and a web of deceit and lies is revealed.

The Nightclub Owner's Wife
ISBN: 978-1070764832

"Nothing hurts more than being let down by the person you thought could never hurt you!'

When Rosie travels to a Greek island to meet up with the mysterious travel writer she has been speaking to online. She has no idea she is about to be reminded of a painful time in her life. This story is set over two decades and tells the tale of a naive young woman seduced by an older man. It is a tale of recovery from the most unimaginable trauma and tragedy. A story of enduring friendships and hope after disaster. It examines number of taboo issues and shows how one act can set off a chain of events and alter the course of life in an instant. It also highlights how one woman can pull her life together and emerge strong enough to carry on. Rosie is a survivor, grieving, hurt and damaged she continues over a decade to find success as a writer, happiness eludes her as she struggles to trust anyone after being let down and hurt by the men in her life. Rosie discovers the man she has come to trust online, is none other than one of the men who has deeply hurt her. A man she loved, and thought would never hurt her. She learns the truth about her life and the acts of others which have led her to where she is now. This is a tale that will take you from the West Coast of Scotland to the Greek Islands, via America. It will keep you enthralled until the last page. It is a story of survival, courage and strength against all odds.

Printed in Great Britain
by Amazon